The
iCongressman

MIKAEL CARLSON

Warrington Publishing
New York

The iCongressman
Copyright © 2014 by Mikael Carlson

Warrington Publishing
P.O. Box 2349
New York, NY 10163

Printed in the United States of America
First Edition
ISBN: 978-0-9897673-2-3
978-0-9897673-3-0 (E-Book)
Cover design by Veselin Milacic

Also by Mikael Carlson:

- The Michael Bennit Series -
The iCandidate

Dedicated to all the risk-takers who have made bold sacrifices to try to make the world a better place.

While the story of Michael Bennit as the iCongressman can stand on its own, a reader will get far more out of his story by starting with the beginning of his exploits. To that end, I encourage anybody who purchased this book to read *The iCandidate* beforehand.

"Social media spark a revelation that we, the people, have a voice, and through the democratization of content and ideas we can once again unite around common passions, inspire movements, and ignite change."
— Brian Solis

"Social media is the empowerment of the individual at the expense of the system."
— David Amerland

-PROLOGUE-
MICHAEL

"I, state your name, do solemnly swear," the Speaker of the United States House of Representatives announces in a formal and somber voice.

After a wild-roller coaster ride the past six months, it's a little overwhelming to be standing with my right hand raised in the Well of the House Chamber, the large assembly room located in the center of the United States Capitol's south wing. Having won a special election while Congress is already in session, I am taking the Oath of Office on the Floor in front of the members. The Clerk of the House received the proper documentation from the Connecticut Election Commission this morning.

"I, Michael Bennit, do solemnly swear," I repeat in a deep, confident voice I hope masks my jitters.

"That I will support and defend the Constitution of the United States against all enemies, foreign and domestic," the Speaker continues from the rostrum. I can't help but notice the five words carved across the front of the large, paneled wood structure: Union, Justice, Tolerance, Liberty, and Peace.

"That I will support and defend the Constitution of the United States against all enemies, foreign and domestic," I echo.

Behind the rostrum are two pairs of black marble Ionic columns with white capitals. An American flag occupies the center with the words "In God We Trust" spelled out in bronze letters above it. Despite being the national motto since 1956, you know the inscription must drive the atheists and secularists crazy.

"That I will bear true faith and allegiance to the same; that I take this obligation freely, without any mental reservation or purpose of evasion."

I am completely lost in the moment. I need to focus on what I'm saying before I commit the ultimate faux pas and ask the Speaker to repeat himself. It is easier said than done under the circumstances though.

"That I will bear true faith and allegiance to the same; that I take this obligation freely, without any mental reservation or purpose of evasion." I actually have a lot of mental reservations stemming from having no idea whether I belong here or not.

"And that I will well and faithfully discharge the duties of the office on which I am about to enter."

On either side of the flag are two bronze fasces consisting of an axe within a bundle of rods, bound together by a strap and representing a classical Roman symbol of civic authority. The Founding Fathers referenced Republican Rome during the formation of the nation, so now these icons symbolize the authority of Congress and the philosophy of American democracy. Like those bound rods in the fasces, the individual states achieve strength through their union under the federal government. Yes, I'm a fountain of useless knowledge.

"And that I will well and faithfully discharge the duties of the office on which I am about to enter." At least, that's the plan.

"So help me God."

I take a moment to again look up at the words spelled out in bronze. In God We Trust indeed.

"So help me God," I repeat, concluding an only slightly different version of an oath I uttered countless times during my military service.

The members in the room break into applause, as do the visitors filling the House Gallery located in the balcony. As my swearing in is the last order of business before recessing for the weekend, the chamber is sparsely populated. There is no assigned seating here so it's difficult to tell who bothered showing up for this occasion and who didn't.

The Speaker of House is here, along with Majority Leader Harvey Stepanik and other distinguished Republicans like Thomas Parker. The Democratic leadership is also present, including the venerable Minority Leader Dennis Merrick. Outside of them, and a small delegation from their parties, it looks like most of the membership got an early jump on their weekend exodus.

It doesn't matter because I'm fully aware who is here. I gaze up at the gallery to find a collection of students applauding along the ledge. It should surprise nobody that Vince, Peyton, Chelsea, Amanda, Emilee, Brian, and Vanessa all made the trip down to Washington to share this moment with me. They are the ones responsible for my being here.

How far we have come from that day where we made a bet I never imagined losing. The entire American History class had to all get an A on a final exam, and if they did, I had to run for Congress. I never would have made the deal if I thought I would lose. My exams were incredibly hard, only they worked harder.

I convinced them to help run the campaign over the summer, and although it was a bumpy ride, they stuck it out in the bitter fight against the incumbent Democrat Winston Beaumont. In the process, the race turned into a circus, my students into media darlings, and my life upside down.

I lost the November election, but apparently I was wrong when I spoke to them after the race. Getting me elected may not have been the point of my decision to run for office after losing the bet, but they managed to make it happen anyway. It took the incumbent getting indicted and a special election, but the result is the same. Here I am.

I end my trip down memory lane to refocus on the gallery. My parents have long since passed, so I have no immediate family joining my students peering over the ledge. The only other person with them is the woman who has changed my life in so many ways. Kylie Roberts was an intrepid independent journalist who first became interested in my campaign to seek revenge on Winston Beaumont. By the time the final votes were cast, she had fully bought into what we were trying to do and became our most ardent supporter. Who knew when I climbed into her car in the parking lot of the Perkfect Buzz that not only would she achieve her goal, but end up dating me in the aftermath?

The speaker raps the gavel to announce the recess and people begin to mill around the room. A few representatives come over to shake my hand, but my welcome to Washington has been anything but warm. Most members simply slink out the door to head for the airport and the flight back to their districts.

I give my former student campaign staff a quick wave and thumbs-up, and then smile broadly at Kylie. Realizing the need to stop and smell the roses, I take a moment to admire where I am standing. You have to hand it to the architects of this building. Their sense of grandeur in designing the Capitol created an extraordinary physical space. Like a Greek temple to Apollo, this room is ridiculously ornate, and conveys an aura of importance of the history men and women create here.

The chamber's lower walls are walnut paneled with light gray marble pilasters, and the peacock blue and gold patterned carpet reflects the electric lighting installed in the mid-twentieth century. It's hard to imagine skylights lit this magnificent room for the first one hundred twenty years of its existence.

Outside of the Oval Office of the White House, the Hall of the House of Representatives is the single most recognizable room in all of Washington. This is the chamber seen by large numbers of Americans every year during the president's State of the Union address. I'm humbled to be standing in the middle of it. You cannot ask for more grandeur and history out of a place of employment.

"I apologize your swearing in was so lightly attended," a voice from behind me declares, breaking my nostalgic moment. "Right before recessing for the weekend is the worst time to get anything done around here. Johnston Albright," he says, extending his hand.

"No apology necessary, Mister Speaker," I respond, meaning it. Given the circumstances of my election, I'm surprised any of the members showed up at all.

"Well, let me congratulate you on your victory. It had to be one of the biggest landslides in congressional history."

Ironically, that's one historical fact I don't know. After losing to Winston Beaumont in November, he was indicted on numerous counts of conspiracy and bribery and forced to resign his seat. While the Republicans and Democrats held primary battles for who would run to take his place, I was already campaigning.

Using the same students who ran my original campaign, and the same social media platforms that gave me the moniker the "iCandidate," we engaged the voters in the district by talking about ideas *and* issues. Whereas I avoided taking a stand in my first race to prove a point, I wasn't bashful this time around. It made a decided difference.

The resulting election a few days ago was not pretty for either the Republicans or the Democrats. We won eighty-six percent of the vote, with the remaining fourteen percent split between the two major parties. What must scare the party bosses the most was the turnout. Special elections usually draw only a small fraction of eligible voters to participate. My victory saw over half of the district cast a vote.

"Thank you, Mister Speaker, I appreciate that."

"I know this all must still be somewhat overwhelming to you," he observes, "but have you discussed joining a caucus with any of the leadership?"

"No, I haven't. It's safe to assume the Democrats won't want me caucusing with them after what happened to Beaumont," I state truthfully.

"I can see where they might be a little bitter about losing one of their most senior voices," Speaker Albright says with a laugh. "The problem is, I'm not sure if you fit with the Republicans either. Some of our members have expressed concerns as well."

"Concerns?" I ask, trying to ascertain exactly where the leading Republican in the House is going with this.

"Yes. Many consider you too moderate in your views to become a valued member of our caucus. I tend to disagree, but I am only one voice," he adds somewhat theatrically. One voice my ass. Who is he kidding? He is *the* voice. Is this what I have to look forward to? I became an official member of Congress five minutes ago and the political games are already starting.

"Mister Speaker, without joining a caucus, I don't get a committee assignment," I explain, as if he didn't know that. Nice job, Captain Obvious.

"I understand," he says in the best fake sympathetic voice I have ever heard. They really do play at a higher level here. "But even if you do join us to caucus, I just don't think we can arrange for you to have a seat on a committee. You understand the difficulty of the situation, don't you?"

I grin, because it's about all I can do. I know their strategy now, and have no idea how to beat it. I may have to get used to the fact that this is going to be a long year and a half.

"Michael, let me give you a piece of advice from a guy who has been doing this far longer than you," the Speaker condescends. "There is a certain way things are done in Congress, especially the House. We all know what the Constitution says, but the document never specified *how* we do business. So over the decades, norms, customs, and processes emerged to best enable us to ... do the work of the people." I want to cough at the statement, but stay silent and accept whatever little gem of advice I'm about to get.

"Learn those processes and abide by them," he continues smugly. "You may fancy yourself a rebel with a cause, but there is no room for aberrant behavior in this building. The parties set the rules here, and you'll be expected to play by them."

"And if I don't?" I say, not as a direct challenge to one of the most powerful figures in Washington, but more out of curiosity. No room for aberrant behavior. What a joke. He smiles and pats my arm once for effect.

"You have strong and determined enemies in this building you don't even know of yet. Don't be quick to alienate the people who aren't." With that, Speaker Albright heads up the aisle toward a set of double doors in the rear of the chamber.

Chelsea, Kylie, Vince, and the rest of the gang give me a series of "what was that about?" gestures and faces from their spots along the ledge of the gallery. Despite the chamber being close to empty now, I don't want to shout, so I point for them to meet me in the lobby so we can start the celebration.

As they climb the stairs to exit the gallery, I survey the room a final time and then glance down at the gold-colored lapel pin announcing my status as a member of Congress. I'm overwhelmed with the pride and honor I feel being here, but I wonder how long that will last. Something tells me I was right about needing to get used to another feeling—that it is going to be a very long year and a half.

PART I

A DECLARATION OF INDEPENDENCE

-ONE-

CHELSEA

Now I understand what the view from Palatine Hill in ancient Rome must have looked like. Although nothing matches the wondrous beauty of mountains, sweeping plains, and great bodies of water found in nature, sitting on the steps of the Capitol and watching the sun set over the National Mall comes pretty close.

The last light of the day is glinting off the reflecting pools, and the sky, only marred by a few wispy clouds, is beginning to take on orange and pink hues. Tourists and students on their eighth-grade field trip wander between the grand museums of the Smithsonian that line the avenues leading toward the Washington Monument. Directly behind the towering obelisk is the newer World War II Memorial framed against the distinctive architectural edifice of the Lincoln Memorial. All these marble wonders combine to create a sight as picturesque as America offers.

I have enjoyed this view countless times over the past ten months. When Congressman Bennit took his seat a year ago, he hired an advisor to show him the ropes on a temporary basis. He made it clear he wanted me to be his chief of staff if I was willing to take the job, a decision that took only moments to make. I joined him in Washington the day after I graduated from Millfield High School last June. Dad was not thrilled with the decision to skip college for a few years, but I promised him I was planning to take classes in my free time here in Washington. That notion is a joke now, for more reasons than one.

I don't know if my expectations were unrealistic, or if we just had a harder time than most in Washington. I learned the demands on any congressional chief of staff are ridiculous, making the enrollment in even a single college course out of the question. It might have been worthwhile if we had been able to do what we came here to.

Since the day he was sworn in, Congressman Bennit has been shunned by the entire political body in D.C. In Congress, there are groupings of members with shared affinities who convene to collectively advocate or vote on policies. These numerous "caucuses" are among the most influential political groups in the House, and Congressman Bennit wasn't invited to participate in any of them.

To make matters worse, neither the Democrats, who choose their committee leaders based on seniority, nor the Republicans, who adopted a selection system using a vote on the Steering Committee, offered the congressman a committee seat. Most representatives belong to one or two standing committees, and as many as four subcommittees, each with its own specialized subject matter and schedule of hearings. The real work of Congress is done in those meetings, and since we weren't invited to play in those sandboxes, we are practically invisible in this building. No committee memberships equals no power or influence.

"I thought I might find you out here," Vince says, sitting down next to me on the steps and running his hand through his short black hair. With handsome Sicilian features and sharp brown eyes, only his age keeps him from being confused for a politician himself.

I always considered Vince the class clown in school, and with good reason. When Mister Bennit enlisted us to help the campaign, we all thought he was crazy to put Vince in charge of media relations. Once we graduated, each of us had a choice to make. Three of us went to work for Congressman Bennit on his staff, and our renowned troublemaker, Vincent Antonio Orsini, assumed the role of press secretary. People back home are still trying to figure out how that happened, but I know. He's brilliant at his job.

"Yeah, I'm nothing if not predictable. At least until the Capitol Police let me on the roof. Heard from the boss yet?"

"No, you?"

I glance down at my phone, as if expecting the damn thing to ring on command, which it doesn't. "No, but I don't expect him to make any progress."

There are a myriad of issues facing America, and Congressman Michael Bennit tried to take them all on. Unfortunately, very few members of Congress take him seriously. He's an Independent who is primed to be defeated seven months from now, so neither side is eager to include him in any debate or discussion. This latest meeting about the looming government shutdown is much of the same, I'm sure.

"You sound defeated already."

"History is on my side in reaching that conclusion," I reply, despondent. "We've been stuck in neutral since the moment we got here. I don't think today will be any different. So much for our grand plan."

"I'm sure it's harder for him. Remember, Chels, the congressman gave up everything for this. We only gave up frolicking in college," Vince reflects, "and spending the prime of our lives with no real responsibilities. We'd be going to parties, playing video games, hooking up with hot girls happy to be away from their parents for the first time ..." he trails off, lost in the land of wishful thinking. We?

"Something tells me you aren't having a problem picking up chicks in Georgetown, Vince," I say, more than a little envious over him having a personal life. I sure don't.

"You sound jealous. I didn't realize you were into girls, too," Vince says to me with a smile that implies so much more. Yeah, keep dreaming, buddy. I don't think he's serious about his lesbian fantasy, or at least one involving me. Over the past year, we've become closer than most siblings are to each other.

"You regret giving school up to do this?"

Vince exhales deeply and smiles, enjoying the view of the sun setting over the Mall. "Nah. I wouldn't trade this experience for anything. College will always be an option," he almost convincingly expresses. Easy for him to say. I gave up a full ride to Yale, Harvard, or a dozen other schools for this.

"Even if we haven't accomplished anything in the year we've been here?" I ply, hoping he is as miserable as I am.

"You know better than anyone that most members of Congress leave office without ever having put their personal imprint on a significant piece of legislation. Lawmaking isn't the principal preoccupation of the people who work in the building behind us — politics is."

"For a media relations guy, you didn't bother putting much spin on that," I muse.

"Eh. Different audience," Vince observes. "After having to deal with two reprimands and a censure over stupid stuff, it's not hard to draw my conclusion."

He's right. Congressman Bennit has been in office a year and is already the most oft-disciplined member ever to serve. The reprimands were a joke, but the censure was more serious. Derived long ago from the need to punish the behavior of legislators, it's a formal condemnation Congress can hand out to the president or their own members. The usual result of a censure is the forfeit of any committee chairs held, but not a loss of the elected position itself.

Since the congressman isn't even on a committee, let alone chairing one, the gesture was symbolic and meant to hurt us in the next campaign. It was a purely political move on behalf of the House leadership, but not a completely unwarranted one. I guess that's what we get for having a leader who doesn't like to play by the rules.

"The Speaker wants him gone," I state definitively.

"Hell, Chels, everyone wants him gone. He's a threat to both parties and the system they established around them."

The inner workings of Congress are hard to grasp, and even more difficult to explain. This lack of understanding is a primary source of angst between politicians and the citizenry that voted them into office. The House and Senate developed rules and customs to help them to operate, and most of them are blatantly undemocratic. It took me months to get used to how the system functions, and I work here full time.

Every two years, newly elected representatives and senators promise to clean up the mess created by those before them. This time, however, we weren't one of them. We never claimed to try to clean up Washington, only to serve the people of the district and the country the best we could. Unfortunately, we learned the hard way that the two are not mutually exclusive. If fulfilling a campaign promise to fix Congress pegs the success needle at impossible, then our promising to be a better representative for the people ranks one notch down at next to impossible.

"Yeah, I guess you're right." Vince is not one for long pep talks designed to raise spirits. I feel worse now than I did before I came out here.

"C'mon, let's get over to the office," he says, standing up. "The boss should be back with Vanessa by now."

I rise, taking a moment to brush off and straighten my navy blue pantsuit. I look back out towards the Mall and the orange ball now dipping below the horizon. I can't shake the vibe that it's an omen for things to come. In November, the sun will likely be setting on our time here as well.

-TWO-

SPEAKER ALBRIGHT

"Are you going to stare out that window all night, Johnston?" my colleague asks from the other side of the spacious room.

"You're not going to let me enjoy one of my favorite trappings of this office, are you, Harv?" I ask the House majority leader without looking back at him.

My picturesque view overlooks the National Mall to the Washington Monument. Admiring the sunset from this spot became a tradition of mine when I took over this job. Office space in the Capitol itself is restricted to the leadership, and as Speaker of the United States House of Representatives, I'm awarded a stunning space to entertain and meet with constituents, allies, and the occasional adversary. This evening, the guest of honor is House Majority Leader Harvey Stepanik, a longtime friend and distinguished congressman from Ohio.

"Normally I wouldn't care, but I have a meeting with the automotive lobby tonight," my ally declares, giving his watch an impatient glance.

"Well, I wouldn't want to keep you from that," I say with a gruff laugh. As a representative from Ohio, Harvey's meeting with the automotive lobby would take precedence over a meeting with the Almighty Himself. The industry accounts for over four percent of the state's gross domestic product, and Ohio is second only to Michigan in automotive production. Success in wooing them means fat campaign contributions, and in an election year, money is everything. "Now that I know this isn't a social call, what's on your mind?"

"Michael Bennit."

"Jesus, Harv, not again," I reply, tired of hearing this character's name. "Every time this guy even meets with other members you come running into my office screaming 'the sky is falling' louder than Chicken Little."

"You underestimate what he's capable of," he replies as I pour us a drink.

"Really? He's been here a year now and do you know what he's managed to accomplish? Absolutely nothing. He's on the outside looking in, and that's never going to change. Keeping him frozen out of anything important is about the only thing we agree with the Democrats on these days. We marginalized him to the point where House clerks exert more political clout than he does, so what are you worried about?"

Harvey swirls his amber eighteen-year-old Macallan around the tulip-shaped glass tumbler. I find scotch drinkers tend to be more worldly and mature, and the forty-four-year-old Harvey Stepanik is about as refined an individual you will ever see come out of industrial Ohio. He plays the political game with gusto, savors new challenges, and doesn't settle for anything below his standards. That includes both the company he keeps and the single-malt scotch whisky in his glass.

"Bennit has two things most people in this chamber don't," he replies, a serious look in his otherwise soft and appealing green eyes. No wonder the voters love this guy. With his brown hair, strong features, and athletic build, he was built for politics in a television age like John F. Kennedy was. "An enviable social media following measured in millions, not thousands, and a mandate from the people in his district to be here." Harvey actually held up his fingers and counted the two things off on them like I needed the visual cues to get his point.

"I think you are overestimating the danger of social media in the political process," I say, taking a sip from my own glass of scotch. "Bennit benefited from a ridiculous amount of mass media coverage in his campaign against Beaumont and still lost. He spent more time on TV than the Kardashians during that race, so winning after the resignation was predictable."

"And I disagree. I don't think we are taking it serious enough. An 'icandidate' has won both special elections held since this beginning of this Congressional session. Bennit broke new ground last spring, and this farmhand from Texas followed suit last week. How exactly am I overestimating the threat?"

"Yeah, I forgot about him," I add, conceding the point. Francisco Reyes is a Texan who won as an independent on the strength of the growing Latino vote in his district. He inspired and motivated them, using the same reliance on social media methods Bennit did. He landed almost seventy percent of the vote while spending almost no money on his campaign.

"Grassroots networks became an irresistible force of American politics, and we did nothing to stop it. Social media is now the new means where unqualified, independent candidates can reach these networks of people and get them engaged in political activity. If we continue to let this grow unabated, there will come a point where political parties will be powerless to beat them."

Damn this guy knows how to plead a case, and being from a safe district, he can afford to be insistent with his opinions. I still don't completely agree with his analysis, but there is no doubt why the party bosses sitting on the Republican National Committee are pushing for him to be the Speaker someday. He is wrong about one thing, though; we aren't letting anything grow.

"We are forcing him out. I've already censured him once and have reprimanded him twice on the Floor," I respond defensively. "He's toast in the next election."

"That's not forcing him out, Johnston. Professional politicians view those types of rebukes as serious, but he views it like a five-year-old getting a 'time-out.' You can agree or disagree with me, but most of the Republicans in this chamber are scared as hell of the trend this guy's started. I bet if we ask the Dems, they would say the same thing. We need to get rid of him permanently, *before* the election."

"You think by cutting off the head you'll kill the snake," I conclude, eliciting a nod in agreement. Forcing Bennit out is a risky endeavor. I worry more about the party being viewed as playground bullies by the public if we push too hard on him.

Harvey swallows the last of his scotch and places the tumbler on my desk before rising out of his seat and buttoning his suit jacket.

"I need to get moving. I don't want to keep the motor heads waiting. Thanks for your time, Mister Speaker." He makes it halfway to the door before I stop him.

"Harvey," I say, causing him to stop and turn around. "Tell the members of the caucus that I will do what I can to push Bennit off the ledge before the campaign season starts." As much as I think it's a pointless exercise, I also recognize the need to keep the Republican membership happy. Harvey is a friend, but he's popular and eager to have this office. If I'm not careful, and don't play my cards right, he could take over as Speaker next January even if we remain in the majority.

"I will. Thank you, Johnston."

"One more thing to remember before you go, Harv. Sometimes the enemy you vanquish is the one that spells your doom. Just ask Winston Beaumont."

-THREE-

SENATOR VIANO

I despise how the House of Representatives conducts business. Sitting here in the House visitor gallery for all of ten minutes, I understand why it's considered the lower chamber. Too many people serve here, all of them wanting their opinions entered into the record so they have something to brag about back home. I guess that's a pitfall of needing to get reelected every two years. I would rather suffer through menopause again rather than have to deal with this on a daily basis.

Following the daily prayer, the Pledge of Allegiance, and approval of the previous day's Journal, the Speaker of the House has the prerogative to start the day with recognition of members for a series of one-minute speeches. To illustrate the gifted cleverness of the men and women of this chamber, these brief orations are commonly known as ... "one minutes." No creativity whatsoever in coming up with that moniker.

Since the issue du jour is our impending government-inspired financial meltdown, it's the topic of choice for representatives asking for unanimous consent to address the House. Speaker Albright rarely makes an appearance to serve as Chair, but the fifty-two-year-old professional politician knows this will be a busy and important day. He is handsome in a lawyerly kind of way, with salt and pepper hair and a moderately expanding waistline. The constant scheming and political worry accompanying his position gives him the appearance of perpetual constipation though.

"I thought I saw you up here. How are you, Senator?" the balding gentleman says as he sits down in the seat next to me. I give a brief smile to the man who was once my right-hand man during the one and only term I served in the Senate. Gary Condrey was a superb chief of staff and shrewd political operator. I miss his counsel and company.

"Fine, Gary, thanks. Yourself?" I mumble, returning my attention back to my smartphone.

"I'm working for one of the dumbest men I have ever met, but otherwise okay. I know you hate this place, so what brings you to the House Chamber?" Gary inquires, knowing full well how unlikely it is I would ever just show up here.

"The continuing resolution."

"Ah. You'll never see it hit the Floor today because of the Hastert Rule." Also known as the "majority of the majority" rule, it's an informal governing principle used to limit the power of the minority party. Speakers of the House have been using it the since the mid-1990s to justify not bringing bills up for a vote. Yes, this is our republic in action. "I didn't realize you missed politics so much, Marilyn."

"I don't. My husband is rich, so what else is there for me to do?" Of course, that's a complete lie. For the better part of two decades, I groomed myself to make a run at an open Senate seat in Virginia. My predecessor was in office for so long, he practically had a room named for him in the Senate wing of the Capitol. When he finally died, I got my shot, and with Gary's expert help, eked out a win against a tough Republican candidate.

My victory was a short-lived one, however. In the six years I served in the Senate, I was never able to raise enough campaign contributions to survive another hard-hitting fight. Virginia is considered a purple state, meaning its citizens will swing their votes to Republicans or Democrats depending on which way the political prevailing winds are blowing. When I was elected, we had it at our backs. Six years later, a stiff headwind caused me to lose in a landslide.

I have spent every moment since my concession speech devising a plan to reenter public life. Support within the Democratic Party for my resurgence as a possible candidate is lukewarm at best. I need something to make me an invaluable asset again, and I will not rest until I find it.

"The Chair recognizes the gentleman from Connecticut for one minute," I hear Speaker Albright announce from his dais. A strapping young man approaches the podium set up in front of the rostrum with a swagger and confidence in his demeanor only gained through military service. With short brown hair and muscular build evident even under his suit jacket, he could moonlight as a bouncer in some hot Georgetown nightclub and the patrons would never guess he was a congressman.

"Is that the guy who ran his campaign on social media?" I ask, tapping my former chief of staff on his arm when it dawns on me who the man I'm admiring is.

"Huh? Uh, yeah, that's Michael Bennit."

Not exactly what I expected. I was too caught up in the struggle of my own campaign to pay much attention to the Bennit-Beaumont media circus. After my horrific loss, I fell into a self-imposed exile and didn't follow the subsequent special election Bennit won a year ago to earn a seat. I always assumed the iCandidate was some homely guy who lived out of his parents' basement. I was wrong. He doesn't look like a politician, per se, but more reminiscent of a leader capable of inspiring people to travel through hell and back with him wearing smiles on their faces.

"When I taught history, the Constitutional Convention was always one of my favorite topics," he begins. "The thought of fifty-five delegates from disparate backgrounds and colonies gathering at the Philadelphia State House every day during a sweltering summer to hammer out a new form of government is such a romantic idea.

"Two and a quarter centuries later, I stand here baffled how the body they labored to create has become so dysfunctional. We are on our fifth continuing resolution for the budget only because both sides are more interested in finding a way to blame each other than sitting down and negotiating. Not only are you adversely affecting the government's ability to perform its function, but more importantly, the negative effects are being felt from Wall Street to Main Street. From volatility in the stock market created by uncertainty, to general unease in the economy, your inability to take action here is having an impact on every American."

I am willing to bet Bennit's class was an entertaining one. He knows what he's doing, at least insofar as his oration is concerned. No wonder his students were quick to join his staff. The Speaker doesn't seem to share my opinion as he sits there pining for the opportunity to shut him up.

"The problem is you collectively don't care about the consequences to ordinary Americans. You're a bunch of sadists, content to drive the United States off a cliff rather than work together." And there is the excuse Albright needed to shut him down.

"Mister Bennit, you are out of order," Speaker Albright commands from his seat in front of the American flag.

"Frankly, I don't give a damn, Mister Speaker. The country is getting screwed by the people in this room and all Americans need to hear why," Michael Bennit declares theatrically.

"Not on the Floor of this Chamber, Mister Bennit," the Speaker responds, rising from his chair and leaning forward aggressively. "What you say to the press gathered outside is your business, but here, I get to arbitrate your language and force you to cease your assaults on members. I am taking back the balance of your time." As chairman, he gets to recognize who speaks and who doesn't, and does so with extreme prejudice.

"Why am I not surprised you want to muzzle me, Mister Speaker? You're one of the ass-clowns driving us toward the cliff."

"Mister Bennit, slanderous language *will not* be tolerated in the House of Representatives! I am going to recommend you be censured for your behavior. Now go take a seat before I instruct the sergeant-at-arms to remove you from the Floor." Bennit thinks about it for a moment then shakes his head, moving to a desk near the rear of the room as Speaker Albright's glaring eyes burn a hole in the back of his head. "The Chair recognizes the gentlewoman from Minnesota for one minute."

"Well, you don't see that every day," I utter, amazed at what I witnessed. His scale of open defiance is almost unheard of in Congress.

"You practically do with him. This will be his second censure to go with at least a pair of reprimands."

"Interesting," I say, meaning it. Since being defeated last election, my quest for angles and opportunities to get back into politics has been fruitless. My primary focus has been searching for a way back into the good graces of my party. Perhaps what I should be considering is a way to stick it to those who abandoned me once my star stopped shining so brightly. Bennit could offer me a chance to both return to politics and get even.

"What's interesting?" Gary asks, consumed with the task of writing an e-mail on his Android phone.

"Bennit is. Nobody racks up such a disciplinary record without making some powerful enemies." I turn to my former friend, ally, and trusted advisor and cover his phone with my hand to command his attention. "What am I missing, Gary?"

"Rumor has it the Speaker and the rest of the Republicans are trying to drive him out," he says, a note of indifference creeping into his voice. Obviously, after the beating he put on Winston Beaumont, the Democratic Party is not keen on jumping to Bennit's aid, regardless of whether doing so would irk the GOP or not.

"I can see that," I say, crinkling my brow. "The question is, why? He's going to lose the next election, right?"

"Probably."

"So why keep gunning for him?" I ask Gary, eliciting an unhelpful shrug.

Bennit has the establishment spooked, and I want to know how and why. Fortunately, I know exactly who to call to find out. There is one person in my sphere of influence who was close to the situation during Bennit's first campaign. Although I'm sure he's not on this rogue congressman's Christmas card list, it won't hurt to watch what happens.

"You have that look on your face you get when you are about to do something crazy. Anything you want to tell me?" Gary asks, sincere in his desire to help me. He must be bored in his current job.

"No, it's nothing," I say, only half meaning it. I may eventually need to loop Gary in to my thoughts, but now is not the time.

"So why the amused face the Joker has in Batman movies right before he blows something up?" Ugh. One thing I could never tolerate about Gary was his obsession with superhero films. The recent serial release of Marvel and D.C. Comics-themed 3D IMAX abortions masquerading as cinema was like Christmas morning for him and a personal nightmare for me.

"Just ought to be fun to see what happens to this Bennit guy once Albright gets done with him."

-FOUR-

MICHAEL

Johnston Albright is my new Robinson Howell. Like my former principal, he desperately wants me out of the building he runs, constantly threatens me, and uses every transgression he can to hasten my exit. The only difference between the two is the Speaker of the House doesn't dress like Mr. Furley from *Three's Company* like Howell does.

The man who has become the bane of my existence only needed two weeks to get a censure resolution drafted and voted on. It probably would have happened faster if not for the scheduled constituent work week the representatives spend in their districts. I hope much of that time was used to explain to the electorate why their government would rather try to destroy the economy than compromise on a solution.

For the second time in my year of political service, I've been summoned to stand in the Well of the House Floor while Speaker Albright reads a humiliating censure for my behavior. This resolution shows the bipartisan spirit in this country is, in fact, alive and well—at least so far as I am concerned. The measure passed by an almost unprecedented four hundred twenty to two vote. Twelve members voted "present," the equivalent of abstaining, and the Speaker did not cast a vote as tradition mandates. Only one person stood with me in voting "no," and I have never even met the guy who cast it.

More than two-thirds of the membership has decided to attend my public flogging, providing a clear picture of exactly how they think of me. Maybe it's not personal. I am the twenty-fourth person to receive a Congressional censure, although the only to have ever received two. Quite the accomplishment, and a dubious claim to fame for someone who is politically castrated. So, perhaps they are present to witness history with the reading of House Resolution 1233. Yeah, wishful thinking.

I return to reality as Speaker Albright gets rolling with the juicy part of the resolution. "Representative Michael Bennit be censured with the public reading of this resolution by the Speaker; and Representative Bennit further refrain from defaming or degrading the House, criticizing the Speaker's personal conduct, and impugning the motives of another member or members by charging falsehood or deception."

Censures are not taken lightly by the Washington elite, even if I have developed a nonchalant attitude towards getting disciplined in this circus fun house. Congress has not historically doled out censures haphazardly, with the last one being Charles Rangel's in 2010. You have to go back nearly twenty years to find the one before his. I earned my two in rapid succession, and harbor little doubt expulsion will be the punishment for my next misstep.

"Is there anything the gentleman from Connecticut would like to say?" I hear Speaker Albright query from the rostrum.

Yeah, I have something to say, but it won't be politically correct. In fact, I have a gesture or two I'd like to make as well.

"Not at this time, Mister Speaker, thank you." I turn and walk up the long aisle to the rear exit under the scrutinizing eyes of my colleagues. As much as a moment like this deserves the middle finger, the footage of the crass gesture would be the lead story on every evening newscast in the country, and the last thing I ever did in Congress.

No thanks to leadership of both parties, enough reporters are here to start our own Woodstock. Connecticut's native news organizations do not employ permanently assigned Washington correspondents, so both the Republicans and Democrats practically bused down state news media to ensure the voters back home hear about their derelict representative. Although her duties with the *Washington Post* are investigative, and don't include covering Congress, even Kylie was instructed to attend.

I wager a guess that the editors at her paper thought it might heighten my embarrassment to be disciplined in front of my girlfriend. In any other relationship, there may be some merit to that. Fortunately for me, Kylie is the most supportive woman I have ever known. She offers the best advice she can to help me navigate the treacherous waters of Washington politics. It's hopeless, but her support is a far cry from anything my ex-fiancée Jessica ever provided.

Although Kylie swears otherwise, I don't belong here. After all my time in Special Forces and in front of a classroom full of students, I fancy myself a doer, not a talker. With so many problems facing this country, I wanted to be a part of the group responsible to help figure out solutions. If such a body of people exists, it certainly isn't Congress.

Now I am left questioning everything I thought and hoped I knew about the American government. As a high school history teacher, I read countless books about how the Framers debated and argued over the document that became our Constitution in the summer of 1787. I always thought that, despite watching the posturing the bloviating politicians engage in on *Meet the Press*, behind the scenes would be different. Out of sight from prying cameras is where the real negotiating, debate, and compromise was done. Damn, was I ever wrong.

"Congressman Bennit," a voice announces from behind me with the volume of a wall of concert speakers. The marble and ceramic tile floors of the Capitol's hallways exaggerate every noise, no matter how muffled. The echo of a single conversation requires both parties to talk at a near whisper unless they want their words broadcast to everyone in the vicinity. On the occasion where a crowd of more than ten people gather in the hall, the resulting din sounds like the end zone of a Seattle Seahawks home game.

"I'm Francisco Reyes, proud representative from the great State of Texas. I'm glad to finally have the honor of meeting you," he says after catching up with me and shaking my hand with serious enthusiasm.

"Please, call me Michael."

"Only if you call me Cisco."

At first glance, this guy is pretty unimpressive. He has typical Latino features—dark hair, dark eyes and a mocha skin that acts as a perma-tan. He may be short in stature, but he strikes me as big in attitude, charisma, and likability.

"Fair enough, Cisco. I want to thank you for being the 'plus one' on my censure vote. Siding with me on anything is the kiss of death around here. Why'd you do it?"

"Since it's apparent we icandidates are automatically persona non grata around here, I figured I would just spend the next six months pissing people off," Cisco says with a smile that leads me to believe he is not only serious, but enjoying his work.

"Yeah, well, you're off to a good start then. This must be a memorable first day for you."

"Are you kidding? It took me forty-five minutes to get in the building this morning because the Capitol Police thought I was a landscaper." I laugh at his self-depreciating humor, although part of me wonders if there is an inkling of truth to his words. "It's not funny. I'm tempted to show up in my lawn mower tomorrow just to complete their image of me."

"At least they are thinking of you. I've become nothing more than an afterthought around here. The sum of my legislative aptitude is the remarkable ability to collect censures and reprimands."

"We all have our talents," he replies with a chuckle. Cisco is a guy's guy. I've been talking to him for two minutes and can already tell he's the Real McCoy politically, and someone I could share a beer with at a Yankee game. "You would think with a looming showdown over the debt ceiling and budget for the hundredth time, the parties would have something better to spend their energy on."

"In my short time in Washington I've learned important things get done only on the precipice of a crisis. Until the political risks of inaction exceed the risk of doing something, both sides are content to play chicken with each other."

"And the rest of America gets screwed in the process."

"Exactly. Tell me something, Cisco. Why did you decide to run for your seat?" I'm assuming he didn't lose a bet, so I am curious why someone would willingly sign up for this. Although I suppose I did too when I ran the second time.

"You know, I followed you during your campaigns. I read every Twitter and Facebook post and watched your online web chats. I was inspired by your words about what the Founding Fathers envisioned for this government. I think Americans were too. I'm here because of them."

"So what do you want from me?"

"I was hoping we could work together to help turn this thing around," Cisco says with noticeable optimism in his voice. His attitude is refreshing, and reminds me of how I felt my first few months here. It wasn't long after that when I realized how pointless that mentality was.

"A year ago that would have sounded great. But go back into the chamber and take a hard look at the people in there," I respond, pointing back to the Hall of the House of Representatives. "They don't exemplify what was imagined in 1787. The vision of the founders is a myth, Cisco, and Americans are self-delusional enough to prefer the myth over reality. There's nothing either you or I can do to change that paradigm."

The Texan looks wounded at my comment, but I just don't have the will to qualify my comments to make him feel better. It is the cold, hard reality, and best he learns now. I wish I had known a year ago.

"Good luck, my friend. I'll see you around," is all I can say before fleeing this building to return to the sanctuary of my office.

-FIVE-
CHELSEA

I escaped the confines of our office and retreated to my spot on the west stairs of the Capitol to admire the sunset and take a short break from another crummy day here in Washington. The chill in the air, even now in early May, causes me to shiver, even wrapped in my favorite white wool winter coat. My butt is freezing on these stone steps, but the serenity is worth the minor discomfort.

"You changed your hair. It looks good," Blake Peoni says in greeting as he suddenly sits next to me. Ugh, so much for serenity. Now that we have established he is observant enough to notice my long swooping curls, what could he possibly want?

"And your cologne still makes me want to gag," I say in retort. Blake is fit, handsome, and has the same Italian features Vince does, but that's where the similarities end. A half dozen or so years older than us, he's more experienced, twice as jaded, and has a soul as black as road tar.

"Good to know your hatred of me hasn't ebbed any over time. It's a pretty view, isn't it?" Blake asks, admiring me more than the setting sun. I keep refusing to look at him.

"This is my spot, and I don't like sharing it." Blake's laughter at my comment annoys me, and the last thing I need is more stress today.

"Do you remember that night after the election when you told me your staff used to meet in the same park we were standing in?" he asks, eliciting a curious nod from me. "You are sitting in the exact place I was when Roger sent me up there to go after you guys. So technically, it's my spot."

"You are turning ruining my life into an art form," I scold, rising from the cold stone to walk away. Blake grabs me by the arm gently, and something about the look on his face and the feel of his hand stops me from jerking away from him.

"I'm sorry, Chelsea. I never seem to say the right thing to you. But I've been where you are. Part of me still is. I see your frustration with the system, with Washington, and even with Congressman Bennit. Nobody understands that better than I do."

As much as I want to leave, I know he's right. The mere thought of my experiences here makes me emotional now. And although I don't want to admit it, even to myself, I desperately need someone I can talk to who can relate to me. I shudder inside to think that person may be Blake, but I sit back down anyway.

"What makes you the expert on how I'm feeling? What are you even doing these days?"

"Nothing of any interest, I can tell you that," Blake responds with a deep exhale. "I am the smallest cog in a huge, multi-million-dollar K Street lobbying machine."

One of the first introductions made to any staffer who arrives in this city is to the advocacy groups housed on K Street in Northwest Washington. The street itself is not the epicenter of lobbyists it once was, but the "K Street" reference serves as a powerful metonym for the entire industry.

"Sounds exciting," I say, completely disinterested.

"It's a sympathy job that was given to me at the bequest of a relative who happens to be close to the lawyer who runs the lobby. At least I can pay my bills, and it does keep me in Washington."

"I guess that's where we differ, Blake. I can't stand this town and won't be able to leave it soon enough."

"Is Congressman Bennit thinking of resigning?" Blake asks, without a hint of sarcasm or arrogance in his voice. He almost sounds ... concerned.

"That's funny. Quit isn't in the man's vocabulary."

"Good. Then you're already winning."

"Winning? This is winning? Maybe I slapped you too hard on that bridge a year and a half ago and jarred something loose," I say, fighting against my own emotions to stay in control. "Being ignored by, well, everybody, and getting censured twice is not winning."

"It is when their sole purpose is to get the congressman to resign, which you said he won't do."

"I thought they were just trying to make us look bad so they could hit us with it during the campaign this fall." In fact, I'm certain that's what they're trying to do. I have no idea where Blake is going with this, or where he's getting his information from. I also have no idea why he's bothering to tell me.

"I thought so too, but I have it on good authority the intent is much more sinister and immediate than that."

"Oh, really? Are you going to tell me who this 'good authority' is, or where you got your information from?"

"It's not important. What is important is they won't stop with a second censure if he doesn't resign on his own. They are going to find a way to try to expel him before the next election."

"Same old Blake. You will never change, will you? Saying it 'is not important' tells me you are full of it. Not that I expect anything less."

"Don't take it out on me because you're mad at him," Blake says, now really getting on my nerves.

"What?"

"You're pissed at your boss because he's not fighting the way you think he should. He decided to play by the rules when he got here and has been paying the price ever since."

"You know his record? Are you seriously telling me you think he plays by the rules?"

"He abandoned social media and tried to be the typical politician. You think he needs to be the maverick the people in the Connecticut Sixth District thought they were electing; only he's not listening to you." Blake pauses a moment to study my face, which I'm positive is betraying me again. "Go ahead, tell me I'm wrong and I'll walk away right now and you'll never hear from me again." Tempting, but even with my guard up against his BS, I'm curious.

"What's in this for you, Blake? Why do you care? Who put you up to this?"

"Nothing is in it for me, other than a vested interest in seeing you guys succeed."

"Yeah, right. Whatever." Blake may or may not be telling the truth, but he's holding back on something, and it probably has to do with whoever is behind him having information "on good authority."

"I'm not asking you to believe me, but I am asking you to trust me, just this once." I roll my eyes at him, but don't interrupt. "Please tell him I want to meet with him. He can choose the time and place, and I'll be there. You're his chief of staff and need to look after his best interests. This is in his best interest."

"And if I feel a meeting with you is not?" I'm on the fence with this, and need some time to think about it. Like so many other times since I have been in Washington, I don't know what the right course to take is.

"Then I'm sure you'll say so when you let him know what we talked about today and it becomes his cross to carry."

-SIX-
SPEAKER ALBRIGHT

"Boy, when the House adjourns for a long weekend, ya'll don't waste any time hitting the road, do you?" the burly voice of James Reed calls out from the entrance of the terminal.

He's right. The House adjourned only a couple of hours ago, and I made a beeline for the departures terminal at Reagan National Airport without wasting much time in between. How he found out about my schedule enough in advance to meet me here will remain a mystery, although I shouldn't be surprised. Information is your primary commodity when you run one of largest and richest lobby firms in Washington.

"How are you, James?" I ask, dropping my carry-on bag to free my right hand and shake his. Hand may be a bit understated. It's more like shaking the paw of a four-hundred-pound grizzly bear.

James Reed could easily be confused with a retired NFL lineman if he wasn't one of the most influential men in Washington. Standing over six feet tall, with a hulking build and graying hair, the large African-American from the backwoods of Kentucky is as imposing physically as he is professionally.

"I'm doing well, Mister Speaker, thank you so kindly for asking."

"What brings the head of Ibram & Reed to Reagan National on a Thursday evening?"

The one reward for making regular campaign donations to members of Congress is access. Universally accepted is the proposition that someone providing financial benefits is afforded ample opportunity to convey their views to any member of Congress. The more money and influence the lobby has, the more access is given, even if that means an impromptu run-in near the ticketing counter at an airport.

"Michael Bennit." Damn, I just cannot get away from this guy for even a day. "Let's move off to the side so we can chat, shall we, sir?"

I follow him away from ticketing to the corridor that connects Terminal A with Terminal B. The huge picture windows and Jeffersonian-style arching domes create a large space which offers at least some privacy so long as we stay away from the shops that line the hall.

"Why are you worried about Bennit, James? He poses no threat to you, your firm, or lobbying in general," I observe, after finding a quiet spot next to one of the windows and away from the horde of people trying to get out of town.

"I respectfully disagree. Every day that renegade remains in his seat is another day that puts our whole system in jeopardy," James responds with his usual southern charm.

"I never thought you would be so prone to over-exaggeration," I say with a smile. It is not returned.

"Hardly. Ya'll are working damn hard to push him out, so I'm willing to bet your members are leery of him, too."

Information is the coin of the realm on Capitol Hill. The best lobbyists make themselves invaluable to members of Congress and their staffs by providing useful information, and often get some in return. James Reed is the best of the bunch, and he often knows more about what is happening here than most lawmakers do.

"I have been hearing some grumbling from the caucus," I say, relaying a half-truth. It's been more than grumbling, as evidenced by the majority leader pleading with me in my office a couple of weeks ago. "He has been censured and reprimanded for his behavior, as has been appropriate. I'm not sure I would characterize it as pushing him out. You still haven't answered my question. Why is the largest firm in the Washington lobby so concerned?"

Lobbying is a huge industry, and one very difficult to define. Federal law requires a degree of official reporting on union and corporate expenditures on influencing public officials, but it only scratches the surface of the amount of actual money spent. The official report claims the tally exceeds three and a half billion dollars a year, but anyone who peddles influence in Washington, James Reed included, will tell you that the number is far greater.

"You don't need me to connect the dots for you, Mister Speaker." He doesn't. Money talks in this town, and when a politician doesn't need money, Reed and the rest of the lobbyists lose influence. This was not historically the case, but it is the modern reality, and people like Reed have made millions cashing in on it. He won't stand by idle and let that change.

"What are you asking me to do?"

"I'm not asking you to do anything, Johnston. I am here to offer my assistance. I can make Michael Bennit go away, and make you the hero for looking like you're cleaning up corruption in Congress. It will get the conservative firebrands in your party off your back and send a message to the moderates to toe the line."

"That sounds like a great plan, but this isn't my first dance at the ball. Everything you do comes at a price. You need me for something, or you wouldn't be here making me late for my flight home."

He offers up a laugh I'm sure is more for theater than substance. I look at my wristwatch, now with legitimate concern that my flight will leave without me. As Speaker of the House, I'm entitled to my own taxpayer-funded jet like the one Nancy Pelosi, a predecessor of mine, used to use. To avoid the appearance of impropriety, given the nation's voracious spending, I choose to fly commercial. The last couple of Speakers started the tradition, one that I am cursing myself for continuing at the moment.

"You are correct as always, Mister Speaker. This effort is pro bono, as we lawyers might say, but I will need your help when the time comes." Somehow his statement is supposed to sound wise and strategic, but his native Kentucky twang makes him sound ridiculous. An observation I'm not dumb enough to ever mention to him.

"Are you going to share the details?"

"It's best that ya'll don't know the details, Mister Speaker. Plausible deniability and all. Just know I'm taking care of it, and when the results come to light, ya'll know what to do."

"With due respect, James, this is beginning to sound like something I don't want to be associated with. I cannot engage in something illegal, or in a conspiracy to entrap a colleague in the House." There, my ass is officially covered in the remote chance he's recording this conversation. In reality, if James Reed is going to use his extensive resources to help get rid of Bennit, I'm all for it providing he isn't planning on offing the guy.

"Yes, I understand your apprehension. The reality is, sir, you will go along with the plan. I mean, how would the party respond to a poor showing by the GOP in November? It's an election year, and you have members in tight races that are going to need … substantial financial support. It would be a shame if the well dried up so close to the finish line."

The threat, while not overt, was received loud and clear. He's got me by the balls, and he knows it. I'm third in line to the presidency, yet the man in the loud, obscenely expensive suit has my political career in his hands and is the one calling the shots. Welcome to politics in modern America.

"Don't let me hold you up any longer, Mister Speaker. Go catch your flight. I'm sure we'll talk again soon," he says with a wink and a big smile, before swinging around and heading for the door leading out of the terminal.

SEVEN

MICHAEL

Directly across the Potomac River from the Lincoln Memorial, and adjacent to the Pentagon, is one of the most beautiful and powerful spaces in the United States. Arlington National Cemetery is six hundred twenty-four acres of rolling green hills where veterans of the nation's conflicts, beginning with the American Civil War, have been laid to rest.

Established during the Civil War on Robert E. Lee's wife's family estate known as Arlington House, the cemetery is one of the most popular tourist sites in the Washington, D.C., area. Sadly, it's also one of the most powerfully solemn places to visit since full military honors are rendered during funerals an average of twenty-seven times each workday.

The grounds of the cemetery are meant to honor those men and women who courageously served the nation by providing a final resting place of peace and serenity. Section Sixty, the burial location for those who gave their lives since the beginning of the Global War on Terror, has been called the "saddest acre in America." It certainly is for me.

"Hey, Leroy," I whisper to the white marble headstone as I squat down beside it. "It's been a long time."

I place a deck of cards as a memento on the headstone. That man loved playing Spades, and as Special Forces soldiers in Afghanistan, much of our downtime was spent in our hooch playing that simple card game with whoever dared to challenge us. Of course, finding fresh opponents was difficult once word of our prowess spread. Our win-loss record in the strategy game was the talk of all the NATO forces stationed throughout that hellhole.

"Wherever you are my friend, I hope you're looking after me. You'd be one of the few who are these days," I say, a tear breaking loose from the corner of my eye. We promised each other that should the worst ever happen, we would spend the afterlife watching over the one who survived. I drew the short straw. "I miss you, buddy."

I stand up, still staring at the Leroy Charleston, New York, SFC, Afghanistan, and the dates of his birth and death etched into his grave marker. He was a good man, brave soldier, and reliable friend. Everything the man behind me isn't.

"You going to just stand there like a dope or are you going to say something?"

"I didn't want to interrupt, so I just thought I would wait until ..." the voice behind me says, trailing off either in deference or fear of saying something stupid. "Did you serve with him?"

"He was my brother."

"I uh ... I didn't think you had a brother," Blake stammers in obvious confusion.

"Look around you. Every man and woman buried here were my brothers and sisters." He is cowed at my response, which wasn't my intention. I let him off the hook. "Yes, Blake, I did serve with him. He was killed by small arms fire during our last mission over there."

"The one you were awarded the Distinguished Service Cross on?"

"Yeah, that one," I say remorsefully.

Blake finally summons the courage to walk over and stand beside me. We remain quiet for a few long moments, enjoying the peaceful calm of the air and surroundings shrouded in the early Friday morning fog.

"I'm not going to lie, Congressman, meeting you here feels a little like something out of a Tom Clancy novel. Congress adjourned for the weekend and everyone headed home. Is there a reason you chose to meet at Arlington?"

"Yeah. Out of all the places around Washington, this is where I'm most comfortable. Take a look at this garden of stone, Blake. The men and women buried in this section gave 'the last full measure of devotion' to their country, as Lincoln put it. Many of the veterans who survived the wars they fought in believed deeply in the ideals of freedom and liberty. They are the only ones inside the Beltway who do. I doubt you understand, though."

"My father was a vet," Blake says, surprising me. I honestly didn't know that. "He died from the effects of Gulf War Syndrome."

"Is that why you wear that Second Armored pin?" I ask, pointing to the lapel on his coat. I may be dressed in jeans and a windbreaker, but dressed in a suit, Blake looks like he's the one who serves in Congress. At least I'm comfortable.

"It was given to me by a Vietnam vet over near the Lincoln Memorial not long before your debate with Beaumont. I was out for a walk, questioning the worth to my former boss and Roger and my loyalty to them. It was that night I was reminded of some things I had long forgotten. To keep reminding myself, I wear this in my father's memory." Blake pauses a long time before continuing. "You remind me a lot of him."

"Is he here?"

"No, he wanted his ashes spread in the Rockies." I nod, not wanting to continue to get any more sentimental with a guy who I'd just as soon choke the life out for what he did a year and a half ago.

"Why did you want to meet with me, Blake?"

"To tell you there's still time to get your head out of your ass." He really didn't just say that to me, did he?

"Excuse me?"

"You heard me, sir. Do you know how many independents have ever been elected to the House?"

"Not many, but who really gives a damn? One reason is because independents don't mix with the GOP and Dem Party elites." I spare him the lecture about how our country adopted the two party political system and how they've worked to preserve it ever since.

"No, independents mix fine. *You* don't mix because you're not like them. A lot of them don't believe in the Constitution, and certainly can't quote it from memory like you can. Congressmen don't come here because they decry the values the people buried here died for."

"Okay, since you're on a roll, tell me something I don't already know."

"Gladly. The people don't want you to try to be one of them. They are waiting for Michael Bennit to be the man they elected, and everyone around you is waiting for you to realize that. How much longer do you plan to disappointment them?"

"You think you have any understanding of the people around me?" I ask, getting more annoyed with every word that comes out of the pompous fool's mouth. Blake has a selfish reason for every angle he exploits, and I want to find this one.

"I think they're frustrated that you're playing their game, not yours," he says, pointing off in the direction toward the Capitol that sits in the far distance.

"What are you talking about?" I ask, incredulous at his ignorance. Does he not know that my disciplinary rap sheet is the talk of both chambers?

"You could never have beaten Beaumont in a traditional campaign. Not in a million years. So you did the next best thing—changed the rules to something he couldn't compete with. You need to do the same thing here."

"It's not that simple," I reply with a derisive snort. "I tried, but some rules you just can't change."

"Are you serious? Will you listen to what you're saying? You're going to stand there and tell me that the man who broke every conceivable rule as a candidate is willing to play by any of them as a congressman?"

"Forget it, Blake. I don't belong here. I can't do the job I was elected to. It's over."

"So you're quitting?"

"No, I'm not quitting. I am going to run again in the fall, get my ass beat, and go find a teaching job somewhere."

"Okay, you're not quitting, you're just too weak to do what must be done. I would never have thought the great Michael Bennit is nothing more than a coward."

That was the last straw. Maybe it was being called a coward, or the emotion of this place in front of the burial site of one of my closest friends, but I felt the surge of anger through my body translate into a physical act that was a long time coming.

I think back to all the pain he's caused. How he hurt Chelsea, did the dirty work for Beaumont, and only came clean about it all when it was too late to help. I think about the past year and all the frustration I've felt. How I've been ignored and rendered ineffective. Right now, in this instant, I have a convenient target to take it out on. I channel that anger into my fist before I let it fly.

Before Blake could even register what was happening, the hardest right hook I have probably ever thrown connects with his left cheek. He pirouettes, stumbles over the grave marker and hits the ground with an audible thud. He writhes in pain for a moment before rolling awkwardly onto his side and climbing to his feet.

"You've wanted to do that for a long time, haven't you, Congressman?" Blake asks, still shaking the cobwebs out. "I'm sure I deserved it."

He doesn't see the next one coming either. Not as hard a swing as my first, the second punch connects with his jaw and knocks him right back down to the ground.

"Go ahead, get up. I dare you," I threaten through clenched teeth. Blake surprises me with a little laugh. Is he seriously taunting me?

"Why? Are you going to kick my ass? Leave me here in a bloody heap for the groundskeepers to find? Go ahead, but I'm going to say my piece."

Blake gets up, his clothes now soaked from the heavy dew clinging to the emerald green grass. He brushes himself off and draws closer, tenderly checking the gash on his now puffy, red cheek and gash in his bloody lower lip.

"Hit me again if you want, but I learned the consequences of not speaking up. I could have fought against spreading the rumor about you and Chelsea during the election, but I didn't. I stayed quiet, and have paid the price ever since."

As a teacher, I always wanted my students to learn lessons from their mistakes. It was a message I explained to them after the man standing defiantly in front of me released embarrassing information about some of Vince, Peyton, and Brian's transgressions. Blake may be a little older, but isn't that lesson a universal one?

"All right, finish what you came here to say," still ready to hit him again if I feel the need.

"You could play by every rule the House has and it would still change nothing about the situation we're all in. Americans have had it with the government. Whether it's a president acting more like a king, or partisans in Congress playing games at the expense of the citizens who put them there, we've reached the tipping point. Enough is enough. We have not been this divided, and this discontented, since the Civil War. It scares me what could happen next.

"You have a once in a generation opportunity. You may not have asked for it, or even wanted it, but America needs you to serve them once again. Not with a rifle in a distant land, but with a voice right here at home. To speak for them, and seize the chance to effect some positive change. I hope you don't waste the moment, because the expiration date on this opportunity is fast approaching."

I hate being lectured, especially when someone is trying to duplicitously appeal to my sense of duty. The feeling is doubly intense when the man doing it is Blake Peoni. But even through my unmitigated anger, I realize he may have a point.

"Please think about what I've said," Blake adds, starting his walk back toward the road heading out of Section Sixty. "For all our sakes."

-EIGHT-
CHELSEA

The congressman returns to the office a full three hours after we thought he would. The only plausible explanation is he shunned the Metro and opted for a long, leisurely stroll across the bridge over the Potomac River and up the National Mall. That's his prerogative, but it left us bored.

"It's not enough that I get censured on a monthly basis? Now you have me contributing to the delinquency of minors?" the congressman asks Kylie when he enters, sans any real shock or annoyance in his voice.

Not relishing the idea of hanging out in the office on a Friday morning when the House is not in session, Kylie had made a pit stop and brought back some adult beverages. Mister Bennit is greeted with the sight of us all holding bottles of Sam Adams. It wouldn't be a big deal if anyone else in the room other than Kylie was over the age of twenty-one.

"You guys realize it's eleven in the morning?" Okay, I suppose that makes it a big deal too.

"We know," is all Kylie bothers to answer.

"It's been a rough week," Vince adds.

"And it's five o'clock somewhere," Vanessa chimes in for good measure, uttering one of the most overused clichés ever. I don't bother saying anything.

"All right, since all of you here can't be a good sign, I might need this," the congressman says while selecting a bottle out of the six-pack. He pops the top off using the opener and takes a long swig. He knows an intervention when he sees one. "Okay, who gets to take the first swing?"

"Don't get all defensive already, honey," Kylie warns. "You're going to hear what we have to say now or you can regret it tonight." She has a way with him. Kylie may be the only person on this planet I've met who can be more stubborn than Mister Bennit is.

The implication of Kylie's comment is not lost on the congressman, and he relents quickly. No couple is perfect, but they are as close to a perfect match as I have ever seen. I thought he and his former fiancée went well together, but not until I spent more time with my mentor did the ugly truth of their relationship start to show.

With Kylie, it is much different. She moved to Washington not long after last year's special election, and since they were inseparable anyway, Mister Bennit moving in with her was a no-brainer. Between his condominium in Millfield and her apartment only a few blocks away, their living situation was covered.

Together, they are a force of nature—strong, unyielding, and undeterred. They have a love for each other I haven't seen since I was a kid. My mom and dad had a great marriage before she died. Even with all the congressman's troubles since he came to Washington, Kylie has been unflinching in her support of him. It's inspiring, in more ways than one.

Kylie Roberts is the polar opposite of Mister Bennit's ex-fiancée, Jessica Slater. Miss Slater was fashion model beautiful, with, long, blonde hair, impeccable fashion sense, and curves in the all the right places. Kylie has more of a girl next door beauty, with dark hair, and a petite, yet powerful build. I asked Vince to compare them once, and he said Jessica was the girl you want to sleep with while Kylie was the one you wanted to marry. Pretty astute analysis, I think.

"What do you guys want to know?"

"What did Blake have to say?" I ask, surely the most curious since I was the one initially approached to set up the meeting.

"Before or after I laid him out with a right hook?"

"You hit him?" a couple of us cry out simultaneously.

"Twice, actually."

"Bet that felt good," Vanessa deadpans. "I've had dreams about doing that." She glances at me and I reward her with a smirk of agreement. I have dreamt about it too, even after having smacked him that night at Briar Point. We tip our bottles at each other and take a sip.

"Let's go with what caused you to go all Rocky Balboa on him," Kylie remarks to give the conversation a nudge forward.

"He called me a coward." Oops, that was a mistake.

"He set a meeting with you just to challenge your honor?" Vince queries, somewhat baffled at Blake's behavior while equally admiring his ballsiness. It's the last thing any of us would dream of saying to him, regardless of how pissed off we are.

"No, he set the meeting to tell me to stop trying to play their game."

"He wants you to play Candyland," I add, a direct reference to the strategy that got us here.

Knowing we could not beat Winston Beaumont in a traditional campaign, we decided to change the rules and force him to play our game. Mister Bennit likened it to beating a chess master by forcing him to play Candyland. We used our involvement as students, social media, and mainstream media coverage of both to do precisely that.

"Yeah, Chels, and he told me to get my head out of my ass in the process."

Vince chokes on his beer as the comment caught him mid-swallow. "He said that?" Vince's admiration level of Blake just went up another notch. Congressman Bennit nods in response as Vince wipes his chin.

"Well, he's right," Kylie offers, getting everyone to turn their attention to her. I guess she is going to lead this charge.

"Oh, not you too?"

"Look, just because you don't want to hear it doesn't make it untrue. I've been covering politics my entire adult life and you want to know what I've learned? People don't want to give a damn."

"I already figured that out, Kylie. I ran on that basis the first time, remember?"

"That's not what I mean. People elect others to run the government and make decisions for them so they don't have to. Hell, most of them wouldn't even want to if given the chance. Americans have their own problems and don't want to worry about things that don't directly affect them or that they can't easily do something about. The only reason they get excited about anything political is when it's about an issue they like, a law they don't, or a person they believe in actually runs for office."

"And you're that man, Congressman," I say, finally getting a chance to chime in on Kylie's monologue. It's one of the few contributions I get to make around here. "Vince, Vanessa, me, and all the others joined your campaign for that reason. People voted for you for that reason. Now we are all just waiting for you to be the leader you need to be."

"Honey, all I'm saying is millions of Americans lost faith in the system a long time ago," Kylie continues after my contribution to the argument. "The pettiness, the partisan politics, the corruption … they all contributed to a collective national blindness for what goes on here in Oz."

"And you want me to pull back the curtain?"

"No, we can't settle for that. Not anymore. We need you to kill the Wicked Witch and set Oz free."

"Oh, that's it? So now I'm Dorothy? I suppose you guys are going to be handing me the buckets of water."

"Damn straight we will be," Vanessa adds, the serious look on her face letting everyone know that the chica is itching for a fight.

"How? We don't have the weapons we once did. I have all of one ally in the House, and I'm pretty sure he's spent too much time in the Texas sun. The media has turned on me, I have no clout or influence thanks to the political parties, and our social media following is dwindling. Even you can't help with that anymore, sweetie, because you can't influence what is reported like you did in the campaign," the congressman accurately points out.

"Since when do we care what the media thinks?" Vince challenges. It's an honest question coming from the press secretary. "We didn't during the campaign. They hated on us for ignoring them, and chastised us for not talking about issues. It didn't bother us then, so why now?"

"It shouldn't. We need go back to breaking all the rules and not caring what the media or anyone else here says," Vanessa implores.

"And use the social media machine we built up to get our side of the story to the only group who matters—the voters back home," I add, taking up the argument. Damn, you'd think we rehearsed this. I guess we are all so passionate about it, we didn't have to.

"Social media doesn't work for us anymore. People have tuned us out," the congressman offers. He's not one to make excuses, so hearing one come out of his mouth is a little shocking.

"How do you know? When was the last time you even logged onto Facebook or sent a tweet?" Kylie demands, probably knowing the answer as sure as we do.

"You think the people back home care? You've seen our polling. What does the Marist poll have us down by? Twenty? Thirty? I'm beginning to feel like Dick Johnson." In our defense, our numbers are much higher than the eight percent of the vote Johnson won in the fall election, but I see his point.

"Yeah, they care," Vince counters. "People elected you to come here because they believe in you. They're down on you now because you stopped engaging them like you used to. They'll hear you out though, especially if we show them the people who run the system are using it to prevent you from accomplishing what you came here to do."

"So, what you all are saying is instead of legislating and representing the people of our district who sent me here, you want me to enlist their support to start a revolution that fundamentally alters how the U.S. House of Representatives operates?"

"If that's what it takes, yeah, that's exactly what we want you to do," Vince states, outlining clearly where we all stand on the matter.

The congressman isn't buying the argument. He has always had a romantic vision of government that the media and his colleagues constantly derided as naïve over the past year. He would have been perfectly at home at the Constitutional Convention. Unfortunately, there is no facsimile of Madison, Morris, or Sherman serving in the Congress.

"Vince, do you have any idea how many revolutions in world history have failed?" the congressman fires back.

"I know one that didn't," Vanessa intercedes. "The American Revolution succeeded against all odds, unless my high school history teacher taught me wrong." Ouch.

"That brilliant history teacher must also have taught you that the colonists were dead in the water without help. You realize there were more French at Yorktown when the British surrendered than colonists."

"Darling, if getting help is the only basis you have to debate this with us, then your argument is pretty weak. If you want allies, let's go out and find them."

The congressman doesn't want to add himself to the long list of new representatives who have wanted to rock the boat only to fail. I get it, but sometimes you have to break something to get it to work right. It's counterintuitive, but true, and although Congressman Bennit is a brilliant debater, he's out of excuses. Vince recognizes it too. Scoring a victory against him is a rare feat for us. The resigned look on his face mirrors the one he wore on the day he made the bet with us our junior year.

"Viva la revolución!" Vince adds, a wry smile creeping across his face as he tips his beer in salute for the fight yet to come. We all follow suit, but in the end, I don't know if the congressman has the will to follow.

-NINE-
MICHAEL

Millfield High School hasn't changed a bit. Not that I expected it to in the year and a half since I left. A lot of time has passed since the last day I worked here, but it still all feels so familiar.

I pull into the parking lot and find a spot reserved for visitor parking near the front door. This is a first for me. In all the time I taught in this building, I never used the front door in an effort to avoid the troll who hides in the main office.

"My, my, the prodigal son returns." Speak of the Devil. What are the odds of a man who rarely leaves his office happening to be standing at the front door the day I walk in? "I didn't think I would ever see you back here, Michael," Robinson Howell sneers.

"Robinson, I think you meant to say *Congressman Bennit*, not Michael. And it's good to see you outside your office, now that it's 2:45 and the students and most of the staff are gone. I'm glad to see your confidence level is improving."

His face goes beet red in a manner that only I seem to be able to bring out. Good to see I'm not losing my touch. He looks like he's about to come up with some semblance of a response when Charlene Freeman walks out of the main office.

"I hope you boys are playing nice for once," she cautions, knowing full well we aren't.

"Yes, ma'am. Robinson here was just telling me how wonderful it was having me back in the building and how he'd love to have me back to teach here if things don't work out for my reelection in November."

"What a very gracious and generous offer," Charlene says with a big smile.

"I thought so. It would be great to work for such a fine administrator again," I say, laying it on thick. Before he goes nuclear, she cuts him off.

"Robinson, will you give me a moment with the congressman, please?"

Howell shoots me a look and storms off, leaving me with the superintendent of the Millfield Public School District. Again, very little has changed since I left.

"Love to have you back to teach, eh? Are they putting LSD in the water down in D.C. these days?"

"It was the best I could come up with on short notice."

"Oh, I doubt that," she says, glancing in the direction Howell disappeared in, "but I would be lying if I said it wouldn't be great to have you back in the school district again. What brings you here now?"

"I owe my mentor a visit."

"I'm sure Chalice is still up in her office, but before you go, I need to apologize."

"For what, ma'am?"

"Congressman, you don't work for me anymore. You can drop the ma'am thing."

"Sorry, it's a force of habit. And I prefer Michael, not Congressman," I say, returning her smile.

"We never apologized to you after the truth about the allegations of the affair came out. More importantly, I never reached out to apologize to you. I should have, and I'm sorry."

I give her a nod, but I'm not sure I can accept the apology. My termination from Millfield was more of a result from the disruption I caused and my insubordination with Howell than anything else. To say I've been sore over the past year because my former employer could not be bothered to issue an apology would be an exercise in understatement.

"Are you serious about wanting to return to teaching if you don't win a second term?" I look off down the hall in the direction Howell sulked off in.

"Charlene, we both know that won't ever happen, at least not here." She nods, understanding that my reemployment would never be accepted by the school board. "But please feel free to mention it in passing to Howell. The token consideration of it would make him go postal."

"You bet. Now, you'd better get up there before Chalice leaves. It was great seeing you again, Congres ... Michael."

* * *

"I apologize, I'm not going to have my lesson plans in on time this week," I announce as I reach the door.

"Oh my God!" Chalice exclaims, jumping out of her chair and moving around the desk in her cramped office to give me a hug. "You look great! How are you, Congressman?"

"Really, Chalice? Congressman? Cut that crap out. You are the very last person I'll ever let call me that. But I'm good, thank you, and yourself?"

"Another year under Robinson Howell and another year closer to retirement," she says with a smile. "Every day I take the bad with the good. Did you run into Jessica while you were wandering the halls?"

I was afraid this would come up. Chalice was always partial to my ex-fiancée, and I'm sure would love nothing more than to see us get back together. She likes Kylie, but until there is a ring on her finger, she will always be rooting for Jessica.

"Chalice," I warn with a look that prompts her to hold up her hands in mock surrender and change the subject.

"So, what brings you home?"

"I flew in this afternoon for our constituent work week in the district."

"Look at you, Mister Jet-Setter."

"Yeah, not so much, but working with the people in the district is about the only part of this job I still enjoy."

"Of course it is. You're a natural problem solver. You didn't answer my question though. I asked why you're *here*."

Chalice has always had a low tolerance for small talk with her teachers. She was an amazing boss and understanding advisor, but she could also be a cut-to-the-chase taskmaster. It would have made her an extremely effective principal. Instead we ended up with Howell.

"To see you. I need some advice."

"Let me guess. Congress isn't what you'd thought it'd be?"

"That's putting it mildly. Don't plead ignorance, Chalice. I know you watch the news."

"I do, but I never put much faith in the accuracy of their reports, especially when they're about you. 'The most effective way to destroy people is to deny and obliterate their own understanding of their history.'"

"*1984*. George Orwell. Very nice, but I have another for you. 'He who controls the past controls the future. He who controls the present controls the past.' That's how these people I have to deal with get elected year after year."

She offers a seat across the desk from her, although I have to move a pile of folders to sit in it. She sits in her own chair, reaching over to turn off her computer monitor to avoid the distraction of e-mail notifications that seem to be pouring in.

"You know, *Newsweek* did a poll in 2011 and found less than forty percent of Americans knew the term of office for a senator was six years. I used that study as a teaching tool and posed the same question to my students. Can you guess how many knew the right answer?"

"I can only imagine."

"Fifteen percent. Just fifteen percent, Michael. The people can't be bothered to know how long their representative's term lasts, so it's no surprise how easy they can be manipulated. Of course, that was before the rise to power of the iCandidate ..."

"Rise to power," I say derisively. "That's a joke. Blake Peoni is telling me to get my head out of my ass, Ky—"

"Wait! Blake Peoni?"

"Yeah, it's a long story. Anyway, Kylie wants me to mix it up with the most senior politicians in the country, and my mutinous staff is encouraging me to start a revolution." Chalice raises an eyebrow. "As in changing the way the House works, not overthrowing the whole government."

"Ah. Well, they're all correct."

"Yeah, I knew you'd say that. But, to be honest with you, I don't think I have any more fight left in me."

"I see," she says with the same disagreeing pout I once got on a regular basis. "Come with me."

"Where are we going?"

"You need a little reminder of who you are, and I know just the place you can get it."

I follow her out of the office and through the adjoining work room to the hallway. There are still a few students wandering the hall, and a couple even give me the patented head nod teenagers like to use as a form of greeting.

"Michael, you were a dedicated soldier," she says as we head down the hall. "You earned the Distinguished Service Cross in Afghanistan, and I know you don't think you deserved it, but you also told me once the mission saved a lot of lives."

"What's your point, Chalice?"

"I'm getting to it, so don't be fresh." She always did know how to keep me in line. "You could have chosen not to run in the special election. You lost to Beaumont, and you fulfilled your obligations to your students for the bet, but you ran again anyway. The voters responded by overwhelmingly sending you to Washington. They asked you to serve once again, and you couldn't say no, because just like your time in Special Forces, your devotion to this nation is part of who you are."

We stop at my old classroom and she walks in, flipping on the lights as she enters. I'm amazed at what I see. Every print, poster, and piece of memorabilia I had on the walls is in the exact place I left it. My room was always the most extravagantly decorated in the building, and not one thing has changed. Even more to my surprise is the layout of the room. The desks are still set up in a horseshoe.

The seating arrangement in a semi-circle gave me a "stage" to work on, and both my students and I came to call it that. It's not a style most teachers prefer, so I don't understand why it was preserved. As I move to the center of it, and look at the seats where my students would have been sitting, I feel like I'm home again. I can almost imagine Xavier, Vince, Amanda, Vanessa, Brian, Emilee, Peyton, and the rest of the honors American History class all staring back at me.

"What do you think?"

"It's just like I left it. Is my replacement trying to be me or something?"

"No, he realizes he's never going to be you. Nobody can. But he is trying to emulate you, and do you know why?"

I hear the question, but I am lost in my own thoughts as I look around the room. The posters of Washington, Lincoln, and Martin Luther King, Jr. still look down on the classroom from their spots on the wall.

"Let me answer that for you. He emulates you because it works. You think you're in this fight with the political elite alone, but you're not. There are a lot of people in this country who feel the same way you do, and they will fight with you to do what must be done. All you need to do is decide to step up and lead them."

"I think the time for that has come and gone," I say with a tinge of regret. Maybe I should have visited six months ago. I'm not sure Blake's pleadings, my staff's intervention, or even Chalice's reminder can make a difference now.

"Let's go back to your Orwell quote. 'He who controls the past controls the future. He who controls the present controls the past.' The last time you taught in this room, that's exactly what you did. I know you can do it again." She looks at her watch and edges toward the door. "It's quitting time for me, so I have to get going. It was great seeing you again, Michael. Good luck."

"Thanks, Chalice. For everything."

The last time I stood in this room, I addressed my students after we lost to Beaumont. Then, as now, I could almost feel the eyes of Washington and Lincoln stare down at me. Back then, I hoped they were proud of what I was trying to do.

I pull my iPhone out of my pocket and select the number from favorites. As I wait for her to pick up, I can only hope Washington and Lincoln will again approve of what I'm about to do.

"Hey, Chels, it's me. Yeah, things are fine, but I need you to do me a favor," I say, waiting for her to ask what it is I need. "Have Blake set up that meeting. If we're going to go all *Demolition Man* and start a war, I'd better find out what heavy artillery I can bring to the fight."

-TEN-
SENATOR VIANO

The Capital Grille offers a stunning view down Pennsylvania Avenue and a panoramic view of the Capitol that makes me yearn for the position I held a year and a half ago. Although my time in the Senate was spent dining at more frequented establishments like the Charlie Palmer Steak, this place still brings me back to the good old days. The food, service, and ambiance are pretty good, too.

That's not saying this restaurant isn't enjoyed by power brokers in Washington. Even with Congress in recess for the weekend, a couple of political players are seated only a matter of feet away from me. Weekends are not high tide for deal making, but hopefully I'm about to make one for myself.

He's late, so I order the pan-seared Chilean sea bass with citrus and pea tendrils and sip on a glass of chardonnay as I wait. When he finally enters the restaurant fifteen minutes late, I can't help but notice he looks like he got hit by a bus.

"Nice cheek, Blake. Did you get mugged or something?" I say, offering the seat on the other side of the table.

"No, a mugging would have been easier. I had the unfortunate experience of pissing off a Green Beret," he explains, taking his seat. Oh, I like this guy already. I just hope that Blake's lacerated cheek, fat lip, and broken ego are not a bad omen for me and what I want.

"So I'm to assume that your damaged face means my request will go unfulfilled?"

"Never assume, Senator. Chelsea called yesterday afternoon, just as I said she would. My little speech got through to Congressman Bennit. He wants to meet you." Excellent!

"Thank you, Blake. I knew you would come through in setting that up," I say, tempering my enthusiasm and taking care to repress my true thoughts. A meeting with Bennit set up by Blake was a long shot, and I didn't have much confidence that he could get it done.

"You're welcome. Consider it thanks for getting me my job. We're even now."

"Even? Oh no, I don't think that's a fair trade. But you know what? I'm in a good mood, so yes, we can call it square." Getting Blake his bottom-feeder job was really a piece of cake, but he doesn't need to know that. "Can you stay for lunch?" Please say no …

"Thank you, but no. Even as a menial laborer, and with Congress out of town, the Washington lobby never rests. Tell me something, Senator. Why are you taking an interest in Bennit? I mean, not that I think he wouldn't appreciate your help. But why now?"

I don't have a high opinion of Blake. He thinks far more of his capabilities than what he actually possesses, and may have been a trusted advisor to Winston Beaumont, but that man was an idiot anyway. Only a fool wouldn't make certain a paper trail detailing illegal activities was destroyed, or better yet, never created in the first place. Now he is on the way to the clink along with members of his senior staff. Blake may have escaped a date with prison rapists by selling him out to the Feds, but being permanently banished to the lowest rung of the political ladder may feel like the same thing.

"The world is an unjust place. I learned that in my reelection campaign, and I think you learned it as well. I'm just looking to ensure another fine representative in government is not cast out because he's politically inconvenient. It's how we can get our payback, Blake."

That sounded believable. Despite my low regard for him, I can't afford to trust Blake. I don't think his agenda will mesh with mine in the long run, so he has to be kept at a distance and out of the loop. I only need him now to gain Bennit's trust so I can do the same.

"Tomorrow, one p.m., the National Archives," Blake says, accepting my ridiculous answer and rising from his seat. "And don't be late. He was a teacher. I know he hates that."

"Duly noted," I say, using the same broad smile I flashed at every stop on the Virginia campaign trail eight years ago. "Have a nice day, Blake. I'll be sure to let you know how it goes."

Blake nods and heads for the exit just as my server arrives with lunch. I have a meeting that I am actually looking forward to for the first time since I lost the election. This could change everything. Yep, the political winds define who wins and who loses, and a front is about to blow into Washington.

PART II

WE THE PEOPLE

-ELEVEN-
MICHAEL

The National Archives Building bears a resemblance to the Parthenon and is situated on Pennsylvania Avenue north of the National Mall. The Archives exhibits important American historical documents such as the Louisiana Purchase Treaty and the Emancipation Proclamation, but the Rotunda for the Charters of Freedom is the part of the building the public comes to see.

It is there where the original copies of the Declaration of Independence, the Constitution, and the Bill of Rights are stored. Two large-scale murals by Barry Faulkner in the Rotunda depict fictional scenes of the presentation of our nation's two most important documents. Both works have more of a feeling of ancient Rome than anything depicting eighteenth-century America.

I have been wandering around the room for the last twenty minutes, finally stopping to admire the Constitution before moving over to the first official document that united us as a people. There are no long lines to wait in like a Six Flags amusement park. Visitors to the National Archives are allowed to walk from document to document as they wish.

"You may be the only elected official in this town that actually comes here," I hear the voice say from behind me. I'm impressed that she's nearly fifteen minutes early for our meeting.

"From what I have seen over the past year, I'm not surprised," I say without turning around.

"Do you have a favorite part?" she asks, joining me in admiring the document encased before us. I don't bother to strain to read the fading text of one our oldest and most cherished artifacts. Instead, I just look directly at her and smile.

"'That whenever any Form of Government becomes destructive of these ends, it is the Right of the People to alter or to abolish it, and to institute new Government, laying its foundation on such principles and organizing its powers in such form, as to them shall seem most likely to effect their Safety and Happiness.'"

"Fitting, considering your present circumstances," she observes, outstretching her hand. "Senator Marilyn Viano."

"Congressman Michael Bennit," I reply in an equally formal voice, "but I prefer just being called Michael. I want to apologize for dragging you here on Mother's Day."

"Don't worry about it," she says with a dismissive wave of her hand. "I have no kids, thankfully. I'm happy to settle for being an aunt. My siblings were the baby factories, giving my parents the desired grandchildren, so they stayed off my back about it."

"Baby factories?"

"Three siblings with eleven kids split between them. All girls, except for my younger brother who had a son that can't manage to get out of his own way in life."

I smile at the senator. She's likeable in a proper, almost British sort of way. Tall and fit for her mid-fifties, she looks like a gray-haired cross between Ellen Degeneris and Dame Judi Dench. Her sophisticated charm is disarming, but something in her cold, calculating eyes tells me this woman can be a very dangerous political creature.

"I'm sure you know all about the situation I have found myself in."

"Most of the country does, Michael," she offers with a dazzling smile cameras must have loved. "Blake filled me in on what pieces I didn't get from the news. The only thing I am uncertain about is what exactly you are trying to do here."

I take a deep breath to collect my thoughts. The reality is I'm not sure what I'm trying to do here anymore. Just as Chalice surmised, Congress isn't what I thought it would be.

"From the moment the First United States Congress met in April of 1789, skeptical citizens expected the worst from the people elected to it. Over the next two hundred twenty-five or so years, we've done nothing but confirm their opinions. I thought when I got elected I could show them there was someone out there who could fulfill the Framers' original expectations."

"Michael, there's your first problem. That's a very naïve approach to politics." I'm glad she isn't planning on going easy on me.

"Yeah, probably. But it's my approach, and not one I plan on abandoning. Unfortunately, I am almost the only person in the House who thinks that way."

"Almost?" the senator queries with a raised eyebrow.

"Believe it or not, there may be another." Exactly one, assuming my first impression of Francisco Reyes turns into a lasting one. "And it's hard to have real discussions and debate about issues without serious people to hold them."

"The partisanship in the House and Senate is the longest running show in Washington. Trying to pass any bill is like watching two heavyweight boxers dance around each other in a ring because both are afraid to get hit with a punch hard enough to put them on the mat. It's frustrating, and the public's become too jaded and cynical to listen to the crap coming out of this town anymore."

"Exactly, and if we don't start restoring America's faith in the political system, the divide will only grow worse until it forms a rift that cannot be healed. Ask Abe Lincoln how much fun governing is when that happens," I add to drive my point home.

"You plan on doing that by yourself?"

"I can't. That's why I need your help." Somehow I sense she already knows that's why I'm here, but I go on to explain my thoughts anyway. She listens intently as we meander around the Rotunda, and then on to the "Record of Rights" exhibit where a copy of the Magna Carta is on display.

"Before you go down this path, you should know what you're up against. Over the last fifteen years, a majority of House districts have become decisively Democratic or

Republican. Three hundred of the seats in the House are gerrymandered to the point where they are reliably safe for the incumbent. Changing that won't be easy, and in fact, will probably be a complete failure."

Congressional districts are redrawn every ten years following the national census. Gerrymandering is a term first coined by the *Boston Gazette* in the early eighteen hundreds to describe a practice where these boundaries are manipulated to establish a political advantage for a particular party. It's just another method politicians have used to reduce the power of the American voter.

"Maybe, but it's those members who don't worry about being reelected and can apply their ideological instincts without fear of retribution back home. Members who feel no political need to court voters from the ideological center aren't compelled to collaborate and compromise. We need to find a way to force them to play ball."

She reflects on my comment for a moment, and I notice this woman is very hard to read. She is extremely intelligent and analytical, but she also doesn't show an overt willingness to share her true feelings on a matter. As an old soldier, I have been taught not to trust reporters or politicians. Now I am dating a journalist and asking for help from a Washington insider. My world is completely upside down from where it was two years ago.

-TWELVE-
SENATOR VIANO

Most freshman politicians in the House are naïve fools. Since the House is the proving ground for Senate, I didn't have much exposure to the laughable tommyrot these political rookies bring to the capital. As much as Michael Bennit falls into this category, I find myself liking him.

His back is up against a wall, and some very powerful people are yearning to crush him. Ironically, some of those people are the same ones who decided to end my political career. Bennit isn't the type to go out quietly, and the fighting spirit he embodies makes him my kind of guy. Unbridled passion, and willingness to battle the elite in this town, is precisely what I'm looking for.

"There are a lot of merits to your plan, Michael. But remember, these people have war chests as big as Beaumont's. In the modern age, politicians devote more time and energy to raising money to run for reelection than any other singular task."

"True, but money doesn't always buy wins. I spent nothing and still came within a hundred votes of beating Beaumont," Michael offers. He's right, but his campaign was unique and largely successful because of free mainstream media coverage. For those not blessed with such an organic level of curiosity, television commercials are the most effective way to reach the population. Networks know this, thus air time for commercials is sold at a premium.

To afford them, a candidate needs to be well financed. The result is that fundraising becomes the primary concern for any politician who ever worried about reelection. It was my Achilles' heel, and maybe the reason I find Michael's proposal so fascinating. But the other piece of his plan is intriguing.

"But you're right, my colleagues do spend an insane amount of time fundraising," he continues. "Because of that, there are few legislative statesmen and women. The number of people in the House who either care about or understand the complexity of national policy issues is non-existent. The result is what we have today—politics eclipsing policy as the default mindset of Congress. That's our angle."

"You're planning on exploiting the incumbents' love affair with ducking tough issues." He nods. Conflict avoidance is a serious motivator for many in Congress, if for no other reason than it can be used against them in a campaign. No politician likes running on their record these days.

"Cards are on the table, Senator. What do you say? Will you help?" The mood of the country is the mystery ingredient in the election process. Right now, with the constant battles over program funding, the budget, and the debt ceiling, the mood of the nation is darker than it has been in a century. That could make the man in front of me the ultimate wild card.

A popular incumbent riding a wave of successes is harder to defeat than a controversial one like Michael Bennit who has accomplished very little. Despite his impotence, the parties are scared to death of this guy. Fear is at play here, and a powerful motivator among the rank and file on both sides of the aisle who must think they're politically vulnerable because Bennit owns social media.

"Your plan is intriguing, Michael, and may even work. However, you are asking for an awful lot without offering much in return," I say coyly. Not that it matters, because I made my decision long before this meeting. He is offering far more than he could ever understand. Maneuvering is always part of the political game, so I might as well uncover any other concessions he is willing to make.

"You're right, I'm not," he says plainly. "And that's the way it's going to stay, unfortunately. I can only offer you a chance to help reshape the political system and appeal to your sense of patriotism to take me up on it."

"I understand. Let me think about it and I'll get back to you." We shake hands, and say our good-byes.

I leave the Archives and head out into the warm spring air, reaching for my cell phone in the process to make a call to my former chief of staff. After a few rings, the call gets sent to his voice mail.

"Gary, it's me. If you're still bored, I have a little something I'd like you to work on for me. Call me."

I press the end button and then select another number from the presets in my phone. This call is far more important.

"We're in," is all I say when the call is picked up.

"Excellent," is the terse reply the Southerner returns. I hang up because nothing more needs to be said, at least over a cell network.

I tuck the phone in my purse and take a deep breath.

"And so it begins."

-THIRTEEN-
SPEAKER ALBRIGHT

"Nathan!" I bellow after reading the text message on my smartphone.

"Yeah, boss," he replies, crossing the threshold into my office.

"What's happening on the Floor?" I inquire with a sense of urgency. I don't get panicked notes from the majority leader. I mean ever.

"Nothing that I know of. They're in the Committee of the Whole to discuss the tax reform bill. Why?"

The Committee of the Whole House on the State of the Union, as it is referred to by its formal name, is a parliamentary device used to expedite the debate and amendment process for certain bills. It is less formal, involves fewer members to have a quorum, and prohibits many of the motions some representatives use to delay passage. The best part is, I get to appoint someone to serve as chairperson and don't need to physically be in the chamber.

My phone vibrates again with another plea from Harvey and I rush past my chief of staff and out of my spacious Capitol office to get to the Floor. The first thing I notice is that the media is here in much larger numbers than usual. Something is not right.

The House mace, an ornamental object long part of the House's lore, is still perched on the lower pedestal, indicating that the House hasn't returned to regular session. It's the official way an observer can understand that the body is assembled in a different form, since every representative who meets in the House chamber belongs to this particular committee. Ironically, it's technically the only one Michael Bennit belongs to.

"About time you got up here," Harvey says urgently, pulling me off to the side. "We've got a serious problem. Bennit offered an amendment to the tax bill."

"Harv, he's an elected lawmaker, whether we like it or not. He's allowed to do that." The Committee of the Whole can recommend amendments to any bill, subject to re-approval when the House returns to session before the amendments are added to the final bill. He hands me a sheet of paper prepared by a member of his staff, and my eyes grow big as I read.

"You've got to be kidding me with this, right?"

"It passed, Mister Speaker."

"What?" I almost scream.

"You heard me. Look at all the media here. The chamber was full of moderates not about to vote no, so it passed. We'll have to kill it on the Floor during normal business when we come out of the Whole."

The Committee of the Whole may vote on these amendments but not on the final version of the bill. At the end of the debate, the bill's floor manager makes a motion to report the legislation, which is happening now. The House then will return to regular session and vote on the bill and defeat this amendment, but that will be done very publically.

"Bennit," I grumble, shaking my head after spotting him over near the side of the chamber. I storm over to him, and as much as I feel like berating him for all the world to hear, I would be out of order and scolded by the Chair. Not a good thing to happen to the Speaker of the House.

"What the hell is this, Mister Bennit?" I say by means of introduction, nodding to the hand holding the copy of the amendment Harvey gave me.

"It looks like an eight and a half by eleven inch sheet of copier paper. Brilliant white," Michael Bennit retorts.

"No, I think it's paper for a laser printer," Francisco Reyes corrects. "You see the texture?" Now I know who orchestrated this little show in my House—the "icandidates." Maybe there is something to Harvey's concerns after all, and that's the exact message being conveyed through the look he's giving me.

"Oh, I think you may be right, Cisco. How did you know?"

"Connections, my friend. You see, I have this cousin who works at Staples and he—"

"If you two gentlemen are quite finished, it's the absurd amendment you offered to our bill that ... what's this say again? 'Suspend congressional and presidential pay, and dictate that the parties work around the clock for a solution to the issue in the event a continuing resolution to fund the government is not passed, resulting in a government shutdown,'" I read from the paper.

The continuing resolution is an appropriations bill Congress uses to fund government agencies if a formal budget has not been signed into law by the end of the fiscal year that runs from October through September. Since the Democrats won't move on spending, I will not allow a vote on the bill since a majority of my caucus doesn't support it.

"Yes, Mister Speaker, I believe that's what it says. Cisco?"

"That's my recollection of the amendment as well, Michael." Oh, these guys think they're so smart.

"This amendment has no chance to get passed when the House comes back to order. I will see to that."

"Okay, then defeat it. Of course, the price tag is a little steep in terms of political embarrassment. I'm sure your caucus will be screaming at you for making them cast that vote," the representative from Texas says.

"Or you can bury it using the Hastert Rule, just like every other bill you don't want to see voted on. I'm sure Americans would just love the prospect of not getting tax relief because you're too busy sparring with the Democrats."

"You gentlemen are apparently not savvy enough to understand the politics involved," Harvey says, coming to my defense. "Turning off the spigot of federal dollars is the only way to keep the Democrats from spending like gambling addicts and driving the country deeper into debt. Not that we should expect independents to understand how government works."

Congressman Reyes takes the dig personally, and he looks like he might actually take a swing at my partner. A small crowd of representatives from both parties is starting to gather around us. Although our voices are being kept low enough to not disrupt the business of the Committee of the Whole, the North Carolinian I appointed as Chairman must be getting distracted.

"As per the Constitution, only Congress may appropriate the money needed to operate the federal government," Reyes explains coolly, almost as if reading from a book. "Therefore, Congress is required to pass separate spending bills every year, and if no such law is signed, all functions of the government not exempted by the Antideficiency Act cease immediately. In order to prevent this interruption, Congress may pass a continuing resolution that authorizes funding of federal agencies at the current level until either the resolution expires, or an appropriations bill is passed."

"I understand how government works, Mister Leader, as does my distinguished colleague here," Michael Bennit points out to Harvey, almost sounding bored with his colleague's verbatim piece of political prose. "The situation you described is not the workings of government, but of the two dominant political parties. If you guys want to play chicken with each other, that's your prerogative. When you hang ordinary American citizens out to dry in the process, well, I have a big problem with that. If that means I had to attach an amendment onto an unrelated bill to get you guys to sit at a table, then damn it, that's what I had to do."

I can feel my blood pressure shoot up. Being in politics for as long as I have, I learned the necessity of controlling my temper and thinking rationally. Hot heads, like Winston Beaumont, whom Michael Bennit defeated, sooner or later make a mistake and pay a steep political price. Despite this, I'm trying to tamp down my emotion so I can speak.

"This isn't over, Bennit," Harvey says, beating me to the punch. "We won't forget this." The comment elicits a smile from both Michael and Francisco.

"We certainly hope you won't," Bennit says, walking away with his new buddy and exiting the chamber. Realizing there won't be a headline-grabbing brawl today, the others gathered around us disperse.

"This is a huge problem, Johnston," the majority leader observes. "If we vote down this amendment, we look callous, and if we don't, we lose our wedge issue with the Democrats."

"I know the stakes, Harvey."

"Two censures and two reprimands haven't forced him out of here, so the members are going to demand a plan."

"There's already one in the works. Now, let's get back to it," I say, ending the discussion as the House returns to order from being the Committee of the Whole. The first order of business will be undoing the damage Michael Bennit just inflicted, but that's not my only concern.

Our confrontation on the floor is going to get some television exposure, and now it dawns on me that the whole episode could have been recorded by cell phone. I don't understand what makes things go viral, but I do understand how unwanted videos can have embarrassing political ramifications. This whole stunt feels orchestrated to achieve that goal, making Bennit more dangerous than I thought.

Of course, there are enough embarrassing reprimands now to all but ensure a victory against him this fall. Bennit's last words to Mister Stepanik weren't meant as a personal slight. He issued a warning. With all the pressure we've exerted on him to resign before the election, I wonder if we've pushed too hard and took him off the leash by accident. As I accept the gavel to bring the House back into order, all I can think of is Yamamoto's quote at Pearl Harbor: "I fear all we have done is to awaken a sleeping giant and fill him with a terrible resolve."

-FOURTEEN-
MICHAEL

The average temperature in the middle of May for Millfield is right around seventy degrees, but today is not one of those days. With a cold front sneaking south out of Canada, it is barely cracking fifty-five, and feels much more like October than the end of spring. With that in mind, I skipped wearing shorts and opted for a T-shirt, light jacket, and jeans for this meeting.

Climbing out of my car and seeing the group gathered around the picnic table at Briar Point State Park brings back a flood of old memories. My campaign with this group of overachievers may have been run out of the Perkfect Buzz coffee shop, but it was hatched at the very table they are now sitting at. Is it possible that was over two years ago?

"It looks like we're putting the band back together!" Vince announces as I reach the picnic table. The next few minutes are filled with warm embraces, man-hugs, fist bumps, and high fives. The hardest part of teaching is watching the kids you spent so much time in the classroom with grow up. Luckily, it's also the most rewarding. I remember each of the young men and women in front of me when they were terrified freshman, and it's wonderful seeing them full of confidence and optimism as college students.

When they graduated, this motley group of friends split and went their separate ways. Chelsea, Vanessa, and Vince decided to put off college and came to work for me in Washington. Brian, the resident computer geek, got accepted to MIT and is studying computer science. Peyton did end up as prom queen as we all predicted, and is now pursuing her dream of fashion marketing at Vassar. Amanda, the numbers wizard who ran our campaign finances both times without landing us in prison, chose to attend the University of Connecticut, and is dual majoring in accounting and business. Emilee is also a double major in education and, gulp, history at NYU. Xavier is playing basketball at Syracuse, and majoring in political science, the poor guy.

They may have chosen different paths after graduation, but they interact like they saw each other a week ago. Each may have new friends and unique experiences from the others, but they are all bound by the events of their senior year. Somehow, I think they will still all gravitate towards one another at a high school reunion forty years from now.

"Good to see you all survived your freshman years in college," I say, remembering the trouble I used to get into at that age. "Any news I should know about?" They all look at each other to see who wants to go first.

"Brian has a girlfriend," Amanda offers, putting him up first in the hot seat. Somewhat surprising considering, other than putting on a few pounds, he's just as dorky as he was in high school.

"The inflatable kind or one that actually breathes?" I ask with a smile on my face. The group snickers, and we spend the next ten minutes getting caught up in everyone's activities and funny experiences. Then it's my turn.

"How's Kylie?" Emilee asks, still petite and sporting short, brown hair, but a far cry from the shy girl that I remember from two years ago. She always liked the freelance reporter who covered our campaign, and felt the most betrayed after she wrote the articles I asked her to when it was over. Nobody was more thrilled we ended up together.

"She's great, thanks for asking. She really wanted to be here to see you, but the *Post* has her on an assignment."

"Have you proposed yet?"

"Not yet, Em."

"Damn, Mister B, what are you waiting for?" Xavier pries. He appears a little more buff than I remember. Still lean and lanky like he was when he set all of Millfield's varsity scoring records, he definitely has spent time in the gym.

"You know, if you like it you'd better put a ring on it," Amanda says, playfully paraphrasing Beyoncé. And yes, I am thrilled that working with teenagers makes me hip enough to know that.

"I keep telling him that!" Vanessa exclaims. And she does, almost every day.

"Mister B—"

"You guys are out of school, so you can call me Michael." They laugh and I realize that is never going to happen. Old habits may die hard, but some never will.

Damn, it is so good having this group together again. There's a certain power to us that makes me feel invincible when I'm surrounded by them. I know that isn't the case, but that is the feeling I get.

"Okay, so how's life been in Congress?" Amanda asks.

"The short story is we were not invited to join a caucus, not on a single committee, haven't gotten a single bill we introduced out for a vote, and we're not included in any discussions about anything."

"Thank you for that rosy depiction of the last year, Chels," I say with a tinge of sarcasm. Chelsea hasn't been happy for a long time now, and even seeing her old friends isn't bringing her out of her funk.

"Oh, and I forgot to mention he's working with Blake Peoni." Chelsea almost spits when she says his name. Everyone looks at me, stunned.

"Really?" Peyton asks.

"Did you fall and hit your head?" Xavier scolds.

"Are you *The Manchurian Candidate* instead of the iCandidate?" Brian quips.

"You don't know the half of it," Vince explains to X. "It's been a fun year for a person in my job. He's already set the disciplinary record in Congress, and even punched Blake Peoni's lights out."

"Twice," Vanessa adds with two fingers extended.

"What?" the group utters all at once, looking at Chelsea and Vanessa to gauge whether they need to flip on their internal lie detectors for Vince.

"It's a long story," Chelsea bemoans.

"You know, Mister B, I can say this since we're not your students anymore, and I pretty much speak for all of us. You're one crazy bastard," X observes. Yep, I still call him "X."

"And yet you're all still here," I say with a smile.

"For now," Brian smirks. "So how will this work?"

"The campaign will hire you as paid interns over the summer. We should still have some money in the campaign account."

"What about after the summer? Once I start this, you know I won't be able to just stop until it's over," Amanda says. I know better than to doubt her.

"You guys will be going back to your respective schools in September, so I don't know what you'll be able to do."

"Mister B, you're always going to be the iCandidate. With a high-speed Internet connection, I could run your reelection from the moon. There will be plenty of stuff to do. Besides, with all the time management skills we learned during those two campaigns, college classes were child's play. We can balance the work."

I have no doubt they can. I made them get signed permission forms from their parents before our first run because I was concerned about their grades slipping. It turned out to be completely unnecessary—most of their grades actually improved. Go figure.

"Okay, so what's the plan? We know you have one." Apparently Brian is eager to get to work. That's good, because I am really going to need his help to pull this off, just like last time.

I explain the plan we have as it has developed so far. There are a lot of variables, and a lot of things we aren't yet sure how to execute. For the next ten minutes, I tell them about my meeting with Blake, and then with Senator Viano, and what that could mean for us this summer. I even loop them in on Cisco, who is the only friend I have in the House.

"Maybe it's my déjà vu kicking in, but this all sounds eerily familiar," Amanda opines, looking around her.

"Amanda's right, it is familiar. Only you guys don't know the whole story yet," Vince says in warning.

"What does he mean?" Peyton asks me.

"Well, if you guys are serious about jumping on this train one more time, you should probably know what you are getting yourselves into. Both the Republicans and Democrats are running excellent candidates against us, and considering my … colorful record … in the House, we are getting crushed in the polls."

"Colorful record is one way to put it," Chelsea adds sarcastically.

"Anyway, we always considered Beaumont to be the consummate politician and a great strategist. Turns out, he was neither, at least compared to what we are up against now. We managed to blindside him because he was ignorant, an egotist, and didn't consider us a threat until it was too late. Now, we're already in everyone's crosshairs and both parties want to parade down Main Street with my head on a pike."

"Seriously? You've been a congressman for over a year and you still haven't managed to work on your motivation skills?" Xavier observes.

"Any other bad news?" Brian asks.

"Yeah, we are probably going to lose this election no matter what we do. There is no Kylie Roberts to come swooping in and put us on the map. This is going to be much harder than the last time."

"What about this former senator you mentioned?"

"I'm still not sure what she will be able to do for me, so consider her a wild card," I state honestly. Senator Viano may be a huge help, complete bust, or anything in between.

"So, is that it?" Brian asks again.

"Noooo," Vince responds. "Tuesday, Congressman."

"Oh, yeah. I sort of stirred up a hornets' nest last Tuesday on the Floor, and now the Speaker of the House and Republican majority leader want to cane me like a Singapore pimp. So don't be under the illusion I'm going to have a *Mr. Smith Goes to Washington* moment that will make this better."

"A Mister who?" Peyton asks, confused.

"*Mister Smith Goes to Washington*. Frank Capra's great American political drama ..." I look around and notice the bewildered faces. Sometimes I forget they are not even twenty, and even giving them quotes from eighties' movies is a hit or miss proposition. "Okay, yeah, never mind."

"So what's the first step, boss?" Amanda asks, sparing me any more explanation.

"The campaign needs a base camp. Coordinate with Chelsea on how to find one. We aren't running this out of the Buzz this time. Then we'll take it from there."

"Viva la revolución!" Vince shouts again. I hope he's not planning on making that our unofficial campaign slogan.

-FIFTEEN-
CHELSEA

It is really awesome being with this gang again. We only knew each other as classmates when we had Mister Bennit for American History our junior year, but that changed as seniors in his Contemporary Issues class. The shared experiences of working on a congressional campaign and a special election allowed us to grow very close. So much so that I barely talk to my old friends Cassandra and Stephanie anymore, and I have known them since childhood. We're just different people now, with far different interests and responsibilities. I hope the same thing doesn't happen to this clan.

"If you have this under control, Chels, Vanessa and I are going to head back to the district office."

"Sounds good, Vince," I say with a wave, and then watch my colleagues walk to their car, jump in, and leave.

"It's great seeing you guys again," Amanda says. "How often do you get to come home?"

"More than you might think. The House is in recess more than it is in session."

"That explains why nothing ever gets done," Brian adds, rolling his eyes.

"It's not all bad. The Speaker of the House likes to ensure representatives have plenty of time in their districts. He scheduled 'constituent work weeks' so members can conduct business out of offices in their home states."

"Yeah, do they really do that?" Xavier asks with a suspicious look.

"Probably not. The congressman does though. What about you guys?" I ask, trying to get off the subject. "You make it back to Millfield much?"

"We're in college, Chels," Peyton replies. "We avoid coming home at all costs unless our parents force us to." The others laugh and nod in agreement.

"There is way too much going on at NYU to ever want to come home," Emilee, once the shyest and most introverted among our group says. "I am sort of tired of living in a dorm though. It's a twenty-five-minute walk to class." Yeah, tell me again why I didn't go to Yale, Harvard, or Marist? Twenty-five minutes. If she thinks that's long, she should try my commute sometime.

"Where do you stay down in D.C.?" Brian asks.

"Vince, Vanessa, six other young government types, and I all rent a house in the city."

"That sounds really cool," Peyton says, almost in admiration that I'm doing something else other than college and managing to survive.

"Yeah, it's okay I guess."

"All right, do the rest of you hear it too?" Amanda says to the others and getting agreements.

"Hear what?" I ask, perplexed. I probably shouldn't be, though. This group of friends knows me better than almost anyone.

"You sound defeated and the campaign hasn't even started yet," Brian observes. Maybe because I think losing is a foregone conclusion.

"I'm fine."

"No, you're acting the same way you did right after the campaign announcement was a bust," Emilee adds.

"And after we lost the election. So, are you gonna tell us what's up or force us to drag it out of you?" Amanda directly challenges.

All the emotions I have spent the last year suppressing well up inside me. I have tried so hard to be strong, but the walls I built up are crumbling. I can't tell the congressman how I feel because he relies on me. Vince and Vanessa really don't understand the pressure of my job, even though they work in the same office. My father can't know I made a mistake by taking this on. With those thoughts, I lose it.

"I can't do this job," I sob, letting my frustration and insecurities spill out. "It's too big for me. We have had a horrible year and it's all my fault!"

Emile gives me a hug, but it does little to stem the tears pouring from my eyes. After a minute or so, my bawling lets up enough for Brian to try to console me.

"I'm sure that's not the case, Chels."

"You don't understand, Brian! You can't. You haven't been with us and seen me fail time and again."

Brian started it. He tried to hide his smile, first by squeezing his lips together, then by turning away. One by one, Amanda, Peyton, and Xavier followed suit until they couldn't hold it anymore and started laughing. Emilee releases her hug and starts doing the same.

How dare they laugh at me over something like this? I feel betrayed by my friends. My insecurity gives way to remorse, and now I feel something else — anger.

"What the hell's so damn funny?" I scream, only prompting them to chuckle even harder. This is beginning to feel like a bad dream I am hoping to wake up from.

"We're laughing because of you," Brian says, pointing out the obvious. "This has been your M.O. since we've known you. You're not failing, Chels, you're just not living up to the incredibly high expectations you set for yourself."

"That's not true! This is different."

"No it's not," Emilee consoles. "Hon, you didn't think you could handle running the first campaign, either. So what happened? You came within a hundred votes of winning against a tough incumbent while not taking a stand on a single issue."

"And then you followed it with the most successful congressional campaign in the history of the country," Amanda continues, still trying to stifle her grin.

"News flash, Chels, in case you didn't notice, you're the also youngest chief of staff in the history of Congress. There are literally hundreds of people around the country trying to replicate what you did. Really, what more do you think you need to prove?"

"None of that means I'm getting the job done in Washington, Brian."

"Has Mister B said anything to you about it?" Xavier asks. I shake my head no, my flash of anger now subsiding. "I didn't think so. I'll bet he thinks you're doing a great job under the circumstances."

"I doubt it. He's been too busy trying to get kicked out of Congress to notice," I smile weakly. It's a start. I haven't had a reason to for a long while.

"Looks like neither of you have hit your stride yet," Brian says with hints of optimism that makes me feel a little better than I did a few minutes ago. I look at Xavier who seems to be relishing this opportunity to work with us again.

"And we're now here to help change that."

* * *

Dorothy had it right in *The Wizard of Oz* — there is no place like home. Most high school kids can't wait to leave home and either head out into the world, or at a minimum, cut the parental strings at college. I would be lying if I said I wasn't one of them. But after a year inside the Beltway, the colloquial name for Washington, D.C., I miss the comfort and familiarity of home more than ever.

I pull into the driveway and kill the headlights on my aging car. My senior year, I was ashamed to have to park it next to a Range Rover and BMW every day during high school and thought that would change once I left. I was wrong. If anything, it's worse on the occasions I drive to work given the flashy cars most politicians and the senior staff drive.

Dad greets me at the door and gives me a huge hug before I can even make it into the kitchen. "Hi, Snuggle Bear. I've missed you so much."

"It's only been a couple of weeks, Dad," I say, probably sounding way more insincere than I meant to be. "I missed you too," I utter before he gets the wrong idea.

I come in and drop my stuff on the chair that once housed piles of college literature. Most colleges don't bother sending out volumes of brochures to prospective students anymore. Everything is done electronically over e-mail and the Internet. My case was a little different once our first campaign got rolling, and schools were going above and beyond to get me and the campaign crew to listen to their admissions pitch.

"How's work? You look a little rough around the edges."

"It's okay," I mumble, hoping that wasn't meant like my emotional redhead self tends to take things.

"Only okay? You know, when you started this job, even when things were bad, they were never just 'okay.' Please tell me you aren't becoming jaded at twenty years old."

"No, I'm not jaded," I say, lying a little. "The job can wear you out at times, that's all. I'll be better after the weekend." Okay, I lied a lot.

Dad knows I'm down, but he also knows I won't talk about it until I'm ready. You can count on Bruce Stanton for two things in this world—showing up to his shift at the factory every day for work and being in my corner. He's taken on the press in our front yard and even got into a fight with

Mister Bennit in our living room. He only replaced that broken end table a few months ago.

"Would ya tell me if you were?" he says with a wink. He knows me too well.

"How's work treating you?" I ask, changing the subject away from anything to do with my chosen career.

"Work's fine, same ol' same ol'. Not that I'm not thrilled to see ya, but what brings all you guys up here?" Dad asks, bringing the conversation back full circle. You'd think working for a politician in a town full of lawyers would make me an expert in deflection, but apparently I can't pull that particular Jedi mind trick on my own father.

"We're looking for some space to run the campaign out of this year," I reply, too tired and emotionally drained to add my belief that the idea is a stupid one.

"You're not gonna use the Buzz again? It worked for you last time."

No kidding. That was the exact point I made, but was overruled. Again. Mister Bennit has spent the last year trying to shed some of the aspects of the maverick image that got him elected in the first place, and the quaintness of running the campaign out of a coffee shop was sacrificed to help reach that goal. As has been the case many other times this year, my opinion was ignored. One more instance of the congressman and I not heading in the same direction.

"The congressman doesn't think …." I trail off and Dad flashes a parental look of concern. He probably already knows, but I don't want to let on how bad I'm struggling right now. I am having a hard enough time keeping it together without Dad getting all gooey, or worse, combative. He is a hard-nosed former Marine, and they have a tendency to do that.

"Are ya okay, Snuggle Bear?"

"I'm fine, Dad. Just really tired. It's been a long day." He nods in understanding, but I know that it will do little to end this conversation.

"Can I ask one more question without you getting pissed at me?" I'd rather he didn't.

"Sure," I say in the most upbeat tone I can muster.

"He's becoming one of them, isn't he?"

-SIXTEEN-
MICHAEL

"Good luck in your meeting. Everything is all set from our end," Chelsea says as I put on my suit jacket.

"He knows where to get seated?"

"All taken care of. He'll be in place five minutes after your appointment arrives to avoid suspicion. He's even bringing a date, if you can believe that. I think it's the girlfriend he says he has."

"Perfect. Thanks, and don't work too late," I warn, heading out of my district office to what I'm sure will be a very interesting dinner. Chelsea thinks this is a terrible idea, and she's probably right. No big deal if I'm wrong, but if I'm not, I'm toast should things go awry.

Our headquarters is located on Main Street in Danbury, a diverse city of over eighty thousand people in the far western part of the area I represent. Millfield is about a forty-minute drive away, assuming the traffic is cooperating. Under normal circumstances, that's where I would be heading after a long day of meeting with people and listening to their problems and opinions on issues. Tonight's meeting, however, is definitely not normal.

I have been ignored by the D.C. lobby since the day I took my seat in Congress. The men and women who make their living currying favor to politicians in the Beltway see no real point in showering me with money, attention, or favor. I am that irrelevant in the U.S. House of Representatives.

A few days ago, while I was getting reacquainted with my former students in the park, a lobbyist contacted my staff to set a dinner meeting with me to discuss how we may help each other on issues of concern to his clients. If that wasn't weird enough, he was adamant that it be hosted here in my home district. Needless to say, I'm very curious to know what this is about.

There are great restaurants all around Danbury, but most of my favorites are on Mill Plain Road near the New York State line. American fare at Four Square and Market Place, Japanese at Bambu, and Italian at Spasi are among the limitless choices in that area. I thought about having this meeting at either the eclectic Rosy Tomorrow's or Irish-themed Molly Darcy's, but decided neither was quite right for a meeting with a lobbyist. Vera's Trattoria is my favorite pizza place, but I had that yesterday. Max 40 and Della Francesca would both have worked, but I like to keep those reserved for dates with Kylie.

In the end, I settled on Prespa, an Italian restaurant that had both the quiet ambiance and good food I was looking for. The drive there from our office only took ten minutes, and after pulling into the parking lot and being seated, I began to doubt the quiet ambiance part as the dining room filled up quickly. Now I'm just happy to have a table. The one perk of being a congressman is you have no problem getting a reservation in town, even at a busy restaurant on the Friday before Memorial Day.

"Congressmen Bennit," the man arriving to my table greets. "William Mashburn. I'm sorry to keep you waiting, sir," he declares with a firm handshake and used car salesman smile. He's a younger guy, probably in his mid-twenties and not senior enough to be a heavyweight at his lobby firm. I chose to dress up for this, meaning I am actually wearing a suit. Other than age, the obvious difference between me and the man I'm shaking hands with is my suit was bought in a Men's Wearhouse at the mall. His is probably custom-tailored from someplace swank like Milan, Italy.

We order drinks, dinner, and for the next forty-five minutes, he listens to my opinions about education, government reform, and spending. Although he is trying to be attentive, I can tell he harbors no interest in what I am saying. After the neatly attired waiter clears our dishes, I decide to end his agony and confront the subject.

"You know, William, I have been ignored by K Street since the moment I got to Washington. I'm more than a little surprised you would meet with me now."

"You don't trust my motives?" William says, feigning surprise.

"Nope. Tell me why we are really having this meeting." Maybe it's my general lack of trust with people, or it could be the three Samuel Adams Boston Lagers I've had, but his slick approach is trying my patience. I glance over to the college-aged pair enjoying their dinner a couple of tables over. They make a cute couple, actually. So she is real, and maybe it is a legitimate date.

"Many of the clients my firm lobbies for were impressed with your actions on the Floor last week. It dawned on us that maybe we erred in our original impression and have dismissed you too soon. Plus, we want to convince each and every member on the merits of our clients' concerns."

"William, you're not here to engage me in a spirited debate about healthcare, environmental causes, financial reform, or any of the other issues we do nothing about. I'll ask one more time, what do you want?"

The lobbyist sends me a cheap smile and fidgets with the napkin placed on his lap. "You're right. Although I find your views insightful, that's not why I'm here." Is this guy for real? Insightful my ass …

"I wanted to give you this," he says as he discretely looks at the tables near us and reaches inside his suit jacket, producing a white envelope. He sets it on the table and slides it over to me.

Is this really how it's done, or am I such a novice that they put on this show special for me? Against my better judgment, I open the envelope and look inside. Not being able to read the print, I pull the check out about halfway and put on my best poker face when I see the amount.

"It's pretty brazen to attempt to bribe an elected representative in a crowded restaurant, don't you think?"

"It's not a bribe, Congressman. Consider it a donation to your campaign in return for services yet to be rendered," the epicene bastard says with a wry smile. I want to jam this check down his throat, along with the rest of my fist.

"You know I can't accept this. It's illegal."

"You need the money, Congressman. Even if it goes in your own personal account instead of your campaign fund, we want you to have it as a token of our dedication to your ideals."

"My ideals?" I question, my voice rising. I toss the envelope back at him, hitting him square in the chest with it. "You obviously don't know the first damned thing about my *ideals* if you thought for a second I'd take that check."

William looks around surreptitiously before slipping the envelope back into his jacket. I pull my wallet out of my jacket and pull out three twenties to pay for my half of dinner. It's not uncommon for lobbyists to pick up the tab for these types of meetings, but after that display, I'm not leaving anything to chance.

"I thought you were a practical man, Congressman Bennit," William says with a hint of disgust.

"No, Mister Mashburn, you thought I was a weak man. You saw the polls, figured I have nothing in my campaign coffers, and realized I was a prime target to get bought. But let me make one thing very clear to you. I am one of the only politicians in Washington without a for sale sign on my office door."

"I'm sorry we couldn't do business together," he says, recovering quickly. His voice is loud enough to be heard by half the restaurant as he extends his hand. Eyes all around us turn their attention on the two of us, and I remember I'm supposed to be playing the role of the diplomatic politician. As much as I'd like to cave his skull in, I have no choice but to shake the slime ball's hand.

"Don't ever call my office again," I warn as I let go of his hand and turn to leave.

"Have a good night, Congressman." The restaurant patrons have turned their attention back to their meals and conversations as if nothing happened. Something certainly did happen though. That was the most brazen setup job I've ever seen, and I fell right into it.

-SEVENTEEN-
SPEAKER ALBRIGHT

My home on the Bull Creek in Charleston is my refuge. We bought this property a dozen years ago, satisfying my wife's need for modern convenience and my own desire for southern charm. The brick structure has high-pitched ceilings, arched doorways, hardwood floors, and plenty of room. It even features a long boardwalk through a marsh to a dock on the creek. It is my definition of serenity, and the perfect place to spend a long Memorial Day weekend.

The house is perfect for entertaining my big campaign contributors and political allies, but tonight was reserved for a dinner party with longtime friends. My wife is a great cook, but events like this get catered from a restaurant downtown I have a special relationship with. We are almost finished with dinner when my cell phone interrupts the conversation.

"Excuse me all, I have to take this," I say after checking the caller ID and absorbing an annoyed look from my wife. "Hold on," I say into the phone after connecting the call, leaving the dining room and walking through the door to the front porch.

"What can I do for you, Mister Reed?"

"Mister Speaker, I trust I'm not interrupting something important."

"No, but my wife might disagree."

"Ha, ha," Washington's top lobbyist heartily laughs. "Then in the name of ya'lls everlasting domestic bliss, I'll make this brief. It's regarding the subject of discussion at the airport earlier this month. Do you remember?" As if I could forget, or he would be remiss not to remind me if ever I did.

"Of course I remember."

"Excellent. A package is being sent by courier to your office. It'll arrive when ya'll get back to Washington on Tuesday. Please be there to receive it. The courier will be instructed to deliver it only to you."

"May I inquire as to the contents of this package?" I ask, fully expecting James not to indulge my curiosity.

"Regrettably, I cannot acquiesce to that request. Suffice to say, when you see the contents, ya'll will know exactly what to do with them." Did he really use acquiesce and ya'll in the same breath?

"Very well," I say, the gears in my head already starting to spin once I get past the distraction of his verbiage.

"I won't take up any more of your time, Mister Speaker. Enjoy the rest of your evening. We'll be speaking again when ya'll get back to town," James commands before ending the call. He wasn't off the line for three seconds when I select another number from my favorites and press send.

The front door opens and my wife sticks her head out. "Johnston, you're keeping our guests waiting," she says impatiently.

"I'll be right in after this call. Promise," I respond, as the call connects. That seemed to be enough to placate my wife who slips back inside and closes the front door.

"Good evening, Mister Speaker," the voice of the House majority leader says on the other end of the line.

"Hello, Harvey. I'm sorry to bother you on a Saturday evening."

"No bother, sir. What can I do for you?"

"I'm expecting some news next week about one of your favorite congressmen," I relay sarcastically. "I thought you might like the courtesy of a heads-up."

"That sounds interesting, Johnston, but a little vague. Can you elaborate on which one of my favorites you're talking about?"

It dawns on me that I will be making two people happy in one night. Both James Reed and Harvey Stepanik are getting exactly what they want in one fell swoop. If I land fat campaign contributions from my wealthy friends at the dinner party, it becomes the perfect trifecta. Life is good.

"When you get back to the Capitol, I'll need you to set up an investigation," I decree, my mind still fixated on previous thoughts.

"Okay. Are you going to tell me who the target of the inquiry is?"

"Michael Bennit."

-EIGHTEEN-
SENATOR VIANO

Washington, D.C., is a zoo on Memorial Day. Between the events at Arlington, the parade near the National Mall, and the services at the various war memorials, denizens know to stay away from those areas at all costs on this holiday. For that very reason, I chose the forty-acre Fort Ward Park, located a mere ten-minute drive from my house, on the west end of Old Town Alexandria, for this meeting.

Fort Ward was used as a Union fort from 1861 to 1865 to defend Washington during the Civil War, or so the sign says. The grounds feature underground shelters, officer quarters, earthwork walls, and cannons situated on the Northwest Bastion where I now stand.

"Interesting spot for this meeting," Gary observes as he inspects one of the cannons following his trek from the parking lot. This place has a historical charm that Bennit would like. It's also nearly empty, despite the significance of the day. It's one of the other reasons I chose it.

"Not exactly Deep Throat's parking garage, but it will do for our purposes," I respond. "How did you make out?"

"You tell me," he says with a laugh, handing me a thick manila folder full of documents.

"Jesus, Gary, this is pretty extensive. I didn't realize you had so much free time."

"My current boss is as ambitious as a doped-up teen with an Xbox. This favor was a welcome diversion because it gave me something to do. The summary sheet is on top," he says, noticing my visual inspection of the file.

I continue to flip through the contents before turning my attention to the printed spreadsheet stapled on top. I scan the list in amazement.

"Damn, that's a lot of names."

"There is no shortage of people looking to emulate Michael Bennit. That list is up-to-date as of yesterday. The deadlines for most states aren't until June, so there could end up being more."

"How established are any these people?" I ask, tapping him on the arm. Gary already has his face buried in his smartphone, but despite his apparent lack of attentiveness, he never misses a beat.

"Varying degrees," he replies without looking up. "Most will probably use the Bennit technique of announcing late to avoid being an early target and riding the wave into November. Although I'm not convinced that will work again."

"Okay, let's narrow this list down to the most viable icandidates in the one hundred strongest red and blue districts. Choose the top fifty of each."

"It'd be easier to target the moderate ones in swing states."

"Yeah, probably, but right now you have Democratic and Republican districts, and very few moderates getting elected from the middle. You know staunch conservative and liberal districts only elect extreme ideologues to Congress. If Bennit is going to change how the House does business, he has to hurt those extremists, not the moderates."

"Tell me something, Senator. You ever danced with the devil in the pale moonlight?" I'm not sure, but that sounded like another superhero reference. Ugh.

"I'm quite certain I have no idea what you're talking about." Gary looks at me suspiciously, and then actually pockets his handheld electronic leash.

"I've known you forever, Marilyn. Not once have I seen you interested in cavorting with anyone like Michael Bennit." The use of my first name instead of my former title lets me know this is a personal question. "The two of you are ideologically different, come from completely different backgrounds, and have seemingly diverse goals. So if this is some sort of symbiotic relationship, I'm not seeing it."

"Are you questioning his motives, or mine?"

"I have spent way too much time in this town not to question everybody's motives." Fair enough. I do the same thing.

"Okay, I get that, so let's start with him. Everything I have found on Bennit says he's non-negotiable. He won't sell out, can't be bought, and has unimpeachable character. I know that's exceedingly rare here, but not unheard of. I know you have all the information I do on him, so why are you questioning *his* motives?"

"Alfred Pennyworth said it best. 'Because some men aren't looking for anything logical, like money. They can't be bought, bullied, reasoned, or negotiated with. Some men just want to watch the world burn.'" I love my former chief of staff like he was family, but enough is enough.

"Really? A Batman reference?"

"It seemed appropriate."

"Do you really think Bennit is out to destroy anything?" Of course, I think I know the answer to that question, but does he?

"No idea. All I know is he's a maverick and my boss hates him with a burning passion. Neither one of those would disqualify him in my mind, but I don't trust him either."

Trust is one of those words that has a different meaning in this town than it does in the rest of the country. Nobody trusts anybody in Washington, so the definition of the word has changed in the crucible of the modern political process. Here, it takes on more of a "willing to work with him without complete fear of betrayal" meaning.

"Okay, what about me and my motives?"

"It doesn't really matter. You know I'm with you whatever you decide to do. But tell me one thing; why is a former senator, who spent most of her life trying to become a Washington insider and player in the system, throwing her lot in with the ultimate outsider?" I grin broadly, keeping my lips pressed together instead of flashing my usual toothy smile. For the next five minutes, I tell him exactly what working with Michael Bennit means for my own ambitions.

"Wow, you thought that through," he comments following an astonished whistle.

"I have a lot of time on my hands these days."

"There are an awful lot of variables to work through in that plan if you dream of pulling it off." He pauses to pull the phone out of his pocket again to silence its incessant vibration.

"That's why I need you. You're the only person I can trust to help make it happen." Not entirely true since I can think of about a dozen better people, but they are all unavailable. Gary was a faithful servant for a long time, and while he may not be the best fox hound on the hunt, he's the most loyal.

"Do you have resources to help him?" he asks, stalling for time while he thinks.

Normally a one-term senator would have nothing in terms of the national resources needed to help with this endeavor. Fortunately, I am no average one-termer. My six year stint in D.C. may have been brief, but my relationship with one special contact, who was my greatest benefactor, may come in handy again. This may not have been the future I anticipated when calling on his services, but it will do.

"I have friends of friends who ran national campaigns and are willing to help with most of them if I so choose that route. Now, let me ask you a question. If I go down this road, are you willing to come along for the ride, or are you happy being penned up in that cage your current boss has you in?"

"You know, sometimes when you cage the beast, the beast gets angry," he says with a sly smile. I guess I'll have to look up which movie that was from when I get home.

-NINETEEN-

MICHAEL

"So the House finally agreed to a fifth continuing resolution that will keep the government funded, at least in the short term," the television pundit says to the camera as a lead in. "The rhetoric only a couple of short weeks ago led most Americans to believe the nation had to prepare for yet another government shutdown. I ask the panel, what changed?"

The last votes for the week are usually scheduled no later than three o'clock on Fridays, so I like to take time with my inner circle to sit down and discuss the events of the past few days. Most of these meetings over the past year have circled around our demoralizing failures. Today is a different story.

"As much as I'd like to say the representatives in the House listened to the polls and hammered out the agreement most Americans wanted, it wouldn't be true," the bald man with the tufts of gray hair on the sides in the studio says. "The passage of the Bennit Amendment to the Tax Relief Act played a huge part in getting them to sit down."

"Is it me, or does he look like an overstuffed Oompa Loompa?" Amanda asks.

"Funny, I was thinking more along the lines of Krusty the Clown." Oh yeah, we spend more time ragging on the pundits when we watch these shows than anything else.

"We haven't heard much out of Michael Bennit since he came to Washington, at least legislatively," the rather manly looking woman on the panel chuckles in an obvious reference to my censures. "But he teamed up with the other icandidate, Representative Reyes from Texas, to successfully tack on this amendment."

"A few more chin hairs and she could be a stand-in on Duck Dynasty," Chelsea observes.

"Or as a member of ZZ Top." Vince, Vanessa, and Chelsea all look at me with the faces of bewilderment I get when I stray into eighties pop culture. "Forget it, way before your time."

"We know the Republicans are livid over this amendment, but they wanted their tax bill more," the bearded pundit adds. "He embarrassed the leadership, but actually succeeded in forcing the parties to cooperate and accomplish something for a change."

"This is what I think most of America expected Michael Bennit to do when he got to Congress. Do you think we'll see more of that?" the host asks.

"We'd better," Vince quips. He's wanted me to mix it up since the day we arrived in Washington. If I told him I decided to walk into the House chamber with a flamethrower, he would volunteer to carry extra fuel.

"He is down significantly in the polls, but he's still popular nationally and carries a lot of weight in the social media sphere, even though he is not as active in it as much as he once was. I wouldn't count him out just yet, especially if he keeps doing things like this."

"Congressman? I'm sorry to interrupt, but Thomas Parker is here to see you," one of my junior staff members says from the door to the office.

Vince, Chelsea, and Vanessa all look at each other in disbelief as I shut the television off. It's not often we get distinguished visitors. In fact, it never happens.

"Send him in. Vince, Vanessa, can you guys excuse us for a minute?"

"Sure thing, boss," Vince says, turning to leave. "But we're going to want details." No doubt they will. That debriefing will come complete with a metal chair and single light hanging from a wire in a windowless room.

"Good afternoon, Congressman. I'm sorry to drop by unannounced."

"It's not a problem. Can I offer you anything?"

"No, thank you," Parker responds politely while looking around. "I've never been in this office before."

"Most every other member of the House hasn't either," I reply in kind. "The reasons for that don't escape you, sir, so what do I owe the honor of this visit?"

"You like to cut right to the chase, don't you, Michael?"

"There's too much small talk in this town already."

"Yes, there is," Parker says with a laugh, "so I'll get to it. I doubt you know, but I have family that lives up in your district. In fact, my niece serves in the Connecticut National Guard with the 1-169th Aviation Regiment."

"No kidding? I didn't know that."

"Yes, sir, she joined up right out of high school to help pay for college. She just got back from her first deployment. It's hard to think of my brother's little girl as a combat veteran," he says, taking a private trip down memory lane.

I don't know much about Thomas Parker, but I do know service to God through the clergy, and to our country through military service, runs deep in his family. He comes from a long line of Baptist preachers, and many of them served as chaplains in various branches of the armed forces. I've heard rumors his family has participated in every conflict this country has fought in since the Civil War.

"What does she do?"

"She's a fifteen tango and just got a slot as a crew chief," he says with pride in his voice.

Fifteen Tango is the designation the Army uses to define a soldier's Military Occupational Specialty as a Helicopter Repairer. It's a fancy way to say her job is to fix helicopters. I'm impressed though, because I know it's a competitive specialty and difficult to progress into a Blackhawk crew chief slot. They have tough jobs, especially when they get deployed to combat zones like Afghanistan. I met more than my fair share of them in my tours overseas.

"So what's the problem?"

"The pilot and the rest of the crew. She's tried everything to stop their sexually explicit behavior. The direct approach, indirect, third party ... Finally she had to file a formal report against them for contributing to a hostile work environment.

Now, she hasn't been physically assaulted in any way, or anything, but—"

"There is a zero tolerance policy for all forms of sexual harassment, especially since such behavior has been well documented to lead to sexual assault," I say, finishing his statement.

"Exactly," Congressman Parker says, happy that I understand the seriousness of the matter.

"And let me guess, the command's done nothing."

"Next to nothing. That's why I'd like you to conduct an investigation."

"You're asking me to intervene?"

"No, just force the leadership to follow their procedures. Are you familiar with Army's SHARP program?"

"Sharp?"

"It stands for something like the Sexual Harassment and Assault Response and Prevention program. Does it ring a bell?"

"Vaguely. It's been a while. I think it was called something else back when I was in."

"Yeah, apparently they change the name every couple of years, but the goal is the same. Anyway, one of the tenants of the program dictates while an investigation is being conducted, the commander is supposed to protect the complainant from acts of reprisal. That includes reassigning the soldier in question, if necessary. They haven't done any of that, and she turned to me when things got ugly during the Memorial Day parade the unit participated in."

"Congressman, you are just as capable of doing this on your own. Why are you turning to me?" It's a legitimate question, but he seems offended at it.

"I assume you are balking because you think this is some sort of political trap," he surmises, studying my face for a reaction.

"Considering my last year here, to be honest with you, the thought crossed my mind."

I glance over to Chelsea who is silently leaning against the wall. To her credit, she is one of the rare people in this world who knows when to talk and when to sit back and listen. The fact that she does not need to interject her own comments and feelings into this conversation is one of the things I love about her. Anything she has to say will be brought up in private, but the look on her face speaks volumes. She doesn't trust Representative Parker one bit.

"Okay, I suppose I can't blame you for that. Look, there are some really good soldiers in that unit. A few bad apples are spoiling it for the rest. But she's my niece, Michael. I don't want my investigation to appear like influence, meddling, or a conflict of interest. She lives in your district, and since you're from a military background—"

"I'll take care of it, Thomas." He doesn't need to say anymore.

"You will?"

"I will look into it and get back to you as soon as I can. In the meantime, tell your niece to keep her head up and her butt down."

"Okay, I'll do that," the man from Alabama says with a smile. "Here is what little information I have on the situation. It should get you started."

I accept the folder from the man and shake his hand. He gives a nod to Chelsea. "Ma'am," he says before walking out the door of my inner office. By the look on Chelsea's face, she's never been called "ma'am" before. Not surprising, considering she's barely twenty years old. When she walks over to the desk, I hand her the file.

"What do you want me to do with this?" Chelsea asks, her hand holding the paper ominously over the trash can. She doesn't like Parker for legitimate reasons. Anything that smells like a favor to him ought to be summarily rejected in her mind.

"Who is our most tenacious case manager?" I ask. Favor or not, I'm not willing to dismiss this outright. If a soldier is indeed in trouble in my state, I'm going to help where I can.

"You can't be serious? You believe this load of crap? Parker is setting you up for something politically embarrassing!"

"Yeah, he could be. The only way to know is to investigate it, which leads to my original question."

"Meghan," she sighs, realizing there is no talking me out of this.

"Have her bump this to the top of her to-do list, please. Tell her to let me know if she gets any push back from the command. I have talked to The Adjutant General on a few occasions, so instruct her not to be bashful with the name dropping."

"Okay," Chelsea says halfheartedly, the unmistakable sound of frustration in the tone of her voice. She turns to leave, but maybe now is the right time for the talk I owe her.

"Chels, you have every right to be pissed. I know you can't stand Parker, or damned near any other elected representative here. And you know I respect your opinion and counsel above pretty much everyone's."

"So why do this? Why do a favor for a man who is one of the leaders of your lynch mob?"

"Simple. His niece is a soldier living in our district. If she is getting a raw deal, we are going to correct that. Not for him, for her."

Chelsea nods, but once again I'm at odds with my chief of staff. I'm about to tell her something she needs to hear when the familiar voice of the woman who is the light at the end of my tunnel enters.

"Was that Thomas Parker I saw walking out of your office?" Kylie asks, beckoning back over her shoulder. I guess the talk will have to wait once again.

"The man, the myth, and the legend. One of the most influential Republicans in the House and the illustrious Chairman of the Congressional Black Caucus."

"And he came to visit you?" she asks with a disparaging tone I'm sure wasn't intended.

"Yeah, he missed *Keeping Up With the Kardashians* this week and wanted a recap," I add sarcastically.

Kylie's a journalist, and a damn good one. So I'm not surprised that she notices tension between me and my chief of staff. There are no secrets between us, and she knows I'm beginning to worry if this job has gotten more to Chelsea than it has me.

"He wanted a favor," Chelsea corrects, clearly not in the mood to enjoy my witty sense of humor. That or it just wasn't funny.

"Okay then. Let's move on to the bigger issue of the day."

"Uh-oh."

"Yeah, uh-oh is right. I had a contact call me to see if I knew anything about an investigation under way. Apparently, a special subcommittee was convened in secret, and based on the results, is about to bring charges to the Ethics Committee."

"You can't be serious," Chelsea says, already connecting the dots on who is the focus of the inquiry. I swear that girl is one more bad day away from going on a serious bender. Considering how horrible I have been at this job, I can't really blame her. She has been the modern version of the Greek goddess Selene trying to keep the wheels on this wagon. She's done an amazing job, but it's taking a toll on her.

"It's already been leaked to the media, so expect your phone to start ringing off the hook."

"Vince is going to love this," Chelsea reacts sarcastically, walking out the door and into the outer office.

"It gets worse. Apparently the evidence against you is pretty compelling. Are you sure you didn't leave anything out when you told me about your meeting with that lobbyist back in Connecticut?"

I briefed her on the meeting in great detail, both before and after. She smelled a rat from the very beginning, and said as much. Mercifully she stopped well short of the "I told you so"

I would have gotten from Jessica when I told her what transpired. Although she was a touch disappointed I didn't break his nose. God, I love this woman.

"Another fabricated scandal," I say with an exhale. "It's starting to feel like old times again."

-TWENTY-

CHELSEA

The walk from the Capitol to our space in the Cannon House Office Building is a short one. Out of the four House office buildings, Cannon is the oldest, and by far, the coolest. We were lucky to score a nine-hundred-fifty-eight-square-foot room there with a Capitol view after the representative who originally had it opted to take Beaumont's old office in the more prestigious Rayburn Building. To our surprise, none of the new representatives housed up in the fifth floor "cages" sucked it up.

I see a group of media breaking up at the House Triangle as I approach it. Located on the House side of the Capitol's East Front, the small patch of land sports a permanent podium that uses the Capitol as a backdrop for press conferences seen on the news all the time. After a quick search of the small crowd, I return my attention to walking just in time to avoid crashing right into one of the Three Amigos.

"Hello, Miss Stanton," Christopher says. The other two also bid their hello. Crap, what are their names again?

"Hey, guys."

"We're actually glad we ran into you. You have time for a quick talk?"

"Sure," I say, not really meaning it.

Chris leads the way with me at his side, his colleagues in tow behind us. I guess he drew the short straw. The Three Amigos, as I like to call them, are the chiefs of staff for three prominent New York Democrats. All short and in their late thirties, they're always together when I see them around Capitol Hill.

We walk along the sidewalk that parallels Southwest Drive between the Capitol and the Rayburn building. Tourists meander past us, so we walk until we're clear of any prying ears. This better be good. If it's not, they will learn firsthand what happens when you piss off a redhead.

"This has been a pleasant walk, fellas, but is one of you going to ever get to the point?"

"We were asked to deliver a message to you and your boss." Yeah, this ought to be good. "Bennit has more support here than you know."

"All evidence to the contrary," I sneer.

"It's true," one of the other Amigos says.

"Our bosses are among them. They don't agree with him on every issue, but wish they could work with him more," Chris laments.

"So why don't they?" I snap. This level of annoyance in my voice can be unappealing, and is probably a big reason I don't get asked out on many dates.

"The press is reporting your boss is about to be slapped with ethics violations," the third Amigo says. "That's toxic in this town."

"No kidding, but that doesn't explain why you didn't reach out sooner."

"The minority leader would flay us if we go anywhere near him," Chris explains. "And the most liberal caucus members have made it very clear that any member caught working with him will face repercussions."

Damn caucuses. In Congress, they are formed by representatives as a forum to discuss issues and make plans to advance legislative agendas important to the membership of the group. There are dozens of them in the House, and the Democratic House caucus is one of the most powerful since each representative from that party is a member. Like its Republican counterpart, that caucus elects the party leadership.

Their bosses also belong to another group called the New Democrat Coalition, Congress's largest group of moderates who often finds itself at odds with the rest of the party. Yes, instead of partying on weekends, eating pizza, and studying for the occasional college exam, this has become my life.

"I don't know if there is anything to these charges against Bennit or not," Chris says. "What I do know is the most extreme members of both parties want him gone."

"Well, the way it sounds, no one in this town has the backbone to stand up to them, so they'll probably get their wish," I say, turning to walk away. My emotions are catching up with me, and thinking about how hopeless our situation is only makes it worse. I can't let these guys see that. I'm about ten steps away before they stop me.

"We know about the other icandidates." I stop dead in my tracks. The discussions I had with Mister B about whatever plan he and the ex-senator are conjuring up have been vague at best. I don't think he has even seen the names, let alone shared them with me. How the hell do these guys know?

"What icandidates?" I ask reflexively. They look at each other before walking over to me.

"Bennit is teaming up with a former senator from Virginia to support the campaigns of a hundred independent social media candidates to run against the most powerful politicians in the House," Chris says.

"How could ... I mean ..." C'mon Chelsea, get it together, I tell myself. "How do you know that?"

"It's not important," Amigo Two says. I really wish I could remember his name. It would make it so much easier to verbally assault him.

"Damn straight it's important. I want to know!" I demand, my redhead temper starting to get the best of me.

"Lots of things get discussed between staff members at a bar over Marlboro Lights and Coors Light, Miss Stanton," Chris says, deriding both my age and implying I'm so far out of the inner circle I wouldn't know that. As much as I want to strangle him, I need to let it go and dig for more information.

"Fine. Why are you guys telling me this?"

"Rumor has it Bennit is avoiding going after moderates. Our bosses are slaves to the powerful liberals in the party. I'm sure Republicans in the Liberty Caucus and other Blue Dog Democrats feel the same way."

"So?" I ask impatiently.

"Michael can change the dynamic of the House if he can pull this off. Our bosses think that may be in the country's best interests. We want you to let him know that if he does, we're willing to work with him."

"Yeah, only we all know that he won't survive this ethics hearing. It doesn't matter that he didn't do anything wrong." It's the truth, and I knew it as soon as I heard. There is nothing we can do to fight this.

"Chelsea," Amigo Three says with a chuckle, "you're his chief of staff. You can't think like that. I know you're new to this game, but you're his top advisor. If he's in trouble, it's on you to get him out of it."

"Most of our colleagues just think you wandered off your school tour and ended up as a chief of staff. Time to prove them wrong," Chris says as he and his two pals head toward the Rayburn Building.

"How?" I call out to them, instantly regretting it.

"That's for you to figure out."

* * *

I made it as far as the grand rotunda of the Cannon Office Building before I break down. Seated on a simple wooden bench nestled among the grandeur of the arched portals and high ceiling, I bury my head in my hands and cry.

I knew the pressures of this job would be difficult to manage, but I never prepared myself for this. There was no realizing that I would have to fashion a plan to keep my mentor from getting kicked out of here. Is he really expecting me to do that? Is that why he's so disappointed in me lately?

"Chelsea?" the soothing voice of Kylie asks as she hovers over me.

"Uh, yeah, hi, Kylie," I say, trying to stifle my tears and hide the puffiness of my eyes.

"What's wrong, sweetie?" she asks, genuine concern all over her face and in the tone of her voice.

I want to be strong. I want to tell her that I just needed a moment of emotional release. I want to pick up the pieces and show her that I have it all under control. "I can't do this anymore, Kylie!" is what I blurt out instead. Yeah, fail.

"Okay, we are long overdue for a girl chat. Let's go."

"No, I can't, I have—"

"It wasn't a request, Chelsea. C'mon, work can wait," she says. She's very compelling. I suppose that's a reason why she's such a good journalist.

Kylie reflexively knows where to go. She doesn't say anything as we leave the Cannon building and walk around to the set of stone stairs on the West Front of the Capitol. With no effort, she leads me right to my favorite spot and has a seat facing the National Mall. It may not be sunset, but I instantly feel better.

For the next ten minutes, I open up to her like I have never opened up to anyone since my mother died. I was just going into high school when I lost her, and although my father did a great job as a single parent, there is no substitute for a girl's mother. Kylie's a little young to fulfill that role, but she's doing a damn good job listening to me spill my guts to her.

"I just can't do this job. I can't be the chief of staff he needs me to be," I conclude, finishing my emotional rant between sobs.

"Then don't, Chelsea," Kylie says so matter-of-factly, it almost sounds insincere.

"You think I should quit?" almost not believing what I just heard.

"Oh, God no. I think you should stop trying to be what you think people expect and just be who you are."

"I'm not sure what you mean."

"Long before I met you guys, I was on a career trajectory that resembled something NASA would launch. I was covering politics for the *New York Times,* and I was in heaven. But I realized all that glittered in Washington was not gold, and I set out to purge the town from the corruption I thought was choking democracy. After all, I was Kylie Roberts. I was untouchable."

"And you got fired."

"Yup. I was pretty resentful about that for a long time. I thought I had made a mistake by straying from what was expected from me. Then I met you guys. A group of students working so hard to get their teacher elected to Congress was inspiring. It made me realize that I was focused on being the journalist everyone expected for so long, I needed to lash out and break away. I think deep down I wanted to be fired."

"But you joined our campaign because you wanted revenge."

"I never said I wasn't vindictive," Kylie says with a laugh and a smile.

"So you think I want to be fired?" I ask, not sure what the point of the story is.

"Not at all. I think you are trying to be something you're not and sacrificing who you are. He didn't ask you to be his chief of staff because he wanted you to be some political sleaze ball. He asked you for the same reason he chose you to run the campaign. He trusts your judgment enough to listen to your advice and let you lead the troops."

"It doesn't feel like he ever takes my advice."

"He's a free thinker, Chels. Believe me, he won't follow anyone blindly, but I don't think him not taking your advice is really what's bothering you."

"What do you mean?" If there is one person's judge of character and behavior I trust, it's hers.

"Michael is like a second father to you. Just like you were always terrified of disappointing your own dad, the same applies here. I know how you feel. When I first met Michael, he was larger than life. I didn't want to disappoint him for different reasons, but I understand what you're going through because he has that effect on people."

"Never seems to bother Vince or Vanessa."

"Vince learned this lesson much sooner than you are. Remember back to when your campaign was first starting? He had his meltdown."

She's right. The day we announced our first campaign at the Perkfect Buzz, Vince tried to be something he wasn't and it turned into a disaster. I had forgotten about that.

"When I started working with you guys, I struggled with knowing that Michael would be a terrible politician if he played by the traditional set of rules. The same applies to your situation. You will be a horrible chief of staff for the same reason, because it's not in either of you two's DNA."

"That's not how people are supposed to act around here. It's all about deal making and schmoozing and networking. I'm not good at any of that."

"You don't know that. You have no clout to bargain with, schmoozing is overrated, and you can't network if the members have been directed by their leadership not to work with you. Nothing that has happened over the past year has anything to do with your abilities."

"What if you're wrong about all this, Kylie?" For so long I have believed everything that has gone wrong is my fault. I'm still not sure what to do or what to think, and I'm getting tired of feeling that way.

"Trust me, sweetie, I'm not."

Kylie and Michael have a relationship most women can only dream about. They are both stubborn, so when they fight, it's epic. But in the end, they are completely in love with each other and loyal to a fault. Even only after dating for a year and a half, they know each other better than most couples who have been married for ten.

"So what do you think I should do now?"

"Frankly? Say screw it and be yourself. Michael needs you to be the same tenacious, fiery redhead that got him here."

"I'm not sure how to start doing that."

"I do," she says, rising and prompting me to get up from my own seat on the stairs. "He's up there meeting with that shark Viano right now. This is as good a time to start as any."

-TWENTY-ONE-
SENATOR VIANO

We are a half hour into this meeting when Michael's chief of staff finally decides to grace us with her presence. She walks in with Kylie Roberts, who's a bit of a tart, but otherwise a capable journalist. Chelsea's eyes are puffy and red from crying, and I'm willing to bet Kylie was acting as a supportive girlfriend. For a chief of staff in this town, she needs to develop a thicker skin. What a weakling.

After greetings are made, Michael quickly gets Chelsea and Kylie up to speed on our discussions with Blake handling most of the questions. I only deal with principals, not questions from the staff. That and I know of the history between Chelsea and Blake going back to their first campaign. Keeping her intimidated and on edge can only benefit me.

"Have you vetted all these people?" Chelsea asks, I suppose getting the obvious questions out of the way.

"It's not complete," Blake replies patiently, "but we are working on it. They all passed the cursory look for anything potentially embarrassing."

"What do you think?" Michael asks her. I am not sure if asking someone who can't legally buy a drink for her political opinion is out of sympathy or legitimate. Hopefully the former more than the latter.

"She thinks going after the extremes is a mistake," Blake says, drawing a fiery stare. "I'm sure she thinks we need to target moderates to get bigger numbers."

"Don't presume to think you know anything about what my thoughts are, *Mister Peoni*." I look over at Kylie who has a look of almost maternal pride on her face. I may have to account for her being more involved in the happenings of the Bennit camp than I thought.

"I was assuming that—"

"You were assuming that I would balk at taking on the most firmly entrenched representatives in the House. That we don't have the resources or time to target entrenched incumbents in heavily gerrymandered districts. And you were most afraid that I would convince Congressman Bennit of all that, which is why you leaked it to the Three Amigos."

"The who?" Michael asks, not quite understanding the reference. I only can guess, but I assume it is some of the staff members I told Blake to reach out to in preparation for this meeting.

"They work for three of the New York moderate Democrats," she explains. "They seem to be very well informed about the senator's plan here. How do you imagine that is?"

"Now Chelsea, we're all on the same team here," Blake chides. Best if I come clean now before she launches into an Alec Baldwin-like tirade.

"I had Blake talk to some of staff members for moderates in the House. I had my former chief of staff Gary Condrey talk to a few others."

"Why would you tip them off like that, Senator?" Kylie asks me. I didn't even know she was invited to this meeting.

"Because I don't want moderates to panic when the word spreads about this," I reply, a little annoyed I have to justify myself to a simple journalist.

"No, that's not why, Senator," Chelsea intercedes. "You cut us off at the knees. It was your way of manipulating us to do what you want. If we fight you on this, and decide to push forward with going after more vulnerable members, you'll have leverage to make us look like bungling fools." Very astute. That was part of my thought process.

"That's patently untrue, Miss Stanton. I discussed this at length with Gary and he advised me that this was the best route to take based on our ultimate goal. We are working toward the same thing." There is no part of what I said that's true, but I almost believed it myself. Damn, I miss politics.

"So you guys keep saying. But if we're a team, then you should start being team players." I am about to say something before Michael stops me.

"Senator, Chelsea is right. I understand the course of action, but it should have been pursued after we had this meeting, not before."

"I understand, Michael. It won't happen again." Not that it matters, because it served its purpose.

"Why are you doing this, Senator?" Chelsea barks without preamble.

"Excuse me?"

"You heard me. Why are you doing this? Let me answer your next question before you ask it," she says, getting up and pacing around the office now. Michael is paying rapt attention, almost confused by her behavior. "When Kylie began helping us during the last campaign, she had reasons she never shared with us until after the election. Turns out they were good ones, but I'm not so sure about yours. I'm not willing to put that kind of faith in you. So tell us now, why are you helping us?"

This little teenager is showing me a side of her I haven't seen yet. I will have to do a little more homework and keep a closer eye on her. Dealing with one loose cannon on the ship is bad enough, but two could be a disaster.

"Are you accusing us of—"

"It's okay, Blake," I interrupt. "I understand your concern, Chelsea. And yours, Michael, assuming she is speaking for you as well. Let's just say I've harbored a lot of resentment toward the elites in my party since my defeat. That's as much detail as I am going to provide."

"That's not good enough," Kylie says, butting in again.

"It's going to have to be, Miss Roberts, because that's all you're going to get. I want to help you change the system. From here, you can either choose to accept my help or not. I've shown you all my cards and have asked nothing in return."

"Yet."

"I'm trying to help you, Chelsea. That's all. God knows you both need it."

"Yeah, right. I don't know what your game is, but I don't buy your reasons for a second. You expect us to believe you are doing all this out of the goodness of your heart? This is Washington, and the very notion of that is laughable."

"I don't think I like what you're accusing me of."

"I don't think I give a damn." She's turning into quite the feisty one, isn't she?

"Chelsea," Michael warns. She's ignoring him, so maybe it's time to test the strength of their relationship. Chelsea is too young to be an effective political player in this town, if for no other reason that so much work is done in restaurants and bars over drinks. Her crying also makes me question her mental toughness. You need an iron will to hack it in this town. Blake would be far better suited for this role, and him being an insider instead of just a liaison would be beneficial to me as well.

"Michael, if you don't want my assistance, I will happily leave you to try to pull this off yourself." He looks at me for a long moment, and I'm convinced he's about to ask Chelsea to leave the room. If he does, her future working for him will have a life expectancy of minutes, not years.

"Senator," he says to me with a serious tone he rarely uses. "I suggest you listen to what my chief of staff has to say, and listen hard." Well, what do you know? He's backing her after all.

"I've had a rough year and I am at my wits' end, but I'm done playing games," she proclaims, not wasting any time seizing the opportunity her mentor just gave her. "You cross us and you'll find out the hard way what your lying tongue tastes like after I rip it out and feed it to you."

I regard her for a moment, quickly glance over to Michael, and then let out a laugh. The girl is finally showing some spunk. I admire that. I may need to rethink my opinion of her.

"Chelsea, you might just make a good chief of staff after all."

-TWENTY-TWO-
SPEAKER ALBRIGHT

Power in Congress may transfer between political parties, but the one constant in the lives of the congressional elite is the power lunch. Between noon and two o'clock, restaurants in and around Capitol Hill fill with members and staff who meet to negotiate and clinch deals. Charlie Palmer Steak is one of the most popular places for these gatherings and, depending on the week, serves about a quarter of the House and a third of the Senate.

"You're late," I say to the majority leader as he takes a seat across from me. The restaurant sports a rooftop with scenic views of the city, but is also replete with private dining areas including the one we're seated in now.

"Sorry, it's already been one of those days. I acquired this as a peace offering." Harvey hands me an innocuous looking manila file folder and orders seltzer water from the waiter while he waits for me to peruse the contents.

"It's a list of names and districts. So what?"

"It is a list of icandidates planning to run in the next election." Oh, not this again.

"Where did you get this from?" I ask, more than a little curious as to where he gets his information. As Speaker of the

House, I get wind of a lot of rumors, but it's nothing compared to what Harvey seems to uncover.

"I have a source friendly with Bennit and willing to do my bidding. Do you notice anything peculiar about where those candidates are running?"

I give Harvey a long, hard look before turning my attention back to the file. I look through the associated districts next to each name again. By a third of the way down the sheet, I know what he is referring to.

"They're all safe districts," I say, scanning harder for one in particular. Members who hail from districts who almost always support a particular party tend to be slackers. Because they never face serious threats, they don't know how to campaign well. They also are the most ideologically rigid representatives in the House, as reflected in their voting records. Taking a hard-line position on controversial issues is fodder for a crafty opponent in a tight race.

"Your district is on the second page. Do you know the lady?" I find the line with my South Carolina district and trace across the spreadsheet at the name of my soon-to-be foe.

"Damn."

"You do know her then?" Harvey asks, amused.

"Yeah, she's a well-respected small business owner and longtime Republican supporter. I never imagined I would have to worry about her, much less face her in an election."

"Welcome to the age of the icandidate," Harvey laments.

"Your district is on this list too?"

"All of our districts are," another voice booms from next to me, deciding to take a seat uninvited. "Good afternoon, Mister

Speaker," he says, before turning to Harvey. "And to you, Mister Leader."

"So you have a problem with Bennit, too, Dennis?" I ask the longtime Democrat and reigning minority leader of the U.S. House of Representatives. Meetings between party leadership rarely happen in public these days, although that was not always the case. While old-school reporters may remember a day where we would all be seen at a restaurant table together, a young journalist would crap his pants if he walked by this dining room and saw Harvey and me sitting with Dennis Merrick right now.

"Fifty of the districts on that list are Democrat strongholds. You're damn right we're worried about him." Dennis is a politician's politician. In his late forties, he has television looks and a disarming demeanor. Coming from Washington State, he is remarkably popular with the hipster crowd that frequents the Seattle coffeehouse scene.

"I think you guys are overestimating the effectiveness of a social media campaign in a presidential election year," I state. "There was nothing else to talk about when Bennit ran in the midterms. Now, everyone will be focused on who will win the White House. Nobody is going to care about virtual campaigns. It's been done."

"That was my initial thought," Dennis says, "but the members of my caucus are concerned that people will be more tuned into social media because of the presidential race."

"Okay, the only thing I know about social media is my teenage daughter's posting of duck faces on something called Instagram and documenting her every activity in Facebook status updates. Harvey, what's their plan? How are they planning to stand out if there are a hundred of them running?"

"I don't know, but I'm sure they have one. These aren't run of the mill lawyers bred for politics. They are teachers, tradesmen, businessmen, and entrepreneurs. Many of them probably built their own dedicated following like Francisco Reyes did down in Texas."

"That's the other reason they are dangerous. In today's media age, we are expected to answer questions about any subject. Let's face facts; most of the incumbents in these safe seats don't have the expertise to argue the issues against some of these candidates. They've never had to worry about mastering many subjects because they win reelections so easily."

Dennis is more legitimately concerned about this than I ever thought. A professional politician to his very core, you always have to be aware of alternative agendas. He will do anything that benefits the Democrats, and would even ally himself with Bennit in a heartbeat if it meant reclaiming the House for his party. Maybe that's something we should consider.

"What's the status of the Bennit investigation?" Harvey asks, getting to the point.

"It's progressing. The evidence is strong, but is still being validated. I'm concerned that there are members of the committee who won't be swayed though," I add, staring directly at the minority leader to allow no confusion that the comment is directed toward him.

"That shouldn't be a concern," he replies. Yeah, right. Everything is a concern when Dennis Merrick is involved. He would vote to abolish the Fourth of July if he thought he could make my party look bad.

"I know how the Republicans will vote," Harvey says, trying to coax a more concrete reassurance from his counterpart. "Are you saying the Democrats are with us?"

"What I'm saying is you don't need to lose sleep wondering if Democrats on the ethics panel will make this a partisan fight. We will follow your lead if it means getting rid of Bennit before November."

"We have a long history with you, Mister Leader," I tell the leading Democrat in my most foreboding voice. "Not all of your pledges of support ever materialize the way you advertise them." I may run the show as Speaker of the House, but I am first beholden to protecting the interests of my own party. This Bennit thing is bad, but getting politically outmaneuvered would be even worse.

"There is no love lost between my party and Bennit," Dennis discloses. "Winston Beaumont may have been a blowhard, but he was our blowhard. Now, because of Bennit, he's spent more time in court than Lindsey Lohan." Yup, definitely a hipster.

"Meaning?"

"Meaning we will not cross you on this, Harvey. On that you have my word," he promises, getting up to leave. "Keep my office in the loop on any developments. Good day, gentlemen."

"The RNC wants this too, you know that, Mister Speaker," Harvey says, once the minority leader leaves our private dining area.

"You trust him?"

"Merrick? Hell, no. He will turn this into a political opportunity to regain the House the first chance he gets. But I do believe he'll instruct his caucus not to interfere with the proceedings in the Ethics Committee."

"Okay. Let's get a press conference scheduled for two weeks from now and fire a shot across his bow," I command. "Maybe he takes the hint and resigns on his own, but at a minimum, it might scare all these independents into not working with him."

"I'll get it scheduled. In the meantime, have the Chairman of the Ethics Committee press forward with the investigation and get a hearing scheduled in August before we hit convention season. Any negative press or public backlash will be buried under the avalanche of media surrounding the nominations for president."

"Let's hope so."

-TWENTY-THREE-
MICHAEL

Even as a congressman from the state, I spend very little time in Hartford. When the occasion calls for the elected representatives of Connecticut to come together for the best interests of our residents, I am usually left out in the cold. The governor, a longtime, flag-waving Democrat and friend of Winston Beaumont, will not even return my calls. But that's not what brings me here today.

The State Armory and Arsenal in Hartford was built in the early twentieth century and is the largest such facility in the state. Located only a quarter mile from the state capitol building, the classical revival-style structure serves as headquarters of the Connecticut Military Department and holds the office of the man currently lined up in my crosshairs.

Major General Timothy Reinert is The Adjutant General of the Connecticut National Guard, and is responsible to the governor and the National Guard Bureau for providing mission-ready forces to support both Army mobilization and state emergency operations requirements. He is a two-star, and the man who ultimately implements policies applicable to all state Guard units. That makes him responsible for their failures as well.

"I'm sorry, the general has asked not to be disturbed," the staff sergeant seated at the desk in the small outer office decrees without looking up.

"That's his problem, not mine," I retort, already cranky that I had to drive up here to storm the ramparts of this man's office because he could not manage to hold a civil conversation with one of my staff members.

The NCO looks up, equally annoyed at the disturbance and my affront to his status as gatekeeper for the state's ultimate military authority. "There are no appointments scheduled so you, whoa ..." he trails off mid-sentence after recognizing me. "My apologies, Congressman Bennit, I didn't realize—"

"Don't sweat it, Sergeant; you're just doing your job. However, trust me when I tell you that I'm also doing mine. Please go tell your boss I'm here to see him, and that he will come out to take this meeting or I will dust off my breaching skills, go all infantry, and kick his damn door in."

"Yes, sir!" the staff sergeant says, probably impressed he just met a politician who actually speaks his language. He disappears into the general's office and shuts the door behind him. The ensuing one-sided conversation with his boss was a spirited one from what I could hear through the door. As a former NCO, I know what it's like to stand in front of an officer's desk and have to tell him something he doesn't want to hear. It's not a pleasant experience.

After a moment, the tall, gray-haired general emerges in his utility uniform, the subdued two-star rank insignia unmistakable in the center of his torso. He is struggling to mask how pissed off he is, and would almost succeed if his eyes didn't give it away.

"Congressman Bennit, welcome to the Connecticut National Guard. It's good to see you, sir." I know I'm supposed to say something equally political, so I won't. Shock and awe is so much more fun.

"Good morning, General. I'm the last person you want to see today, so drop the façade and cut the bullshit." Perfect. You don't get any more non-political than that without dropping an f-bomb or two. He grins, maybe appreciating the fact that I'm not here to be coddled.

"Let's head into my office," he says, leading the way. His office is typical of most military men, adorned with various plaques, framed shadow boxes, and gifts from various units he served in and commanded. Almost every service member has similar "I love me" walls, but the higher in grade someone climbs, the more extensive the décor. General Reinert has managed to cover all four walls of his office.

"As I told your staff member, sir, I cannot interfere with an ongoing investigation," he says, getting to the point. Usually, I prefer being called Michael, but this isn't one of those moments.

"No, General, you told Meghan she doesn't understand the military and should mind her own business. That's just half the problem you and I have today, though. You then asked her to tell me that if I have a problem with that, I should come see you so you can tell me to get lost to my face." I watch the blood drain out of his. "Go ahead, I dare you."

"My apologies, Congressman, I intended no disrespect."

"Yes, you did. You know my background. I was a NCO, and dealt with officers who were jockeying for the next rank all the time. You don't reach your position without being politically astute, so I will hazard a guess that your purposeful avoidance of me was probably ordered by the governor."

General Reinert exhales, and I know I'm right on target with my comment. Now he relaxes, given the knowledge that I understand his actions without him having to tell me. I have a flight to catch back to D.C., so it's time to get this done.

"This isn't about you and me, or the politics that rule our respective worlds," I say. "It is about a young soldier who is having a bad time of it and some men who may be behaving in a manner that neither of us condones."

"Yes, sir, but we don't know if their behavior constitutes harassment yet. I cannot interfere on your behalf," Reinert concludes, the double meaning of his statement not lost on me. He will face consequences if he consents to any of my requests.

"Then it's settled."

"What's settled, sir?" the old soldier asks, confused as to whether I missed the point of his statement.

"General, when the governor calls after hearing that I was spotted in the building, you are going to tell him that you told me I'm an amateur and to go pound sand."

"I am, huh?"

"Yes, you are. Then you are going to hear through an imaginary source that a soldier under your command may be having issues with sexual harassment in her unit. You will direct the command to perform a fair and speedy investigation, and order that commander to remove her from any situation where alleged behavior may be repeated for her protection."

"Imaginary source? Look, I know who her uncle is. The governor—"

"Will never find out the subject of this discussion," I say, cutting him off. "You can make up a reason why I was here. Where you got the information about the NCO in question from isn't my concern. Soldiers talk, especially in headquarters buildings. In the end, you will be the firm leader enforcing your zero-tolerance policy on harassment, while having the cover of not doing it for me. Agreed?" As if he could say no to that.

"Agreed."

"Excellent," I say, turning to leave his office.

"Congressman Bennit?" he says, stopping me before I hit the door. "Congressman Parker hates your guts. This isn't a political favor, so why are you doing this?"

"'All Soldiers are entitled to outstanding leadership; I will provide that leadership. I know my Soldiers, and I will always place their needs above my own,'" I recite from the NCO Creed. Every sergeant worth a damn should be able to quote it from memory.

"'I will bear true faith and allegiance to the same,'" he replies from his own oath with a nod. "You could try to score political points publically over this if you wanted to. Why aren't you?"

"Because a soldier who just wants to do her job has a problem she needs our help with. She doesn't care about me, you, or anyone else's political scorecard."

"Despite being a former Green Beret, you know that's not how business is done in Washington, or even here for that matter," General Reinert laments.

"No, sir, it isn't. But imagine the problems we could solve in this country if it was."

-TWENTY-FOUR-
CHELSEA

"This is my spot, Blake, go find your own," I say as he takes a seat next to me on the Capitol steps.

"We've covered this. It was mine first, remember?" Damn, I forgot that part.

"Fine. Just sit there with your mouth closed or you'll find yourself swallowing your teeth."

Blake looks like he has a witty comeback in mind, but wisely thinks twice about it. It's just after lunch, and I wanted to spend a few quiet moments outside in this beautiful weather before returning to the grind of the day.

July is coming to the capital, and with it oppressive heat and humidity typical for that time of year. Today is gorgeous though, with the thermometer only reaching the low eighties and humidity unseasonably low. Too bad it's being ruined now.

"Any plans next week for the Fourth of July?"

"I thought I warned you not to talk to me."

Blake resumes watching the people mill around the Capitol reflecting pool below us. I can't stand the guy, but maybe I'm being too hard on him. While I'm not one to forgive and forget, I am stuck working with him now that we are allies with Senator Viano.

"No, I don't have any plans," I say. I'm direct, and about as nice as I can force myself to be.

"And your boss?"

"It's one of his favorite holidays. He will be watching stuff blow up somewhere."

"I'm never going to get you to like me, am I?" Blake comments, changing the subject after a long, serene pause.

"You have no idea how unlikely that is." That may be the most truthful statement uttered anywhere near this building today.

"More or less unlikely than you ever trusting Senator Viano?" Blake asks. So that's why he's here.

"Very slick, Blake. I don't trust either of you. None of us do." I have daily meetings with Brian, Peyton, and the gang, and they are very vocal about their reservations with Viano and dislike of Blake. Say what you want about my generation, but we do know how to hold grudges.

"I don't blame you, at least in one regard. I don't trust the senator either." Well, that's news.

"So why get her teamed up with the congressman?"

"You guys needed help. She approached me a while back, and I thought it made sense to at least make the introduction to a possible ally and let you all make the decision," Blake explains in a manner that almost sounds sincere.

"But you don't trust her?"

"No. I've know the senator for a very long time, and she can always be counted on doing whatever is in her own best interests. For some reason, she looks at working with Bennit as an opportunity, so your interests are aligned. So long as they stay that way, she will fight like a pit bull for you guys."

"And when they aren't aligned?"

"We'll need to walk around with steel plates on our backs to deflect the daggers she will try to stick in them."

"Great, there's something to look forward to." I study Blake for a moment, looking for any indication he's lying to me. My BS meter is much more active than it was back in high school, probably because the people in this town make it go off so often. It's quiet right now, which has me both concerned and curious.

"Why are you telling me this? What's your angle?"

"You like to accuse me of always having an angle," Blake says with a series of small laughs. "You accused me of that backstage at the debate once, remember?"

I actually do remember. In the heat of watching Mister Bennit wipe the floor with his boss, he pulled me aside to warn me that Beaumont could get desperate following the thumping he took. Blake was right, but conveniently omitted that it was he who would try to embarrass us through a baseless claim of an affair.

"Given our history, Blake, I can't see you as the altruistic type."

"Altruistic. Good word. I'm not going to pretend to be anything of the sort, Chelsea. I'm not perfect, but I'm also not the guy I was back when I worked for Beaumont. I want you to trust me again, and I know it will take a long time to ever get to that point."

"You want me to trust you, or Congressman Bennit to?" I ask, wondering if there was an implied meaning to his choice of words.

"Both, but I want to start with you. I need to start with you."

I stare into his eyes and see a pain I've never seen before in him. It's the kind of thing you only read about in stories printed in *Glamour* or *Elle* magazine. For the first time since I met Blake, it actually feels like he is opening up and being genuine. I feel like there is a lot of emotion dammed up inside him that is about to come pouring out, and I am lost in the moment of it.

"I hate to interrupt ... whatever this is ... but we have a situation," Vince says from behind us. I turn to see Vince staring at us with a furious look on his face. I'm not sure if it's because he sees me with Blake or because of whatever prompted him to come find me here.

Vince stares at Blake with one of those looks you see in mob movies right before someone gets whacked. While I'm pretty sure the Orsini family doesn't have any real organized crime connections, he is Italian through and through. Of course, Blake is too, so this could turn into an episode of *The Sopranos* real quick.

"What is it, Vince? What's wrong?"

"Speaker Albright just announced a press conference."

-TWENTY-FIVE-
SPEAKER ALBRIGHT

Three press rooms serve the House of Representatives for members of the media who report on Congress. These "galleries" are controlled by a committee of journalists who qualify for press credentials to cover various media events. For this particular announcement, I cashed in a couple of favors to get every media organization who wanted to attend approved. For that reason, this room is packed full.

I stand in front of the lectern with the seal of the United States House of Representatives on it and against a light oak backdrop that features panels comprising the Capitol dome in the foreground against a translucent American Flag. To my right stands Harvey Stepanik, the majority whip, and several senior Republican members of the Ethics Committee.

Since this is a bipartisan effort, House Minority Leader Dennis Merrick joins us on the left along with the minority whip and his contingent from the committee. I get a nod from one of my press assistants who is liaising with the correspondents to get the timing right since this will be broadcast live.

"Good afternoon, ladies and gentlemen," I say in greeting before going on to introduce the others on the dais. That completed, I get into the heart of the matter. "I'm here to announce today that the House Ethics Committee will hold a formal hearing on alleged violations by Representative Michael Bennit."

There is a chorus of sharp inhales from the media in the room, the looks of shock on their face betraying their usual stoic demeanors. I'm caught off guard by their reactions because I know this was already leaked to the media. Hell, I leaked it. Ethics violations aren't exactly an uncommon occurrence here. This is the U.S. House of Representatives, after all, and when reporting scandals ranging from sexting to piles of cash hidden in a freezer, it takes a lot to rile this brackish group.

"An eight-member bipartisan adjudicatory subcommittee convened several weeks ago and issued a document yesterday concluding allegations against Mister Bennit are supported by clear and convincing evidence. The violations in question include: maintaining an improper relationship with a lobbyist, inappropriate acceptance and misuse of campaign funds, accepting money for influence, and accepting a bribe."

The initial display of shock among the correspondents in the room is replaced by more cynical looks and gestures as I read the charges. Bennit may not be the media darling he once was, but he's still well regarded among journalists in the jaded House press corps. They may be tepid about running with this story, but their editors won't be. A scandal with Michael Bennit's name attached to it is ratings and circulation gold that no news organization will choose to ignore.

"A formal hearing will be held prior to the August recess. As we have had only one other hearing of this nature since 2002, I will make the formal process available through my office. I will say that it will involve a trial-like session involving formal charges with lawyers for the House acting as prosecutors and Bennit's lawyers, should he choose to employ any, defending him. I will now take your questions."

The room explodes in a cacophony of shouted queries from the floor. I wasn't expecting this reaction. The press in the Capitol Building is usually far more muted and less hostile in their questioning. Normal business aside, even scandals are not typically met with this brazen response.

I answer the first few questions deftly and even defer to the minority leader who seizes the opportunity to prattle on about the imperative to clean up corruption and abuse in the House. My intent was not to turn this into a partisan battle, so I take the reins of leadership back on this lynch mob for the last few questions.

"Mister Speaker, there is an allegation making the rounds on social media that claims these charges were fabricated in an attempt to discredit Michael Bennit ahead of the November election. Can you comment on that?"

Where the hell did that come from? I have had my staff monitoring social media sites for a few days now and heard nothing. I am not happy that I've been blindsided by this question, and I can only hope it doesn't show.

"I cannot comment since I have not seen any such allegation, but—"

"The story was broke by a small political blog and is a trending article on sites like Reddit and Digg, Mister Speaker. It claims that Republicans and Democrats are in league to expel Representative Bennit. It further states that all of the evidence you previously mentioned was fabricated to that end."

"Thank you for the recap. Is there a question in there?"

"Yes, sir. Are you stating that these reports are untrue?"

Crap. I take a sip of water from the glass on the shelf of the podium to buy time. I was handed this evidence by the head of the most powerful lobby in Washington. I have no idea how he got it, and can safely assume he's covered his tracks on it. But what if he didn't? Honesty is never the best policy in American politics, but I don't want to get caught in a lie either. I need to find a way to deflect this and get out of here.

"The subcommittee found no reason to question the validity or authenticity of the evidence. The accused is a social media guru, and I'm sure he'll put forth several defenses in light of these accusations all over his Facebook page," I say in a mocking tone. "However, these serious allegations are not going to be tried on the Internet or in the court of public opinion. Mister Bennit will be afforded every opportunity to explain his actions at the committee hearing. Social media will play no role in our decision. Thank you for your time today," I finish, ending the news conference.

My attempt at a clean getaway was anything but smooth. The press in the room shouted question after question, many of them pretty good ones. What was supposed to be a bombshell about the illegal activities of Michael Bennit has started to turn into a conspiracy over who is framing him.

Bennit has this uncanny ability to enchant the media in a way few others can. Even after they realized he used them as pawns in his race against Beaumont, they are still willing to give him the benefit of the doubt. I understand why, since even I got caught up in Bennitmania when it was all the country was talking about. I guess that's what my colleagues fear most about him.

Personally, I think we are only making the situation worse. Michael Bennit is going to lose in November anyway, and probably lose big. Going after him may only reinvigorate his bastion of social media followers. If that somehow happens, then we may actually have a real problem.

Unfortunately, it's out of my hands. I can fight this, but too many people want it to happen now. Money, politics, and power are the engine of this town, and if I want to keep my seat at the table, I have to play my role. I may be third in line for the presidency and set the agenda for one of the two bodies in the legislative branch, but right now I feel I have no power at all. In that way, I'm not unlike poor Michael Bennit.

-TWENTY-SIX-

MICHAEL

Thomas Parker's workspace is on the second floor of the marble monster that is the Rayburn House Office Building. Next door to my modest digs in the Cannon Building, it is the newest and biggest of the three structures that provide office space and hearing rooms for all four hundred thirty-five representatives elected to the House.

Parker is a political veteran of the House, and ironically one of the fifty Republican districts we targeted for a run by an icandidate. As a senior member, he gets a really nice office, and I can't help but be impressed just walking in. Just one room in this suite measures twenty-five by forty feet, under a ceiling that has to be twenty feet high.

I get an assortment of strange looks as I walk past his staff and am shown into his impressive inner office. Now I know what lepers must have felt like in the Middle Ages. The mood changes when I see the large man's face light up when I enter.

"Mister Bennit!" he says in an enthusiastic greeting I'm not prepared for.

"Mister Parker, good to see you again."

"What brings you to the Rayburn Building?"

"You do. Or more specifically, your niece does," I say, assuaging his concerns that this might actually be a social call from the most radioactive politician in town.

"You investigated?"

"Not exactly," I say, getting the anticipated look of chagrin from the man in front of me. "I went up and paid a visit to the adjutant general."

"I have to admit that's much more than I expected. How did it go?"

"I threatened him, he patronized me, you know the drill. In the end, he realized helping a young sergeant was in his best interests on several levels. To make a long story short, I received a call from him an hour ago. He took care of the situation."

"Michael, I can't thank you enough. Really, I owe you one for this." The seriousness of his voice makes me perk up.

"No you don't. It was my pleasure to help," is all I say to see just what he's implying.

"Michael, you did me a favor when you had no business having to. I don't forget things like that. In this town, favors like this mean a lot, and I trust you will find a way for me to repay it."

He's right, that's exactly how this town works. Favors are the oil that keeps the machine working, as dysfunctional as it is. I have never participated in the experience, given my black sheep status.

"Congressman, I appreciate what you're trying to say to me, but there is no quid pro quo here. I didn't do this for a political advantage. I did it because a young soldier was being victimized by a failure to adhere to process, nothing more. When I tell you it was my honor to help, and that you don't owe me anything, I mean it."

"You're a rare breed in this town, Michael. Honor and integrity are not traits you see around here often."

"According to your colleagues, you don't see them in me either," I say with laugh. "I have a staff meeting to get to. Please send your niece my regards and please let me know if General Reinert doesn't follow through on his promise."

* * *

The walk back to the Cannon building is a short one, and after spending a couple of moments chatting with some junior staffers in the outer office, I walk into my sanctuary to find Chelsea, Vince, Vanessa, and Kylie waiting for me. To my surprise, Blake is also with them. I can only wonder how he survived this long in a room with Chelsea in it.

"So, what's the word?" I ask, stopping to give Kylie a kiss.

"The committee said it will meet before the August recess to make a determination on the allegations and recommend appropriate sanctions."

"Memorized that, did ya, Vanessa?" I ask, eliciting a smile from my one-time pupil.

"They're trying to bring a quick end to this before they all flee town and have to answer questions," Chelsea concludes.

"And it'll work. After a few days of coverage, the media will refocus on the conventions and the race for president," Kylie adds.

"Well, we hoped they would ask the tough questions following the Speaker's press conference and that didn't happen, so we shouldn't be shocked about any lasting coverage."

"It's still a two-party town, love. Until that changes, the Dems and the GOP will hold sway over the mainstream media. Information is the lifeblood of news organizations and they control the flow. Doubly so during the rare times they agree on something."

"Like getting rid of me," I say with a shake of my head. The others nod. "So why are you here, Blake?"

"Funny, I've been asking the same thing," Chelsea mumbles, with no attempt to hide her annoyance at his presence.

"The senator asked me to act as a liaison between you and her. She wanted me to bring you up to speed with where we are in the planning."

"Do we really need her to help with this?" Chelsea asks.

"She's right, Congressman. It's not like we haven't done this before," Vanessa says, picking up the argument.

"Successfully," Vince chimes in with a sideways glance at Blake. That dagger went right between the ribs.

"You can't do this without her," Blake says in defense. Unfortunately, he's right.

"Wanna bet?"

"Vince, as much as it pains me to say so, Blake is right," I interject. "We may have done this before, but not on a national scale. We don't have the ability to pull it off in such a short time frame without help."

"Our information tech guys say everything is ready to go for each of the one hundred candidates."

"Vanessa, can you coordinate with them to have Brian take a look at their work?"

"That's not going to be necessary, Congressman," Blake says, a little too quickly and defensively for my tastes. "Senator Viano says we have it handled."

"And I really don't give a damn what she says, Blake. Brian is my IT guy and has a group of people I will put up against the best the senator can hire any day. If I say he's to be involved, it's not a matter open for discussion."

"I will relay that to the senator, but she's not sold that volunteers can get this done. For the record, I disagree with that assessment based on firsthand experience."

Vince, Kylie, and Vanessa all smile weakly at the props he showed our once fledgling campaign. Blake will never be the most liked guy in the room, but I actually think over time my little staff will warm to the idea of having him around. All except maybe Chelsea.

"Nothing is stronger than the heart of a volunteer," I tell him. "And trust me, there are plenty of others throughout this country who are looking to be the next Chelsea, Vince, and Vanessa for an icandidate. It will all be for nothing if we don't survive this hearing in two weeks, though. With that said, Blake, could you please excuse us. I need to talk to my staff about prepping for my impending firing squad."

-TWENTY-SEVEN-
CHELSEA

Anybody who got lost and stumbled into Room 2129 of the Rayburn Building would instantly know something momentous and important was happening. In this case, it is the Ethics Committee hearing on the charges leveled against Congressman Michael Bennit.

When the chairman gaveled the meeting to order at ten o'clock this morning, it was already standing room only. In a rare spectacle, every committee member was present and seated in this cavernous room at four long, stepped rows, measuring fifty feet from one side to another. The mahogany work surfaces are curved slightly, creating an arc around the focal point of a single table where the person being questioned is seated.

None of these members' staff is in view, but they are never far away. In Congress, we tend to disappear from public view when cameras are around, and in this particular hearing, there are dozens of them to record every moment of testimony from each witness.

Mister Bennit is not present for the parade of individuals being called to testify. I am left with Vince and Vanessa to watch and report how things are unfolding. As it stands right now, the congressman will be the last to testify and the only person to speak in his defense. As one might predict from a hard-nosed Green Beret, he opted not to hire an attorney.

We listen to the lobbyist tell his tale, admitting no fault in the process. He was simply making a requested contribution to a campaign fund. He would never believe it would be inappropriately handled. Yeah right.

Chairmen of House committees wield considerable power. Hearings are usually a forum for testing ideas against reality, or providing experts and interests affected by proposed legislation a chance to provide their input. Most of those proceedings are orchestrated, or even scripted, by the staff of senior members. This isn't turning out to be any different.

After a break for lunch, a photographic expert is called in to verify the authenticity of the pictures and dispel any notion that the images were altered. I am sure the pictures are authentic, and pay scant attention until the last person before the congressman is summoned to testify.

I let out an audible gasp when the final witness called is Congressman Reyes. I already know he is about to perjure himself when he raises his right hand and repeats the oath being read to him. He takes his seat at the table and the final act of this drama begins to play out.

For the next fifteen minutes, he proceeds to claim Michael Bennit took him into his confidence about a scheme he devised to earmark money for personal use since he knew he would not be reelected. He went on to claim, laughably, that the congressional salary was not enough to cover his expenses and that he needed some cash.

The questions being asked are softballs, and not a single representative on the committee is asking for details or proof to substantiate the allegations. The entire proceeding is scripted, and each of Reyes's answers well prepared in advance.

"Congressman, your testimony here has been invaluable in substantiating all the evidence presented before it. I commend you on your honesty, and the courage you show by appearing in front of this committee today," the chairman says. "I know this must have been difficult considering you and Mister Bennit were close friends."

"Yes, we were, and this has been very difficult for me to do. However, I believe that if we are to rid the country of the corruption that plagues our government, we have to go to great lengths to publically expose it. The men and women Americans entrust with the reins of leadership should be of impeccable character and of the highest moral order. To root out the ones who aren't, we have to put them on display for the entire country to see. I believe this is the best way to accomplish that."

I feel like my insides have been ripped out. I have been afraid to message the congressman with this because betrayal of this magnitude is going to destroy him. Mister B is fiercely loyal to those around him, and Congressman Reyes is his closest friend and ally in Washington. I just never saw this coming.

Congressman Reyes gets another round of congratulations from the committee members, and his testimony completed, leaves the table and walks up the aisle. I glare at him as he walks past me, refusing to make eye contact. I can't let this go. I have been boiling with emotion all morning, and now I've reached my breaking point.

"I'll be right back. Stay here," I tell Vince as I slide out of my seat and follow the congressman from Texas down the aisle. I hear Vince and Vanessa come up from behind me, and I give them a nasty look over my shoulder.

"What? You think we'd miss this?"

"What the hell was that, Congressman?" I shout as I catch up to my quarry in the hallway outside of the meeting room.

"Excuse me?" he says, startled.

"You heard me! You came to us crying about how all politicians are liars. Congratulations, it only took you a couple of months to become one of them."

Congressman Reyes looks around at the small crowd beginning to gather. Drawn to the commotion, staffers and media begin to circle. You can count on someone recording this.

"I did what I felt I had to do," he explains, measuring his words carefully.

"Leave him alone, Chelsea," Congressman Bennit says as he weaves through the crowd to get to us. "Please accept my apologies, Congressman. My chief of staff is a little emotional and got caught up in the moment." Reyes nods, and then walks off, causing the gaggle to begin to disperse.

"What are you doing?" I ask my mentor. "Do you know what he said about you in there?"

"I can only imagine, but confronting him publically isn't going to fix anything. Let's focus on what I need to do in there."

I am at a loss. Where is the Mister Bennit that would have channeled his Special Forces training and ripped the soul out of this traitor's body? Why is he being so passive in the face of treachery?

"You can't let this go!"

"Chelsea! They got to him," the congressman snaps. I've never seen him react like this. "There's nothing we can do about it now. Life sucks, and sometimes when you place your trust in someone, they turn on you. We have to get past it. The damage is done. All we can do is move on like we planned and hope for the best."

"They are calling for you, Congressman," Vanessa says from behind me.

"Congressman, the plan won't work anymore," I argue, grabbing his arm as he attempts to pass me. "If you are ever going to listen to me, it has to be now. The footage won't be enough. Not anymore. You need to take the filter off and stomp them. Do something every person in this country will crash YouTube's servers trying to watch."

"Like what?"

"Like the most epic, impassioned, blood-thirsty rant you can muster to splash on every Facebook page in the country. You need to be the Army NCO who pisses napalm and has a degree in Murphy's Law. Show this country what being a leader means, and be as obnoxious as possible in doing it. You need a performance so good even ESPN will show highlights of it."

"That's your advice, Chels?"

"You hired me to advise you, and that's my advice, take it or leave it. If we're going down, then our foxhole better be full of spent brass and grenade pins when we do."

"Nice speech," the congressman says with a beaming smile. "You have been hanging around me way too long. Your dad would be proud."

Vince and Vanessa are smirking at my little tirade. They may think it's funny, but I'm dead serious. I can't go on like this, and if our days here are numbered, I want to make it worthwhile.

"Are you going to listen to me or not?" I ask with way too much attitude.

"Don't get your red hair tied in a knot. You had me at 'blood-thirsty rant.'" I smile for the first time since our meeting at Briar Point. "If spent brass and grenade pins are what you want, you're gonna want to watch this."

-TWENTY-EIGHT-
SENATOR VIANO

"Pictures don't lie, Mister Bennit! They have been authenticated as real and one hundred percent unaltered. Yet you sit there making denial after denial. How do you respond to that?"

Michael has been in the hot seat for over an hour now, and the hearing has grown increasingly contentious as each member gets a chance to exact their pound of flesh. Lawyers are not allowed to badger witnesses unless they get elected to Congress. Here, almost anything goes.

"Do you believe everything you see in pictures?" Michael asks. He has his back to me, but I can still hear the hint of a smile in his voice. I may no longer be a U.S. Senator, but the skills that once got me here are as sharp as ever. I know when someone is being baited.

"No, but these pictures tell a compelling story."

"What about video? Do you believe everything you see on television?"

"We don't have any video."

"Yes, sir, but if you did?"

"I don't like commenting on a hypothetical, but yes, although I understand it can be altered, I generally believe what I see on video." Where is he going with this?

"Excellent," Michael says as a young man gets up from his seat along the aisle and moves to a television monitor situated along the wall. He powers on the unit and nods to Congressman Bennit. "Then let me offer some evidence of my own. I took the liberty of fast-forwarding to the good part, but we have the whole thing for anyone who is interested."

The committee almost unanimously leans forward with their heads cocked to the side to stare at the images playing before them. When the part of the lobbyist pulling the envelope out comes up on the screen, it freezes. Visible behind them is a man taking still shots with a camera under a napkin.

"A little background before we continue. Previous testimony submitted to this committee alleges that it was a concerned citizen taking pictures with a cell phone of what he thought was something shady. Ironically, that information was vetted and certified as fact during the investigation." Michael looks back at the video theatrically, and then back at the committee in mock confusion. "I admit, I don't work at the Apple Store's Genius Bar, but does that look like an iPhone to anyone in this room? No, I'm pretty sure it's a Nikon dSLR."

The video continues, showing the events at the restaurant as they really transpired. The room gasps when he throws the envelope back at the lobbyist. After Mashburn tucks it into his pocket, the video focuses on the individual working the camera before freezing again.

"The concerned citizen in question, widely reported to be from Danbury, is one Logan Tyler, a twenty-three-year-old resident of Chevy Chase, Maryland, and employee of the lobby firm Ibram & Reed." I pause to let the muffled grumbles in the room subside before continuing. "Trust me when I say it was pretty tough to track that bit of information down. Hit play again, Brian. Oh, by the way, this is Brian Carlite, a former student of mine and the man who recorded this ... interaction."

He gives an awkward wave to the room. Damn, that's who that is. He wasn't sitting next to the rest of Michael's staff, so I never could make the connection.

Bennit must have figured out he was being framed for something and smartly arranged to record the whole sordid thing in high-definition. He was even patient enough to let this play out to ensure the media were here to witness the treachery. As the video rolls, it is now apparent to everyone in the room with an ounce of common sense that Michael was set up.

"In case anyone is curious," Michael says as a voice over, "the reservation for the cameraman was made immediately following mine. The hostess was slipped a hundred-dollar bill when he arrived at the restaurant to seat him at this particular table. I have her name, her sworn statement, and even the serial number of the C-note she was given. Amazing how the thorough investigation you guys conducted wasn't able to uncover that."

James is not going to be happy when he hears about all this. He may be a brilliant schemer, but he just got sniffed out and played by a guy he probably didn't think was capable of doing his laundry. It is dawning on me that I may have underestimated him myself.

The video clicks off and the chairman confers with one of his staffers. Most likely, he is receiving instructions from the Speaker or the minority leader.

"Thank you for that spirited defense, Mister Bennit. However, despite the compelling nature of the video footage, I feel that it's best to let the whole House decide your fate. I think the motion to recommend your expulsion should be approved by this committee and sent to the Floor."

So much for common sense. Welcome to the U.S. House of Representatives. I'm not upset about it, but things are not going as predicted. That in itself poses a major problem for me. A slam dunk reason for expulsion is morphing into the biggest sham in American political history right before my eyes.

-TWENTY-NINE-
MICHAEL

"Why am I not surprised you would reach that conclusion, Mister Chairman?" I ask without bothering to hide the disdain in my voice. My staff was equally divided over whether the video would be enough to dismiss the charges. Chelsea somehow knew they would stay the course, and she was right.

"What are you implying?"

"Only that in the face of overwhelming evidence to the contrary, you have reached the conclusion I'm guilty and recommend an undeserved punishment to curry favor with the leadership."

"I resent that assertion!" the chairman barks into his microphone. Yeah, truth always hurts, doesn't it?

"Thomas Jefferson once said, 'Experience hath shewn, that even under the best forms of government those entrusted with power have, in time, and by slow operations, perverted it into tyranny.'"

"Mister Bennit, I will not stand idly by while you demean this panel!"

"Then stop giving myself, and every other American, just cause to do precisely that! I cannot make more of a mockery of these proceedings than you already have, Mister Chairman. Is this really what …"

I see him make a slashing signal across his neck and I stop talking when I notice my microphone is no longer on.

"Mister Bennit, we have warned you that you are here to testify about your actions, not pander to the cameras in the room by impugning the members of this committee. If you are not capable of restraining your speech, we reserve the right not to let you talk at all."

Okay, I have played this game long enough. DaVinci was dead-on when he noted, "Nothing strengthens authority so much as silence." I have been silent for over a year, and I think my time for quiet assent needs to end. If social media fodder is what Chelsea wants, by God that's what she's going to get. I'm sure C-SPAN will like this, too.

"Well, since I don't need this microphone anymore …"

I rise out of my chair and grab the bottom edge of the long, rectangular wooden table I'm seated at. It's heavier than I thought, and I'm thankful that one benefit of having no influence is the extra time I can spend at the House gym. With all the strength I can summon, I flip the table violently up into the air. Papers I had on it go flying, as does the microphone they switched off on me. The large table crashes to the ground in a deafening roar, causing everyone on the committee to recoil right out of their chairs.

The looks on their faces are priceless in light of my aggressive reaction. Fear, anger, surprise, and contempt sum up the majority of what I see. The method may be unorthodox, and maybe even extreme, but it has the desired effect. For once, people who love to hear themselves speak are mired in a blissful silence.

"Do I have all your attention now, ladies and gentlemen? Good, because today's lesson will only be given once," I announce, now channeling my time in the classroom. The area between where my table was once set up and the semi-circle where my jury now sits reminds me of my classroom.

"You're out of order, Mister Bennit, and I will have you removed from this hearing!" the chairman yells into his microphone, now standing and leaning forward after finally recomposing himself.

"Stow your threats, Mister Chairman. My first day of basic training was the first time I had short hair, the first time I wore shiny boots, and the *last* time I feared *anything*. So sit your ass down in that chair and listen for a change, because what I'm about to say is important."

"I ... uh ... this is—"

"Mister Chairman, Low-T isn't an excuse for either lack of hearing or the inability to follow simple instructions. Now maintain bottom to top lip contact before I beat you with that microphone and then jam it down your throat until you stop twitching."

There is a collective gasp at the ferocity of my comment. I expect the chairman to protest further, but he doesn't. I'm not sure if it's out of fear or a genuine curiosity about what I'm going to say. Either way, I have the floor and need to give the most important speech of my life.

"Why are we here today? If this committee was going to discipline me regardless of the evidence presented, why are we wasting taxpayer money on this circus?" I ask to the members of the committee before me. "Outside those doors are over three hundred million Americans counting on us. *We* are the people the citizens of this country call on to be their voice and solve their problems. Yet, most of the laws this body passes aren't worthy for Americans to write out on a Post-It note and take a dump on.

"Our citizens are the people we work for. *They* are the ones living life up close, personal, and in the trenches. They're taking on all the challenges of pursuing the American dream in close quarters combat. And what support do they get from their government? From this body? None."

I hazard a look at the press in the back of the room. Although this speech is going to be seen, heard, and discussed on every imaginable media outlet and social media site, I am careful not to appear to be playing to the cameras. The correspondents, who moments ago looked like they were collectively ready for their naps, are now paying rapt attention as if this were the story of the century.

"And no, I don't mean reaching into the pockets of others to support giving them a check and a pat on the head. I mean real support and an optimism that tomorrow is going to be better for them than today is. To make their lives easier and their families more secure through sound policy and competent administration.

"Life is hard, and when they get knocked down, it should be us inspiring them to get back up each … and … every … time. We need to set the example of perseverance, endurance, tenacity, and a singular drive to 'get it done' in the face of any challenge or obstacle."

I move the length of the tiered wooden bench where the committee is seated. Only a few bother to make eye contact with me. Only now, even after more than a year here, do I realize just how much control is exerted on them. These people serve many masters, and their constituents aren't one of them.

"This Congress doesn't do that. We are the laughing stock across the world because we stand on the steps and sing patriotic songs when enemies attack our country. We allow our spy agencies to target our friends and own citizens. We let political enemies be harassed by agencies because of petty vendettas. Our foreign policy is not the stuff of a world superpower, but of a schoolyard bully.

"Sure, you get the partisan outrage from Capitol Hill, but no solutions. The Affordable Care Act, stimulus plans, immigration reform, Bush tax cuts—we wax poetic about these issues in front of the cameras and then are content to use them against each other. No law is perfect, but instead of even attempting to make them work for the public, we use them as political grist for the media while we sit on our asses, secure in the notion that Americans are too consumed with their own struggles to care.

"That's not legislating, it's cowardice. It's a failure to lead, and this branch of government needs to lead. It needs to step out of the shadow of the divisive presidents we've had over the past three decades and show Americans what can be done when we debate, discuss, and compromise on issues. We need to restore American faith that we are here to make their lives easier and more prosperous, and for no other reason. Instead, we have this," I say, theatrically gesturing around the meeting room that is dead silent.

I have said what I needed to say. I could go on, but a good soldier knows when it's time for a tactical retreat. I take a few steps toward the center aisle to signal my rant is nearly complete. I stop and look back to the pensive faces of the committee members who only moments ago wanted me drawn and quartered.

"A warrior is someone who stands between the enemy and those he holds sacred. There are others out there like me who are willing to do the same. I will proudly stand with them between you and the millions of Americans who think this Congress, and this government, has lost its way. If you are so blinded by your party allegiance that you think I should be expelled from this body, so be it. Send this resolution to the Floor for all of America to see."

With that final volley, I walk up the center aisle towards the set of doors in back of the room. I feel every set of eyes and camera lens in the room following me. If my mission was to make an impression, it's safe to call it a resounding success. If it was to get kicked out of Congress, well, I probably made that happen too.

Even if the original charges are dismissed, a resolution to expel me for my antics here will go to House floor. I am sure every single person in the room feels the same way as they watch me leave without saying a single word.

-THIRTY-

CHELSEA

"Congressman Bennit, you're now being called the 'iCongressman' because of all the social media attention you're getting following the ethics hearing. Can you comment?"

"There's nothing really to comment on. I should have stayed more engaged with social media from the day I got here. That was my mistake. Had I done that, I would have been called the iCongressman all along." If he had listened to me from the beginning, he would have been.

"So you are okay with it?"

"I wish Americans were using social media to comment on things of substance instead of this carnival I'm in, but I'm glad they're getting involved in the political process again."

You would think I would be used to getting ambushed by the media. In a scene eerily similar to what happened on my front lawn during our campaign oh so long ago, we were accosted trying to get into the Cannon Building. Ten minutes later, the congressman is still answering questions.

"Congressman, what about reports surfacing that you orchestrated the story about the involvement of the House leadership and lobby firm Ibram & Reed to hide your illegal actions?"

"You guys are all capable journalists, so stop allowing yourselves to be spoon-fed and do some digging of your own. If I told you I found a Thai hooker with a snorkel on, lying flex-cuffed in a bathtub full of cherry Jell-O at Johnston Albright's house, would you take my word for it, or would you verify it first?"

"That's not a believable claim."

"Neither is yours," the congressman says with an amused laugh. "I have to get going, folks. Thanks for the chat," the congressman says just before we weave our way to the entrance.

We led every newscast and found ourselves on the front page of every newspaper the day after his spectacle in the hearing. Headlines reading "Flipping Out," "Congressman Flips Off Committee," and "Flip You!" screamed from the pages of the *New York Times, Los Angeles Times, Chicago Tribune,* and every paper in between.

As evidenced by the horde we just encountered, the story hasn't lost any interest in the four days since. The talking heads have been going nuts over the Bennit hearing on the cable news channels every night. Panels of experts have nearly started riots on their sets over their defense of one side or another. Mister B may have reignited 'Bennitmania' with the American people, but he's got the establishment tearing themselves to pieces on television.

"A hooker and Jell-O?" Vince asks the congressman when we move into the grand foyer and are far enough away from the press to not be concerned about anyone overhearing. Vince is known for some classic one-liners of his own, and is beaming like a proud father that his boss is still equally capable. It's been a while since we have heard one.

"Too much?" he asks in reply.

"No, it's good. I can't wait to see that on YouTube," Vanessa chimes in, already no doubt thinking about the headline for it.

We make our way down the hall in silence, saving any further discussion for the quiet privacy of our sanctuary. Walking in, I conclude it's not so private after all. The flurry of activity of the staff is something I've never seen before.

"Okay, will one of you please tell me why am I suddenly being bombarded with tweets about hookers and Jell-O?" Kylie demands playfully as we cross into the congressman's outer office.

"Priceless! It won't be long before that's trending," Brian observes, content with the prospect of making sure that happens.

The congressman gives Kylie a kiss and a hug then waves us all into his office, Vince closing the door behind us. The gang all headed south down I-95 from Millfield yesterday. Pissed that they missed the fireworks at the committee meeting, they aren't about to skip the show at the final vote on the House Floor.

"Since we're only campaign staff, are we allowed to talk about this here?" Amanda asks, sensing that there probably is some line between official and campaign duties.

"They are about to throw me out on my ass. Ask me if I give a damn," the congressman says pleasantly, but with a tone that lets us know what he thinks about the rules right now.

"Let's start with you, Emilee," I say as we all take our seats on the couches and chairs in the office.

"The aptly named 'Congressman Flips Out in D.C.' is setting records at YouTube. So far, over forty-five million views in the first twenty-four hours and over three hundred million in the last four days." The congressman whistles, and even Kylie looks impressed. I'm not surprised. Politicians doing something unexpected rates right up there with stupid pranks and cat videos in terms of what people will invest a couple of minutes to watch.

"The best part is they are following the link to our site we posted at the end of the video," Brian adds. "I checked Google Analytics this morning."

"Google what?" Peyton asks.

"Analytics. The short explanation is it allows us to track where web traffic comes from. It's very exciting."

"You make me so hot when you talk geek," Peyton responds playfully. "Please don't stop," she pants as she unbuttons the top button of her shirt. Brian turns bright red before trying to continue.

"Uh, yeah, uh … anyway, uh …"

"Peyton, knock it off or we'll never get through this. Another thirty seconds and Vince will start baying over there," the congressman scolds with a laugh. It's been almost two years since we were all in a classroom together, and yet nothing feels like it has changed.

"Anyway, the hyperlinks from YouTube account for almost eighty-five percent of the traffic that visits the *Meet the iCandidates* website I set up. Many of the drop offs from the main site are to individual icandidate sites in districts. Our allies are getting a lot of traction."

"All the icandidates announced their campaigns on Monday night after the hearing," Amanda reports. "They have gotten a huge bump in the polls because of all the publicity surrounding us."

Amanda has taken on the role of liaison between our campaign and the others. Congressman Bennit made it very clear to us that he didn't trust that being left to Blake and Senator Viano. Much to my dismay, he is warming up to the former. I'll question his sanity when he trusts the latter.

"Publicity is an understatement," Vince states. "The media has gone ballistic over this. Watch this."

Vince turns on the television and tunes into CNN. Sure enough, they are talking about us on their morning show. He then flips to a few others. *Fox & Friends, Morning Joe,* and *CBS This Morning* are all the same. *GMA* and *Today* had moved on to other stories, but no doubt we got some attention on those programs as well. Congressman Bennit is the hot topic of the week, and all of the networks are cashing in on us again.

"Like, where are they getting their information from?" Peyton asks. Vince shakes his head and we all look at Kylie.

"I may have leaked an item or two and pointed others in the right direction," she says coyly.

"Nice!" Xavier, Emilee, and Vanessa say in unison.

"I'm sure your current employer will just love that," I add. It's no secret that the relationship Kylie has with the *Washington Post* is a tense one. Even working as an investigative journalist, they have shielded her from covering almost anything to do with Mister Bennit to maintain the appearance of integrity and unbiased reporting. Probably a smart move on their part, but she isn't on board with the decision.

"Not one bit, but screw them. I have been on the sidelines long enough."

"Okay, I hate to be the guy who brings up unpleasant subjects again, but what are the odds we survive the vote tomorrow?"

"Afraid you're wasting your summer again, X?" the congressman chides.

Xavier asked the same thing back when we first started the campaign for Mister Bennit two years ago. He was a great basketball player in high school and knew that he would eventually land the scholarship he earned to play at Syracuse. He didn't want to waste his time back then, but somehow this is different.

"No, it's not like that Mister ... Congressman B."

"Mister is fine, Michael works too."

"Yeah, that's still not gonna happen," Vince opines from his spot along the wall.

"Honestly, it's good working with you guys again. I don't want it to end tomorrow," Xavier confesses.

"It's not going to," Vanessa reassures, "but where do we stand?"

"They are going to win by forty votes according to the majority whip's staff," Peyton says with a flip of her hair.

"How do you know that?" Kylie asks.

"I spent some time last night at Ebbit's something-or-other. Some guys started hitting on me and said they worked for the Democratic whip. I played the dumb college girl visiting a friend at GW, and by the third drink, they were telling me anything I wanted to hear."

"You got served in one of Washington's most notorious restaurants within stone's throw from the White House?" Congressman Bennit asks incredulously.

"Yeah, why? Is it hard?" I just shake my head as the others let out a chuckle. I love Peyton, and while she may come across as a dumb blonde, that girl is one of the slyest people I know.

"There's no way we can make up that many votes in a day," I say, dejected. I wish I could be more optimistic, but I've been in this town a year and I get crushed every time I do.

"I don't get it. Why would they vote 'yes' if they know about the video? Why would they support a lie?"

"Some of them don't condone flipping tables at committee hearings. Other members are all hanging their hats on Congressman Reye's testimony," Vanessa practically spits while saying. She loathes disloyalty.

"The extremes in the media are doing the same. That clip of his testimony is being shown again and again to provide cover for their favorite candidates so they can vote 'yes' to please the leadership."

"I still don't get it."

"They can't hide, Peyton, so they need political cover. Usually Americans are too apathetic to care what goes on here. Thanks to all the Facebook and Twitter comments, constituents are paying attention now."

"Yeah, the traitorous bastard's lies are going to sink us."

"Just when you guys thought you had a friend down here, right, Vanessa?" Amanda asks. She shakes her head in disgust.

"He'll get his, but you'd better tell him to stay away from me until then," Vince adds with the dramatic pounding of his fist into his open hand.

Kylie and Michael share a smile, one that I used to see in school between two people sharing a secret. What could they possibly be hiding? I begin to wonder what I'm missing. I'm certain it's not something he has shared with me, so now I need to know why he is leaving me in the dark again.

-THIRTY-ONE-
SENATOR VIANO

"Let's end with predictions. Is Michael Bennit going to survive tomorrow's vote to expel him? Ryan?" the host asks the one of the guests being shown on split-screen via satellite as she winds up her interview.

"I don't think so, no."

"Gabe?" the attractive brunette queries her other guest.

"Bennit did nothing wrong. Vulnerable incumbents won't vote to expel him."

"So he'll be spared?"

"Yes, he will."

"Thank you both for being with us this morning."

"They still are talking about this?" Gary booms from the adjacent white sofa when he sits down.

When I was in the Senate, the only time staff was ever allowed in my house was during the extravagant parties I would throw with my husband. He is out of town so often, it was the only time he ever interacted with anyone in my political circles.

Gary is more than just staff, and he doesn't technically work for me anyway. I have been running a low profile since I partnered with Bennit on this icandidate experiment, so having him meet me here was the logical thing to do.

"Every channel," I respond, muting the huge flat-screen television mounted to the wall. "What have you learned?"

"James is panicking. He's got Ibram & Reed calling in every marker they have trying to keep this thing afloat."

"He doesn't like to lose."

"Yeah, that's apparent. He must have the leadership of both parties tied in knots. They had a meeting and agreed to do whatever it takes to keep their caucuses in line. As of this morning, they have the votes to get rid of him, but it's going to be much closer than everyone thought."

"Giving away the keys to the castle, are they?"

"Something like that. Even my boss is getting in on the action."

The Bennit expulsion has become a political risk for the members, so they will demand concessions for their votes. The House is filled with opportunists, so they will leverage this to get pork barrel spending for their districts, choice committee assignments, and anything else they can think of.

"This is coming together much faster than I ever dreamt. Each of the one hundred icandidates is climbing in the polls, so the establishment has to be getting very scared."

"It's going to be standing room only tomorrow, so I'll save you a seat."

"Thanks, Gary. If all goes as planned, I should be able to rescue you from your life serving the weak and helpless congressman you got saddled with."

Gary nods in assent. He's my loyal soldier, trusted confidant, and soon we will once again be the toast of this town. I just feel bad that it will be not soon enough to spare him the agony of working for a buffoon.

"Anything you need me to do, Senator?" Gary asks.

"No, we let tomorrow play out before we make any moves. I need you to keep your ear to the ground though. Michael is less than forthcoming with me about his plans, and I prefer not to get blindsided again."

Gary regards me for a moment and I know what's coming next. He hasn't quoted *The Amazing Spiderman* in a while.

"We all have secrets: the ones we keep ... and the ones that are kept from us."

-THIRTY-TWO-

MICHAEL

I am not sure if it is because today is the eve of a month-long recess or if it's the uncomfortable subject of my dismissal, but everyone is eager to get on with the show. Floor speeches kicked off at nine a.m. and have dragged on for the last four hours. I tuned C-SPAN on the TV in the office and watched as the battle lines were drawn. What has transpired is not your typical Republican–Democrat partisan fight. Representatives from both sides called for my ouster while others came to my defense. It was surreal to see a split having nothing to do with ideology.

With only a half hour until the scheduled vote, Kylie accompanies me down to the Capitol. My staff is already hanging out in the gallery, since getting seats will be harder than scoring something on the fifty-yard line at the Super Bowl. As we reach the doors of the House chamber, I share a moment with my beautiful girlfriend.

"Would you have ever predicted a year and a half ago that it would come down to this?"

"Honestly, no," she answers, "but I wouldn't trade the journey for anything."

"Speak for yourself. If I could do it again, I would have taken the blue pill."

"The matrix isn't real, Neo," she says with a laugh. "You know you wouldn't change a thing. Whatever happens in there, Michael Bennit, I will always love you."

"I love you too. You know, this reminds me of the time during the Constitutional Conven—"

"No time for a history lesson right now, dear," she says playfully.

"I know. Catch you on the flip side," I say with a wink and enter the chamber for what will probably be the last time.

* * *

"The Chair recognizes the gentleman from Texas for five minutes," I hear Speaker Albright say as I enter the chamber.

Cisco stands at the small podium in the Well and greets the other members in the chamber. It's a full house this close to the vote, so I grab a seat toward the back and wait for the party to start.

"A lot has been made of my testimony on Monday," Cisco says in preamble, "and I have come to understand that there are members of this House that are basing their votes solely on my remarks to the Ethics Committee. Bearing that in mind, I wanted to clear a few things up about my relationship with Congressman Bennit."

Most of the representatives in the room are paying scant attention. Even the Speaker, who is serving as Chair for this session, looks bored. Well, they are about to get the shock of a lifetime as Cisco spends a minute or two outlining how we met and became friends.

"So when I testified at the hearing, it was the hardest thing I had to do. Not because it was about my friend, but because I had to *lie* during the whole thing."

The Speaker's head shoots up, questioning whether he just heard what Congressman Reyes just uttered. I would pay money to see the looks on my staff's faces up in the gallery right now. Chelsea verbally berated him outside of the committee room following his testimony and wondered why I stopped her. Now she knows, although will be pissed I kept it from her.

"You see, I was approached by the majority whip with a proposition, one I can only assume was on the behalf of all the leadership in this body. I was offered millions of dollars in earmarks for my district and even several plum committee assignments in return for false testimony against Michael Bennit."

There is a collective gasp in the room and Speaker Albright has to bang his gavel several times to bring the room into order. Guess they didn't see that coming.

"I waited until today to come forward with this, mostly because I wanted to see if the promises were upheld. They were. If you check House Resolution 871, you will see an earmark for eleven million dollars for my district. Also, yesterday I was named to a coveted seat on the House Banking Committee. Now, I would love to say I earned those, but ask yourselves a question. How do I, an independent, get granted such rewards when the other independent here is systematically ignored?

"I suspect most of you won't take my word for this. It may be because I'm new, or an independent without party affiliation. Maybe you just hate Hispanics and think I should be cleaning your pool instead of making laws." Of course he had to get that line in.

"But for those of you who are curious, I can let you listen to the whole thing because I recorded it." He holds his smartphone in the air as a prop for all to see. I would surmise the representatives in the room are divided as to whether he should hit play. I know the media want to hear it, knowing they are always yearning for a good show.

"The men and women Americans entrust with the reins of leadership should be of impeccable character and of the highest moral order," Cisco continues after replacing the phone in his inside suit jacket pocket. "To root out the ones who aren't, we have to put them on display for the entire country to see. I believe this is the best way to accomplish that. I yield the balance of my time to the Chair."

Quoting the line he used at the end of his committee testimony is a nice touch. The House erupts in chaos as Cisco departs the podium. I get up, since I am the next to speak as the gavel crashes down repeatedly in a vain attempt to quiet the chamber.

"Glad that's over. I've missed hanging out with you, man," Cisco says with a pat on the arm.

"Me too. I'm sorry you had to perjure yourself in the process."

"I dare them to go after me," Cisco says, probably hoping they do. He is itching to give that testimony.

"We'll catch up when this is all over and I'm done explaining this to my staff."

"Yeah, good luck with that!"

"The Chair recognizes the gentleman from Connecticut for five minutes."

With the bomb Cisco just dropped, the Democrats have to be smelling blood in the water. Partisan politics runs deep these days, and although they may have conspired to oust me from Congress, there is no way they will pass up the opportunity to unseat the majority whip come Election Day. Since the whips in both parties are the enforcers who ensure discipline among their members, they make juicy targets.

"Thank you, Mister Speaker." The House quiets as I assume my place at the podium. I am thinking about exploiting the rift Cisco just caused, and every person in this room is looking forward to a good five-minute show as I lay out my final defense. Sorry to disappoint them, but it's time for them to make their decision with no time to think about it and live with the consequences.

"I yield my time back to the Chair," I state to the shock of the entire room.

"Are you sure, Mister Bennit? I took the liberty of bolting all the desks and chairs down," the Speaker says to a smattering of laughter.

"Mister Speaker, if I wanted to hit you with a chair, a couple of bolts aren't going to stop me," I say with a smile as I leave the podium and wander up the center aisle.

The Speaker gets the vote under way, and I go cast mine. The House votes utilizing an electronic system that requires a plastic card with a photo ID be inserted into a terminal. The red button on the systems is to vote "nay," a green button for "aye," and a yellow button for "present" which is basically an abstention. I insert my card, punch the red button and remove my card, placing it in the breast pocket of my suit jacket.

For anyone who has ever been bored enough to watch C-SPAN, votes in the House are usually allotted fifteen minutes. In reality, the outcome is usually determined in a third of the time. There is no assigned seating on the House Floor, so I choose a spot along the center aisle with a good view of the voting board in the upper gallery behind the rostrum to watch my imminent demise.

Members' names are displayed on a blue, backlit panel above the Speaker's dais, and when a member votes, a red, green, or yellow light appears adjacent to his or her name. Showing both the votes of individual members and a running total of "yeas" and "nays," I watch as the total of "aye" votes climbs toward the magic mark of two hundred eighteen.

Even with indisputable evidence and the admission of Cisco about lying to prove his own point, it's a tie six minutes into the vote. I managed to sway enough members over to my side to make this interesting, but it doesn't look like it will be enough. Maybe I underestimated just how badly they want me out of here.

Thomas Parker takes the adjacent chair and watches the same unchanging screen I am. There is only one vote in the entire chamber that still needs to be cast, and it belongs to the man now sitting next to me. No doubt what he wants.

"Losing by one vote is a painful way to end your political career, Congressman. Of course, it doesn't need to be that way. You did a favor for me once, and now I want to offer to return it."

"I told you, sir, there was no quid pro quo with me helping your niece. That is just as true now as it was then."

"Yes, so you said. But real truth is that *was* then, and this *is* now. There are certain political realities you have to face, especially while sitting here and watching the clock on your political career tick down." And ticking down it is, now under eight minutes to go. "I am willing to vote 'present' to leave the vote as a tie if you ask me to."

"Congressman, a tie is a loss because the Speaker will simply break it with his vote."

"You know, I could be persuaded to bring along a friend or two to ensure that doesn't happen, but favors like that don't come cheap."

"I'm sure they don't."

"Look, Michael, let me reason with you. I may be an ultra-right wing conservative, but I'm a Christian. The people of my district may think you're a liberal Yankee, but they also think you're a good man. I can sell this to my constituents back home." I wouldn't consider myself liberal, but I can see how the people in his district might view me that way.

The offer is a tempting one. While my staff and I already decided that we can lead the icandidates from the sidelines should I lose this vote, it's preferable for me to lead them from the front. Of course, I need to be here to do that. The prospect of my political survival is looking less likely by the second.

"So what do you say?" Parker asks, looking to strike the deal.

"Have you read Christopher Marlowe's *Doctor Faustus*, Congressman?"

"I have. You think you're selling your soul to the devil? I'm uncomfortable with the thought of how making a deal with an old preacher like myself compares to dealing with Mephistopheles." I close my eyes and grin.

"No, sir, I'm not comparing you to the devil or his messenger. But you need to realize that I'm definitely not Faustus either. My ex-fiancée was an English teacher, and she brought me to that play. I learned a valuable lesson from it."

"Which was?"

"Some deals, no matter how great they sound in the present, aren't worth the final price."

Congressman Parker shifts in his seat, somewhat stunned that I rebuffed his offer. It is very un-Washington like, especially given the stakes. It amazes me how being honest in this town really throws people off their game.

"I see," is all he manages to utter.

"Excellent. Now go vote your conscience, Congressman. It's what the good people of Alabama elected you to do."

I don't bother watching him move off, instead settling my eyes back on the vote board. It only takes forty-five seconds for the small globe light next to his name to switch to green. From his dais, the Speaker is grinning from ear to ear in a way you only see in graduation pictures and weddings.

The vote count reads two eighteen to two seventeen and I know it's over. I can't help but think about what my former students are thinking. Vanessa will be livid, decrying an unfair system. Xavier will be upset. Amanda and Emilee will be dejected. Vince will want to off someone and Brian will think about finding a way to steal their identities. Chelsea has always been the emotional one, and tears will be pouring down her face.

I will not hang my head. I refuse to let them see me defeated. When the results of this vote are read, I will stand in the Well of the House to hear my expulsion, turn, and exit with the same dignity I came here with. I'm not giving the people in this room the satisfaction of seeing me leave in shame.

It's hard not to feel demoralized though. I have never been one to deal with failure well, and this is no exception. In the spirit of sportsmanship, I understand the need to be gracious in defeat on the playing field. Losing always led me to work that much harder. But this is life, not sports. Just like when I was Green Beret, the thought of failing is wearing on my soul, despite the face I'm putting on it.

I wasn't able to do what the people elected me to. I can blame the system, or the people toiling under it, but in the end, it is my responsibility. The people of my district deserve better than what I was able to deliver. Maybe, in the end, this expulsion is the best thing for them. Perhaps they need someone who can navigate the political waters of Washington, something I was warned time and again I don't have the proper disposition to do.

With just under two minutes remaining, I can feel a set of eyes studying me. I have been watched for my reactions as this has played out from everyone in this room including the media, members, and visitors in the gallery. I can even feel the beautiful, yet weary eyes of Kylie set upon me. But this is different.

Searching for the origin of this feeling, I see Congressman Parker standing in the Well of the House Floor. When he notices me watching him, he does the most unexpected thing this legislative body has seen in decades.

-THIRTY-THREE-
SPEAKER ALBRIGHT

I watch Michael Bennit sit in a seat along the aisle and stare at the blue tally board projected above me. He's remained like that for the last several minutes, and I find the stoicism he's displaying admirable. Most of the lot in this chamber would be trying whatever last minute antics and tactics they could to save their hides. Instead, he watches impassively, expressionless, and with a confident placidity that almost makes me envious. I'd be a nervous wreck.

I turn my attention to Parker who is talking to the clerk when I witness one of the most politically horrific sights of my career. I watch in horror as one of my closest political allies signs the back of a red card and hands it to her. I am confounded. He changed his vote for Bennit. I check the display next to me to be sure it wasn't my mind playing tricks on me. It wasn't. The muted cacophony of voices in the filled room escalates into a roar, and I shoot off the dais like The Flash over to where Parker is standing.

Members can change their vote at the voting station during the first ten minutes of a fifteen-minute vote. After that time, any change must be done by handing a card to the Tally Clerk on the rostrum. With a minute and a half left, my own personal Judas did just that.

"What the hell do you think you're doing?" I demand, as I storm up beside him in the Well.

"Calm yourself, Johnston," Parker states as he slips his pen back inside his suit pocket.

"Calm myself? Calm myself? You just changed your vote! Why? What deal did you make with Bennit?" I yell, causing everyone in the immediate area to stop what they're doing and take notice.

"I didn't make a deal with him. I tried, but would you believe it? He turned me down."

"You expect me to believe that?" I question, glancing back at the clock to notice there is only a minute left.

"I don't really care what you believe."

"So you changed your vote because of what, your conscience?"

"It's not a concept I would expect you to understand, Mister Speaker, especially in light of the events that brought us to this moment." I need to try a different tactic.

"I am the Speaker of the House," I softly say to my longtime colleague to avoid the prying ears of those around us. "You know the favors I can do for you and your entire caucus. I am a much more powerful ally than enemy. You know that."

"'And I saw, and behold a white horse: and he that sat on him had a bow; and a crown was given unto him: and he went forth conquering, and to conquer.' Revelations, chapter six, verse two. You have gone too far this time, Johnston. While politics is a hard way for an old Christian preacher to make a living, I cannot tolerate what you are doing to an honest man. I might not agree with Bennit politically, but he deserves to be here."

Damn! Fifteen seconds left.

"Look, Thomas, you don't understand what kind of pressure I'm under. As my friend, I need you to help me make this happen. There are higher powers in play here."

"There is only one higher power I answer to," Parker says pointing with his index finger and looking up. "'But I will forewarn you whom ye shall fear: Fear him, which after he hath killed hath power to cast into hell; yea, I say unto you, Fear him.'"

I watch as the final seconds tick off. In that time, seven more votes switch out of the "yea" column. Arguing with Thomas Parker is a moot point now. Time expires, and now that the vote is over, the official Congressional Record will show the resolution to expel Michael Bennit was defeated by eight votes.

This news is not going to be received positively by my political allies. The people I have to deal with do not respond well to failure, nor accept excuses when it happens. I wasn't lying when I said powerful forces had their hand in this, and I'll be hearing from them soon.

-THIRTY-FOUR-
SENATOR VIANO

"How the hell did he pull that off?" I ask Gary, who took his nose out of his phone to watch the final result of the vote and resulting uproar on the House floor.

"No idea, but it's impressive," he muses in thinly veiled admiration. He told me earlier that his boss told him this vote was a lock, despite Michael's theatrics during the committee hearing.

"It's not impressive, it's ridiculous! And to trust Reyes to play that little game and not betray him in the process? Who does that?" I can't help but think they must be old Army buddies or something, because that level of trust is unprecedented in this town.

"Again, impressive."

"Or stupid."

"No, it only would have been stupid if it didn't work."

Gary brings up a fair point. Reyes and Bennit were smart enough to fool the smartest politicians in the country. The leadership of both parties was so smug about this vote that they never realized they were set up to fail by a couple of political novices until the final votes were cast.

Michael is on the Floor, shaking hands with the men and women who I presume took his side in this fiasco. I can't hear what is being said from up here in the House Gallery, but there are some spirited arguments all over the place between members down below.

"Damn."

"This throws a small wrench in your plan, I think," Gary astutely observes. It does.

I never thought for a second he would survive this vote when it came up. When I was first told of how they planned on getting rid of Bennit, I formulated my scheme around that. Of course, I could not have known about Michael's counter-surveillance move, nor known that he would use that cowboy from Texas to embarrass the leadership of both parties on the Floor. He is far shrewder than I give him credit for.

"I may still be able to control them even with Bennit in the picture."

"I doubt it, Senator. You may have picked them, but he is their leader. They emulate Bennit, and he's a messiah now. After this Houdini escape, they'll be waiting for him to walk on water next."

If I were religious at all, I might be offended by the inappropriate Christian references. Unfortunately, he's probably right. There is no reason for the icandidates to stop following Michael now.

"Perhaps it's time to begin reconsidering our allegiances." My former chief of staff and longtime trusted advisor eyes me suspiciously.

"You're playing with fire if you decide to cross ..." He cuts his warning short after realizing there are too many people around to discuss this in public. He leans and whispers, "I signed on to do this with you because your patron is a powerful voice in this town. I don't want to be on the wrong side of him. You told me the same thing."

"That was before I realized Bennit may be stronger. Gary, Michael survived this against all odds. How long do you think he will be down in the polls up north in Connecticut? With all the social media fuss and the news coverage of this mess, he'll probably win that race now in a walk. If even half the icandidates win their races, it's a game changer that provides us a lot of leverage."

"It's risky," is all Gary says, turning back to his phone which is now blowing up with notifications.

"But it's an acceptable risk."

"If you say so," he concedes, still sounding unconvinced.

I had a favorite professor during my undergraduate studies who was a survivalist. He would take nature trips to the deepest parts of the Alaskan woods for a month with nothing more than a tent, sleeping bag, and hunting rifle. He had one piece of advice for all his students I never forgot—no matter how good your first is, always have a Plan B.

When I ventured into politics, I often had multiple instances of Plan B lined up in case things went haywire. My benefactor, the man who helped me win my Senate seat, takes it several steps further. He goes deep into the alphabet, often referring to changes in direction as "Plan G." I was convinced my original plan would work because the very thought of

Michael Bennit surviving the joint effort to expel him was simply laughable. For that reason, I never spent a lot of time developing a contingency. One is forming now, though, and I need my former chief of staff on board to pull it off.

"Gary, if two independents can cause this many problems, can you imagine what will happen when a group of them comes to town to face off with the Washington establishment?"

"Yeah, like the Dark Knight says, 'We find out what happens when an unstoppable force meets an immovable object.'"

"Precisely. Let's make that happen."

-THIRTY-FIVE-
CHELSEA

"Dad, this is a pretty expensive place," I observe, admiring the atmosphere after our waiter delivers the appetizers.

"Nothing but the best for my little girl. When was the last time we had a father–daughter night out?" he asks, knowing full well it's been a while. "I know you've been really busy and stressed and wanted to treat you to someplace nice."

My father is one of the most frugal men in America. He has an old school work ethic and belief in saving your money that Americans, caught in the frenzy of materialism that defines today's society, have long forgotten. He is a man who saves money by bringing his lunch to the factory everyday instead of eating in the cafeteria. A trip to the local Taco Bell would be an expensive night out for him on any other occasion.

"Excuse me, are you Chelsea Stanton by any chance?" a slender woman in her mid-thirties says when she approaches the table.

"Yes, I am," I respond, to the amusement to my father.

"I'm so sorry to interrupt your dinner. I just wanted to say I see you on television and watched you during your first campaign. You are such an inspiration."

"Thank you, that's very kind."

"Good luck to you and Michael Bennit next month," she wishes before departing.

"It's beginning to feel like old times again," Dad observes once she is out of earshot, referring to our experiences in the first campaign run.

"After being invisible for over a year, I'll take it."

Not that we have had any problems with that since what we have come to call "the flip." That day in front of the Ethics Committee changed our fortunes, and the failed attempt to expel the congressman turned it into a circus. Social media has turned out to be the driving force that propelled us to Capitol Hill and the anchor that managed to keep us there.

Over the summer, we were losing handily to both candidates from the parties. Now, barring another October surprise like the last one, we should have no problem getting reelected. I understand why the congressman wants more though.

"I know you had a tough year, Snuggle Bear. Do you regret your decision skip college?" Uh-oh. I already know where this conversation is going. I'm one parental lecture away from feeling like I'm in high school again. No wonder Peyton, Emilee, and the others never visit home.

"I know I disappointed you when I didn't go to Yale, but it's not like I don't ever plan on attending."

"I didn't realize ya were. When?"

"Dad ..."

"I'm just asking. I know you're really busy down there. How do you plan on fitting college into your schedule?" he asks sincerely.

Busy is an understatement. Running one campaign as an eighteen-year-old was daunting. Helping run a hundred of them at twenty is ridiculous, especially since the congressman and Viano decided to target the most influential, senior, and well-financed members of the House. It is having a dramatic effect though.

Speaker Albright is fighting for his political life in his own district against a rather tenacious and aggressive icandidate there. It is much of the same over the other ninety-nine districts we are fielding virtual campaigns in. We are giving them as much expert guidance and social media advice we can. With three weeks to go it will only get busier.

"I don't know. I'll think about it after the election."

"Then you'll have the start of the next Congress, then some scandal or major issue to work, and before you know it you'll be campaigning again." Maybe not, but I'm not ready to tell him that yet.

"What's your point?" I ask a little too sharply. Terse replies like that caused us a lot of tension during my senior year.

"My point *is*," my father replies with a warning glance, "that it's easy to get caught up with the reasons to forego school."

"I know." I'll say anything to end this conversation. I'm sure he senses it, too.

"Snuggle Bear, I will always support you in whatever decision you make. Ya know that. But you also have to know that Bennit will not be a politician forever, and you won't always be his chief of staff. I just don't want ya to end up unemployed with no degree and no job. I don't want ya ending up working in a factory like I did."

His words break my heart. He is the hardest working man I have ever met. After Mom died, he dedicated his life to ensuring I wanted for nothing growing up. I don't want to hear him talk about himself like that.

"Dad," I say, reaching across the table to take his hand, a lone tear rolling down my cheek. "I'm not going to blow college off, but I had to do this first. I'll make you proud of me. I promise."

"You already have, Snuggle Bear."

-THIRTY-SIX-
MICHAEL

"You were the first guy to crash through the political wall, so you were bound to get bloody," one of the ladies says on my right.

"I agree. You are a true pioneer like Henry Ford or the Wright Brothers, or even baseball general manager Billy Beane, to use a more modern example. You redefined how the public elects their representatives in the first campaign and are taking on the extremes of our two political parties in an effort to change Washington now. You should be commended on that."

"Ladies and gentlemen, Michael Bennit," one of the hosts says as the audience's applause reaches a crescendo.

"Thank you," I say to the crowd, "and thank you all for having me." As the cameras roll prior to commercial break, I shake the hands of my hosts. This is a new experience for me. As the iCandidate, I shunned anything resembling mainstream programming and focused everything on social media. Now I am finishing my banter with the ladies of *The View*.

This is a different election, though. When I ran two years ago, the idea of being an icandidate was unique. Running the campaign using nothing but social media created enough buzz and headlines without much effort. With one hundred two icandidates all vying for attention in the social media sphere, it's a little harder to generate that level of interest.

Vince urged me to make a run on the talk show circuit to dial up the visibility for the rest of the icandidates. After focusing so long on using Google Plus, Facebook, Twitter, and Instagram to reach voters, dealing with television programming is a departure from the norm.

Of course, we didn't stop there. The video of me doing the top ten on *The Late Show* went viral almost overnight and cracking jokes on *The Colbert Report* is all over Facebook. People share everything these days. The only question is, will all this be enough to sway people's opinions on Election Day? We almost won without talking about a single issue, so I suppose anything is possible.

"You were great!" Kylie exclaims, giving me a big hug and kiss when I emerge from the dressing room.

"Thanks, hon. I feel like I oversold it too much."

"No, it was perfect. It's still a little strange seeing you on television though."

I've never been comfortable in front of a camera. One of the benefits of running as the iCandidate is not having had to. Now, even with the iCongressman moniker, I know that avoiding them is impossible.

"I'm sure my Twitter feed will let me know if you're telling the truth or lying to me once this episode airs."

"Hungry?"

"Starving," she says as we exit ABC Studios. "Let's go to that little place in the Village we like."

"You got it!" The studio is on Sixty-Sixth Street on Manhattan's west side, so we need to catch a cab to travel the nearly fifty blocks to Kylie's old stomping grounds. I move around the oversized UPS truck parked on the curb and extend my arm.

"Look out!" Kylie shouts as she yanks my other arm violently, pulling me off balance and into her in the process. A yellow cab goes screaming by, missing me by mere inches. I am definitely losing my Special Forces reflexes.

"Well, that almost sucked," I say, catching my breath. "He came out of nowhere."

"That's a lousy way to get assassinated," Kylie says, peeking around the truck and peering down the street before trying to hail another cab.

"What do you mean?"

"Call me crazy, but it looked like he tried to swerve into you."

"Okay, yeah, you're crazy. Do you really think someone is trying to bump me off on a busy Manhattan street on the off chance I need a cab leaving a studio?"

"Okay, probably not," she says dismissively as a taxi pulls up next to us. Something in her voice tells me she is far from convinced.

THIRTY-SEVEN

CHELSEA

The house lights come up and the three candidates shake hands on the stage. Tonight's debate wasn't as entertaining, nor was it the epic beat down as the one two years ago, but the result was the same. The congressman owned it.

Scheduled three weeks ahead of the election instead of the week before it like last time, the debate was once again held at Western Connecticut State University in Danbury. They did a fantastic job hosting our first, so it was only fitting they hold it again. At least we knew what to expect this time.

The debate will probably land some good ratings because of the social media fervor we stirred up again. With the media presence, it feels like a case of déjà vu. The ten-point lead the congressman carried into tonight's debate will grow overnight. No need to spend a sleepless night worrying about catching our opponent this time around.

Emilee, Brian, Amanda, Peyton, and Xavier all went back to school when classes started in September but still made it back to town for the debate tonight. Some of them had long drives here from school, but none thought classes were more important than being here for this. Even with the additional responsibilities of college life, each has been very active on the social media front in support of all the icandidate campaigns.

Congressman Bennit comes backstage and gives a kiss to Kylie. She embraces him, whispering something in his ear only intended for them. Kylie has been on edge since they got back from their NYC trip a week ago for the congressman's interview on *The View*. She hasn't said why, but her attitude has changed a little and she has been clingier then I have ever seen her.

Breaking the embrace with Kylie, Mister B doles out the hugs to the rest of us. Even Vince, Brian, and Xavier get in on the act with a sort of man hug that guys are known to engage in. As a teacher, he was always careful to avoid any physical contact with us outside of a high five or fist bump. Oh, how times have changed. He's gone from a well-respected and liked teacher to cherished boss.

"How did it feel to come into a debate as the frontrunner?" Amanda asks.

"I wasn't really looking at it that way."

"You might not be, but I know I am," Vince proclaims to the delight of the group. The congressman sighs, and shakes his head.

"You guys have been out of my classroom way too long. Let me share a little story with you."

"Uh-oh. Here comes today's history lesson," Amanda says, channeling the old expression we used before the congressman's lectures during our first campaign.

"You're lucky you don't have to live with him," Kylie says, rolling her eyes.

"This is a short one, I promise. There was this kid who started his career by working paper routes, selling magazines door-to-door, and reporting for duty in his grandfather's grocery store to earn money. Through those experiences, he learned the value of a good work ethic and to never take success for granted. Like us, he did the impossible, and made it when everyone didn't think he could. He was a millionaire by age thirty-two, but he wasn't content to stop there like many others would have. There was much more out there to accomplish, and he did."

"So who was he?" I am trying to recall all the lessons we received from Mister Bennit, but this one isn't ringing any bells.

"The Oracle of Omaha."

"Who?" Peyton, Xavier, Emilee, and Vince all blurt out simultaneously.

"Warren Buffett," Amanda says with a smile. "He runs Berkshire Hathaway, one of the most powerful investment firms in the world."

"Glad to see the tuition dollars you are spending at UConn are well-invested," I compliment with a wink. An accounting and business major ought to know about him.

"I'm not seeing the point."

"The point is, Peyton, that Warren Buffett was a consummate entrepreneur and worked hard to become the billionaire and the world-renowned financial expert he is today. He could have retired decades ago, but it wasn't in his nature. It's not in mine, either. We may be leading our race, but this election is about more than winning reelection.

"The icandidates," Kylie says, making it clear to anyone who had yet to figure out where we are going with this.

"Their success is our success. Without them, I will spend another two years in Congress like I spent the last one, and I refuse to do that. Tonight was a big win for us, but the fight isn't over. You guys were mad at me for not including you in my plan to teach America a lesson about how they vote in elections during our first campaign. I'm not going to make that mistake again. I need your help, because the final surge starts tomorrow."

* * *

We all went out to dinner following the debate, and it felt good having something to celebrate for a change. Now on my way home, I feel the need to stop somewhere first. I park the car and gingerly wander down the path as the large iron behemoth looms ahead. I hear the clicking of my heels against the metal decking once I reach the bridge, only stopping when I assume my traditional vantage point in the middle of the span.

Blake can lay all the claim he wants to my spot on the steps of the Capitol, but the old iron bridge across the river at Briar Point State Park is mine. The last time I was on this bridge this long after sunset, I was threatening him with my Dad's old Ka-Bar knife. Now he practically works for our campaign. It's amazing how times change.

I almost wish Blake had been able to come to the debate tonight. He would have enjoyed watching Congressman

Bennit handle the issues with ease and respond deftly to all the questions about the censures and reprimands. There were no epic fails like Dick Johnson bungling the order of articles in the Constitution, but there were still plenty of one-liners to keep social and mainstream media buzzing.

I look out past the bend in the river to the center of the town I grew up in. So much has changed. Three years ago, I was a high school student just trying to figure out who I was and who I wanted to be. Two years ago, I was running an underdog campaign for my favorite teacher that became a media sensation. A year ago, we were trying to learn how to navigate the treacherous political waters inside the Beltway. Today, I feel like I have come full circle, again wondering the same things I did three years ago.

I've had moments over the past year where I felt ... I don't know, proud. Dressing down Senator Viano last summer was one of them, but the satisfaction I got was short lived.

I'm envious of my friends who went on to college—they work hard on the campaign without facing the crushing responsibility of working on the staff. They have been invaluable to our effort, but on their terms. It makes me wonder what would have happened if I chose a different path.

Who would be chief of staff if I had decided to go to Yale, Harvard, Princeton, or the dozens of other schools that offered me full scholarships? Would he trust Vince enough with that responsibility? I love him like a brother, but I'm not sure Vince is the right guy for the job. Maybe Vanessa could have done it. Eh, he probably would've hired a professional political operative who could have done a better job than I did.

Unless what Kylie said is true. That he does value me more than I know. I need to know what he thinks, but he's not talking about it, at least not to my face. How do I ask him? Is it easier just to move on with my life?

I pull the thin, ivory envelope out of my coat pocket and look at it in the light of the moon. I received the letter in the mail earlier today but didn't want to open it before the debate in case it was bad news. Breaking the seal and extracting the contents, I realize how much rides on what is written on this sheet of paper. I'm not sure if only seeing a single paragraph is a good sign or not.

Since the ambient light is not enough to read by, I flip on the flashlight feature of my phone. The seal of Harvard University jumps off the top of the page. The letter is short, to the point, and takes my breath away.

Dear Chelsea:

I received a notification from our Admissions Office that you were inquiring about the status of the scholarship you were offered two years ago. The short answer is, yes. There will always be a place for you at Harvard, and we would love to have you attend this spring. Please contact my office if you would like to discuss this further.

Warm and cordial regards,

Andrew Stemple
President, Harvard University

-THIRTY-EIGHT-
SENATOR VIANO

Tarrywile Mansion in Danbury is a beautiful example of the "shingle style" Victorian-era American home architecture. The gable roof with multiple dormers, large chimney stacks, and Doric columns constructed in a semicircular fashion around the veranda makes it no wonder it was entered on the National Register of Historic Places.

Virginia has its own beauty, but there are few places on Earth prettier than New England at the peak of foliage season. This estate is over seven hundred acres of red, yellow, and orange clad trees that scream autumn like no other place in America. The air is a cool fifty degrees and is invigorating without being frigid. There are dozens of trails here, perfect for clearing one's head amongst the quiet serenity of drifting leaves and whispering evergreens.

There are two picnic areas in the park, and I make my way back to the one of which is located in the wooded grove off the lower Mansion parking lot for the meeting I set up. I find Blake and Gary waiting for me when I get there.

"Good morning, gentlemen. Blake, I hope you're not too hung over after partying with Michael's college-aged staff last night."

"They're not twenty-one yet."

"I was in college once, Blake. It never mattered to me. So, where do we stand?"

"The country watched Bennit seal his win last night. Not the resounding win he had a couple of years ago against Beaumont and ..." Gary trails off and snaps his fingers, mentally searching for the name of the man who became a political punch line and YouTube favorite for his Constitutional gaffe.

"Johnson," Blake interjects, filling in the blank of the otherwise forgettable Republican candidate in that race.

"Right, that's it. Anyway, Bennit will win pretty convincingly, sans any last minute debacles. The GOP candidate will be second and the Democrat a distant third."

"That man is like a phoenix. He was a pile of ashes a couple of months ago. What about the rest of the icandidates?"

"Feeding on his success," Blake says. "Eighty percent are within striking distance or already within the margin of error of the polls. Of the remaining twenty, we are going to win five races with no problem and lose the other fifteen."

"Impressive showing for a bunch of no names. The country is embracing this movement far more than I thought they would."

"Never underestimate a grassroots effort on social media," Gary resolves.

"What about Albright? Is the Speaker going to keep his seat in South Carolina?"

"It's too close to call," Vince explains. "Amazing, considering how conservative that district is. He had a commanding lead just a few weeks ago, but his poll numbers have tanked since. Tough place to be in, and I remember the feeling well. His campaign is starting to panic."

"'You can't come to any harm when you're falling. It's the landing part you have to worry about,'" Gary pronounces.

"Iron Man?" Blake asks.

"No. Danger Mouse."

"Nice one."

"Are you two quite done?" I snap as Blake and Gary look at each other sheepishly. Really, enough of the superhero quotes. When he comes to work for me at the end of all this, I swear I need to banish them from his vernacular. "Don't encourage him, Blake."

"Sorry, ma'am."

"Don't apologize, just get on with it."

"It looks like Harvey Stepanik will win his contest," he says, refocusing on the task at hand. "The Dems may lose their whip, though, and I would bet the minority leader goes down too."

"They stayed on the sidelines for much of the Bennit expulsion disaster, so I'm surprised it's not the reverse. And Thomas Parker?

"He's safe. Changing his vote played well in that district and the icandidate there wasn't as keen to run against him after that."

A gust of wind sends a swarm of leaves blowing past us. Instead of shouting over the wind and rustling leaves, I wait for the squall to subside.

"So we could potentially win eighty-five of the hundred races?" I ask, just restating the obvious because I don't really believe what I'm hearing.

"Eighty-seven of one hundred two, actually. We weren't counting Bennit and Reyes. So long as no bombs get dropped, it could be a historic election night."

"Do we expect any October surprises?"

"Our opposition research guys don't seem to think so," Blake replies. "They vetted each of the icandidates thoroughly before turning their attention to researching the competition."

Of course, it helps when there is nobody left to do research against you. Part of the plan was to utilize every reputable oppo outfit in the country to work for us. It was an expensive proposition, but extravagances like this are a perk of being filthy rich and having some deep pockets supporting my efforts. The political parties were able to eventually line up some resources, but we got the pick of the litter.

"Many of them are riding Bennit's coattails," Gary observes. "He has gone viral in social media again and his approval rating nationwide is through the roof. The mainstream media isn't covering him with the tenacity they did last time, but that isn't stopping America from talking about him."

I have underestimated his appeal from the beginning. He is the average guy's politician this country has begged for. While most insiders gasped in horror when he flipped that table at his hearing, the rest of America shouted, "Hell yeah." He makes politics more real for the country, and because of that, they can relate to him. One more example of the magic that is Michael Bennit.

"We are on the threshold of a turning point in American politics," I state, knowing one of my small little group doesn't know the half of it. I can't resist sharing a knowing smile with my former chief of staff.

"Let's hope so," Blake says, oblivious to the double meaning of my words.

"Blake, you have done an amazing job with this effort, but I guess I shouldn't be surprised that you came through in the clutch. It runs in our family. Your father would be very proud of you."

"Thanks, Aunt Marilyn. I'll see you back in D.C."

With that, Blake heads back to his car leaving me alone with Gary.

"Do you think you can trust him? He's getting a little cozy with the Bennit camp."

"I think he'll do the right thing when the time comes," I conclude, knowing there is a danger that his loyalties are divided.

"So when will you tell him the plan?"

The most dangerous part of this plan is the variables involved. Michael Bennit was not supposed to survive his expulsion, and having done so, has made life far more problematic. Now the decision on how I play this lies with his reaction to my proposal. Either way, I will become a major player in national politics again. Whether it is as an ally or enemy remains to be determined.

"Let's see how the election goes. It all hinges on how Michael responds to my offer. If he agrees, we will need him with us immediately. If not, well, I'll need him to do his part in a different way. Either way, I don't think Blake is ready to hear what I have to say yet."

-THIRTY-NINE-
SPEAKER ALBRIGHT

"The members of the Republican National Committee are seething right now! It's bad enough having to fight off the Democrats, but having to face serious threats from independent candidates is inexcusable," the scratchy voice screams at me through the phone.

"The Dems aren't having any better of a time with it," I utter in my defense. I have my own reelection problems and don't really give a damn how upset the RNC is. I take a sip of my morning coffee as the tongue-lashing continues.

"Only I don't give a damn about them! I care about our prospects of winning the presidency and keeping the House. We don't have the resources to win the White House and fight off all these social media independents. We were counting on you to remove that threat for us, and you failed!"

The Republican National Committee provides national leadership for the Republican Party in the United States and is responsible for developing and promoting our political platform. They ran the national convention to select the candidate for president back in August, and are responsible for coordinating fundraising and election strategies. Each state and many counties have smaller committees governed by a national committee, of whose chairman I am currently getting chastised by.

"Settle down, Phillip. The races are tight, but we can still pull most of them out. Just dedicate more resources to them." Actually, they don't look good at all. I may pull out a win if this huge blitz on television works, but as it stands right now, many of my colleagues won't be returning to the next Congress.

"We have a presidential race to win, Johnston. What resources do you think we have available?"

"What do you think I can do about that?"

"Accept responsibility that you screwed up and pray we don't lose the House in the process." With that, I hear the phone disconnect, ending the terse conversation.

I am fighting for my own political life down here, so I don't know what he expects me to do. I have spent millions on advertising, and this most recent ad buy will only increase that exponentially. I am spending every waking moment out campaigning—something I have never had to do in my conservative district. Today, I have a ridiculous schedule, with five campaign stops and an evening fundraiser to attend. I take the television off mute as the pundits on the CNN morning show continue to discuss the congressional races across the country.

"This is completely unprecedented," the short-haired female panelist says to her cohorts. "This many independents being competitive in congressional races have never been seen before in American history."

"And they are social media candidates," the show's host interjects. "Bennit got tremendous coverage because he was a novelty. That uniqueness has worn off, so why is this current crop getting so much air time?"

"I think it's a reflection on the mood of the country," another well-respected pundit concludes. "People watched the viral video of what happened in the House when they tried to force Bennit out. People realized they are tired of settling for whichever candidates the political parties choose and want other options. Michael Bennit has inspired this icandidate movement that provides precisely that."

"Johnston Albright is widely considered to be the architect of the effort to expel Michael Bennit. Does the blame for all this fall on him?"

"I think that's the safe assumption to come to. If he had left Bennit alone to serve out his term, I don't think he could have sparked the surge in social media popularity we are seeing nationwide."

"Bunch of crap!" I exclaim, slapping my mug off the ornate end table next to the couch and sending it skittering across the room. I am not taking the fall for this. Someone has been talking to the media behind the scenes and trying to pin this fiasco with Bennit on me. Had they listened in the first place, there would be no icandidates and, a couple weeks from now, no Michael Bennit.

Instead, I was forced to push the issue against my better judgment, and he used that to his advantage. Now all the politicos can talk about are Bennit and these virtual candidates. The very premise of that is almost unheard of in a presidential election year. The race for the White House still leads the news, but the messages from both candidates for president are getting lost in the noise surrounding what the media is calling "a historic independent movement in Congress."

I hear the doorbell ring but am content to let my wife answer it. After so many years of political service, she has become a brilliant gatekeeper here at home. Nobody gets through her if they are visiting unannounced.

"Johnston, there is a James Reed here to see you," my wife says from the entrance to the living room after a few moments. Okay, almost no one. You have got to be kidding me.

"Thanks, hon," I say, setting the remote down and getting up off the couch. I give her a kiss on the cheek as I pass her. "We'll be in the study."

I greet the large Kentucky lobbyist and wave him down the hall into my small library. The walls of the room are covered in floor to ceiling bookcases filled with ancient-looking works, of which very few I have bothered reading. I offer him a seat on one of the red leather couches and take a seat in one of the facing high back chairs.

"Ya'll have a beautiful room here," the man says in preamble, admiring the fine furnishings and inhaling the sweet stench of cigar smoke that still leaves a musky scent in the room.

"Thanks, but I'm sure you're not here to admire the décor. What's on your mind, Mister Reed?"

"Did you watch the Bennit debate last night?" I nod. That man has a gift for making issues relevant to his constituents, and by extension, upping his likability in the process. The debate was a resounding victory for him, even if he didn't humiliate his opponents like last time.

"Then you also noticed the bump in the polls all his minions received as a result."

"Yes, I did. But they are short-term gains that I don't think will hold until Election Day."

James smiles thinly. "I disagree," he says, pulling out a manila file folder from his leather valise and handing it to me. I eye him wearily before reading the contents of the first page.

"What the hell is this?"

"A contingency plan. Let's call it Plan G." That comment makes me wonder what happened to the other plans after "C," but I let it go. "I am offering a way out of the situation you created."

"I created?" I ask with an indignant tone. "Practicing a little revisionist history, aren't we?"

"I don't look at it that way, and neither does anybody else, including the RNC, DNC, and most other political action committees and lobby groups. Now, I know what you're about to say next, Mister Speaker. Ya'll think just because my man got caught setting up Bennit that it will blow back on me. Trust me when I say, it won't."

"And how do you know that?"

"Because, I just do."

I read a little more of the contents in the file, but it's hard to focus. Even with the disaster the committee hearing laid on the doorstep of Washington's most powerful political lobby in a very public way, James Reed has the clout and financial resources to weasel out of any responsibility for it.

"This is based on a lot of presumptions, the first of which is the election of more than a handful of these icandidates."

"Yes, that is why it is called a contingency plan. But should we be faced with more than two icongressmen next year, we have to have an agreed upon tactic to reduce their impact. This is it." I wince at the term. The media have fallen in love with it, just like they did with "icandidate." I swear I want to pass a law that prohibits the use of i-anything. Sorry, Apple.

"Agreed upon? I haven't agreed to anything," I say, snapping the folder closed and tossing it on the cherry finished table between us. "I won't bring this to the Floor."

"Actually, Johnston, you will," James adds, staring at his fingernails as if assessing their length, "or you won't be Speaker much longer."

"I don't respond well to threats, Mister Reed. Do you really think you can waltz into my house and threaten a democratically elected representative to do your bidding?"

"We both know that democratic principles died a long time ago in this country. But, should you persist to cling to that illusion, let me remind you that the selection of the person who holds your position is the most undemocratic thing in American politics. I did not put that process in place, but I have no compunction over using my influence to ensure it works to the benefit of my firm and those like us."

Unfortunately, he's not wrong. If Americans ever really knew how the sausage was made in Washington, they would riot in the streets. Voters no longer call the shots. People like Reed do.

"You're afraid you are losing your hold over the members. Perhaps, in light of this threat, that is not a bad thing."

"Everyone has a right to petition their government in a democracy," James lectures, "and it's our responsibility to listen to their concerns and bring them to the people who can affect change. We explain the real world impact of the ideas ya'll dream up, and it isn't corrupt to do so."

This guy can lay it on thick. It doesn't take ten minutes in office to learn an enormous part of lobbying activity is busy work to justify lobbyists' big fees. It's a multibillion-dollar industry, and one you mess with at your political peril. Unless you don't need them, like Reyes, Bennit, and the host of the candidates they are running to replace us. No wonder Reed is so scared. Not only could he lose millions of dollars, but something of far greater importance inside the Beltway—influence.

"That's a bold assertion to make considering you just told me we don't live in a democracy."

"Don't play word games with me. What we choose to let America know and what the truth really is are two separate things," James fires back. "You know that better than most people, Mister Speaker."

The gentle knock at the door interrupts the conversation at the perfect moment. The door remains closed, my wonderful spouse knowing from experience that face-to-face meetings are not to be barged in on. "Come in," I announce just loud enough to be heard on the other side of the heavy oak door.

"I'm so sorry to interrupt," she tells James before acknowledging me. "Your chief of staff is here, honey. He asked me to tell you your first campaign stop is in an hour and you have to get going."

"Thank you, dear. Please tell him I'll just be a moment longer," I respond. James Reed rises as my wife closes the door the study.

"Election Day is going to be important for your political future, Johnston. You think two icongressmen are bad? I watch the polls, too. If you manage to keep your seat, you will have to deal with a new crop of independents beholden to Bennit and Reyes. The only thing left to determine is exactly how many. Either way, both political parties will be putting pressure on you to come up with a solution to the problem."

"And you just handed me it," I conclude, already knowing where the powerful lobbyist is going with this. He lets a smile escape his lips. I imagine it is exactly the satisfying grin a cat would have when the mouse realizes he's cornered.

"Failure to act decisively will be a sign of weakness. The Republicans may turn to new leadership, assuming the Democrats don't take the House back." Just from the way he said that I can tell he has already talked to members of the Democratic National Committee and other power players in that party.

They will do his bidding if it means they can own Congress again. They are in no danger of losing control of the Senate, and if their candidate wins the White House, they could have complete control over the legislative agenda for the next two years. The GOP will do everything to avoid that from happening.

"I believe you have a rally to attend so you can save your skin," James says, turning towards the door. "Don't let me hold you up. I can show myself out. Good luck, Mister Speaker, I hope we have a reason to talk after Election Day."

-FORTY-
CHELSEA

I'm never going to get any work done today. One of the downsides of working in a fully functioning coffee shop is you don't get a moment of peace. I'm sure that's why the congressman originally wanted to find a space of our own to run the campaign out of.

We had no money when we ran the first race, so the offer to use the Perkfect Buzz as our headquarters was quickly accepted. Laura, the timeless owner of this Millfield institution, was offended when she heard we were thinking about alternatives for this campaign. Of course, the real reason for my pushing to be here is not so straightforward.

I realized my dad was right when I brought it up to him that we were shopping for space at the beginning of the summer. Mister Bennit is not an ordinary politician, and the more he acted like one, the less popular he was becoming. He was losing his identity, and I can put up with the small interruptions if working out of Laura's haunt helps him realize his true nature.

Well, that's half of the story. Even while away at college, everyone is still involved, but everything is done over Skype now. The fact is I miss working in these cozy confines with

Kylie, Brian, Peyton, and the rest of the staff like we did in the last campaign. Kylie is also working down in D.C., so it leaves just me, the congressman, Vince, and Vanessa running the show here in addition to the legion of volunteers eager to be a part of Vince's "revolución."

With five minutes to go before a staff meeting with the volunteers, I go to the counter for some caffeine. Laura refuses to let any of us pay, and I wonder if the tab we've racked up in free coffee could be construed as an illegal campaign contribution. That makes me smile.

"Chelsea? Hi, I'm Rick Schemm from the *New York Times*. I'm doing background on the Bennit campaign. Do you have a moment for some questions?"

The *New York Times*. Kylie's old employer. Two years ago, I would have freaked out doing an interview. Despite getting ambushed on my front lawn during our first campaign and facing a horde of journalists during the post-election press conference Mister Bennit set up, I never got comfortable with the idea. Even during my first few months as chief of staff, I let Vince handle those requests. Given everything that has happened since, I'm amazed how much has changed.

"Sure, but I have a meeting in a few minutes so it has to be quick."

"It's two days after the debate," Rick says, turning on a Dictaphone, "and recent polls have you winning in a landslide with over sixty percent of registered voters casting their votes for Michael Bennit. Any comment on the success you're having running a social media campaign again?"

"Sixty percent is a good number, but it still means there are forty percent out there whose vote we need to earn. You guys may be calling it a landslide, but we look at it as having more work to do." And that's the truth.

"How much time is Congressman Bennit devoting to working with the other icandidates around the country?"

"We have mostly volunteers helping with that effort, when they are needed. The congressman represents the Connecticut Sixth District, and reaching out to the people here has been his focus." Also true, but I wonder how many people actually would believe that.

"Last question. You were a key player in all the drama surrounding this campaign last year. Do you miss it?" Some of it more than you might think, but I can't say that.

"There is plenty of drama watching all these independents run for seats in the House. It's nice that Americans are focusing on a call for change in Washington instead of allegation as to whether I slept with my teacher."

"Thanks, Chelsea."

"No problem, Rick. Enjoy your coffee," I say with a smile. Yup, we have definitely come a long way the last couple of years.

* * *

The staff meeting with the volunteers in the district went fine, but I miss having everyone here. As much hard work and long hours the first two campaigns demanded, it was bearable because we all became good friends and had a good time with it. Now it feels more like work. The only way we make up for the lack of physical presence is through a daily videoconference Brian set up. It's a poor substitute, but at least we can still meet, coordinate our activities, and share a few laughs.

"Someone on Richter's staff got diarrhea of the mouth on Twitter yesterday, so I have been helping with damage control," Amanda explains.

Amanda and Peyton are the firefighters for the icandidate effort. When a crisis pops up, campaigns turn to them for guidance because they know we had to deal with our fair share of surprises back in the day. Since the last two campaigns were focused on getting our teacher elected to Congress, another of our big changes is the roles we play. Instead of working locally in our district, we are trying to get a hundred people chosen by Viano, whom we've never even met in person, elected across the country.

"Do I dare ask?"

"He made a couple of off-color racial comments and called a female detractor an 'uneducated tramp only good for soliciting on a street corner.'"

"Ouch."

"Yeah, he's in pretty hot water right now," she concludes.

"Being a racist and a sexist doesn't boost one's likability." It also makes me wonder where Viano got some of these people. "Keep me informed. Peyton?"

"I have had to deal with a couple of dumb Facebook posts and tweets, but nothing that epic, thank God," she reports to the group.

"Okay, thanks, Peyton. Bri?"

"Hash tag icandidate trends on Twitter almost nightly. If you count Reyes's and our campaigns, likes on Facebook pages are steadily increasing. Blogs across the country are writing about our little movement, some, ironically, calling it a 'revolución.' How do you suppose that happened, Vince?"

Vince and Vanessa are sitting next to me, but they logged on to our Skype session with their own computers. I look over to see the wry expression on his face.

"Great minds think alike?" he posits, clearly letting us know through his look where the bloggers got that gem from. Vanessa takes it upon herself to smack him on the head. Yep, just like old times.

"Anyway, we can't really complain about the social media traction we're getting," Brian finishes.

"Nor what it means for mainstream coverage," Emilee chimes in. "My afternoon class got cancelled, so I spent the time looking at TV and print reporting on a couple of dozen campaigns. It's not exactly Bennitmania from two years ago, but they are getting a respectable amount of free press."

"Comparing anything to our first campaign probably isn't fair," Vanessa concludes. "We were rock stars." Yeah we were. No police escorts are needed this time around.

"Speaking of stars," Peyton interjects, "nice game the other night, X. Eighteen points against Duke is pretty impressive."

"Thanks. I wish I could contribute more ..."

"We understand, believe me," Vanessa says. "The fact that you have done this much and still been able to balance classes and hoops is incredible."

Five days before the election and all we really have to do is just engage in small talk. Xavier is on the periphery of this effort, but we are all proud of how well he is doing as a freshman on the college basketball scene. While the others grill him on what it's like to be a big-time student athlete, all I can think about is how to get through Election Day.

The challenge is not to get Mister Bennit reelected, but to keep working on getting him some help in Congress. The icandidates are polling extremely well according to Marist, Quinnipiac, Gallup, and the dozen other groups taking the country's political temperature on a nightly basis. It is going to be a race to the finish in most of those contests. Their staffs are doing the majority of the work now, and all we can do is be there for them in case something pops up they can't handle.

It's not exactly the drama-filled ending our first election had, but it beats being smeared all over the nightly news. I don't miss the angst of those couple of days, but I do miss the adrenaline rush. That's not to say we shouldn't expect to see a few surprises in other races, but for ours, the outcome is almost assured.

I sign off the video conference and notice Congressman Reyes walk into the Buzz with a handsome Asian man at his side. What the hell is going on? I leave my post in the corner and greet the two men at the door.

"Congressman Reyes, it's great seeing you again. What brings you all the way to Connecticut?"

He is looking around the room, admiring the décor and the flurry of activity around us. About a third of the volunteers stayed behind after our staff meeting and are only now retrieving their coats and belongings for the trip home.

"Hello, Miss Stanton," he says, returning my firm handshake. "I'd love to say I travelled all the way up here because I need a triple espresso, but truth is, we need to have a chat with your boss, and it requires an in person meeting. Do you think he can spare a moment?"

-FORTY-ONE-
MICHAEL

"For you, I have more than a moment," Congressman Bennit says as he gives our only elected ally a handshake and hug accompanied with a couple of hard slaps on the back. Kylie rolls her eyes at the display of man affection. "Cisco, it's five days until the election and you're taking a road trip?"

"I got all my lawns mowed early," he answers with his typical self-effacing cultural humor. "If it wasn't important, I wouldn't be up here freezing my ass off. You need to hear this. Can we talk here?"

Mister Bennit looks at Cisco's friend and then back at Laura who is finishing cleaning up behind the counter so she can go home.

"Laura is through here, so we have to get going, but there is a quaint little restaurant around the corner still open I think." The Asian man nods.

"I will never understand your decision to work out of the coffee shop again, so I guess it will have to," Cisco adds. "Not that you don't run an impressive operation from here."

"My chief of staff believes in keeping me well-caffeinated, so this works. Give us a minute to grab our coats," I say, indicating I want Kylie and Chelsea to be there for whatever this is. "We can do the introductions on the way."

We retrieve our coats and head out into the chilly New England evening. We walk through the parking lot to the front of the Perkfect Buzz and then make a right, heading down the sidewalk towards the center of town.

"Okay, Cisco, who's your friend?"

"Terry Nyguen," he says, shaking my hand. He also introduces himself to Chelsea and Kylie as we walk.

"Terry is a senior coordinator for the Freedom Coalition for Responsible Government. You ever heard of it?"

I look back at Chelsea, hoping she has. There are so many organizations based in Washington that it is near impossible to know them all and still do my job.

"A think tank dedicated to the spirit of the constitutional convention that decries ideologues and promotes moderate candidates in races across the country," Chelsea says. Yep, that's why she runs my staff.

Think tanks are research organizations and advocacy groups that delve into public policy areas ranging from political strategy to business policies. Most are non-profit organizations, while others receive funding from wide-ranging interests including "concerned citizens" and even governments themselves. They can be incredibly partisan or not at all, making distinguishing between them nearly impossible for anyone not an insider.

We enter the little bistro and settle into a corner booth where we can enjoy some privacy. After my last restaurant run-in with somebody I don't know, I almost wish I had Brian here to record this again.

"I can't say I have ever heard of you, Mr. Nyguen. Especially odd considering I'm probably your poster boy." Not to mention he looks like a mercenary, with his short haircut and military demeanor. I've served with sergeants major who were less intimidating than this guy.

"We're a small operation that provides financial backing and political advice to moderate candidates willing to work to find a consensus in Washington. You have never needed us before now."

"And from our experiences, you haven't had a lot of success in your objective," Chelsea adds, clearly meaning to test him.

"A prospect I also hope will change shortly. I understand your apprehension—"

"Which is why you approached Cisco instead of coming directly to us," Kylie finishes. Always the journalist, she is digging to get to the bottom of exactly who this guy is and why he's here.

"Honestly, yes."

"You need to understand something, Terry. Trust is not something we have a huge supply of these days. Now you show up here, days before the election, and expect us to buy whatever it is you're selling?"

"Hear him out guys. Please," Cisco pleads. We all nod, but hardly give him a ringing endorsement to continue.

"I don't expect you to buy anything, Miss Stanton," he says, leveling with us. "You can choose to ignore everything I have to say here. All I am asking is for you to hear me out. We can take it from there."

"Go ahead, Terry."

"Congressman Bennit, are you aware there is a rumor floating around that you plan on uniting the icandidates under one political banner once they are elected?"

"You're kidding, right?" Kylie asks before a word can slip from my mouth.

"No, I'm not. Are you planning on forming a third party if all these independents you are helping win?"

"No."

"Someone in your camp says you are." He looks at each of us, clearly trying to gauge our reactions. "These ideas don't come out of nowhere, and the source of this rumor has to be someone well informed, because it's gaining traction."

I begin to think of the people close to the campaign, but quickly realize I am looking at things the wrong way. Maybe not in my camp, but issued a visitor's pass to it. I look at Chelsea to see if we are on the same page.

"Viano," is all she has to say. I agree with her, but I don't want to air the laundry in front of this guy. I don't trust him enough to let him in on our relationship with the former senator.

"We can figure out if that's the case later, Chels, but right now I want to know why it matters."

"It doesn't, insofar as it only leads me to the next piece of information. Are you familiar with Ibram & Reed?"

"You can't spend a day in the House and not be."

"They were the ones who helped run the little operation to get the congressman sent packing out of D.C.," Chelsea adds. "William Mashburn was one of their employees."

"You may want to reconsider using the past tense, Miss Stanton. They aren't done yet."

"What do you mean?" Kylie asks. I am not sure where Terry gets his intel from, but it's clearly news to the woman who lives for uncovering underhanded dealings each day for the *Washington Post*.

"I don't have specifics, but my sources are telling me they are looking for a way to help the leadership neutralize any independent that gets elected."

"I haven't heard anything of the sort," Kylie retorts, clearly upset that she may be getting scooped by some guy at a think tank. "That firm has bunkered itself to fight off a pending federal investigation of framing an elected official. They wouldn't dare make another play so soon."

"Yet they are. They may be hiding from people like you in the media, but it is still very much business as usual for them behind closed doors. Their crusade against you experienced a setback in their eyes, nothing more."

"Why?"

When I was in a classroom, it was the question I loved to ask my students. It's one thing to know when the American Revolution happened or who was involved in the women's suffrage movement, but understanding the why is the relevant part.

"That's the real question, isn't it? I only can offer a theory. People have come to understand getting elected to Congress costs a lot of money. It is a truth that has been propagated for decades now by the very interests we are talking about. Your first race showed a campaign could be competitive without that level of financial support."

"And even if they look at the first race as a fluke ..."

"Success of a hundred independents using the same model isn't," Kylie says, finishing Chelsea's statement.

"You are changing that paradigm and it's scaring the wits out of some very powerful people, and I don't mean just the smooth-talkers at Ibram & Reed. There are other people out there that could make things dangerous for you, and I mean more than just politically."

I look over at Cisco who meets my stare. Now I know why he brought Terry here to meet me, and why he did it in person. In the age of NSA scandals about wiretapping, electronic communication could be compromised. You can't assume what your enemy's capabilities are and aren't. Great, now I'm thinking like the author of a spy novel.

"Who?"

"I don't know, and that's what makes me nervous. We know Ibram & Reed's motives, along with some of the other power players. We can watch them. It's the unknowns that make me nervous."

"One hell of an assertion you're making, Terry, considering you have no specific information to back it up."

"Unfortunately, Congressman, what I'm telling you isn't based on anything concrete. There is no imminent threat, so to speak, but something we wanted to make you aware of."

"We being …?" Kylie asks, fishing for answers to who this guy really is.

"We being us." Yeah, that helps.

"Having people target us is not outside the realm of possibilities. We're poised to cause more casualties than Jack Bauer in this election, Michael." Cisco knows how to speak my language.

I am amazed at just how surreal my life has become. Three years ago, I was a simple history teacher getting ready to ask my girlfriend to marry me. Now I'm having a cloak and dagger meeting in a restaurant, seriously discussing whether someone might try to kill me.

"You're not taking this seriously, are you, Congressman?" Chelsea inquires.

I honestly don't know what to think. I don't know Nyguen's credentials, or how he came across any of this information. He could just be a guy making this up to get closer to our campaign. He could be a false flag planted by an enemy to distract us. Who knows? Despite my misgivings, my gut tells me to trust what he's saying. And I have firsthand experience in knowing that trusting that intuition in combat keeps you alive.

"Chels, I'm used to being shot at, but it's not something I would ever want to expose my staff to. Dodging bullets is not in your job description, so if there are threats being made, I want to know about them. Have we received any?"

"Nothing out of the ordinary. Anything that comes through has been passed on to the Capitol Police as usual."

Threats against Congress are more common than most Americans know. House Speaker Sam Rayburn had a cross burned on his front lawn in Texas during debate on civil rights legislation in the 1960s. There was a sharp increase in the number of threatening communications during the health care reform debate in 2010. Republican Eric Cantor even got his campaign office window shot out. If all that isn't enough for me to take this seriously, there's the assassination attempt on Gabrielle Giffords in early 2011.

"How concerned should we be?" Kylie asks, taking this even more seriously than I am. It was of her opinion that the driver of the taxi outside of ABC was aiming to run me down. I may have convinced her of the absurdity of it being an organized plot, but she has been weird about it ever since. This conversation is simply feeding that initial paranoia.

"And don't answer with one of your cryptic responses," I add for good measure. The corner of Terry's mouth turns up. Forget military. I am beginning to think this guy either was CIA or FBI, or still is.

"I don't believe the national committees and PACs will take defeat lying down. I know the lobby industry and major contributors won't. If Ibram & Reed is unscrupulous enough to frame you when you were ineffective and ostracized, I'm afraid of what someone may try to do to silence a more powerful voice."

"Meaning what?" Chelsea asks, channeling Kylie's concerns.

"Blackmail, intimidation, threats, and even assassinations have all been used in the past. There is no reason to think they won't in the future. I am saying you should watch your backs."

I see the fear flash in Kylie's and Chelsea's eyes. We are days away from the election and I can't have them peeking over their shoulder looking for ghosts. I want to take this warning seriously, but I can't afford to have the two most important women in my life getting consumed by it. "You must read a lot, Terry, because you are starting to sound like a Brad Thor novel," I utter, articulating an earlier thought in a futile attempt to ratchet down the tension.

"I do actually. And what I have learned is all good fiction has elements of truth in it that makes it believable. Look, I don't know for certain if you are in any physical danger, Congressman. All I am saying is that you are getting tangled up with groups of people with a lot to lose if you pull off this coup. You think Beaumont was desperate to keep his seat? It's nothing compared to what the card-carrying members of that club will do to keep their power."

Yeah, I'm sure that reassurance is going to put Kylie and Chelsea at ease.

-FORTY-TWO-
CHELSEA

"Is this what you did on the last Election Day? Stand on a bridge and wait for the polls to close?" the familiar voice calls out as his footfalls echo off the bridge decking.

I love autumn, but the one thing that sucks is it gets dark way too early once daylight savings time ends and we turn the clocks back. So to see my town bathed in the oranges, purples, and pinks of a beautiful November sunset, I had to break away from the chaos while they remain open for another three hours.

"Blake, if there is one thing for certain I know in this world, it's you cannot lay claim to this spot."

So much for having some time to myself to think. With one of the most important decisions I will ever make hanging over my head, an interruption from the likes of Blake Peoni was the last thing I needed. I'm vulnerable enough as it is.

"Wouldn't dream of it," he says coming up beside me and leaning on the railing of the bridge. We quietly enjoy the view for a few moments, but since I have him here alone, I might as well dig for some information.

"I have two questions to ask you, if you're up for it."

"Shoot."

"Why do you wear that ridiculous pin on your lapel? I noticed it right before the election two years ago and I've seen you wearing it every day since."

"It's a bit of a long story," he dodges, straightening the triangular pin with his index finger and thumb. "Let's just say it's a memento I was given to remind me of my father and a pledge to be a better man than I was."

"Is it working for you?"

"Is that your second question?" he asks playfully.

"No, that was part B of the first one."

"This is starting to sound like a pop quiz. Yeah, I would say it's working. That was a pretty tame first question, so what's your second one?"

"If you are a better man like you say you are, why are you working with a snake like Viano?" Blake spins his head around and looks at me with a mix of confusion and consternation. I meet his deep brown eyes with a hard look of my own.

"What do you mean, Chelsea?"

"Blake, you're part of Senator Viano's inner circle. You've already told me you don't trust her. Are you really going to stand there and tell me with a straight face that you don't know she's trying to screw us?" I shake my head and turn back to admire my view.

"She hasn't let me in that far yet. I don't think she trusts me enough to let me in on whatever her scheme is."

"Why wouldn't she?"

"Because she knows what I did to you guys two years ago and understands I swore never to do it again. If she's up to no good, she will only let me in once she thinks she has the leverage to make me do what she needs me to."

"Jesus, Blake, how did you get mixed up with her to begin with?"

"That's a complicated story. Let's leave it at sometimes you don't get a choice in the matter."

"Whatever." I never get the full story with this guy.

"Chelsea, are you ever going to find a way to trust me?" he asks with weird sincerity in his voice. Now I turn to face him, the wind whipping my strands of red hair that sprung loose from under my white knit hat.

"Are you ever going to give me a reason to?" I demand, realizing it's too late to stop myself from opening up.

"I asked first." Blake reaches for my face and gently brushes the strands of red hair to the side. His touch is so gentle, so caring. I haven't experienced that in a long time.

"Chelsea, I promise on my father's grave that I will not let anyone hurt you or Michael Bennit again so long as I can help it," he promises. "If it means I have to take a bullet for you to prove that, then that's what I'll do."

Before I could stop myself, I put my arms on his chest as he wraps his arms around my back. We share a soft kiss, and for a moment, there is nothing else in the world but us. No year of hell in Washington, no campaign, no politics, and no letter of acceptance to Harvard. Then I realize whose arms I am finding solace in.

"I can't do this, Blake," I say, pushing him away. I try to fight back the tears as I hurry past him. "I'm sorry!"

"Chelsea, wait!" I hear him say, but I don't turn back.

What the hell am I thinking? I rush off the bridge and onto the well-travelled dirt path back towards the parking area. I only slow my pace when I'm sure he's not chasing after me. The last thing I need in my life right now is all the complication that comes with any personal involvement with Blake. My God, what have I just done?

-FORTY-THREE-
SENATOR VIANO

There are few things more thrilling to the politically minded than a presidential election year. Between the contest for the Oval Office and the phenomenon that is the social media candidacies of over a hundred independents for the House, the media is so elated they have been doing cartwheels for weeks.

Now that we have finally reached Election Day, coverage is at a fever pitch. Networks are paying rapt attention to what the viewers want to see more of and are desperate to give it to them. Considering how tuned in the country is, the competition over who calls what races first will be as staunch as ever.

"Exit polls across the country are telling the story of this election. America is fed up with politics as usual in Washington," an analyst says from in front of a huge display of the United States, "and that is being felt in the ardent conservative and liberal districts where social media candidates are running. These exit polls indicate that many of these races will be decided with the final votes cast ..."

The knock on my hotel room door interrupts the trance the cable news coverage had me in. Probably for the best as it's almost time to head to Millfield.

"Blake?" I ask after answering the door. "This is a pleasant surprise. Come in." What the hell does he want? It's not like I wasn't planning on seeing him in an hour.

"Thanks," he says, entering my hotel room suite and looking around. "Where's Wonder Dog?"

"I assume you mean my superhero-infatuated former chief of staff. It's Election Day. He's handling his duties for his current boss. His absence has been noticed of late so he can't exactly skip out on holding his boss's hand as he loses an election."

"I suppose not."

"I'm just getting ready to head to the coffee shop. Something on your mind?" Not that I really care if something is or not, but he wouldn't be bothering me otherwise.

"Yeah, there is. What's your plan?" The question isn't bothering me so much as how he is asking it. While there is no way he could know with any certainty what is in store on this big night, I have to wonder what he's been able to deduce.

"My plan? What do you mean?" I reply, stalling and fishing for more information at the same time.

"Senator, I've known you my whole life. I grew up listening to you and your political adventures at the dinner table at Thanksgiving. You don't help people out of the kindness of your own heart. You are doing this for a purpose, and it's time you let me in on it."

Isn't that bold of him? I have toyed with the idea of looping him in, but I can't be sure whether I trust him yet or not.

"Okay, Blake, you've earned that much. I do like Michael Bennit, but you know what I think of the House of Representatives. There is a reason the Senate is known as the 'upper chamber.' Anyway, I will never get support as a traditional candidate again after the Democrats abandoned me. So, I want to run as the first icandidate in the Senate."

"I don't believe you," he says with a dismissive wave of his hand.

"I don't give a damn if you believe me or not. It's the truth and whether you accept it or not is your problem."

"You can run again any time you like, Aunt Marilyn. You have connections and financial resources and didn't have to help Bennit for that."

"I believe social media candidacies are the future of elections in the United States, but doesn't it makes sense for me to want an unassailable proof of concept that running as a virtual candidate can work? We have demonstrated the viability of running an election this way, regardless of tonight's results. Now I plan to march a new wave of icandidates into the Senate in two years," I lie. A convincing one, if I may say so myself, but a lie nonetheless. "And since when do you think you have the right to question my motives? That's pretty ballsy, even for you."

I can almost hear the gears turning in Blake's head. I have him back on his heels, questioning everything he thought he knew. There is an old adage that claims "the truth will set you free." It's a load of crap. In politics, the truth only gets you in trouble. Lies are much more convenient.

"If that were true, you would have told me from the beginning. No, there's more to it you're not letting me in on."

"You are your father's son, Blake." I pause, putting my coat on and thinking exactly how I want to put this. I still need him on my side. "You know, I loved my brother to death, but he could be a crazy ideologue when he wanted to be. Everything was about sacrifice and honor with him."

"You talk as if that's a bad thing."

"It is when it is both unappreciated and unreciprocated. Do you really think the people of this country give a damn about his sacrifice? About anyone's for that matter? Sure, they pay it lip service, but all anyone really cares about are themselves. They prove it day after day and election after election. It's why we are in the same place now that we were thirty years ago. Americans cannot be bothered."

"And you're any different?"

"No, I'm no different, with one major exception. I care enough to educate myself and am willing to make the tough decisions for them."

"You sound like a despot," he scoffs, clearly not buying my benevolent women of the people routine.

"You used to agree with me, remember? Why do you think you worshipped Beaumont once upon a time? I got you in the door with him because you were two peas in the same pod."

"Don't compare me with Winston Beaumont."

"Why? Does the truth hurt? You may be engaging in some revisionist history, but we all know the truth. That crisis of conscience you had was nothing more than weakness. You may pat yourself on the back for taking down a scoundrel, but you'll be remembered for your disloyalty and nothing more."

"How I am judged for my past actions isn't as important to me as how I want to be judged for my present ones," he says, sounding like a quote on morality. "I know you're up to something, and since you feel compelled not to include me, I'm going to assume it's not in Bennit's best interests. Or mine."

"Assume away, Blake. I don't require your approval or your counsel."

"No, but you do require the congressman's. If I think for a second you are working against him, I will do everything I can to freeze you out." That's an empty pledge coming from Blake. He doesn't hold any standing with Michael or his campaign staff, and I'm annoyed that he dare challenge me like this.

I was right when I made the decision not to loop him in. I almost caved after the debate and am sincerely happy I went with my gut and didn't. Blake's loyalty to Michael, his staff, and his combativeness towards me leads to another problem. I planned to include him at some point, but now the price is too high. Things have changed, blood is not always thicker than water, and I can't count on him being in my corner. I need to find a way to get him removed from the situation.

"I have been nothing but helpful to Michael, and I will continue to be long after you are nothing more than an afterthought. With all the challenges he faces, I am beginning to think you are a bigger problem for him than you think I am."

"Keep believing that, Aunt Marilyn. I'll be watching you." With that, Blake leaves the room, the door closing behind him.

"That's right, Blake, keep watching. Maybe you'll finally learn how it's really done in Washington," I say to myself once he's gone.

-FORTY-FOUR-
SPEAKER ALBRIGHT

"It's now seven p.m. and polls have closed in seven states. We have some projections both in the presidential race and the closely watched congressional races."

For the first time in my political career, I am more interested in the congressional races than who wins the presidency. The race to become the next president will come down to just a handful of swing states as usual. The Republicans still hold dominion over the South, Midwest, and Texas. The Dems still own the Pacific Northwest, New England states, New York, New Jersey, parts of the Rust Belt, and California. Per usual, the contest comes down to the voters in Pennsylvania, Ohio, Florida, and Virginia. I only half listen as the analysts on CNN drone on about precisely that.

My political career hangs on the ability of social media to get people to the polls. Watching the first Bennit campaign, the world saw what a capable social media candidacy could do. Not only did he reach people and establish a rapport with them, it became a motivated grassroots effort that showed up at the polls. But that was then and this is now. Now he's the iCongressman, and the question for tonight is whether he can spur the other independents running virtual campaigns to similar turnouts.

"There are seventeen independent candidates running in districts where polls are closed, and we are ready to announce some early results. In Georgia, we can proclaim Michael Garcia winner over the Republican incumbent. The other races there are too close to call. In South Carolina, it looks like Speaker of the House Johnston Albright will keep his seat, but two fellow incumbents have fallen. We project Independents Mickey Stevenson and Pamela Russell will claim the seats in districts that have been Republican held for a generation."

I listen as the anchor announces similar results in Kentucky and Indiana. This is a nightmare.

"The Democrats are also falling victim to the icandidates. We can now announce that five-term incumbent Geraldine Cantera from Vermont has lost her seat to Jeremy Penton. And in Virginia, Democrats Kenneth Michaud and Brett Gemmell, serving strong blue districts around Richmond, have also been defeated."

I wish I could take solace in knowing that any of those seats were vulnerable. They weren't. Had there not been independents running, the incumbents from both parties would have won easily.

Unfortunately, that's not the case, and it's all because of that damned Michael Bennit. How could one man create so much havoc with so much unmitigated regularity? Harvey was right—he was a threat. The only disagreement now was whether we needed to get rid of him or let political natural selection run its course.

"Mister Speaker?" my chief of staff asks after knocking and poking her head in the door. "They are ready for you in the ballroom, sir."

"Thanks, Elizabeth. I'll be right down." She nods and closes the door behind her.

I don't really feel like celebrating my own victory. I have now been elected to this seat seven times, and in the first six elections, could barely contain the excitement and enthusiasm bursting inside me. That's just not the case tonight.

"We are on the verge of a historic election night in America," I hear the politico say before I punch the power button on the remote.

It will be a historic election, all right, but for all the wrong reasons. I have watched the talking heads prattle on all night about just how seismic a change tonight's results will be in the House for the next Congress, and I am actually physically ill thinking about it.

I stare at the now dark television as if I were still watching it. I'm at a complete loss. I fancy myself as the type of leader that has all the answers. It is that prowess that got me elected by my party to lead them in the House of Representatives.

If they had only listened to me from the beginning, we wouldn't be in this mess. Bennit would be making his concession speech about now and I would be at the head of another wave election that propels Republicans to a large majority. Now ...

Bennit has survived everything that has been thrown at him since he entered politics. Winston Beaumont went after his staff to embarrass him and that backfired. He tried to mire the fledgling campaign in a scandal about an affair with a student, and that was enough for him to be reelected, but alienated Blake Peoni enough to present evidence to have him indicted.

So Michael Bennit made it to Washington after all, and survived two reprimands, two censures, and a vote to expel him. I did my part to end his influence, and now I am lucky to survive my own reelection as a result. The man is made of Teflon, and anyone who goes after him pays political consequences.

And that is the problem. The party will turn to me to find a way to limit his influence and power. The task is much harder than it was last summer once the final numbers come in and we find out how many independents were elected tonight. Scandals, ostracizing him, disciplining him … none of that will work now. The path is clear. Someone will need to get drastic in dealing with Michael Bennit if he's going to be stopped.

-FORTY-FIVE-
CHELSEA

The weather is mild for early November, meaning it was in the low sixties during the day and is only dropping to forty-eight degrees Fahrenheit tonight. It also means all the people crammed into the Perkfect Buzz is causing the shop to get stuffy.

I slip out the door and walk past the half dozen smokers who are calming their nerves by sucking down Marlboros. Since we decided against a ballroom again, the congressman asked Laura for permission to rent and erect a party tent in the parking lot. Other than a small pool of journalists and photographers allowed in the coffee shop, the rest of the media are set up there for what will hopefully be a victory speech. The tent is big enough to hold a small army, and the far end has a raised podium framed against the backdrop of the largest American flag I have ever seen. Not the most elaborate setup, but very Mister Bennit.

Wanting to be left alone and not accosted by the press, or by Vince who is canoodling with them, I head into the parking lot and away from the tent. I don't get far before Emilee catches up to me.

"You can only avoid him for so long," she says, stopping in front of me. Wait, what? I look around to see if anyone is planning on joining her, and am relieved when I realize she's alone.

"Don't worry, everyone is busy either chatting with volunteers or lighting up Twitter and Instagram. What's going on with you?"

"What do you mean?"

"Chels, we've been friends for a while now, so don't play dumb and expect to get away with it," she chides. "Why are you going out of your way to avoid Blake?"

"I didn't realize I was."

"Please. You've got me feeling like I'm back in high school. You look like a girl trying to avoid making eye contact with a weekend hook-up during study hall. So look at me and tell me why you're avoiding Blake or I'll start making stuff up."

As much as I don't want to tell her, I know she's already figuring it out. I am reluctant to open my mouth, and am sure the guilt is all over my face. That was all the confirmation she needed.

"Oh … my … God!" Emilee screeches, covering her mouth in shock.

"No, it's not that. We just kissed, I promise."

"Just kissed? Oh, Chelsea, please tell me you had some mouthwash with you for afterwards."

"Emilee—"

"Vince and Peyton are going to flip when they find out."

"Which is why they're *never* going to. It was a mistake, nothing more. Promise you won't say anything?"

"Say anything about what?" Kylie says from behind me. Damn it! Can't anyone get a moment alone around here? I can only guess how much she heard.

"Nothing. Girl stuff," I say, instantly regretting the lame response.

"Girl stuff, eh?" she says, looking down at her chest. "I'll try not to be insulted. This wouldn't have anything to do with you playing kissy face with Blake Peoni, would it?"

It's a cliché, but my jaw literally drops and hangs open. I'm stunned speechless. I try to say something, but the words get caught in my throat. My dirty little secret isn't much of a secret after all.

"How ... I mean ... you couldn't ..."

"Chelsea, I'm a journalist. Being observant comes with the territory. You might despise Blake, and hate being in the same room with him, but you've never avoided eye contact with him like you have tonight. It wasn't hard to hazard an educated guess as to why." I have a new found respect for Kylie's investigative powers.

"This isn't happening to me," I say, hanging my head in shame. If she knows, how long will it be before the congressman finds out, or the others for that matter?

"Don't sweat it, Chels. I tried to keep my crush on Michael a secret from the day I met him. It took months before I got the nerve to show him how I felt, and even longer before we made it public. Your secret is safe with me."

How can you not love Kylie Roberts? She's almost like the big sister I never had. Maybe she kind of regards me as a surrogate for the little sister she disowned and is now sitting in a jail cell for complicity in crimes committed by Winston Beaumont. Either way, it's nice she has my back.

"Thanks, but it's not the same. It was a mistake, and it won't happen again."

"Right. Keep telling yourself that," she says with a smile and a wink. "I actually came out to find you guys. It's getting close to eight o'clock and we are hoping they call our race quick once the polls in Connecticut close. C'mon."

* * *

"We are on the verge of a historic and unprecedented election night," the NBC anchor exclaims to the camera, "and I don't mean in the race for the presidency. While that race is a dead heat in the Electoral College, we are also watching what's happening in the congressional races across the country. All four hundred thirty-five seats are up for grabs, and some of the results are shocking.

"We have called the races in just a third of the contests, and we have already seen fifteen independent candidates defeat well-established incumbents from both parties. There were a total of a hundred ten independents running, with all but eight part of Connecticut Congressman Michael Bennit's effort to elect icandidates. Many of those races are still too close to call."

"Not this one!" someone shouts from the back of the coffee shop to the delight of everyone.

"As we approach the eight o'clock hour, polls will be closing in seventeen more states and we'll be able to update the tote board for at least some of the one hundred seventy-two electoral votes up for grab in them. We'll also have results in some key congressional races. One in particular is for the iCongressman Michael Bennit, whose resurgence in popularity is all the talk around America tonight as he leads this wildly successful surge of independents upsetting established candidates across the country."

Another cheer surges out of the crowd and I look around for the congressman, only to realize he isn't in the room. I look to Kylie who only mouths "Viano" to me. I am left with the eerie feeling that we are about to find out exactly what the cost for her help these last few months is going to be.

-FORTY-SIX-
SENATOR VIANO

"You've completely lost your mind, Senator," Michael says to me. I knew this would be a hard sell, but his reaction is a little more aggressive than I expected.

"Are you paying any attention at all to what is going on tonight? Do you understand the implications of what is happening?" I adamantly question. "We are on the verge of history. Dozens of independents are going to get elected tonight, and they are going to be looking at you to unite and lead them. This is your chance to step up."

"The very nature of being an independent is being free to represent your constituents without the undue influences of a political party and their ideology. That's what this movement is about."

"That's a naïve line of thinking. There's safety in numbers in politics. It's the reason why political parties came into existence in the first place."

"I don't need a history lesson, Senator. We spent the last couple of months convincing people to take a chance and vote for change. We called it a revolution, the definition of which is the forcible overthrow of a social order in favor of a new system. We are doing it at a ballot box in lieu of rioting in the streets. America has become impotent because of partisanship in Washington. Adding a third party does not rectify that, it exacerbates it."

"I didn't realize you considered this a revolution."

"Apparently you haven't been listening to Vince." Viva la revolución. Now I get it.

There were three truths about Michael Bennit I came to understand as I prepared myself for this discussion. The first is he can debate a topic with the best of them. Watching him dismantle Beaumont and Johnson is still a YouTube favorite two years later, and makes *The Daily Show* highlight reel whenever the topic of inept politicians comes up. The second is he is incredibly stubborn when his principles are being compromised. The third, and most important, is to win any argument with him, you have to appeal to his sense of duty.

"Independents won't stay that way for long. Sooner or later they will be swayed to toe the line with one of the parties, unless they have a strong figurehead to guide them. Americans are giving you this opportunity to do just that. You served your nation as a Green Beret, and now your country needs you again, Michael. They need you to serve and to lead. To complete the mission they are voting to set you on tonight."

I watch as he squints at me, and at least for a moment, I think I may be getting through to him. So much rides on this moment. I have rehearsed this conversation time after time, and convinced myself that I could bring him along to my line of thinking. It will make everything go much smoother for me if he does.

"I see your point," he says, causing a smile to creep across my lips. Yes!

"I'm glad we could come to an agreement," I say with barely controlled enthusiasm. "A new political party under your leadership will be a powerful force in national politics."

"Do you know what the Spanish-American War and the Vietnam War have in common?"

"No, but I think I'm about to be treated to one of your history lessons." He smiles, but the surging enthusiasm from moments ago is tempered by the thought of one of his boring lectures.

"In 1898, the Democratic Party and a cabal of industrialists were pushing for American intervention in the Cuban revolution against Spain. When the U.S.S. Maine mysteriously exploded and sank in Havana Harbor, they got the war they wanted.

"Similar circumstances existed in the Gulf of Tonkin when the U.S.S. Maddox engaged several North Vietnamese attack boats. A second incident supposedly occurred two days later that compelled President Johnson and Congress to take a more active role in Southeast Asia. We both know how that turned out."

"Is there a point to all this?" I ask impatiently. History is for fools because it has no apparent relevance to the present. Only sentimentalists care about such trivial things.

"You saw my first campaign as the country's first icandidate as an opportunity. You helped create a conflict with the Republicans and Democrats by helping me assemble a coalition of independents to run against them. Now you are using their impending success tonight as your U.S.S. Maine and Gulf of Tonkin Incident to advance an agenda.

"I may not know what your scheme is, but I know enough to not go along with it. I appreciate the support you have given me and the icandidates this fall, but there is no quid pro quo on this. If you were ever left with the impression there was, you are greatly mistaken."

"Michael, I think you have completely misinterpreted my intentions," I say defensively. The denial was a reflex, because I didn't expect him to blindside me like this.

"No, I don't think I am. For the first time, I think I'm finally starting to understand them."

Screw this, the time for niceties are over. He needs to know who he's dealing with.

"You don't want to make an enemy out of me," I say in my best menacing tone. He matches my hard glare and doesn't back away one inch.

"You're right, I don't, but will if I have to. A third party is the wrong course and I won't be manipulated or bullied into taking it."

Michael looks at his watch and then back at the coffeehouse. It must be after eight now, because I sense this conversation is over.

"You're not the man I thought you were."

"I guess not, assuming you thought you could push me into this against my will. You're correct about one other thing, too. Americans need a leader they can count on to make the tough decisions and act in their best interests regardless of the ramifications. Unfortunately for you, they've found him."

"So you've made your final decision? How unfortunate for you. All you've done is make an enemy tonight."

"If that's your attitude, Marilyn, then I'm not sure you were ever a friend to begin with." He used my first name for the first time ever. It is a subtle, yet telling shift in the dynamic of our relationship. "And yes, I have made my decision, and there's no level of deceit, manipulation, or treachery you or anybody else can use that will change my mind."

With those final words, Michael heads back in the direction of the Perkfect Buzz. There is no need for me to follow—I'm no longer welcome there after this conversation. As I watch him walk away, I can only lament that he was a tougher nut to crack than I thought he'd be.

"No level of deceit, eh?" I mutter to myself. "We'll just have to see about that."

-FORTY-SEVEN-
MICHAEL

I sneak back into the coffeehouse and am greeted by guests mired in an eerie silence punctuated only by the occasional tense verbal ticks. I was beginning to think they announced I lost when Kylie finds me.

"They are getting close to calling our race," she whispers urgently. "Where were you?"

"Around back making out with Marilyn Viano. Sorry."

"Ew, that's just gross," she replies with a grimace. "If you're going to better deal me, it better be for a Victoria's Secret model. I have an ego to stroke. Seriously, I know that look you're wearing. What's going on?"

"We've got a problem, but I'll tell you about it later."

We move up closer to the giant plasma television Laura has mounted to the wall to listen in on the coverage. The channel selection has rotated through Fox News, CNN, and ABC over the past few hours, and has now settled on NBC for the final announcement. During presidential election years, electoral vote tallies trump everything. Americans want to know who the next chief executive is going to be. This is definitely not most years.

"Polls are now closed in many of the New England states, New Jersey and the ever-important swing states of Florida and Pennsylvania, and we have some races to update you on," the anchor comments into the camera. "Before we get to the electoral numbers, let's look at a couple of key congressional races where independents are making historic gains."

For the next several minutes, we watch contest after contest get called in surrounding states. Of the races that featured an icandidate, we won two of three. There are a great many that are still undecided, the analysis being the margin of victory in those races will be razor thin. I know how that feels—I lost by less than a hundred votes two years ago.

"C'mon, get to ours!" Vince shouts. He's not known for his patience.

"Let's go!" another voice chimes in until the crowd sharing the room with us begin shouting at and taunting the television. I can barely hear now over the cackle.

"Shhhhh! Quiet down everybody!" the usually reserved Brian chastises from in front of me.

"And now, we turn our attention to the Connecticut Sixth District and the race of the man who has helped lead this surge of icandidates tonight," the anchor says.

The graphic on the television first zooms onto Connecticut, and then our odd shaped district colored yellow is a sea of blue meant to represent the political affiliation of the incumbent. A set of three graphics pops up featuring the Republican in a red square, the Democrat in blue, and me in the yellow. Maybe I should have started a third party just to get that color changed. I hate yellow.

"They love to drag this out, don't they?" Chelsea rhetorically asks from next to me. She's not quite the bundle of nerves she was last year. None of us are.

"This contest went late into the night two years ago, but we can call it early tonight. After seeing an approval rating that dipped well below fifty percent, Michael Bennit has rebounded to retain his seat in a convincing win ..."

The rest of the announcement is drowned out by the thunderous cheer erupting from the gathering at the Buzz. It is the first time we've gotten to celebrate the result on an election night. Two years ago was a very different emotion, and the special election in the spring, although a convincing win, lacked any of the dramatic coverage you see when the entire nation goes to the polls in November.

I gladly accept all the handshakes and hugs from all the people around me who worked so hard. The victory is equally sweet for my staff, especially the ones at college who seemed desperate to get caught up in the moment once again. But for as happy as I am, something dark is nagging at me and I can't seem to get it out of my mind, no matter how hard I try to tamp it down.

* * *

"I don't know about you guys, but I'm completely smoked," Xavier says, crashing awkwardly into one of the plush chairs tucked into the corner of the coffeehouse.

"I wasn't this tired cramming for final exams last year," Peyton says, sprawled out in her own chair.

"You guys do this every day?" Emilee asks Chelsea and Vince.

"Yeah, sorta. Although life in D.C. isn't nearly as intense as an election day is."

"C'mon, guys, you're in college. You can't tell me you aren't used to nights a lot later than this," Vince challenges.

"Yeah, but most of those involved a drink in my hand," Amanda states.

"La, la-la, la-la," I sing out with my fingers plugged into my ears. My avoidance is less the fact that they aren't legal, but more because I still think of them as my students.

"Nice victory speech tonight, Congressman," Vince says. "You struck the perfect tone." The others all chime in with their agreement.

"Thank you, all," I say with a playful bow. At that moment, Brian and Vanessa return from the other side of the shop. I may be tired of staring at the TV, but that doesn't apply to them. "What's the word, guys?"

"You can tell the network news guys are tired. They're getting increasingly cranky," Brian opines. "Ohio went blue, as did Florida. Looks like the Democrats will win the White House."

"A surprise, but that only makes the majority in the House that much more important to the GOP."

"There are going to be at least a dozen recounts, and they have only called ninety-five of our hundred races, outside of you and Congressman Reyes."

"And?" I ask. Having to pose for pictures and shake the hands of a few hundred people tonight, I am a little out of the loop as to what is happening nationwide.

"And if nothing changes, it looks like seventy-seven of the icandidates upset forty-five Republicans and thirty-two Democrats for seats."

Everyone in the room erupts in applause, including an exhausted Laura who is still cleaning up behind the coffee bar. It is an amazing accomplishment, and not hard to understand why the media was making such a big deal about it tonight.

"I have a question, Congressman."

"Shoot."

"Why were you getting questions about a third party after your address?" Vince asks.

"I thought it was just me! I got, like, five questions about it," Peyton adds.

"Nope, I got three myself," Vanessa points out.

"I got two," Xavier stammers, half asleep in his chair.

"So did I," Amanda murmurs, now seated on the floor and rubbing her temples.

"And now we know why," Kylie chimes in after Laura lets her and Blake in the front door and then locks it behind her. "The press was expecting to hear about the eventuality of forming a third party. Naturally, they were curious why they didn't. I can't imagine where they got the idea from."

"I'll give you three guess, but you'll only need one."

"Senator Viano," Chelsea answers just to keep everyone on the same page. Blake sits on the table next to her, prompting her to get up and choose another seat without looking at him.

I have no idea what that's about, but I hope Kylie fills me in on whatever drama is brewing between them now.

"Explains why she spent so much time in the tent tonight," Vince laments.

"Why would she want to form another political party?" Brian asks, just verbalizing what everyone in the room is wondering.

"Yeah, is there something I'm missing here?" Peyton poses, looking around for help.

"What aren't you telling us, Mister B?" Time to come clean.

"Senator Viano approached me right before they announced our win to convince me to unite the independents under the banner of a new party."

I expected everyone to be a little more shocked, but nobody shows more than token surprise. I anticipated something like this from Viano, and so did Kylie, but the fact everyone else did as well shows how little trust she earned with the group. All eyes turn to Blake, some out of curiosity and others flashing contempt.

"Got something you want to tell us, there, buddy?" Vince asks in a threatening tone. There is no love lost between those two.

Blake launches into a narrative of his suspicions and the story she told him when he confronted her in the hotel room tonight. His explanation is sound, but most of my college-aged staff isn't impressed. I'm not sure if I am either.

"You believe *her*?" the quietest and most sensitive to betrayal amongst us questions.

"No, Emilee, not for a second. Viano is nothing if not an opportunist. She has something up her sleeve so sensitive she won't share it with me."

"More importantly, why should we believe *you*?" Amanda asks in the most disdained way possible.

"You don't have a good track record in the honesty department, Blake," Peyton chimes in.

"You're the one working for her. This could just be a part of her ruse," Brian concludes.

"I wish I could give you all a convincing reason to believe me," Blake says in his defense, "but I know I can't. I'm not going to ask you to trust me. All I can tell you is everything I said is one hundred percent true. Whether you believe me or not is entirely up to you."

"That's an easy decision," Vince states.

"Why do we really care about Viano?" Amanda asks, trying to figure out the relevance after a few awkward seconds tick by.

"For one thing, it's about to become the next big story. If she laid groundwork for this in the media, they are going to wonder why we are changing our minds."

"It's bigger than that, Kylie," Blake corrects. "I just did some rough math in my head. Vanessa, you said there were forty-five Republicans and thirty-two Democrats losing their seats, right?"

"Yeah, why?

I do some quick math of my own. "Oh, crap."

"What?" Chelsea asks, finally saying something with Blake in the room. He looks at her, and then the rest of the group.

"Subtract that from the current balance of power and you get seventy-nine Independents …"

"One hundred seventy-eight Republicans and …" A shiver of dread creeps up my spine.

"One-hundred seventy-eight Democrats," the love of my life finishes.

"A tie?" several of the staff say at once.

"I didn't think that was even possible," Amanda states.

"In a traditional two-party system, it isn't," Kylie responds. "Add even one independent into the mix and the odd number of representatives no longer matters."

"What are the odds of there ever being a tie?" Emilee posits.

"I think there's a better chance of getting struck by lightning on the way to claim a Powerball jackpot at high tide, during a full moon, when Mercury is in retrograde."

"You know the media is going to go bonkers over this if it holds up," Vince correctly surmises.

"What does that mean for us?"

I lean back in the chair to let this new found knowledge sink in. In my wildest dreams I never imagined something like this would happen. Assuming the results stay this way after all the recounts and lawsuits. There will be no shortage of those, given this new political reality.

"Did I ever tell you guys about the kid who couldn't add?" I ask, honestly forgetting what I have and have not told them over the years since we shared a classroom together.

"Oh, God. Here comes today's history lesson," Vince deadpans to the rest of the group.

"Math teachers love to inspire their students by telling the tale of this eccentric German kid who could never manage to do well on his exams. They rant and rave that he was clueless, and if he could learn to do it, so could they. Any guesses who I am talking about?"

"Albert Einstein," Brian answers, probably having heard the story before.

"Gold star for you, Bri."

"So that wasn't the truth?" Peyton asks, disappointed. She may have been one of the students the math teachers were trying to encourage.

"Not even close. Einstein was a mathematical prodigy, and better at calculus at age twelve than we will ever be. He believed school was holding him back, and was so advanced that he probably should have been teaching the class."

"So who started the lie?"

"A 1935 article in *Ripley's Believe It or Not!* is widely considered the source, but that's not the point."

"They made it up? Crap, I knew I shouldn't have used them as a source in my last essay," Xavier laments. I seriously hope he's kidding.

"How does this possibly relate to us and a tie in the House?" Amanda asks, still massaging her temples.

"We're the new Einstein. Everybody thought we couldn't play the political game, but are now figuring out that we're more of a threat than they ever imagined. We're now the brightest blip on the radar of some very powerful people who stand to lose a lot of influence and money because of what we helped pull off tonight."

I think back to our conversation with Nyguen a few days ago and wonder what's going through his head now. If he believed we might be a target then, what would he say about creating a power vacuum in the House? When contemplating the fallout of our little revolution, this would have been at the end of my list of possible consequences.

I meet Kylie's eyes and don't like what I see—fear. My job is to protect her and make her feel safe. What I see is the opposite. I see the love of my life terrified at the possibility that anything Terry Nyguen said would come true. We can handle scandals and smear campaigns, but once he introduced the element of physical danger, Kylie started to become unhinged.

"The stakes have gone way up from once upon a time when we only wanted to beat the incumbent congressman from our district. I need you guys to be vigilant about what you are doing in school. Be careful who you get close to, what you post on social media, and where you go. Most of all, watch each other's back."

"Do you think they could come after us?" Peyton says with a hint of concern. Considering she was one of Beaumont's targets during the first campaign, it would figure she would be most sensitive to a possible repeat of that trauma.

I am purposely watering down this warning, and Chelsea and Kylie both know it. Scaring them is counterproductive, and we don't really have any concrete information. I value honesty and integrity, but I also value not terrifying my staff without good reason to do so.

"I don't know, Peyton. The game has changed. Getting some independents elected is bad enough, but having no majority party creates a whole new set of problems. Both parties will go nuts trying to get a majority, and I don't need a Magic 8-Ball to tell me it's a real possibility if they get desperate enough."

"But why us?" Vanessa asks. Kylie glances at me and then handles the answer to the question exactly like she thinks the political elites will. It is also the reason why she may be more fearful than ever.

"Because you guys led the movement that just broke the U.S. House of Representatives."

PART III

FORMING A MORE PERFECT UNION

-FORTY-EIGHT-
SPEAKER ALBRIGHT

My conference room on the second floor of the Capitol offers a view of the Mall from its three windows as majestic as the one from my office. Under these vaulted ceilings, and classically designed walls with ornate gilded moldings, is the only place I can get a moment of peace since legislators have begun to reassemble for the lame duck session.

Nothing substantial usually happens during the last session of the year. It's only been a week since the election, and congressmen who have lost their seat are not eager to vote on bills after being cast out by the people in their districts. And for this particular session, there have been a lot of casualties. The seismic shift of political success has left us with an untenable situation.

There is a loud series of raps at the door before it opens, and my most important appointment of the day enters. I have been engaged in meeting after meeting since the moment I set foot back in town. The capital is in an uproar over the results of the election, and honestly, even I'm stunned at the result. Lawsuits are pending in states across the country, and the media is going crazy with their coverage to cash in on the drama. In the end, I don't think it will matter. Despite the legal maneuvering and pressure being applied, the result will be the same, and we have to figure out how to handle the consequences.

"Come on in and have a seat," I say, pointing to the large, twenty-five-foot-long mahogany table. "I'm glad you decided to accept my invitation."

"I was a little surprised to get it, Mister Speaker," Blake Peoni says, taking his seat at one of the high-backed chairs surrounding the table.

He's probably not as surprised to receive it as I was in needing to send it. In my dealings with James Reed, I came across some information that Blake worked as a minor functionary for the Ibram & Reed firm. That in itself is unimportant until you consider he moonlights as a liaison between Marilyn Viano and Michael Bennit. A strange relationship considering Reed is so bent on removing Bennit. Politics may make strange bedfellows, but this is the equivalent of Yankee fans rooting for the Red Sox to win the World Series.

"Things are pretty sensitive down here in Washington. I honestly almost decided not to send this invite."

"I almost didn't accept it," Blake says glibly. "What can I help you with, Mister Speaker?" The direct approach. I can work with that.

"I need a question answered. Does Michael Bennit know who your current employer is?"

Blake grasps the small triangular pin on his lapel. It looks like something military, but it is not a unit I'm familiar with.

Either way, he somewhat unconsciously straightens it and says nothing.

"I didn't think so. I find it odd that you would be working for a man like James Reed while working with Marilyn Viano to support the Bennit campaign."

"Mister Speaker, I'm not sure where you're going with this, but I don't like it. I don't owe you any explanations, so make your point or I'm out of here."

"No need to get defensive, Blake, I'm not playing games with you. This isn't an attempt to blackmail you or manipulate you in any way. The way I see it, you're between a rock and a hard place."

"What makes you say that?"

"Marilyn Viano and James Reed are like oil and water. They are supporting different goals, yet you are working for both. Sooner or later, something has to give. It's like playing in the middle of a busy street—you risk getting hit from traffic in both directions."

Blake says nothing, apparently trying to figure out how much I know. After a few moments of awkward silence, he finally says something of interest.

"If you're trying to figure out where my loyalty lies, the answer is neither," he says with hardness in both his voice and eyes. The response surprises me, although I doubt he's telling me the truth. "My loyalty lies with Bennit."

"Michael Bennit. Washington D.C.'s own caped crusader," I muse. "I know all about your history with him. You ran quite the smear campaign for Winston Beaumont before he got issued an orange jumpsuit. Do you think Bennit is ever going to trust you, especially after you finally tell him who your current employer is? Believe me, he won't."

"Don't be so sure, Mister Speaker."

I get out of my chair and move over to one of the windows facing out on the Mall. It's a gray day, matching the mood in this town. Tourists mingle between the monuments and museums of The Smithsonian, oblivious to the atmosphere in the Capitol they helped create on Election Day.

To a lesser extent, Blake is too. Michael Bennit may have meant well with his push to get independents elected, but the result is a crisis never before seen in the lower chamber. The U.S. House of Representatives is set up to work in a two-party system. It requires a minority and majority party to function and an influx of representatives with no party affiliation upsets the balance of power. A third party coming into existence, as the rumors spreading like wildfire around town have been speculating, is a bad dream. Having no majority party and no consensus on a Speaker is a certifiable nightmare.

I think back to the file Reed handed me before the election. It's the nuclear option, but I think it's the only one I'm going to be left with, and I'm going to need a strong player to get it passed.

"After everything that happened between you and Bennit, you still think he trusts you?" I turn and face him. "Does his staff?" That strikes a nerve with him.

"We have a history, yes, but I'm not going to give any of them a reason not to trust me moving forward. Ever."

"I understand, and that is admirable. Let me ask you an unrelated question. Both parties are going to do whatever it takes to sway the icandidates to their side. Do you think any of them will?"

"No, I highly doubt it," he answers gruffly.

"I don't either," I say with a forced grin. Under any other circumstances I would never say that, but I'm guessing the new crop of icongressmen will be last people either the GOP or Democrats can persuade, at least in the short term.

"So we're going to have a major problem in January unless we do something about it now. And if I'm right, when this thing finally blows up, Bennit is going to be under all kinds of pressure I don't think he's prepared to handle. Push is going to come to shove in this town, and when it does, is Michael Bennit going to be turning to you for help?"

I let that question hang in the air for a moment for Blake to ponder. He has to know he will never get in Michael Bennit's good graces. Even if he did, nobody in that camp would ever trust him. Time to play my hand.

"You are going to be the one on the outside looking in. Unless ..." I cast my baited hook in the water to see if he bites.

"Unless what?" Bingo.

"Unless you help me fix it. Blake, I'm not here to threaten you, or milk you for information. We are heading into a very turbulent time for this government and I want your help getting us through it. I'm here to offer you a job. I want you come to work for me."

-FORTY-NINE-
CHELSEA

I'm twenty years old and officially tired of watching the news. Since the election, it has been nonstop coverage of what they are billing as "The House in Crisis." It's a ridiculous notion, since the government isn't going to collapse because there's no majority party.

Not that the media sensationalizing things should be a surprise to anyone. From idiot weathermen reporting three inches of snow as if it were a blizzard, to the over-hyped birth of a royal baby in England, you can always count on the media to blow things out of proportion. Yet, we all tune in, so maybe it's really us who should take the blame.

"There has to be all kinds of dealings going on all over town and with the host of independents who just got elected. What are the odds that one or more of them can be swayed to join a party and end the gridlock?" the moderator asks another panel of "experts."

"I think it's very likely. Washington operates on promises and back room deals—"

"No, no, no, no, no," another panelist interrupts. "Haven't you been paying attention at all to this icandidate movement? The men and women who got elected by running inexpensive, social media campaigns are not going to even engage in discussions over it! Their allegiance is to Michael Bennit, and they will not—"

I hit the power button on the remote. I've hit my limit of nonsensical political analysis for the day. The congressman says even he would be surprised if all of the icandidates who won remain loyal. There are too many carrots and even a few sticks both parties will wield to entice them to the dark side of the force.

I grab my coat and let everyone know I am leaving the office for the evening. It may be the first time I will be home before nine p.m. since I started this job. I make my way down to the lobby, happy that the day is behind me.

"Chelsea, wait up!" I hear as several sets of shoes cause a clatter that echoes off the walls. Okay, maybe not.

Rushing up to greet me are the Three Amigos, Chris and the other two whose names I still can't remember. I think for a fleeting second that I need to correct that, and then I remember that I don't plan on being here much longer.

"You got a quick minute to talk?" one of them asks.

"Not really," I say, still trying to preserve my hasty exit home.

"Trust me, we will make this worth your while."

"All right, what can I do for you?"

"Not here," he states, beckoning me to follow him down the hall before ducking into one of the twenty-three committee rooms located in the building.

"Okay, this is a little creepy," I relay, more to make them uncomfortable than any fear I might feel being alone in a room with three men.

"We have some information for you that we would like to exchange for a favor," the Second Amigo says, ignoring my comment.

"I've learned the hard way not to make arrangements like that blind," I state defiantly. "You want to play strip poker, you are going to have to take your clothes off first and we'll take it from there."

Not the best metaphor I could have come up with. The three men look at each other while my impatience grows. The only thing worse than annoying a redhead is keeping one waiting.

"You're getting good at this game, Miss Stanton," Amigo Three says.

"We've heard rumors that there's a bill getting vetted by the OLC."

The Office of Legislative Counsel is an obscure institution responsible for the language of new legislation introduced to the House. Please tell me they are not keeping me from a rare dinner at home for a piece of useless information. "Okay ... that happens all the time. Get to the point."

"We heard the drafted bill is a rules change forcing all of the independents elected to the House to declare allegiance to the caucus of a political party."

I'm floored. That has to be the most ridiculous thing I have ever heard. Aside from it being questionable constitutionally, why would either party head down a path that would earn them the ire and wrath of the American people?

"We know what you're thinking, because we thought it too. So we checked around and found the staff members who wrote the bill. It came from the Speaker's office."

That bit of info from Amigo One, a.k.a. Chris, is even more stunning. Almost all of the leg work of drafting bills and negotiating the final form of proposed legislation is done by staff. Representatives to Congress rarely do the dirty work of writing bills themselves anymore. If the Three Amigos are to be trusted, then confirmation from staff members is all the proof I need that something is afoot.

"We're not asking you to take our word for it. You can check up on it on your own. We just wanted to point you in the right direction."

"Okay. What is it you want in return?" The three of them look at each other again. Do they share a brain or something? Just spit it out already.

"We've heard the assertions and counter-assertions about Bennit forming a third party around the ... What are we calling the icandidates now?"

"The icongressmen," Amigo Three answers.

"Right. The latest rumors are Bennit will form it with sole purpose of working to bring consensus to the chamber and get things done. True or false?"

"I hate to disappoint you guys, but we have never had any intention of forming a third party. Sorry."

"Is that the truth? Seriously, it's important you level with us," the Third Amigo pleads.

The talk about this new party stuff is making me nauseous. When I see Senator Viano again, it will take every ounce of willpower to tamp down my redheaded tendencies and not wrap my hands around her throat to squeeze the life out of her. I want to smile at the thought of that, but with these guys, it will convey the wrong message.

"It's the truth, cross my heart. Now, tell me why it matters."

"Our bosses are ... interested in finding a way to work with Bennit."

"You know, you said that to me once before and came up with all sorts of excuses as to why you couldn't. So tell me, what the hell does that mean?" The temper is starting to come out, causing the Three Amigos to put their heads on a swivel looking at each other again. "Will you guys stop friggin' looking at each other and just ... out with it! My God, does everything in this town have to be mysterious? I'm tired, hungry, and want to go home."

"If you were interested in forming a third party, or something along those lines, our bosses would consider joining."

"You're saying you would leave your parties?"

"Under the right circumstances, yes, that's exactly what we're saying," Amigo Two clarifies.

"And we're not the only ones who think that way," Chris adds.

"I think you could compel a lot of moderates to join your cause." That was from the last remaining Amigo. It's like trying to have a conversation with a set of stereo speakers.

"I will relay that to the boss."

"Thank you, Chelsea. Keep us in the loop."

I start to walk away and then stop. "Guys, don't take this the wrong way, but what the hell are your names?"

"I'm Chris," Amigo One says.

"I knew yours."

"Then ours should be easy enough to remember. I'm Chris as well, and so is he," Amigo Three says with a smirk.

"Three guys named Chris. I should have known." I think I will stick with Amigo One, Two, and Three.

We say our good-byes, exit the committee room, and head our separate ways. They have given me a lot to think about, and I know my dream of calling it an early night is now vanquished. I head back up to the office to tell the congressman what I learned, knowing tomorrow is going to bring a scramble to find out just who our friends and enemies actually are.

FIFTY

SENATOR VIANO

Breakfast is my favorite meal of the day. With my husband gone almost all the time, it is the only couple of hours where I'm not bothered. Except, of course, when Michael Bennit takes it upon himself to sit in the seat across from me.

"I don't remember inviting you to sit down," I say smugly.

"And I don't remember either asking or giving a shit," he responds in kind. I dab the corners of my mouth with a napkin, half tempted to get up and leave him with the check.

"Just don't flip the table until I'm finished eating. How did you find me?"

"Turned out to be easier than trying to pronounce the name of this place," he quips, ordering a coffee when the waiter comes by.

La Chambre aux Oiseaux didn't seem that complicated to say, but then again, Michael Bennit is a bit of a Neanderthal. For those who failed high school French, it translates to The House of Birds and has been my favorite eatery for more than a decade now. Not only is it close to where I live in Old Town Alexandria, but the food is beyond reproach.

"At least you showed up without a trail of reporters."

"I managed to lose the paparazzi on the way out of town. How long have you known about the resolution?"

"Which one?" Best to remain coy and find out how much he knows.

"I didn't realize we were seated at the kids' table, Marilyn. Maybe we should move this meeting to a McDonald's PlayPlace so you can feel more at home—"

"Did you expect this Congress to stand idly by while you threaten the way they've done business for decades?" I interrupt, getting the point. I already know what he's talking about. "Lobbyists are going crazy and are pushing our current crop of legislators to regain control of the situation. You are removing money from the political equation, and it is making them very nervous."

"You're telling me lobbyists are behind this?" Oops, time to back track a little. I need to keep my composure and watch my tongue.

"No, I'm telling you they are prodding the parties to go in the direction the leadership was already heading. Independents are loose cannons most fear will disrupt the operation of the House. To limit the upheaval in political order, they will force you all to caucus with a political party."

Most of America would have no idea what I just said, nor would they care. The inner workings of Congress are of little interest to the public, and this will be no different. The citizens of this country elected Michael and his misfit toys to do a job and don't want to hear excuses as to why they can't do it. There is no way the majority of the population would understand that the independents are being sabotaged before even starting.

"They have to know we might form our own party and caucus because of this. Our current winner-takes-all approach to elections in this country doesn't work well with a three-party structure, and its creation will lead to instability like you see in Europe's parliamentary systems. It makes no sense that they would push for this."

"You've publically stated you won't form a third party."

"And if I do, now they can paint me as a liar and deceiver," he says, finally figuring out a part of the game.

"Now you get it," I condescendingly affirm.

"They're playing with a live hand grenade. It's still a possibility. Forcing us to join a caucus—"

"Join *their* caucuses, Michael, not caucus with a third party."

"Thus eliminating the havoc created by having no majority party in the House and reestablishing the system in place that makes committee assignments, selects the Speaker, et cetera, et cetera, et cetera."

"Precisely."

"That's why you were pushing for this on Election Night. You knew it would come to this."

I take a long sip of my own coffee as the waiter arrives with his. Maybe this meeting is more beneficial than I thought. I long assumed I could not sway Michael over to my line of thinking, but perhaps I misread him again.

"People are running around Capitol Hill like it is raining razor blades. What do you think their next step is?" he inquires.

"They need to pass this during the lame duck session. The votes of the outgoing members are key, and providing cover for those lucky enough to get reelected is a top priority. On occasion, the House will pass rules that take effect for the next Congress. This is one of those moments. They'll announce the new resolution on the Sunday morning talk show circuit— *Meet the Press, Face the Nation, This Week, Fox News Sunday ...*"

"So I need to talk to the independents by then and get them on board for our own party."

"That would be my line of thinking. The rules bill is going to pass—there will be enormous pressure put on the members to vote yes. If you form a third party the day it's signed, you undermine their efforts—"

"Leaving them all the political downside without any of the upside." Wow, he actually gets it.

Michael regards me after draining the rest of his cup of coffee. I will never understand the allure of being a caffeine junkie. I can almost see his mind in overdrive trying to process what I told him, looking for flaws in the plan. There are none. Everything is working just like I originally hoped it would. Maybe I should have approached him far earlier in the process instead of trying to ambush him on the night of the election. Perhaps all he needed was a chance to get used to the idea.

"Who would run this new party?"

"We would," I respond, leaning forward in my seat. "You from the House and me when I announce a Senate run next year using the same template in the midterm elections. If we can command sizable numbers in both houses of Congress, we will have succeeded in forming the third party Americans are desperately calling for."

Michael spends a few moments thinking about what I said while the waiter refills his coffee. One thing I love about this restaurant is that the service is impeccable. Once the cup is brimming with steaming java and the waiter moves off, he brings up the subject I was wondering if I would hear.

"We've been getting a lot of threats lately."

"You're a congressman. Threats come with the territory. I used to get them myself. I'm sure you've received some before today."

"Not this many."

"You're a national figure now. Even more than you were when you were the iCandidate. Are these cyber threats or letters?"

"Both, but a lot more letters. It feels almost ... planned."

"I'm assuming you're smart enough to bring these concerns to the proper authorities."

"Of course. They haven't gotten anywhere with their investigation yet." Part of me would be surprised if they did. If a threat is not immediately determined to be credible or imminent, things move remarkably slowly.

"Maybe someone thinks they can intimidate you. Independents by definition are not united and make easy targets."

"You don't think that lone crazies are just coming out of the woodwork?"

"I have no idea, but look at the timing. It would be pretty damn coincidental."

Michael is one of those rare leaders who thinks about others before himself. A trait he picked up during his military service, no doubt. I am certain this line of questioning is out of concern for his staff more than himself.

"Do you think creating a third party will make it stop?" I exhale, taking a moment to look like I am thinking of an answer.

"If they are mentally unstable people looking to make the six o'clock news, no, the threat's won't stop. If it's a planned effort by some groups to influence your vote, then it will. There is strength in numbers, especially in national politics."

"Okay," he says, finishing the rest of his second cup of coffee before getting up out of his seat. I've never met a man more fond of caffeine. "Thanks for the coffee. I'll be in touch."

"No problem. I'm here to help if you need me. We'll chat soon."

I can only smile to myself as he walks away.

-FIFTY-ONE-
MICHAEL

"He should be here any minute," I hear Chelsea say from my office as I pass by the other staff outside my door.

"He's here now," I say with a smile, crossing through the open door into my office with Cisco right behind me. Fresh off a landslide victory for the ages in his Texas district, he's eager to mix it up. I notice Amanda, Emilee, Peyton, and Brian are all present on the Skype session connected from a laptop to the big screen television on the wall. "Is X going to join?"

"He's got an away game tonight and is in transit. I briefed him on what's going on before he left. He sends his best."

"Who's he playing, Chels?"

"UNC." Oh, that's going to be a good game.

I give the love of my life a kiss. It may be the middle of a workday with media sharks chummed into a feeding frenzy, but Kylie still made it here to this meeting. I know she is still having problems adapting to her role as an investigative journalist with the *Post*, but her being here shows how fed up with her job she is. She wants to get in on the action.

"Before we start, I have a question," Amanda says over our videoconference. "Why are they going to this extreme? I mean, it doesn't make any sense to me to force people in Congress into a political party's caucus."

"This is the most backward thinking organization in the history of the world," Cisco remarks, starting the explanation. "I'm surprised they face forward when they walk. So when Congress tries something dramatic and unexpected, fear is always the default explanation."

"To answer the second part," I continue, "although there's nothing in the Constitution that specifies it, a two-party system emerged in this country. How we elect our representatives in a winner-take-all format historically has protected that reality, and how we govern is dependent on it."

"Congress is set up based on a system of a majority and minority party," Kylie clarifies to the group. "The majority party elects the Speaker of the House who theoretically sets the legislative agenda—"

"And is third in line to the presidency should something happen to the president and vice-president," Chelsea interrupts.

"Correct, but it's even deeper than that. The majority sets the House rules through a very important committee. This Rules Committee is effectively controlled by the leadership of both parties, and since they appoint the members, they can replace anyone who is disloyal."

"And if the independents form a new party?" Brian asks.

"They are counting on the fact that we won't. Or at least some of us won't join one and just elect to remain independent and caucus with the Republicans or Democrats.

If they siphon off enough off our numbers, we face the same problem we had when it was just Cisco and me."

"This is giving me a headache," Vanessa says, rubbing her temple. "Is this even constitutional?"

"I doubt it," Cisco says. "But it doesn't matter. It's a House rules issue, so the courts won't intervene. They have no business telling us how to conduct our business. Even if they wanted to for some reason, it would take forever to decide even if it went straight to the Supreme Court. We elect the Speaker of the House on January third. There would be no time to undo the damage."

"So you're saying the Republicrats are going to succeed in making every one of our icandidates choose a side, knowing many of them will resent becoming a part of the system they campaigned against." Emilee is taking this very personally. We use the term "Republicrats" when we speak derisively about both parties. It gets used a lot.

"If it passes, yeah."

"Will it pass?" Peyton asks after taking all this information in. Cisco and I nod simultaneously.

"There's no reason it wouldn't during this session," I explain. Cisco and I will probably be the only two who vote against it.

"There is no way in hell they will agree to join a party caucus—any party," Amanda states adamantly. She is in a position to know since she was one of my firefighters for them during the campaign. Between her and Emilee, they are familiar with all the people who ran as icandidates.

"Don't be so sure of that. Yes, they are ideologically different, but all moderate. You worked with them, but you need to remember who we got the list of names from last summer."

"Viano," Vanessa answers, seeing my point.

"God, I'm so tired of hearing her name," Peyton adds with a roll of her eyes.

"Yeah, well, I had to see her face. I met with her over in Alexandria this morning to confirm what I was thinking."

"I hope you hid the body well," Kylie says with an evil grin. "I don't want you to be joining my sister behind bars." I have thought Kylie would be at least a little upset at the image of her little sister living out scenes from *The Shawshank Redemption.* Quite the opposite is true. She isn't shy in vocalizing her hopes that the dog in *The Pirates of the Caribbean* runs off with the keys to Madison's jail cell.

"As tempting as that was, she gets to live another day," I say, returning the smile.

"I'm surprised she's not pounding your office door down," Brian quips.

"Uh, I may have left her with the notion that I'm on board with forming this third party. Sometimes letting people hear what they want to hear is the best way to get them off your back."

"You'd better not be using that tactic with me, Michael," Kylie interjects from across the room. The comment draws laughs from the room, but I'm pretty sure she was at least partially serious.

"We found out about her plan the night of the election, but I think Viano has been advancing this agenda since the first time we met. Somehow she's convinced she holds enough control over the incoming icongressmen to pull off creating a third party."

"Okay, help me out here. If this has been Viano's plan all along, why does the Speaker think this bill will force all of us into either GOP or Dem ranks?"

"No third party exists, and we have stated categorically what we have no interest in forming one," Cisco answers. "Why wouldn't he?"

"So Viano is playing him?" Peyton asks, muting the microphone just long enough to yell at someone I presume is a roommate before turning her attention back at the screen.

Cisco looks at me and I know what he is thinking. We had a lengthy chat following my meeting with the former senator about who could be orchestrating all this. The only image either of us could come up with is the grey haired "Architect" from *The Matrix Reloaded*.

"Someone has to be manipulating this from behind the scenes," Kylie concludes. "Viano is a smart woman, and she has connections but is not enough of a player in Washington to do this alone."

There is a light rap on the door and Blake walks in. In an instant, the feel of the room has an icy edge to it. Blake has the effect on my staff these days.

"So the remaining question is who has enough power, money, and influence to pull that off if it isn't Viano?" Vanessa poses, doing her best to ignore Blake's intrusion.

"Jack Reed," Blake states, closing the heavy oak door behind him. I turn to Chelsea in time to see her clam up. "He's the founding partner of Ibram & Reed, the country's largest and richest lobby firm."

"I know who he is, Blake," Chelsea scolds.

"That was for the benefit of those fortunate enough not to work in Washington, Chels," he defends, pointing at the images of Amanda, Emilee, Peyton, and Brian on the screen. "He's the one pulling the strings."

"Viano's lapdog wants to offer his opinion," Vince taunts.

"No, Vince, dogs are loyal and people *like* having them around," Vanessa piles on, about as happy to see Blake as Vince is.

"Is it really prudent to discuss this with him here?" Chelsea asks me. "He's just going to go running back to Viano and tell her everything we say." I'm not so sure about that, but Kylie beats me to the punch.

"Let's find out what he thinks first. So how about it, Blake? How do you know Reed is behind this?" she asks bluntly from over near the window.

"Because, until yesterday, I used to work for him."

"What?" the group collectively screams, including my four staff members joining us virtually over Skype. I quickly look over at Chelsea who looks like her puppy just died. The wounded look on her face tells me she didn't know.

"How did you end up getting that job?" Vince asks, seriously looking like he wants to rip Blake's throat out. He was persona non grata in political circles after turning over the evidence and testifying against my former arch nemesis, so it's a valid question.

"After my ... falling out ... with Beaumont, employment in politics was a little hard to come by. My aunt called in a favor or two and got me the job."

"Okay. Who the hell's your aunt?" Vanessa sounds like a pissed off interrogator at a big city police department grilling a murder suspect.

"Marilyn Viano," I say, guessing, but stating it like I wasn't. He nods at me.

I put two and two together pretty quickly while Kylie and my staff recover from being stunned to launch into a verbal berating of Blake. I hear epithets ranging from "despicable jackass" to "lying piece of crap" being hurled at him.

Everything that has happened since the day I decked him at Arlington National Cemetery is starting to make more sense. Senator Viano has been plucking our strings like a banjo this whole time. I don't know what her end game is, but it definitely is not combining forces to jointly run a political party.

It also bothers me that Reed is involved, but it qualifies her original statement at breakfast. She mentioned lobbyists, but I think she meant Reed. How he has enough juice to get the Speaker to do his bidding I'll never know, but his fingerprints are on that bill for sure. The questions are why and where we go from here?

To his credit, Blake is standing there and taking everything my staff is dishing at him without defending himself or ticking down a litany of excuses. There is something to be said for that. Maybe Blake isn't a lost cause after all. He has credibility problems which he did make worse. I don't appreciate being kept in the dark either.

"Okay, enough," I demand, putting an end to the verbal caning. "I think you should have shared this information with us long ago, Blake, don't you?"

Blake hangs his head and stares at the floor, not wanting to meet my stare. "Yes, I should have. I'm sorry."

"However, you guys all need to realize that he didn't have to tell us at all. We may have found out eventually, but he stood in this room and faced the fury when lesser men would not have. That takes character and courage, so I think we need to ease up on him for the time being and plan our next move."

I get grudging approval from some of the staff, along with Cisco and Kylie, although it is clear that others don't agree. Vince is ready to grab him by his coat and violently defenestrate him. Chelsea is biting her lip so hard she's practically bleeding.

"So, how do we stop this?" I hear Emilee ask, but I am lost collecting my thoughts.

"Congressman?" Vince asks, trying to get my attention.

I look at Vince, and then take my time to stare each and every person in the room, or joining us virtually from afar, in the eye. The revelations about Blake only add a little more drama to a year that has been a wild journey. We all thought it was over after the election, but now realize this roller coaster just blew through the station for another run. Normally I would welcome an endless ride on Millennium Force at Cedar Point, but this is ridiculous. Oh well, it is what it is.

"We spent our first campaign trying to teach Americans to pay attention to the people they elect. Two years later, it looks as if they started to learn the lesson. Now we have a new crop of students: the people who got elected, and those who think they can control them."

"Are you implying we use the same lesson plan?" Cisco asks, dubious at the notion of the same "mission profile" working again for this. He may have used teacher's lingo, but guaranteed he'd rather default to his Texan roots and use his cowboy boots to start kicking people's asses.

"Sort of. We have built an incredible social media foundation in the country, so let's leverage it to engage the public and see if we can stir them up. That's part one."

"Do you really think you can go the social media route again and expect results?" Kylie asks. She's right, we may have over-relied on our virtual presence.

"The elites are only now realizing that the country is changing. Good or bad, social media is a fixture for a lot of people, and they have been slow to recognize its effectiveness in communicating and mobilizing them behind a cause. We can only hope they remain ignorant."

"What's part two?" Brian asks via Skype.

"Part two entails reaching out to the other independents that will be joining us in January to see how many would jump ship. Then we convince them not to."

"Okay, I'll buy into all that," Amanda concludes. "Is there a part three we should know about?"

"Yeah," Cisco answers, "we figure out how to give Congress a political wedgie." Well said.

-FIFTY-TWO-
SPEAKER ALBRIGHT

"That's because you don't understand social media, sir," the intern pronounces with an irritating condescension. "You can't make things go viral, they just do."

"Then how has Bennit managed to do it twice?"

"Luck? I don't know how or why, but people love him and his story. But just because it's happened twice doesn't mean it will this time."

"Let's hope not," I say, meaning it.

Michael Bennit is the master of social media. He nearly beat Winston Beaumont exclusively using it, falling only because of some last minute allegations. He trounced his opponents the second time around in a landslide that makes Secretariat's 1973 win at the Belmont look like a photo finish. Then there's how he and his icandidates managed to pull out huge victories earlier this month.

"Mister Speaker," my secretary says from the door. "The majority leader is here to see you."

"Send him in. Thanks, we'll continue this later," I say to the intern who looks like he's barely hit puberty. He passes Harvey on the way out who gives him a once-over as he leaves.

"You pulling your staff out of high school now?"

"You'd think so. He's an intern giving me a crash course on social media. I'm trying to figure out how concerned I need to be about Bennit's latest online blitz garnering too much attention from the American public."

"Are you thinking of trying to beat him at his own game if it comes to that?"

"No, I'm hoping it doesn't get that far. We are keeping the media preoccupied with election fallout and Americans are tired of hearing about politics after enduring this last election cycle and have turned to Christmas shopping."

"So why the cram session?" Harvey asks, an amused look creeping across his face.

"I'm trying to formulate a plan just in case. Unless you have a better idea on how to beat Michael Bennit."

"I do, actually. With a bat while he sleeps." He took that literally, but part of me likes the idea.

"Don't think I haven't thought of that. I'm hoping someone does it for me," I say with a laugh.

"Considering the current political climate in this country, you may get your wish. I'm surprised you're still here since we're adjourned for Thanksgiving," the majority leader says, pulling up a chair and changing the subject. It's bad form to discuss in detail the desire to see a political enemy lie on the ground in a bloody mess, no matter how much you want it.

It's Friday, and the last vote was held right after lunch. As tradition dictates before any holiday, the members head for the airport almost immediately after the last business is conducted. The three days before Thanksgiving is a constituent work week back in their districts, but no real work ever gets done.

"Just tying up some loose ends. You?"

"We're actually heading to Thanksgiving at my brother's place in Boston, so we figured we'd just stay in D.C. until Wednesday. But enough of my travel plans. I have news."

"Whatcha got?" I'm somewhat relieved that I didn't need to hear the gory details of Harvey Stepanik's itinerary.

"The House Independent Caucus Bill just made it out of committee. Unanimous vote."

How did it ever come to this? No party outside of the Democrats and Republicans has held a majority in either house of Congress since before Lincoln started the War of Northern Aggression. In fact, they have never even held a significant minority until now. It is just lousy timing that it happens on my watch.

Most third-party or independent candidates choose to caucus with one of the two major parties in exchange for committee assignments or influence. Not this lot. They are being stubborn about breaking ranks, causing a major problem when it will come to selecting the next Speaker of the House. Despite our best attempts, not one has been lured by the carrots we are dangling in front of them. And with Michael Bennit leading the cause, they aren't going to respond to the stick part of the approach either.

"A unanimous vote is a good sign. It means Merrick and the Dems are playing ball," I observe, trying not to hint at the concerns I have about this.

"Yeah, well, it better work. Your job may rely on it." I can always trust Harvey to take my concerns for a spin on the dance floor. He doesn't want us to lose our majority in the House, but I'm sure he's not experiencing any anxiety over me losing my job.

"I understand the political ramifications, Harvey. We just have to figure out how to keep this from becoming the next big thing to hit Facebook. Bennit has no other cards to play. So on that note, on your way out, have my secretary send the kid with the pimples back in. I need him to explain to me again what the world's fascination with Twitter is."

-FIFTY-THREE-
MICHAEL

"Congressman? Blake is here," Chelsea says from the entrance to my office.

"Show him in. You know, I would prefer if you'd stick around for this." She turns and eyes Blake who is waiting patiently in the outer office.

"No, I'm good. It's getting late and I need to get some Christmas shopping done."

"Oh, God, don't remind me. I haven't even thought about it, let alone started it. Good luck with yours."

"Thanks. I'll send him in. Have a good night, Congressman."

"Thanks. You too, Chels."

Chelsea walks out and tells Blake he can enter. Damn, is she ever pissed off about this. I am reminded once again that I need to have a long overdue heart to heart chat with my former prize pupil.

"Good evening, Congressman," Blake says, taking the seat I offer him on the small sofa across from mine. I toyed with the idea of having this conversation across a desk, but I have a hard time forcing myself to be that formal.

"Evening. Glad you could make it."

"I watched you on *The Daily Show* last night. Really nice job, although I really think you should have taken Jon Stewart's challenge of flipping his desk. The viral value of that would have been astronomical."

If you want to change public opinion, *Meet the Press* isn't going to get it done. *The Daily Show* and *Colbert Report* have mainstream appeal, and that's what we need right now.

"I'd be lying if I said it wasn't tempting."

"You working mainstream television programming is still taking some getting used to. It made sense during the campaign, but I'm a little shocked you decided to continue appearing on them." Blake pauses for a moment before continuing. "You don't think a social media campaign will work for this, do you?"

"Not this time. Not by itself."

"Why not?"

A viral social media campaign is not much different than any other movement in history. The only difference is how it materializes and how the message is communicated. For all grassroots movements, there is one fundamental truth someone needs to understand—to work, they have to be something people can rally behind.

"Americans don't understand how this affects them. People will talk about it, but they won't demand the action it's going to take to make a difference."

"So, the fact Twitter hash tag 'silenced' is constantly trending is meaningless?"

"Meaningless is a strong word. People's opinions matter, but in this instance, it won't be enough to change votes. We may have demonstrated the power of social media, but we also have to understand its limitations."

"Is that why I'm here?"

"Sort of. I need some advice. You did some unsavory things for Winston Beaumont, didn't you?"

"Too many," he answers meekly.

"If you were trying to intimidate someone into voting a certain way, or taking a course of action, how would you do it?"

Blake thinks about it for a second before the realization of what I'm talking about hits him like a tsunami. Blake may be a lot of things, but dimwitted isn't one of them. I can't understand why Marilyn's opinion of her nephew is so low.

"You're talking about the threats you're getting?"

"Yup. Tell me something. This rules vote is pretty much a lock, yes?"

"Outside of you pulling off a small miracle to defeat it, I'd say so."

"So if a group is behind sending them, what is the endgame?"

"They are trying to push you into something willingly."

"That's the conclusion I came to, and thanks to your aunt, I think I know what."

"The third party."

I give him a look of agreement without saying anything. He gets the message, then looks over his shoulder to the closed office door.

"Chelsea doesn't trust me. Is that why she isn't here?"

"Nobody trusts you, Blake. Not my staff or anybody else's. I'm not sure you'll ever get over that stigma, but maybe for once that's an asset and not a liability."

"What do you mean?" he asks, genuinely perplexed.

I take a moment to think about how I want to do this. Offending Blake is not at the top of the list of things I give a crap about, but this situation is critical and I could really use his help. I don't want to manipulate him into saying yes, but I also don't want to give him an easy reason to say no.

"How many Democrats do you know in the House?"

"Almost all of them. Not that any of them would give me the time of day."

"I was hoping you'd say that. I have a mission I'd like you to consider taking." I go on to tell him my plan. I decide to play it straight and lay all my cards on the table. It's a different approach than anyone else in this city would use, and I pride myself on owning that approach here.

"I'm fighting a war on multiple fronts here, and I can't do it alone. You are my Manhattan Project, so to speak. You're the best hope I have for victory."

"What if I say no?"

"Then say it. You have that right."

"I'm not sure I'll ever find work in this town again if I do this for you."

"Not going to lie to you, Blake, that's a real possibility."

He closes his eyes, and then opens them, focusing on an imaginary spot in the space in front of him. He is lost in his thoughts, and I'm not about to interrupt his thousand-yard stare. By the time he looks up at me, I already have figured out what he's about to ask.

"Look, if you're fishing for a job offer, you're not going to get one out of me. I'm only just beginning to trust you, and the opinions of the people I rely on the most aren't even that far along. And trust me when I say that'll be an uphill climb."

"How uphill?

"Think the cliffs at Pointe du Hoc between Utah and Omaha Beaches in Normandy." He misses the reference but gets the gist. He goes back to weighing his options, playing with the Second Armored pin he's been wearing on his lapel since the first election in the process.

Despite our social media effort, I think the success of defeating this bill relies on Blake's decision. And while Chelsea is … less than thrilled … in trusting him to pull it off, I know he's the only one who can. It's a high stakes gamble considering how many times he's lied and deceived us. Something in my gut is screaming to follow my intuitions and trust him, and after surviving multiple tours in Iraq and Afghanistan with the Special Forces, I learned to trust that gut a whole lot.

"Do you think these threats against you and the staff are real?" he asks with a look of genuine concern on his face.

"I don't know, Blake, but God, I hope not. Either way, I will not allow myself to be coerced into anything."

"Okay, I'll do it."

"You realize what I'm saying, right? There are no promises of anything for doing this?"

"I understand, but you need to know something first. Speaker Albright offered me a position on his staff to help this get passed." That catches me a little off guard, and my response is reflexive.

"Really? Did you accept it?"

"No. I don't want to work for him, but I was keeping the option open."

"Does anyone else know about this?"

"Not until I let it slip with the rest of the information you want me to leak."

"You scare me a little, Blake," I say with a smile, but meaning it.

"I'll let you know how I make out," he says, reaching out to shake my hand. As we walk to the door, I have to ask.

"Blake, why did you decide to help?"

He looks at me and smiles. "It's what my father would have wanted me to do."

-FIFTY-FOUR-

CHELSEA

Union Station is an iconic landmark in D.C. More than just a transportation hub, it also offers a variety of stores I can peruse for gifts while being afforded easy access to Red Line of the city's subway system. I'm window shopping more than actually planning on buying a gift. Dad is almost impossible to find Christmas presents for.

"Hello, Miss Stanton," the deep bass voice of Congressman Parker says after seeing me in front of the aptly named Street Level Shops.

"Good evening, Congressman. I didn't realize you shopped here too."

"Normally, I don't, but the missus is out of town and there is a great little cigar shop right over there," he beams without a hint of guilt. "And you?"

"Trying to find ideas for my father."

"I know there is a nice little cigar shop right over there," he says with a laugh. It's probably the only store he knows of in this small shopping area.

"It may come to that," I lament, reciprocating the smile. "Before I forget to ask, how's your niece making out with her unit? I haven't heard any updates."

He smiles, probably shocked I remembered. Most elected officials can't be bothered to remember what they ate for breakfast, and staff members only generally care about what their principals do. Of course, no one will ever accuse us of being like most elected officials.

"They finally got the issue sorted out and she is doing much better. She's going to make a helluva crew chief."

"I have little doubt about that. Thank her for her service on my behalf," I say as I start to leave.

"I will. Before you run off, I was wondering if there is something else you could help me with, since I've run into you here."

Ugh. The deal-making here never ends, and I am getting tired of it. I don't feel much obligation to help, even after he saved the congressman's political career. He's a big part of the reason I have to buy jugs of Advil at the local Sam's Club.

"I will do what I can."

"Rumors are like Louisiana mosquitoes on Capitol Hill—they are everywhere, annoying, and if you spend too much time around them, will suck the lifeblood right out of you."

No argument from me on that terrifying analogy. I hear the bayou is beautiful in its own way, but I don't ever plan to find out for myself. The closest I ever plan on getting there is through watching old episodes of *Duck Dynasty*.

"Did you hear Blake Peoni accepted a deal to work with on Speaker Albright's staff?"

The blood drains out of my face. I have a pale complexion to begin with, but now I'm sure I look like a bed sheet.

"No, I guess you haven't."

"I, uh ... do you ..." C'mon, Chels, get it together. "How solid is your information, sir?" I ask, finally regaining at least some composure.

"Very," he states confidently. "I'm not trying to play gotcha with you, Miss Stanton. I only ask because he worked for Winston Beaumont, and he and I ... well, let's just say we live on very separate planets ideologically. Fact is, I don't trust Blake very much. I have no idea why the Speaker does, but I consider it my job to protect my party if he isn't going to. I know you don't care much about that, but I also know he was working with you guys."

I can barely speak. I want to respond. I need to respond, but I can only focus on tamping down the surge of emotion I'm feeling. He lied to me again. He pretended to care about me and even kissed me. How could I be so stupid?

"I wish I could tell you more, Congressman, but I honestly don't know anything," I mutter as the tears form in my eyes. I'm losing the battle with myself, and Congressman Parker sees it too.

"I can see this blindsided you as well. I'm sorry if I upset you. Have a nice evening, Miss Stanton. Good luck with your Christmas shopping," he says with the same concerned look my father gives me before walking off.

I find myself standing in the middle of this national treasure, surrounded by people, yet utterly alone. Alone. That word has a lot of meaning for me these days. So many lies and so much deceit. I feel like a shipwreck survivor, clinging to a board and adrift on a wide open sea by myself. Even the people closest to me have seemed to abandon me.

I walk back to the safe confines of my office through the frosty early December air. Although it really isn't safe anymore either, is it? The congressman seems to be keeping as many secrets from me as Blake has. Has he lost his trust in me, too? Would he bother to tell me even if he hasn't?

Trusting people has never been my strong suit. Maybe that's the one thing I always had in common with my favorite teacher—we both take a while to warm to people. So why is he embracing Blake now instead of me? Blake, the lying, coward of a man who doesn't have a shred of integrity in his body. Why would Mister Bennit, a man who epitomizes the very word, betray his own principles so egregiously? Has Washington changed him that much?

Forget it. I can't take this place anymore. I wipe the tears from my eyes and grab my coat and purse. I have been betrayed for the last time. By Blake, by the congressman, by anyone here. When I get emotional, I get irrational, and right now, I don't give a crap. I look around my office for what will probably be the last time. They can mail me my stuff for all I care, because I'm going home to Millfield and never coming back.

FIFTY-FIVE

SENATOR VIANO

"The infuriating bastard lied to me, Gary!" I exclaim as I barge into his office in the Longworth House Office Building. Well, it will be his office for a short time longer since his boss lost the election to one of my future minions.

"You're just figuring that out now?" The perplexed look on his face leads me to believe he came to that conclusion days ago. I miss having him as my chief of staff for that very reason. He sees the things I sometimes don't.

"I thought he was just engaging in some political posturing. I didn't think he'd have the balls to go against me on this."

Bennit has hit the media circuit hard in the days after our little chat at breakfast. I seriously thought he was just playing it up like he was fighting the good fight. We do that in Washington all the time. Each and every call I had with him was cordial and cooperative. At least until the last one.

"He strung you along. I'm not sure if I'm more impressed he thought of that or managed to get you to buy it."

"What are you saying, Gary?" I ask in my patented accusatory tone.

"You're a political genius, Senator. That's why I liked working with you, and still do. The fact that he successfully pulled the wool over your eyes is more than a little impressive. That's all."

"Are you sure that's all?" I ask my longtime confidant, "Because it looks like you have more to say."

Gary gets up from his desk, stretches, and walks over to the credenza on the far wall. His office is not spacious, but is roomy enough to be comfortable in so long as you like prints and tchotchkes of various superheroes. I don't, so there were relative few of such adornments when I was in the Senate. Now it looks like Marvel Comics threw up in here. Hope he doesn't plan on putting this crap up when he comes back to work for me.

"You should just consider working with him," Gary says, pouring himself a drink from the glass decanter without offering me one. He knows I won't accept it anyway.

"I tried, and this is how I was rewarded."

He smirks, and then takes a long sip of his ... whatever it is. "No, you maintained the guise of working with him while you plotted against him. Your problem isn't Michael Bennit; it's that you keep underestimating him."

"I made him the iCongressman, damn it! He would be *nothing* without me. Even if he managed to win reelection, he'd be more irrelevant in this town than two-day-old chewing gum! The icandidates were *my* idea. I selected them, I helped them—"

"Behind the scenes, Senator. You may know all that, but neither they, nor the person they will take their cues from, understands that."

"Precisely why I won't work with him. As long as Michael Bennit is in office, he will be looked at as the leader of the independents in the House. It doesn't matter if we form a new political party or not." I notice the change in Gary's face, and know what he's going to say, and I don't want to hear it. "I know you're going to say 'I told you so,' so just don't," I warn.

"Okay, so you need to find a way to remove Michael from the picture. Permanently," he surmises, heeding my advice to move the conversation forward.

"Yes, and I think I have a plan to do it. You are aware of all these threats Bennit is getting, aren't you?"

"I've heard the rumors."

"Then I'll assume you also figured out who is behind it."

"James Reed."

"Correct. He is trying to force the issue on the third party idea. Apparently he isn't convinced this bill is going to do it for us."

"Bold move for one of the most prestigious lobby firms in the country to be involved in something like that," Gary correctly surmises.

It is a risky move as much as it is a brash one. The name of his firm has already been tarnished by being involved in ousting Michael last summer. If he were ever tied to this, it would destroy them. James probably thinks there is nothing that could ever lead an investigation back to his doorstep. Of course, he thought that the first time.

"Let's use his tactics to our favor. Michael is concerned about the welfare of his staff. These threats are starting to get in his head because he cares more about the people around him than doing his job. It might not take much to force him out. We just have to send a louder message."

Gary is about as shrewd as they come, and that's saying something in an environment where every politician thinks they're Marcus Aurelius and every staff member acts like Niccoló Machiavelli. Of course Beaumont's chief of staff, Roger Bean, was of the same opinion of himself before his Brooks Brothers suits were exchanged for Day-Glo orange prison garb.

"Marilyn, you're playing with fire now. You've tried crossing Bennit, and if this backfires, you'll be doing the same thing to Reed. Just how far do you plan on taking this if it doesn't work out the way you hoped?"

"I have spent my whole life trying to build the contacts and resources I needed to get elected to the Senate. Once I was there, I was on top of the world. Politics is my life, Gary, and I want that life back. Neither Michael Bennit nor James Reed is going to stand in my way."

"You didn't answer my question," Gary correctly observes.

"How far would I go?" He nods. "As far as I have to. Now let's get to work."

-FIFTY-SIX-

MICHAEL

"Any luck?" I ask Vince as he jogs the last strides down the hall and stops next to me.

"None. She isn't at home, hasn't been to the office, and isn't responding to her cell, texts, or e-mail."

"Okay, now I'm worried. This isn't like her at all."

Worst case scenarios start to spinning through my mind. Now I know what parents must feel like. After a career in special operations for the military, it takes a lot to faze me. This qualifies. Vince shares my concerned look.

"What do you want me to do next? Call the Capitol and Metro Police?"

The thought that something may have happened to Chelsea sends a shiver down my spine. "Have you called her house?"

"Yeah, countless ti—"

"No, I mean her dad's up in Millfield."

"Uh, no, we haven't."

"Okay. Get in touch with her dad first. If he hasn't heard from her, sound the alarm and sound it loud."

"Got it."

"Good. Don't waste any more time talking to me."

Vince runs off back down the hall and I take a deep breath. With all the pressure on me going into this meeting, having to agonize over Chelsea is the last thing I need. But if anything ever happened to her, I could never forgive myself.

"They're ready for you, Congressman," Vanessa gently prods after emerging from the committee room we reserved for this gathering. She knows what's at stake, but also shares our fears about Chels. Here goes nothing.

* * *

There isn't a sound as I walk down the aisle to the front of the room. There are at least a couple of dozen representatives here, representing both parties. The vast majority is what Americans would call moderates and their party bosses would call traitors.

Politicians are really nothing special once you stand among them. Most of the men and women in this room could easily disappear into the anonymity of any group of affluent Americans. However, like most driven and successful people, they do have an ego and want to be admired and respected. Most of all, they want to be reelected every two years, meaning they find a way to not stand out in any negative way.

"Thank you all for coming," I say to the group. I'm honestly shocked so many came. I expected less than half this number.

"Michael, are you going to create a third party?" someone in the group asks without any introduction. Damn, I really don't want to do this without Chelsea here.

"Cutting right to the chase, aren't you, Tom?" I reply with a smile to the Republican representative from Arizona. "The answer is no, I have never intended, nor do I ever intend to create a third party."

"Why not?" a colleague representing some district in Northern California asks.

"Because I don't think a third party goes a long way to heal the divide in this chamber. If anything, it makes it worse."

"I disagree," he responds, taking up the argument. I forgot he is a strong third-party advocate, once even running on the Green Party ballot. "All we need for a three-party system to be successful is a courageous political leader to lead a break away from the current system. Many of the people here think you're that leader, Mister Bennit."

There is a smattering of applause, but I'm unmoved. I am concerned though. I need these people to vote against this bill, not for it in the hopes that I will go the third party route.

"I appreciate the vote of confidence, but it's never, *ever* going to happen."

"Do you hate political parties that much?"

"I don't hate them at all. Political parties have served the citizens of the United States well for a couple of centuries now, but the paradigm has shifted in a way most Americans find untenable. There is an ideological rift that has formed between Republicans and Democrats that make our whole system of government ineffective. If you don't believe me, think back to the last time so many members from both parties willingly sat in the same room together like you are."

"Never," the attractive and intelligent congresswoman from Pennsylvania scoffs. I have listened intently to some of her floor speeches, and she is incredibly articulate and very fair. Formerly a successful and driven small business owner, she's the type of boss people would line up to work for. I am still getting used to the fact that not everyone who serves in Congress is a lawyer. "But what's your point?"

"I'm glad you asked. I feel that creating a new party would further divide the House, but creating a new caucus would bring many of us together."

The room erupts into side conversations and I'm reminded of my days in the classroom. During countless discussions, students would engage in the exact same behavior.

"The bill coming before the House won't allow that unless a third party is created," one of my colleagues interjects.

"That's true. It's also why that bill needs to be defeated."

"But there is no majority party! How will we elect our next Speaker of the House?"

"Do you seriously think that the situation won't work itself out when the next Congress convenes? I'm focused on the long-term here."

"Okay, let's back up for a second. Is this caucus for us, your icandidates, who?"

"There's room for anyone who wants Congress to actually work. It's not about ideology—it's about the common understanding that what unites us is stronger than what divides us and that differences can be worked out."

"Do you *really* think that will work?" Damn, I didn't realize people from Alaska were so pessimistic.

"Yeah, I do, and for one simple reason. This caucus is our *Fight Club.* You all remember the first rule of *Fight Club?*"

"You never talk about *Fight Club*," a moderate from Oregon enthusiastically answers from the back of the room. The group chuckles, including the two elected women in the room. They might not have been huge fans of the movie, but Brad Pitt with his shirt off is a draw, regardless of the subject matter.

"In this case, you never talk about what happens in our caucus. Nothing gets leaked to the media. You leak to the media and you will never be invited back. Ever."

"Do you really think this is going to make a difference, Michael? I mean, even if we break with our party-line votes and find common ground, do you expect us all to agree on every issue?" Again, Alaska?

"No, I don't expect us all to agree with each other on everything. I also don't think we'll inspire all four hundred thirty-five members of the House to join hands around the Capitol reflecting pool and sing *Imagine* while Speaker Albright smokes weed and strums an acoustic guitar."

Everybody ponders that mental picture for a moment. Some are enjoying it a little too much.

"There used to be a day where statesmen engaged in raucous debates in caucuses about various issues. Of course, America never heard about them because they were private. Now pressers are held by representatives acting like *Sportscenter* anchors who give the highlights of every caucus meeting.

"The purpose of a closed-door session is so we can have real debates with each other without having to censor our views. We need a secure forum to have frank conversations with each other or the legislature will continue to get nothing done."

"That would be a refreshing change," one of the young Democrats says from the back of the room. "Every caucus meeting I attend now is about fundraising and how to screw the Republicans."

"It's no different on our side. And as a moderate, my pragmatic desire to compromise is never appreciated."

There is a smattering of agreement, although a few congressmen from both parties take umbrage with the comments. Apparently not everyone is sold on joining my caucus. Now I begin to wonder if the only reason some of these people are here is to report back to the party leadership for both sides.

As the side conversations rage, Vince walks up the aisle and hands me a folded piece of paper. It reads:

Spoke to her dad. She went home to Millfield. She quit on us.

A rush of emotion surges through me. On one hand, I'm relieved to know she's okay. The threats against us are starting to have an effect on me, too. The specter of her being kidnapped, or worse, was almost paralyzing. On the other hand, I'm confused as to why she would up and leave, especially considering everything going on. She had to know it would make us worry. There is a collision between the most important meetings of my political career and one of the most important people in my life, and I have to make a decision what to do. It takes a fraction of a second.

"I hate to have to cut this short, but I have to go."

"You're leaving now?" one of my colleagues asks.

"One thing you'll learn about me is I am a firm believer that people are more important than politics. And right now, I owe one of them a long overdue heart-to-heart. Vince can answer most of your remaining questions about what we're trying to do here, and feel free to reach out to me about anything he doesn't answer to your satisfaction. Thanks for coming everyone."

I head up the aisle to the doors at the opposite end of the committee room. I know dozens of sets of eyes are on me because of my abrupt departure, but I don't feel them. My mind is already up in Millfield, thinking about what's going on with my cherished student, valued staff member, and someone I almost consider a daughter.

I am not one who believes in regrets. I firmly believe such thinking is a waste of time and energy. But for the first time in a long time, I feel those regrets along with pangs of guilt. Chelsea would not up and leave without good reasons, and somehow I feel like I missed all of them.

-FIFTY-SEVEN-
SPEAKER ALBRIGHT

Capitol Beat is a new political news program run by one of the twenty-four-hour cable networks. They are putting a special together to discuss the lack of a majority party in the House and what it means for the country. Obviously, the bill I introduced is a hot topic for the program since it is the only solution to the problem unless most of the independents defect. So far, none of them have, despite our best efforts to woo them.

Harvey Stepanik joins me in my office as the producers of the show set up the shot and the equipment dogs get to work with the audio and lighting for our interview.

"He's meeting with the moderates."

"When?"

He looks at his expensive wristwatch. "Right now, actually."

"Hm. Bennit must have finally figured out he was tilting at windmills relying on the whole social media thing again. How many showed up?"

"I don't know. Too many though, from both sides. He's still dangerous," Harvey concludes, glancing back at the techs setting up.

"You don't really think he can sway anyone from our side to go independent?"

"I don't think he has the political skill to make that argument. I don't think he can entice the Dems either, but it makes me wonder what he's doing."

"Do you have anyone in there sitting in it?"

"Of course, but we won't hear anything until after we are through with this."

"We're almost ready for you, gentlemen," one of the producers interrupts as the techs finish setting up for the interview.

* * *

"We are joined now by the Speaker of the U.S. House of Representatives, Republican Johnston Albright and the Majority Leader Harvey Stepanik. Thank you for joining us today."

"Thank you for having us, Wilson." The sixty-six-year-old and graying, Wilson Newman has been a political analyst most of his adult life and the host of *Capitol Beat* since it went on the air. He has a timeless Sean Connery look, or so my female staffers have told me when they swoon over his image on the television.

"This has been one of the more contentious lame duck sessions the country has seen in a while, and it is all because of the rules bill that you are readying to introduce to the floor. Can you explain to our viewers what the purpose is?"

"As you know, after the results of the last election were certified, we ended up with an unprecedented situation where there is no majority party for the House in the next Congress. Having no majority party is a threat to how our chamber does business. All this bill does is changes our rules to force representatives to caucus with a major political party. We don't dictate which one," Harvey says from beside me.

"Even if it is a third party?"

"Correct," I say. Of course, we're counting on them not creating one.

"You gentlemen realize that this is wildly unpopular with people—only nine percent support the bill," Wilson says frankly.

The problem with conducting opinion polls about issues is you are dealing with a very uneducated sample. Americans don't have the faintest clue about what this bill means for them, or for the country. There is confusion among the population even with more familiar laws. According to a 2013 Gallup poll, forty-five percent of Americans supported the Affordable Care Act while only thirty-nine percent supported Obamacare. They refer to the same law.

"I think there is a lot of confusion in America over this bill being propagated by its opponents."

"You're referring to Michael Bennit and Francisco Reyes?"

"Among others, yes," Harvey answers.

"Why do you think that is, Mister Speaker? I mean, are they purposefully misleading the public?"

Thank God for the friendly confines of *Capitol Beat*. Like most political news programs, it leans toward a particular ideology and asks softball questions designed to keep it in good standing with core viewers. The liberals have their shows, and we have ours. *Capitol Beat* is one of them.

"Congress is probably America's least understood institution. What our citizens need to realize is that Congress is both a system and a culture. This bill only applies to how the House of Representatives does business and really doesn't affect the average American."

"That's not what Representative Bennit is asserting. He is claiming via social media that this is an assault on the country's desire to see independent candidates play a larger role in a government long beholden a two-party structure."

"Some people see a conspiracy behind everything," Harvey dismisses with his charming smile and a little laugh.

"So there is no truth to some of the comments being posted to Twitter that the leadership of both parties are scared to death of the type of campaign reforms this new wave of independents could introduce to make it easier for more like them to join their ranks in Washington?"

"None whatsoever. I'm surprised that tweet didn't include a selfie of Bennit wearing a tin foil hat." Suddenly I am very happy for my social media cram session with the intern. I'm going to have to write him a great letter of recommendation.

"Social media aside, even some of the mainstream media are saying passage of such an unpopular bill could end the Republican and Democratic parties," Wilson points out.

"People want their government to work," Harvey says, beating me to the response. "This bill will ensure we can continue to conduct the people's business with no disruption.

I'm sure with proper leadership, both parties will flourish for a long time to come."

That bastard. Proper leadership is a subtle jab at me. He just openly made himself a candidate for Speaker while sitting right beside me for this interview.

There is nothing worse than fighting wars on multiple fronts. Not only do I have to deal with Bennit, his yahoos that will be sworn in next year, and apparently a host of moderates looking to team up with him, but now a conservative in my own party. I knew Stepanik had designs on my office, but I never thought he would be this shameless.

"So, if this bill doesn't pass, do you think it could be an end of the two-party structure?"

"First, I am very confident this bill will pass," I say, seizing the momentum from the majority leader. "But if for some reason it doesn't, I don't think electing independents is going to become a frequent occurrence in future elections. Americans have simply expressed a desire to get better results out of Washington, and I am convinced the two-party system is perfectly capable of delivering those results despite the poorly chosen paths we have been led down in the past."

Take that Harvey. If you want my job, you're going to have to take it from me.

-FIFTY-EIGHT-
SENATOR VIANO

The political lobby has practically become members of the congressional family. If the news media are the half-siblings to the political elite, then lobbyists are first cousins. Their numbers are greater than the journalists who cover Capitol Hill, and from their purses and wallets spurts the lifeblood of American politics, at least until recently. The campaign contributions they deliver on behalf of their clients guarantee their status and build an easy road to success.

The huge sums of cash they doled out are the primary reason American politics has transformed into a high-stakes game of *Monopoly* over the previous generation. In 2006, over two hundred eighty-seven million dollars were donated to candidates for the House and Senate during that election cycle. Three elections later, that sum grew exponentially. With that much money comes considerable leverage and power.

As the black Lincoln Town Car screeches up against the curb where I am waiting, I begin to wonder just how desperate he is becoming. If there is anything I know, it's that the true power brokers in Washington are not going to let one man ruin the gilded age of lobbying. Too much money and influence is at stake to allow this to continue.

I climb into the car next to the large man who says nothing in greeting. Mirroring the current mood in town, he is less than amiable.

"What? Not even a good morning?"

"Marilyn, we've been good friends far too long for me to engage in petty pleasantries or mince words. Ya'll told me Bennit was on board with creating a third party. Now he's out running a huge campaign against it. Which is it?"

"I told you what he told me, nothing more and nothing less."

"Then you were a fool to believe him. He either played you, or ya'll are playing me. I sure hope it's the former and not the latter. Either way, this is becoming a colossal failure and I've no one to blame but you."

"Let's talk about failures, James. You had me approach him with the idea of running icandidates and funded the venture so you could create a private legislative army of independents loyal to nobody but you. You laid the groundwork to get rid of Bennit, but you failed because he foiled your plan. Turns out he is much smarter than you thought."

James clenches his lips together angrily. He does not relish being shown up, and enjoys having his failures flaunted in front of him even less.

"And the disastrous third party idea?"

"An attempt to save your hide by setting up an organized party you could easily seize control of, but he hasn't bitten yet," I counter. There is no way Reed is laying the blame for this fiasco on me. I don't care how long we've been friends.

"I get the feeling you did that more for yourself than for me."

"So you come up with the crazy bill to try to force the issue, only it's already going sideways on you. Forcing the independents to caucus with a political party was a stupid idea. If I couldn't soft sell them into uniting under a party banner, you should have known you couldn't hard sell them into it."

"I never intended that bill to go to the floor. It was more of a prop to use against Albright."

"A prop he's now taking into an actual fight."

"Apparently."

When Reed first approached me with idea, I thought it was brilliant. Imagine having a cadre of politicians in Washington literally in your back pocket and willing to vote any way you choose. All we needed to do was get Bennit to start the ball rolling and then oust him from the House.

Getting him expelled should have been the easy part, especially when you have the Speaker of the House helping you. Fear is a fantastic motivator, and everybody, including the Democrats, wanted Bennit gone because of it. Unfortunately, it didn't work out that way and we've been forced to keep changing plans ever since. The third party idea may not have been exactly what Reed wanted, but it would be close enough.

What we didn't expect is Bennit's ferocious argument against its formation. He has been an honest broker since I met him, and I never dreamed he would lie straight to my face. With that off the table, the rules change. James having

Speaker Albright introduce it is the only way to force the issue and restore order.

"So you helped create this meltdown in the House that threatens the stability of the entire two-party system and your control over it. Michael Bennit is getting politically stronger by the day, so you have zero chance of ending up with a legion of independents to control like you wanted. So, tell me, how do you plan to put the genie back in the bottle?"

"I've been in this town a long time, Marilyn. Much longer than you," he says, looking over at me for the first time. "Washington is like a powerboat you see in those speedboat races. You never really control it. You just hope you can manipulate it enough to reach the finish line without crashing. I didn't get to where I am today by giving up just because Plan A doesn't pan out."

"Does your Plan B include a campaign of threats to an elected official to force him to vote the way you want him to?" James flinches a little.

"I don't know what you're talking about."

"Yeah, right. I've been around Washington for a while too, you know."

We've known each other for a long time, and he was influential in getting me my seat in the Senate. Of course, part of me believes he was instrumental in me losing it as well. James Reed isn't straight with anyone, even his closest friends. I shouldn't expect it now.

"I know you're working behind the scenes on this vote. What I don't understand is why you aren't including me?"

"You really think I should trust you, Marilyn?"

"No more than I should trust you, but our friendship is strongest and most satisfying when we're going in the same direction."

"Are we going in the same direction?"

"If that direction is me being put into a position to help you, then yes, it absolutely is."

"Then convince Bennit to let that bill pass."

-FIFTY-NINE-
MICHAEL

"How did you find me?" Chelsea asks as I reach the middle of the bridge.

"I love this place as much as you do. It's where I'd come to think things over too," I respond, taking a deep breath and admiring the scene.

"My dad told you, eh?"

"Yeah, that probably had something to do with it."

Briar Point is one of the magical places in town. Millfield is the typical New England village, complete with town green, historic buildings, and a lot of charm. The old iron bridge that crosses the river provides the most majestic view of all of it. It's been closed to vehicular traffic for decades, providing a great vantage point without fear of being run over by a truck.

A light dusting of snow fell overnight, marking the transition from the stunning foliage of autumn to a winter wonderland. Thanksgiving is behind us, the holiday shopping season is in full effect with only three weeks until Christmas, and the snow covered trees are now a reminder that winter is coming.

If the puffy red eyes didn't give it away that Chelsea's been crying, then the tear tracks on her cheeks pounds the point home. She's in pain, and I feel ridiculous for not having realized it much earlier.

"You scared the crap out of us, Chels. We were worried something happened to you."

"I know. I'm sorry. I didn't think about that. I just needed to leave."

"Why?"

"I failed you," she finally says, ending a long, awkward silence between us. I want her to open up and tell me what's wrong, but I want it on her terms. I am just happy that's the route she's going.

"Oh yeah? Since when?"

"I left. I'm running away from you, and Vince, and Vanessa. I'm leaving because I can't handle it."

"Getting away to get some breathing room and perspective is not quitting, Chels," realizing that her shift from the past to present tense means she is probably referencing the bigger picture. Now I at least think I know one thing that's bothering her. She's made her decision and can't come to terms with it.

"It's more than needing a break. Look what's happened … with Blake, and with Viano. I just can't keep doing this job anymore. All the lies, hidden agendas, political posturing, betrayal … I don't know how people live like this. I can never be happy working at a place where nobody can tell the truth."

Chelsea's waterworks start again, and she dabs at her eyes with a ball of tissues she pulls from her pocket. My heart aches for her, and I understand her sense of betrayal. Coming from the military, getting used to that has been just as hard for me, but I'm also not twenty years old and fresh out of high school.

"Integrity is a foreign concept where we work. Not only do the elites in Washington not have it, most can't even spell it. So yes, we have to deal with people who lie and manipulate, but there's a universal truth you need to understand."

"What's that?"

"People are going to lie and manipulate at Harvard, too."

Chelsea's head jerks around so fast I feel like I sprained something just watching her. I don't know if keeping it a secret that I knew was the right or wrong thing to do. Maybe it would have been easier on her if I had told her, but I could never find a way to bring it up.

"I've known about the letter from Harvard for a while." From the look on her face, it's clear she didn't have a clue I knew, or how. "The first call the president of Harvard made was to the office. He tried to explain to me that the scholarship no longer applied and wondered who would be better to break the bad news to you, him or me."

"I don't understand. The letter said it was still good."

"I know. It took me a well-invested three minutes to convince him what a colossal mistake not offering you a scholarship would be."

"How? Why?" is all my chief of staff manages to stammer out.

"All I did was explain to him that you will probably be one of the most powerful women in Washington someday, and that it would behoove him to ensure you are a valued

Harvard alum when you are. As for the second part, why wouldn't I?"

"You want me to leave the staff?"

"Oh, God no. Not having you work would be like going into combat without my rifle."

"Then I really don't understand."

"Chels, I don't get to make life decisions for you. I was thrilled when you decided to come to D.C. after you graduated, but I also knew that you would leave to attend college someday. If that is what your heart tells you to do, I would never stand in your way."

"You could ask me to stay."

"I could, but I won't."

"Why?"

"Because I know you would. It's who you are, but I see the toll it's taking on you. This is a personal choice, and I will not interfere with you making it. Just make sure you are doing it for the right reasons. Running away because you feel betrayed by a guy you like isn't one of them."

Chelsea wears shock on her face for the second time in the span of two minutes. Even in class, it was rare that I was able to do that, let alone twice in a conversation. More so in the year and a half she's been by my side in D.C.

"You knew?" she manages to stutter out.

"No, I'm a guy, and thus an idiot when it comes to recognizing a woman's feelings. Or so I was rather *harshly* reminded."

"Kylie told you."

"In my defense, I knew something was wrong, but never got around to asking. That's been a common theme between you and me since we started this journey. I haven't communicated very well with you. I got so caught up in everything we were doing, both before and since the election, I never stopped to think about how it was affecting you. Or Vince and Vanessa for that matter."

"Did Kylie tell you that, too?"

"No, I came up with that on my own after some quiet reflection." Chelsea looks at me with a hint of disbelief in her eyes. "It's true." More disbelief. "Okay, she helped with the quiet reflection part when she stopped talking to me." That got a smile out of her.

"I thought you knew everything," she responds, seemingly perking up a bit.

"Ha! I'm going to let you in on a dirty little secret teachers will never admit to their students. When we're up in front of the class, we pretend to know all the answers. But the truth is, we learn just as much from our students as they do from us."

"I'm not your student anymore."

"No, but I am yours."

"I don't understand."

"Chels, we were on a sinking ship from the moment we stepped foot in Washington. So you know what you did? What Vince and Vanessa did? You grabbed pails and started bailing. While I was running around playing the role of the typical politician and failing miserably, you guys kept us afloat. The biggest reason we were even in a position to get reelected is because of you."

"I didn't know you felt that way."

"That's because I've done a horrible job telling you how I feel, and for that, I'm sorry. I'm an old combat vet. Sometimes I still find it hard to open up. I have always trusted your judgment, Chels. I have never lost faith in you. You need to know that, even if I don't always seem to be following your advice."

"I'm not always right. Blake fooled me into thinking he cared about me. Then he betrayed us again to get a job with Albright. I thought maybe he'd changed, and I'm an idiot for believing that." Oh, she's really going to beat me up over this next little gem.

"He's not taking any job with the Speaker."

"Yes he is. Parker told me he was," she says, thoroughly convinced of that fact. Our ruse seems to have fooled everyone, including her.

"He was offered. The acceptance part is something I asked him to spread. He's not taking a job with Albright, just acting like he is."

"You asked him to … You know, this is why I can't do this job anymore!" she cries, flabbergasted at the news.

"Can't is a word of defeat. You can do it and have been, it's just you don't want to anymore. Honestly, I don't blame you one bit. In your shoes, I'd probably be making the same decision. You have done nothing but sacrifice for the campaign, for me … It's time you start taking care of yourself and do what you want to do."

This is a lot for her to take in. I never appreciated how bumpy a ride the last year and a half has been for her. Chelsea is incredibly smart and much stronger than even she knows. Out of fear of displaying weakness, she has kept a lot of emotion bottled up inside of her until the dam finally burst. I feel guilty about how much of that I'm responsible for.

"So you're okay with me going to Harvard?"

"No, I'm not just okay with it, I expect a front row seat at your graduation. I am very proud of you, Chelsea. What you have been able to accomplish in just a few short years is nothing short of astounding. You're not old enough to have a drink and you're the veteran of three political campaigns and some very important lessons that we tried to teach the American public."

"I feel like a history lesson is coming."

"For once, no, but there is a request coming. We've been through a lot in the past year and a half. We survived reprimands, censures, and an expulsion vote. We work with an ally we can't trust and an old enemy we have to. The political parties are bent on destroying our influence and, to top it all, we've been getting a boat load of threats against our lives. Through it all, you have stood right next to me, for better or worse. I have no right to ask, but I need your help one last time before you go up to Cambridge."

Chelsea has the look of reluctance on her face. It was probably the same look I had when I realized they all aced their final and I had to run for Congress in the first place.

"Help doing what?"

"We have one more lesson I need your help to teach."

-SIXTY-

CHELSEA

The meeting is just about ready to start. I'm not one to condone speeding, but in this instance, I'm glad I broke that particular law to get here. I drop my purse and coat on a staffer's desk and march into the congressman's open office. The rest of my staff gawks at me, but I don't care.

I walk in and immediately see Vince, Amanda, Peyton, and Vanessa. Emilee, Brian, and Xavier must still be at school finishing up their final exams. I turn to see Blake standing next to the sofas at the end of the congressman's inner office. I walk briskly up to him and summon all my anger, hurt, and frustration over the past year.

"Hi, Chelsea," Blake says, not seeing this coming.

I cock my arm back, pivoting my hips and keeping my eye on my target just like Dad taught me. My fist connects with his cheek with a satisfying *whack* sound. I don't have Mister B's strength, so he just staggers back, off-balance. Damn, I wanted him to go down. I grab him by his suit jacket and ram him up against the wall, my forearm pressing against his neck. This works too.

"Why did you kiss me?"

"What the hell's wrong with you?" he barks, struggling to check his now swelling cheek.

"Answer the question! Why did you kiss me?"

"Ugh, you kissed Blake?" I hear Vince ask, now recovering from the suddenness of my assault on Blake.

"Shut up, Vince!" I scream over my shoulder. "Why?" I repeat, turning my attention back to the man I have pinned against a wall.

"Because I'm falling in love with you."

"Oh, please!" Vince interrupts again. "Don't buy this BS, Chels. Never trust a naked guy who offers you a coat."

"I said shut it, Vince, or you're next!"

"Vince, not for nothing, but she means that. Remember, she's a redhead, so I suggest you cool it," I hear the congressman whisper to him.

"Why should I believe you? Why should I *ever* believe you?"

"I don't expect you to. George MacDonald once said, 'To be trusted is a greater compliment than being loved.' Unfortunately for me, when it comes to you, I want both."

There is nothing but sincerity in his eyes. Since the day I met Blake I have studied his eyes for signs of deception. Considering whom he worked for at the time, I had no choice. So many decisions I've made, and so many I still need to … ah screw it.

"Okay," I say, and with that, I kiss him as hard as I can. It's only the second kiss we've every shared, and it feels even better than the first. When our lips finally part, I can feel every set of eyes in the room on us.

"I'm going to throw up," I hear Vince mutter under his breath.

"Whoa," is all Blake can say.

"Now, let me make one thing very clear to you. If you cross me, the congressman, or anyone else in this room, I will rip off each of your limbs off and laugh as you bleed out. I mean that."

"I believe you."

I release him and then turn to face my friends and mentors. Kylie is standing next to the congressman, arms wrapped around each other's backs. She has the look most women have when watching romantic scenes in the latest chick flick. Vanessa and Emilee share a similar look. Vince is not trying to hide his disgust, looking like he just ate some bad sushi. The congressman just looks … I don't know, content?

"Okay, where were you guys in the discussion? And please don't say you were discussing the latest threat to our lives." I'm not eager to discuss my actions. It's a delay tactic, as I'm sure the grilling will come at a later date.

"No, we are avoiding the subject of our imminent demise," the congressman says, giving a quick glance to Kylie. He then obliges by telling me all the details of the plan I should have been told all along. Now it makes perfect sense, making my temper tantrum up in Millfield look that much more childish. I'm actually still a little angry about that, but now's not the time to vent.

"I don't know, like, this seems so shady," Peyton concludes.

"Glad I'm not the only one feeling that way," Amanda seconds.

"That's because it is," the congressman deadpans.

"Didn't we run our campaign on the promise we wouldn't do stuff like this?" Amanda is not handling this idea very well.

"Look where that got us," Vince states. He's always been the one most eager to mix it up. "If you're not willing to play with fire, you can't cook dinner."

"That's a ridiculous analogy, Vince!"

"Politics is a dirty business. You can't appreciate what we've been through from the cozy confines of Vassar, Peyton!"

"You're a sellout, Vince!" Amanda scolds.

"Excuse me?"

"You heard me. When we ran against Beaumont, we sat around for hours castigating him over this exact behavior. We swore we would do it different. Look at us now."

"You're not down here in the trenches with us, Amanda. Don't think you can pass judgment—"

"Don't you dare—"

Under normal circumstances, the congressman would let this debate rage just as he did in the classroom. Always the teacher, he has never been shy about allowing us to voice our opinions. It's the one thing he's trying to bring back to the lower house of Congress, but this is already getting testy, and that's not tolerated.

"Enough! Both of you! Play nice in the sandbox, or no milk and cookies for you after recess."

"We're not children, Congressman."

"Then stop acting like one, Vince."

Vince is bold, and his confidence has done nothing but grow in the time we've been here. He's brazen and brash, but he's also smart enough to know not to press the issue with the congressman. He has been like a father to Vince, and there is no one my friend and colleague holds in higher esteem.

Mister Bennit takes a moment to walk over to the window and stare out at the gloomy day that's enveloped the Capitol. "Remember that day back at Briar Point when I asked how you beat Bobby Fischer at chess?"

When we ran our first campaign, none of us had any idea what to do. We were going to try to win the traditional way until Mister Bennit pitched the idea of running a campaign completely over social media. It was a fresh approach that the press latched on to and the people loved, but at the time, none of us knew it would work.

"Yeah, you said we had to make him play Candyland," Vanessa answers.

"And we did. It's a game we've played very well, only there's one small problem now."

"Everyone knows that's our game," I say, more to Vanessa, Vince, and company than to the congressman.

"You got it."

"I don't see the point. What does this have to do with our plan?" Peyton asks.

"When everyone thinks you're playing Candyland ..." I decide to finish his sentence, if for no other reason that it's the first time in a long while we've been on the same page.

"Play Chutes and Ladders."

-SIXTY-ONE-
SPEAKER ALBRIGHT

"I need everyone to stand up and step away from their desks right now!" I hear a voice boom from outside my office. What the hell?

"Mister Speaker, please step away from your desk," one of the two uniformed Capitol Police officers announces as he steps into my office. I comply immediately, a shudder of fear making its way down my spine.

"What is this all about?"

"Have any of you opened any mail today?" he responds without answering my question.

"I asked you a quest—"

"Sir, there has been a credible threat against you. Now answer my question. Has any mail been opened?"

"Uh, no, I haven't opened—"

"Has any been delivered today?" the officer asks, cutting my secretary off.

"No. We haven't received any yet," my clerk offers, appeasing the urgent appeals of the officer.

"You're sure?"

"Yes, sir." He turns and mumbles something into the radio microphone clipped to his shoulder as another officer approaches me.

"What is this all about?" I demand.

"The Capitol and all legislative offices are on lockdown. Envelopes containing white powder were mailed to at least several prominent representatives," the officer explains.

"Good Lord," is all I can mumble. "Is it anthrax? Is there any cause for alarm?" I ask nervously in quick succession. "Tests are being run now," the officer replies curtly.

"When will you know?" I almost shout.

"Sir, I need you to calm down, please. I am giving you all the information we have. I know this is stressful, but you have to be patient. The situation is still developing."

I feel like a fool for letting my nerves get the best of me. I take a couple of long, deep breaths and try to regain my composure.

"Do you at least know who the letters were mailed to?"

"We are searching the entire mail system right now, Mister Speaker. As of right now, we've identified three targets, all members of the House."

"Who?"

"You, Majority Leader Harvey Stepanik, and Minority Leader Dennis Merrick. They were intercepted in the mailroom after an anonymous tip was phoned in. We still need to determine if there were any others sent."

"They targeted the leadership. Someone doesn't like what's going on in Washington," I surmise, but nobody is listening. The officer would rather be doing anything else other than holding the hand of a politician, so he meanders over to join the conversation his colleague is having with my secretary and a staffer.

For the first time in my life, I am legitimately scared. Not for my political career or for losing a vote, but for my life. Threats are a way of life when you are a prominent elected representative, but this is different. It's the first time somebody may have tried acting on one of those threats. Nothing like this has ever happened to me personally.

This is eerily reminiscent of the 2001 anthrax scare where letters containing anthrax spores were mailed to several news media offices and Democratic U.S. Senators Tom Daschle and Patrick Leahy. Five people died and seventeen others were infected during a time where the nation was already on edge following the terrorist attacks on 9/11.

"Sir, your office appears to be clean, but the building is locked down, so please don't attempt to leave," the head of the Capitol Police detail says to me once he finishes talking on his radio. "I will leave an officer here with you."

"Do you know who sent the letters?"

"No, sir, as I'm sure my fellow officer mentioned, the investigation just started. Right now our primary concern is ensuring the safety of everyone on Capitol Hill. The National Archives, Supreme Court and all surrounding buildings have been evacuated. All Senate and House office buildings are locked down. We are trying to determine if—"

The radio screeches and the officer again steps away. A few awkward moments pass. I don't know what I should be doing. I want to help, but I have learned it's best to let the professionals handle the situation. The Capitol Police are like the Secret Service for members of Congress, and their instructions are law in a crisis like this.

"I have to go," the officer says after rushing back into my office with a look of grave concern on his face. "Since you are the Speaker of the House, I need to inform you that at least one letter containing a white powder was delivered to a member of the House and it was opened."

"Oh my God! Who was it delivered to?"

"The office is being evacuated and the occupants transported to G.W. for observation," he relays, ignoring my question.

"I asked who it was delivered to," I demand anxiously.

"Michael Bennit."

SIXTY-TWO

MICHAEL

Working in a high-risk workplace like Capitol Hill means dealing with threats most Americans will happily never have to experience. Biological contamination is one of them. Fortunately, being a logical target for any terrorist, domestic or otherwise, means there is a whole suite of protocols first responders are drilled on in the event of a crisis.

Anthrax is a serious disease caused by *Bacillus anthracis,* a bacterium that forms spores that remain dormant until the right conditions bring them to life. Of the three types of infection, inhalation anthrax is most severe. In 2001, nearly half of the cases of inhalation anthrax ended in death.

During my time in Special Forces, I was vaccinated against anthrax prior to my first deployment overseas to a combat theater. The vaccine is not available to the general public, so nobody else on my staff is. For that reason, we were immediately evacuated to George Washington University Medical Center for treatment while tests are performed to determine if we have been exposed.

"How's she doing?" I ask Chelsea, who returns from her shower dressed in hospital scrubs. To prevent further exposure, we all were required to shower and change clothes. Chelsea was the last to go.

"They sedated her. She's pretty shaken up. We all are," she responds meekly.

The blood curdling scream was probably heard in Baltimore. Ashley is one of my newer junior staffers, joining the ranks six months after I got elected. One of her responsibilities is to sort and open the mail.

She has been trained to spot suspicious envelopes and packages, but there wasn't any telltale warning signs on this one. There was a return address, no apparent signs of danger, and proper postage affixed. It wasn't until she opened it and the white powder spilled on her desk did she know there was a problem. The note just heightened the panic.

"How long are we going to have to wait before we learn if we're going to die?" Vince blurts out.

"That's not funny!" Emilee cries out.

"I wasn't trying to be, Em."

"Still not cool, Vince."

"Take a deep breath, guys," I console, trying to ratchet down the tension. "We're not going to die. If the tests come back positive, we'll be treated with an antibiotic. Early detection and treatment is the key, and we are in the premier facility in the world for both." Everyone looks at me, probably wondering how I can state that with such certainty. "I have a little training in this."

My phone vibrates for the hundredth time. This one is a text from Cisco who is pleading for information. I type a quick response and hit send. Friends help you move, real friends help you move dead bodies. Friends like Cisco will do everything in their power to make sure you don't end up one.

Minutes pass in silence, each of us left to wonder if this is a serious attempt to infect us or a cruel prank. Fortunately, the office was not nearly as full as it usually would be. Many of my junior staffers were out performing errands, and my old students went out for coffee. When Ashley opened the envelope, only Chelsea, Emilee, Vince, and I were in the office.

"How's Kylie holding up?" Chelsea asks, finally breaking the long silence.

"Scared to death. She's here, waiting in the visitors' room for the all clear with Brian, Peyton, Blake, and Amanda."

As if on command, a doctor comes into the room along with several officers from the Capitol and Metro Police. Anthrax is not communicable between people, so there is no risk to them. Even so, I regard the fact that he is not wearing a surgical mask as a good sign.

"Congressman, I'm Doctor Fleming. I have good news. Initial tests have come back negative for anthrax in your bloodstreams." There is an audible sigh of relief from all of us. The officer he walked in with speaks next.

"We also have the initial results back from testing the powder in the envelope. It was not contaminated with any known pathogen or toxin. It is just plain baking soda."

"We are going to keep Ashley here overnight for observation, just to be on the safe side," the doctor informs us. "The rest of you are free to go."

* * *

The reunion in the waiting room was a tearful one. At once, the wave of relief led to embraces that felt like they lasted hours. Kylie was especially emotional, and even when she let go of our hug, she clung to my arm tight enough to where I was losing the feeling in my hand.

Everyone is on edge, but overall, we are coping. Threatening e-mails and letters are one thing, but this was a much more surreal experience. After about a fifteen-minute impromptu group therapy meeting, we all started going our separate ways. Given our state of mind, no work would get done tonight even if we did have access to our office. The police won't let us return until tomorrow.

Chelsea is still a little shook up by the whole drama, but is handling it better than she would have a few months ago. I think Blake may already be having an influence on her. Once they leave, Kylie and I are left alone in the waiting room. We're about to follow suit and get out before they decide to draw more blood when my favorite secret agent ninja slips into the room.

"I was wondering if you would show up," I say to Terry. "Please tell me you have something more than the police do."

"I wish I could say I do," he laments. "There is no real information to give other than what was contained in the letters."

"Did you expect anything less, honey? He is only the senior coordinator for a think tank. Why would he?" Kylie challenges, baiting him to tell us who he really works for and what he actually does for them.

"Are you still going to stick with that story?" I ask him.

"Yes," he states plainly. A man of many words, isn't he?

"Yeah, right," Kylie utters in disgust.

"Okay, so tell us what you do know. The envelope had a return address. Have the police tracked it down?" I ask. The authorities said they were investigating the source of the letter, but haven't bothered to update us.

"Two zero six Washington Street, Boston, Massachusetts. I'm surprised you didn't recognize it, Congressman."

"I didn't realize I should," I reply, racking my brain for any idea why I should know that address. I'm at a loss.

"It's the physical address of the Old State House that sits next to the intersection of State and Devonshire Streets."

"Ah, crap," I bemoan in a moment of realization.

"What?" Kylie asks, both confused and concerned. "What's special about that place?"

"Nothing today," Terry tells her. "But on March 5, 1770, British Army soldiers killed some civilians there."

"It's next to the site of the Boston Massacre, hon."

"Oh, you've got to be kidding me."

There's some symbolism for you. Things were tense in Boston that year as relations between the citizens and the British soldiers stationed there deteriorated. A mob formed around one British sentry and harassed him until eight of his comrades showed up. Things escalated, and they fired into the crowd, resulting in the eventual death of five colonists. It was one of a series of formulative events that eventually led to shots being fired at Lexington Green and the onset of the American Revolution.

I struggle to draw a comparison between that incident and present day. Are we the soldiers or the hapless colonists on the wrong end of the rifle? Or am I reading too much into it? Maybe they were just hinting that these letters were intended to be a prelude to a modern day massacre.

"Do you have anything else, Terry?"

"As I said, we're still—"

"So what are you doing here?" Kylie interjects, the impatience dripping off her tongue. Does she think he's at fault for not somehow divining this would happen and warning us?

"Searching for information I don't have so we can continue our inquiry."

"What kind of information?"

"I need to know what your letter said."

"Important principles may, and must, be inflexible. The price for dishonesty is death. This envelope has anthrax, and now so do you." I only looked at the note for a few seconds before clearing my staff out of the office and calling the authorities, but I will never forget those words for the rest of my life.

"Abraham Lincoln," Terry says, recognizing the quote.

"I'm impressed. I figured it would take a Civil War buff or history teacher to pick up on the first sentence."

"Does it mean anything to you?" Kylie asks, inquiring if there is some hidden, darker meaning behind the quote.

"No, but it wasn't the same typewritten text as the others."

"What did the others say?"

"The harder the conflict, the more glorious the triumph. This envelope contains anthrax."

"That's it?"

"From what I've been told, yes," Terry states blandly.

"Do you recognize the quote?"

"Thomas Paine," I tell her, before turning back to Terry. "It sounds like a history buff targeted the leadership in the House. Different parties, different roles, different opinions."

"Yeah, but it's forced. Someone is trying too hard, and that implies a conspiracy," he states with an unnerving amount of confidence. I don't see it.

"How so?" Despite being on edge about the attack, Kylie is eager to get to the bottom of this. All her fears almost became reality today.

"Your note was different than the others. I think the others were a smokescreen, and why an anonymous tip was phoned in before they were delivered. The message of this attack was aimed at you. Someone thinks they can influence you by scaring you."

-SIXTY-THREE-

CHELSEA

Our relationship is only a week old, and we haven't really had much time to enjoy it. I have not had a lot of boyfriends, but whenever I started dating a guy, I felt giddy with excitement. It was new, fun, and … exhilarating. Of course, that was all before I took this job.

Blake and I have spent a lot of time together, but sadly, most of it has been work related. We have a bill to defeat, and have been doing everything we can to ensure that happens. Essentially, that means working long days, endless nights, and little sleep to prepare for either when the sun comes back up. Our romantic dinners have been limited to pizza and Chinese takeout in the office. It also means my quality time with Blake tonight, as with the last several, has been spent working over as the clock ticks toward midnight.

"Ah, this sucks," Blake says, stretching in the chair across the desk from mine.

"Stop your whining. You worked on Beaumont's staff. You're used to this."

"Actually, we never worked this hard, except once and a while during a campaign."

"I guess that's why you're here and Beaumont isn't." I look up to gauge his reaction. "Sorry, I didn't mean for it to come across like that."

Blake smiles, and I'm happy he didn't take my comment the wrong way. He is still sensitive about the time he spent with his former mentor who now has several felony convictions. I learned that the hard way.

"Forget it. I know what you meant."

"Good, because I'm not sure I can handle any more stress piled on right before Christmas."

"Is the fake anthrax attack still bothering you?"

"No. Well, yeah, but that's not what I meant."

"You haven't finished your shopping yet, have you?"

"No, and now I have one more to shop for," I say, giving Blake a playful smile he eagerly returns.

"Well, at least all the threats you guys were receiving seem to have stopped. That reduces the stress a little."

"I only wish that were true," I say, instantly regretting it.

"What do you mean? I spoke to the congressman earlier and he says you haven't gotten more than one or two since the anthrax scare."

This has been wearing on my conscience since I started doing it three days ago, so without explanation I open up the bottom desk drawer and reach way in the back behind the hanging file folders. Finally grasping what I was looking for, I pull out the bundle of letters and set them on the desk.

"Are those what I think they are?" he asks, staring at the bundle. Yes, rocket scientist, they are.

"So much for the threats stopping, right?"

"Holy shit, Chels, Congressman Bennit doesn't know about this?"

"No, and if you breathe a word of it to him, you will wish you had anthrax when I get done with you." I'm a redhead and that is not an idle threat.

"Why would you do this?"

"Because it's my job to protect him. His focus needs to be on winning this vote four days from now, and he can't do that if he's spending every waking moment worrying about us."

"But there could be something in there—"

"There is nothing in any of these we haven't already seen," I interrupt. The Capitol Police have their hands full investigating the anthrax scare the media is still obsessing about, so they don't have any interest in more creepy letters.

"But—"

"This upcoming vote means everything to us. If it succeeds, all the work we've done to this point is for nothing. We need this rules bill to be defeated to do our job, even if the media and the rest of the country don't care."

I don't tell him it will be the last vote I am ever involved in. He doesn't need to be privy to that information. I guess that's why I am working so hard. I want to leave on a positive note. It would be one of the few I've had here.

"Have you talked to Kylie about this?"

"Are you kidding? She is an emotional wreck right now. She thinks she's in danger of losing him to something terrible."

Blake spins the stack of letters on the desk and reads the envelope on top. I can tell he's quietly mulling things over, and I begin to wonder if he disagrees with my decision.

"He's going to be pissed off if he learns about this."

"Probably."

"You don't care?"

"Everyone is either upset, pissed off, unhappy, worried, or stressed out these days. Amanda is angry at our tactics, Brian is annoyed we gave up using social media to influence the vote ... I can't make anyone happy, so I've given up. All I am trying to do is get us through this session of Congress—everything else will work itself out after that."

Blake stares at me with an expression I can't quite place. Our relationship is brand new, and although we have known each other for a while, we don't really know each other. For all the time I have spent trying to read him for deception, I never paid attention to any of his other emotions.

"What? Are you pissed off at me, too?

"Hell no. Quite the opposite, actually. I'm proud of you."

"Uh, okay, that's not what I expected. Why?"

"Because, Chelsea, you are doing what you think you need to do to protect your boss, consequences be damned. Now you're acting like a chief of staff."

-SIXTY-FOUR-

MICHAEL

No less than a half dozen freshman representatives sleep in their offices. Some don't want the hassle of maintaining a residence in the district, and others do it to as a public relations stunt for the benefit of the voters back home. I did it myself for a while until Kylie found work in D.C. When she found an apartment, she asked me to move in with her. It is technically her place, but it's really ours.

Many politicians choose to live outside the District of Columbia in Virginia, but Kylie is too much of a hipster for that. Having lived in the East Village of Manhattan for so long, I wasn't surprised when she chose a new, chic building north of Massachusetts Avenue. Earning the moniker "NoMa," it's an up and coming neighborhood conveniently located just four blocks north of Capitol Hill and Union Station. I can walk to work if I choose.

The apartment itself is reasonably priced and more than spacious enough for the two of us. The furniture was all transplanted from her NYC walk-up, and we collaborated on the décor, which is to say she picked it all. I still maintain my place back in Millfield because I legally have to, and because she'd never let me keep most of my furniture.

With a mere four days left before the vote which will determine the political direction of the government and how the House of Representatives functions, I am doing what any good representative would do under these circumstances — Christmas shopping. Hey, there's only eight days left until Santa comes and I've done nothing. Thank God for whoever invented the online shopping cart.

My notebook computer in my lap, Sam Adams in my hand, and credit card melting due to overuse, I occasionally glance up at CNN on the flat screen hung on the wall. The coverage of what is going on in this lame duck session has been unimpressive, and what they have reported is generally wrong. News coverage strongly influences political behavior, but the media are a capricious bunch. Nostradamus couldn't predict which stories they cover and which get ignored.

Obviously, the anthrax scare from a few days ago is still dominating the headlines as investigators scramble for answers. It may have only been innocuous baking soda, but it's more than enough to distract the media. As a result, the events surrounding this rules bill introduced in the lame duck session have been glossed over.

Political pundits still dwell on the fact there is no majority party, but none are concerned about the latest tactic to address that situation. Any outrage we managed to spark and stoke on social media has fallen off in the wake of the faux-attack. As I feared, nothing we have done on that front will translate into action. I thought it was a long-shot before, but now relying on social media to affect change is an impossibility.

Since we first found out about this bill a month and a half ago, we worked tirelessly to defeat it using every tool available to us. Media, social media, pressure from constituents, and even through trying to broker deals. None of it worked, except to inspire people to constantly let us know they wanted us dead. Thank God those threats seemed to have abated. Now, all that's left is the Hail Mary play I sent Blake out on.

The *Washington Post* has stopped Kylie from working on the two biggest political stories of the year: the debacle that was my Ethics hearing and subsequent expulsion vote, and the anthrax scare which still has Capitol Hill tied up in knots.

Without her tenacious attitude to lead the way, the press lost interest in pursuing the perpetrator of my witch hunt last summer. I guess trying to frame an elected representative for bribery doesn't rank as a scandal in this day in age.

The trail went cold fast, and despite the obvious involvement of Ibram & Reed, most investigative arms of news organizations moved on to alleged voter fraud following the November election. Unfortunately, the FBI and other watchdog groups are not having much success either, although they don't have papers to sell or viewers to entice, so they are still officially working on it.

Now the dog has a new bone to chew on, so the old one is left out in the yard. The anthrax scare is the shiny new media toy, and all their resources are devoted to endless coverage of it. Of course, they haven't added a single shred of analytical value or new information to the discussion or investigation.

To compensate for her perceived lack of value, Kylie is putting in some overtime by writing about the rules bill on the side. Part of me believes she's doing it to distract herself from the threats and the white powder scare. I can't say I blame her for wanting the distraction.

Unfortunately, there is little interest being generated in the stories she is sending out. The woman who could have gotten my grocery list printed during our first campaign is now suffering from a dry spell that makes the Gobi Desert look like a tropical rain forest. To say it is frustrating for her is an exercise in understatement.

Speaking of the devil, Kylie comes in and slams her purse on the small kitchen island, then tosses her coat on the ground. She may not be a clean freak, but this is aberrant behavior even for her.

"Tough day, honey?"

"I don't want to talk about it."

She sits next to me on the couch with her legs tucked under her and buries her head into my chest. I drape my arm around her and kiss her forehead, pausing long enough to enjoy the pleasant scent of the fruity conditioner she uses on her hair. It's the smallest things in life like this I enjoy most.

"Do you ever wonder if this was all worth it?"

"What do you mean?" She lifts her head off my chest and cranes her neck to look up at me. I think the question caught her a little off guard.

"I mean, do you miss the days after I lost the first election where we just crashed at your apartment and only left to shop for groceries and rock out to Dead Rocking Horse at the Bowry Ballroom?"

Kylie has never been a mainstream music fan. She's adamant in her belief that a select few choose the winners and losers in the music industry. It's how we end up having to endure the obscene lack of talent and publicity antics of people like Justin Beiber and Brittany Spears. Living in New York, she became an ardent follower of bands few others know about. Dead Rocking Horse is one of them, and if people ever had the chance to hear them, they would own the Billboard Top One Hundred.

"We were unemployed then, Michael."

"I didn't say there weren't a couple of *small* downsides."

"Small downsides?"

"Yeah. 'Money is something you need in case you don't die tomorrow.'"

"Is that your favorite *Wall Street* quote?"

"'Greed is good' has already been adopted by everyone else in this town," I answer, paraphrasing the actual line. Even being a history guy, Oliver Stone's 1987 hit starring Michael Douglas as the venerable, yet despicable Gordon Gekko, is one of my favorite movies.

"You're going to lose the vote on this bill," Kylie responds, suddenly up shifting from light to serious.

"I know."

"You don't sound upset about it. If that's the case, maybe you should just vote for it." Uh-oh.

"Why would I do that?"

"Maybe the threats against you might end. People will stop sending you white powder everyone thinks could be laced with anthrax, or ricin, or any other biological agent that could kill you through the mail."

"Please tell me you aren't serious."

"I'm dead serious!"

"Kylie, I am not going to be blackmailed into voting for something I don't believe in!" I exclaim, getting a little heated at the notion of it all.

"You are going to lose anyway."

"It doesn't matter. I will not compromise my principles because someone threa—"

"Even if the threat becomes real? What happens when someone really does try to hurt you, or Chelsea, or any of us?"

"Honey, I can't afford to think that way. I have a job to do, and I will never be scared me into voting for something I don't believe in. You know that. I love you, and I love my staff, but if I change my vote out of fear for my safety or anyone else's, I don't deserve to be here."

She doesn't want to hear those words, but she knows I am right. Kylie is driven, independent, but also very protective. She's scared, and isn't realizing the fear of the unknown is clouding her judgment.

"I'm sorry," she says, tabling the argument more than conceding the point. "What's the plan to defeat this bill now that nobody is paying attention?"

"I'm hoping for a miracle, like maybe the mainstream media waking up and doing their jobs." She scoffs at the notion. "What?" I ask sarcastically. "You don't think the media will accurately portray what's going on here?"

"I work for the established media and I wouldn't trust them to give the weather report in the Sahara. The noise about the tie in the House and the white powder gives them higher ratings than a rules bill Americans don't understand. If you are expecting the media to suddenly shift away from that, you are going to be disappointed."

Kylie has not been aloof in her dissatisfaction with her current employer. It isn't working for them she has a problem with, it is the constraints they have put on her. She loves journalism, but just as she learned with the *New York Times* before they fired her, she's usually at odds with their agendas.

"I think it's time we seriously discuss something. I want to take our relationship to a new level." Wait, what?

"Uh ..."

"No, not that. I can wait for that." She sits up and looks me dead in the eye. "I want to come work for you."

"As tempting as that sounds, it's a horrible idea," I say, trying not to sound relieved. It's not that marrying Kylie is not high on my agenda, because it is. I'm just not quite ready for that level of commitment considering what happened to me with Jessica.

"With Chelsea leaving, you need a new chief of staff: that's Vince. When he moves up, you'll need to replace him. Vanessa doesn't like working with the media, so she's out. I want to be your PR person."

I don't say anything. It's not that I don't want her to work for me, because on some level, the idea does appeal to me. On the other hand, happy personal and business relationships rarely coexist between people. Kylie is fearful and wants to be with me every minute she can. This request is an extension of that. She prepped the battlefield well in this conversation, and I need to avoid any landmines.

"Vince isn't going to be the chief of staff, is he?" she says, squinting at me as she does when drawing conclusions. I wait too long to reply, and now I'm about to have another problem. "Oh my God, you promised it to Blake, didn't you?"

"Not exactly."

"Not exactly as you didn't, or not exactly as in you didn't want to tell me?"

"I don't know, both?"

"Hm," she says with a disagreeing look. "Why would you ever even consider him working on the staff?"

"Maybe I see something in him everyone else doesn't."

"I think you fell and hit your head or something. He's a lying scoundrel who would betray you in a New York second to advance his own agenda. You treat your staff like family. Do you really want him to be a part of it?"

"I'm not sure that's true anymore. Besides, Chelsea is dating him now. That does make him a part of it," I say in my defense.

"I'm not sold on that being a good idea either, but that's her choice." My God, we sound like parents discussing our daughter bringing home an edgy guy, covered in tattoos, and driving a van.

"You know, it dawns on me that he was dating your sister," I recall, alluding to the brief relationship Kylie's sister

Madison had with Blake when they were both serving on Beaumont's staff.

"Ew. Don't remind me."

"If things had gone a little differently, he could have been your brother-in-law."

"Okay, seriously, you're making me gag here."

"Imagine that wedding …"

"Stop it!" she chastises and hits me with a throw pillow. "Thanks so much. I'm going to have night terrors tonight with that image in my head now."

We share a laugh, and it is a welcome respite from the growing tension over this vote, Chelsea almost leaving, Blake's role, and a host of other things. Now we can add Kylie's newly revealed desire to leave journalism and come to work for me.

The thought of her becoming her sister came to mind, but I bit my tongue. Kylie was always critical of Madison for becoming a press secretary who thought nothing of lying to everybody for Winston Beaumont. Madison retorted by classifying her as a second-rate journalist clinging to an unreachable idealism. It's a touchy subject to bring up with her, so there's no reason to broach that subject right now or I may get hit with something harder than a throw pillow. Like a lamp, or a coffee table.

"Is Amanda coming around at all?" she asks, suddenly getting more serious again.

"No. If anything, she's even more adamant against what we're doing."

"I know she's an idealist, but it's not like you're signing a pact with Satan. You'd think she would see that."

"Honestly, I see her point. I don't know if what we're doing is the right thing."

"A lot is riding on this vote. If you lose, the Speaker fixes one problem and creates a myriad of others. I don't know how much longer the country will tolerate a broken government. Your scheme with Blake is the only bullet left in your rifle. What are you going to do if it doesn't work?

"Simple. Pray for America."

-SIXTY-FIVE-
SENATOR VIANO

Bells in every clock on the House side of the Capitol and throughout the three office buildings representatives work in sound twice to summon members to the floor for a vote. When you want to intercept one of them, all you need is the route they take to the House chamber and the patience to lie in wait. The only catch is if they work in the Rayburn Building and take the small Capitol Hill subway. Then you're screwed.

Stalking Michael Bennit on a freezing cold December day right before Christmas is hardly what I would have foreseen last summer. I didn't expect him to even be here. He is leading a charmed political life, and I have had to adjust my plan accordingly on a couple of occasions because of it. This is no different.

"A little cold out here to be setting an ambush," he says, his hands stuffed into the pockets of his long, dark, wool overcoat.

"Drastic times call for drastic measures, especially when a certain political ally stops taking your calls."

"The easiest way I know to stop being used as a marionette is to cut the strings. Wouldn't you agree?"

"I would, only I never intended for you to think of me as a puppet master." More like I wanted you to know I was. "We shared a common goal, Michael, and we still do."

"I doubt that. Tell me what you really want, Marilyn," he says, continuing the walk to the House.

"I want to help you bring order back to Washington. It's what I always wanted."

"Yeah, I know, and you think a third party is the way to do it." I need to be careful here.

"I do, but it's not the only way. I know you met with the moderates. Including them was a shrewd move, especially considering the credibility we earned by not going after them in the election."

Michael doesn't dispute me using "we" which is a good sign. The fact that he hasn't used his special ops training to break my neck is another. "I like the idea of forming a caucus, regardless of what happens with this bill," I continue, not meaning a word of it.

"I asked what you wanted, Marilyn, not what you thought about it." Ouch.

"Okay, here it is. I want to be involved. I told you I'm running for the other Senate seat in Virginia next election as an Independent. I want to form a caucus just like yours in the upper house."

"You figured out how to hedge your bet very effectively."

"What do you mean?"

"If this vote passes and we form a party, you're in a position to run for the Senate as our only high-profile candidate. If we don't, you still can hitch your star on the caucus and accomplish the same end."

"Is that a bad thing?" I ask. "I have told you I want to get back into the Senate. This helps both of us."

"What happens if we win the vote today?"

"There is no prayer of you winning this vote," I say, trying to stifle a laugh in the process. "And if you think you are going to sway the moderates to vote against it, you're badly mistaken. They won't because it isn't going to make a difference, you know that."

"I do."

"So, you just have to figure out what your next move is once it passes. I can help you with that."

"You really think I can ever trust you?" he says, stopping and confronting me.

"I don't expect you to trust me. But this is Washington, D.C. Nobody trusts anybody here. The only thing that exists is political alliances, and they work only as long as our agendas are the same. Right now, they are. We might not see eye-to-eye on how we get there, but the goal is the same, and you are going to need every person you can in your corner supporting that come next year."

It's a long shot, but one worth taking. With so many plans falling through over the last six months, I need something to cling to. The hard part about being desperate is not appearing that way. Michael looks hard at me, but says nothing. And nothing is not a "no."

"I have to vote. We'll talk after the session ends," is all he says before turning and striding toward the doors leading to the House side of the Capitol.

Either Bennit is a trusting fool, or I am just that good of a liar. I head off toward the visitor entrance, happy to be mere minutes from escaping the frigid arctic temperatures gripping the capital. Now I only have to watch the events unfold and figure out how to best deliver what I promised to James.

SIXTY-SIX

SPEAKER ALBRIGHT

I reserved only a couple of hours for debate on the resolution. As it only applies to House rules and not the American people, we are doing this for our benefit and not that of the country. There will be no corresponding bill in the Senate, at least not this term. If there is ever a surge of independents into that chamber, they will be faced with the same challenges we are dealing with now.

Not that I expect that to happen. Getting elected using social media in a relatively small congressional district is one thing, but convincing an entire state to vote for you is quite another. It is the one reason why so few independents are elected to the Senate, and why the ones who are hail from among the smaller states in the union.

Of course, the social media aspect is the great equalizer. As the numbers of American adults who use some form of it has grown, so does the threat that the big money and large staffs once needed to run campaigns are no longer necessary. Bennit has proven that in the House, so I suppose it could also be applied to the Senate, and maybe even the presidency.

But that is a future problem for others. I am focused on the here and now. Most of the members are already in the chamber, looking to vote and get this piece of business behind us so we can catch flights back to our districts and enjoy the holiday season. For those who lost in November, they can also mourn the end of their political careers.

I gavel open the start of the vote once the final resolution is read by a clerk. To determine where any bill stands on passage, my Democratic counterpart and I rely on the whips of each party to bring us the headcount. The Republican Whip reported that I may have lost a smattering of moderates, but that the rest of the party is with me. The Democratic Whip reported the same thing to Dennis Merrick.

Moderates. They are a plague on the good order of modern politics. The die-hards of each party call them either DINOs or RINOs; a derogatory moniker meaning *Democrat In Name Only* or *Republican In Name Only*. In recent sessions, we have forced them to toe the party line, but with Bennit around, they are wild cards.

I know he hosted a meeting among them, but I am being told that most won't sacrifice their standing with the party to go with him on this vote. I have been assured of the same thing by the Dems, so I'm not too concerned when the first moderates begin voting "nay."

The larger concern is why the hard core Democrats haven't made their way over to vote. I'm probably overreacting, but there is a lot of activity at the long table in the front of the chamber where the party leadership sits. There is a lot of discussion going on over something that was settled days, or even weeks ago.

Harvey Stepanik gets my attention and I climb off the rostrum and meet with him on the side of the room.

"What's going on?" I ask, more out of curiosity than concern.

"We lost some moderates."

"We knew we would. Why haven't Merrick and the rest of the Democrats started voting yet?"

"I'm not really sure," Harvey says, looking back over his shoulder at the gaggle formed around the table where Merrick is holding court. "It's probably nothing."

I've been in this town too long to believe that. There's something afoot, and I need to find out what it is while there is still time to do something about it.

"Find out, Harv. Quickly."

I return back to my seat in front of the huge American flag that serves as a backdrop on the wall. By the time I get there, the meeting has broken up at the table in front of me. A couple of dozen Democratic members head to cast their vote, their cards in their hands. Merrick looks over at me and squints before joining them. For the first time since introducing this bill, I realize that we may have a serious problem.

SIXTY-SEVEN

MICHAEL

A satisfying look of panic creeps onto the Speaker's face when the first dozen Democrat votes show up. An up or down vote is a fifty-fifty proposition on paper, but most bills never make it to the Floor unless the Speaker knows exactly what the result will be. At least, that's how it *used* to work.

During George Washington's two terms following the ratification of the Constitution, a rivalry grew between the two Federalists John Adams and Thomas Jefferson. Their incessant disagreements led Jefferson to form the Democratic–Republican Party, which ironically contains the historical seeds of our current two-party system.

The word "Democratic" means *will of the people,* while the word "Republican" implies *rule of law,* and Jefferson's party held the presidency for the first quarter of the nineteenth century. They later split into the parties we know today, but have only become so polarized and mistrustful of each other over the last several decades. Now we get to see just how far that rift has grown.

"You always end up with the best seat in the house," Cisco says, plopping down in the adjacent chair. "Wasn't this the seat you watched your political career almost flicker out from?"

"Yeah, but since it didn't, it's become my lucky chair."

"The Dems look like they are ready to vote. Sure you don't want to take the bet?"

"No thanks, brother. You've taken enough of my money this year."

Francisco is the kind of guy who will bet on anything. I've only known him for six months or so and lost over a dozen bets to him. You would think I'd have learned sooner.

The tally on the blue board keeps incrementing, now with a couple of liberal Democrats joining their Republican colleagues in voting for the resolution.

"You ever hear of Shays' Rebellion?"

"Gueverra?"

"Not that Che. It was an armed uprising in Massachusetts between 1786 and 1787. Daniel Shays was a veteran of the American Revolution and one of the leaders of the uprising."

"You and your history lessons," Cisco says with a roll of his eyes. "I would have failed your class."

"Probably. Anyway, the rebellion was ignited by a postwar economic depression and harsh government policies to solve the state's debt problems. Protesters started by shutting down courts, stopped hearings on tax and debt collection, and became increasingly radicalized. They formed a militia to seize the federal Springfield Armory in late January of 1787 and continued their resistance until a June skirmish with government troops left them beleaguered."

"Please tell me you have a point to this."

"I always do. The rebellion sparked in a political climate where people were being very vocal in their call for reform of the Articles of Confederation. It ended up affecting the debates that ultimately shaped our Constitution."

Cisco looks at me, waiting impatiently for the explanation. I make him sweat it out for a minute while a few more votes pop up on the board.

"And?"

"Even if we lose this vote, I have to hold out hope that we can still shape things to come for the better. I want our revolución to shape America's future just like Shays' did."

"You sound like a defeatist. This vote isn't close to over yet."

"No, it isn't. But you're watching the same board I am. You can't be optimistic. Some of those people who voted for this bill were at our meeting."

"They don't matter. It really all comes down to what Merrick does," Cisco opines, ever the optimist.

Cisco maybe the most real legislator the country has ever elected. We share the same detest for the partisan political process, but he enjoys this game immensely. Given my only real desire was to provide my constituents with real representation, I'm not as thrilled to play the game. He relishes playing the role of outcast and maverick, and loves having the power of tying the elites in knots.

"I'm surprised you didn't bring popcorn."

"I did. It got confiscated by the sergeant-at-arms. Something about not maintaining proper decorum." The scary thing is, I'm not sure if he's kidding or not.

"You let that stop you?" He reaches into his coat pocket and pulls out a small rectangular red bag.

"I brought Skittles instead."

I shake my head as he opens the package. Cisco is right about one thing, this whole vote really does hinges on what Merrick does. However, as the next five Democrats who vote all cast "yea" ballots, I question where he is getting his optimism from. I'm convinced we are going to lose this battle.

-SIXTY-EIGHT-
CHELSEA

"I just got done talking with the minority leader," Vince says as he eases into the seat next to me. I am so engrossed texting Peyton and Amanda from my phone that I didn't even notice him.

"What did Merrick have to say?" Vanessa asks from the other side of me.

"Not much."

"Do you know what he plans to do?"

"I don't know. He lost his seat, so it's a crap shoot. Where are Peyton and Emilee?" Vince asks after noticing our absent friends.

"I just texted them to get over here." Seats were almost impossible to save up here in the visitor's gallery for this vote, so I'm hoping Peyton and Emilee hurry. Final exams are now over on college campuses throughout the country, so most of our campaign team physically made it to Washington. Xavier is missing due to his sports obligation, but he sent us a message wishing us luck, which is more than I can say for one of my friends at the moment.

"Is Amanda still not coming?"

"No."

The more Amanda thought about the tactic the congressman used with Blake, the less she liked it. She became more and more vocal in her dissent in the days leading up to the vote until she disengaged altogether and then announced she couldn't be a part of this.

Her defection from our merry band has hit the congressman pretty hard. I suppose it was only a matter of time before one of us found ourselves in a crisis of conscience over a tactic and decided to leave, but it still stings. Amanda was always one of the most dedicated in our little group. Vince isn't taking her absence well either.

"Have you heard anything from other staff?" Vince queries, making me think he has money on the result.

"The Three Amigos told me on the way here that their bosses would be taking a big risk and they weren't sure what they would do."

Vanessa taps me on the arm and points. "We're about to find out." Even Brian takes his nose out of his smartphone long enough to see the activity on the Floor.

Sure enough, the Democrats are beginning to make their way to cast their ballots. Five minutes into the vote and only the Republicans and some of the moderates have cast their votes. Right now, we are losing very badly. The first group of Democrats voted for the resolution, but this is the moment of truth. The ballot cast by Minority Leader Dennis Merrick will go a long way in knowing what the rest of his party will do.

I didn't see it flash up on the board. It wasn't until the House erupted that I realized what happened. The little globe light next to Merrick's name switched to red for "nay" and I realize we're still in the fight. Democrats are now voting against the bill in droves, and the numbers get tighter in a hurry. They are not putting up a united front, though. There are some defections, so will it be enough?

The commotion in the chamber reminds me a lot of the day they tried to oust Mister Bennit. Congressman Reyes helped drive the wedge between the parties to win that vote, and the congressmen decided to try it one more time. One thing in the world of a two-party system we can count on: Republicans and Democrats will never trust each other enough to cooperate for very long, even when it is in their best interests to do so. Today is no exception.

The rumor Blake was going to work for the Speaker worked to our advantage just like Mister Bennit thought it would. Since he was still friendly with many Democratic staffers, he leaked news that the GOP quietly struck a deal with Bennit and the icandidates to freeze them out. It was this blatant fabrication that Amanda took umbrage with and decried as the petty politics we swore not to engage in.

She may be right, but it also has worked enough to put doubts in the mind of Democrats about trusting the GOP enough to work with them. The consequences are too high for either party to make a mistake when the balance of power in the United States House of Representatives is at stake. As a result, they are overwhelmingly voting against the bill.

Of course, he never told the moderates of the plan, curious to see if they would go with him on their own. Most of them did. This is an early test of their loyalty to our cause. If the votes of the moderates who are returning are any indication, there will be over a hundred representatives in our caucus at the start of next Congress.

"What'd we miss?" Peyton asks as she sheds her coat and moves into our aisle. I point to the tally board behind a very upset Speaker Albright.

"Damn! That's close!" Emilee observes. "Aren't you allowed to be on the House Floor to watch this?"

"Yeah, but there's nothing for me to do down there so I thought I'd sit up here and watch it with you guys," I respond.

Besides, if this ends badly, I'm not going to want to be down there when I get emotional. There are only a few minutes left, and we are winning by only a handful of votes. We may have managed to get a majority of the Dems to go against the majority party, but this is still far from decided.

-SIXTY-NINE-
SPEAKER ALBRIGHT

Two dozen votes are left to be cast, all from Democrats, and by a quick look, half will not be returning for the next Congress having fallen victim to Bennit's icandidates. In the time I have been Speaker, only two Floor votes have surprised me. The first was the day Parker changed his vote to keep Bennit in the House. This is the second.

In modern politics, Floor votes are never a surprise. Well, almost never, as current history shows. The Hastert Rule allows me to decide what gets voted on, and party whips tirelessly effort to report where members stand on each and every issue to be decided. The system is designed to avoid embarrassing surprises by utilizing both. I guess that is one more change Michael Bennit is bringing to Washington.

Six more ballots are cast and I make up some ground. Apparently some of the Democrats didn't buy what the minority leader was selling and broke ranks to do the right thing. I need nine more votes to go my way and I will still win, even in the face of betrayal by the insufferable Dennis Merrick and his band of backstabbers.

Six more votes go up on the board and I lose the ground I just gained. What is wrong with these people? Don't they understand what is at stake here? Not only the drama of not having a majority party, but what all these independents able to vote with no accountability means?

When the first "present" vote pops up, I know it's over. The remaining dozen representatives all lost their seats, and aren't willing to draw the ire of either party should they ever want to run again. In my mind, it's cowardice. They could have been the difference between victory and defeat.

As the seconds tick down, the game is up. I gavel the end of the vote and announce the result. The words taste bitter coming out of my mouth, and I feel the sting of defeat. It's the last piece of business to be conducted by this Congress, so with little in the way of ceremony, I bring a close to the session. Everybody is in a rush to get out of here. Everyone, except possibly Michael Bennit, that is.

I climb down from the rostrum and track him down in the middle of the center aisle. It's embarrassing that I had to fight through the small crowd of congressmen and women who were taking a moment to extend their congratulations to the maverick.

"Bennit! How the hell did you pull that off behind my back?" I shout, forgetting any manners or proper behavioral conventions.

"I don't think I owe you an explanation, Mister Speaker," he states defiantly.

"No, you don't, but I would like to know anyway."

Michael weighs it in his mind for a few seconds. "I told the outgoing minority leader that if they supported the amendment, I would convince all the icandidates to join the Republican Party."

"Dennis Merrick would never believe that. You had help."

He shrugs. There is something more, but Michael Bennit isn't going to divulge it, not that it matters. Regardless of how he managed it, he exploited the ideological Achilles' heel that defines the modern Congress. Republicans and Democrats haven't trusted each other in decades, and Bennit used the rift against us.

"All you've done is destroy a process that has worked in this country for over two hundred years."

"Mister Speaker, not having a majority party is not the end of the world, despite your panicked attempts to color it that way. Are you really implying that a country who landed a man on the moon half a century ago can't manage a simple ballot process in one of its houses of Congress?"

"Our political structure relies on the two-party system. Americans need that to keep their government functioning."

-SEVENTY-
MICHAEL

"Keep their government functioning? Is that what you call this?"

I open my arms and look around the room for the dramatic effect I probably don't need given the absurdity of his statement. The men and women around me, dressed smartly in suits and other business attire, may look serious, and tell the voters they have the solution to the nation's problems, but it's a farce.

In Congress, politics trumps substance every time. The weakness of most political firebrands these days is that they often put partisan warfare ahead of all other considerations. Policy outcomes are a secondary concern—the greatest desire of modern politicians is to make sure their side wins and the other guys lose at all cost. That's the game, Chutes and Ladders.

"Americans went to the polls in November and elected us because they've lost faith in how that system functions, Mister Speaker. You can't understand that because you, along with the media, propagate the myth that this country is so ideologically torn, cooperation can't exist. You've promoted the fiction for years that only the party who owns a sizable majority can get anything done, only the American people aren't buying it anymore. While there will always be ideological differences in this country, they are not nearly as vast as you wish they were."

"And what happens when this experiment of yours fails?" he says with a certain smugness and unsettling certainty. No wonder politicians never work toward common goals anymore—they are too busy undermining each other to bother.

"That's a fairly large presumption on your part, sir, but assuming that's the case, Americans will figure out who's to blame and look to rectify the problem in the next election."

"It amazes me you think people are smart enough to realize that, let alone willing to go to the polls to act on it."

"I do believe they are, Mister Speaker, and I also believe we are in a new age of political engagement. Social media makes them that way."

"You're a grunt, Bennit, nothing more. A poor soldier who wandered into a war he shouldn't be fighting. You don't understand modern politics, don't understand how the system works, and ultimately don't belong here."

"Do you know who a grunt is? He's an exhausted, dirt-covered, camouflaged, and heavily armed son of a bitch who has protected the flock by keeping the wolf away for over two hundred thirty years. He's done more for this country than any career politician ever has."

"This isn't over, Bennit. You have no idea how powerful the people are who want to see you destroyed. They will stop at nothing to make that happen, and believe me, they never lose."

"Here's a little history question for you, Mister Speaker. Do you know what King Leonidas, George Washington, and Michael Bennit all have in common?" He just looks at me. "We were all underdogs who kicked the crap out of the smug bastards who didn't think they were capable of losing."

"Leonidas lost at Thermopylae," Speaker Albright says with a "gotcha" grin. Really? Fine, here comes today's history lesson.

"Yeah, he did, but then came the naval battle in the Straits of Salamis which forced Xerxes' retreat back to Asia. He left Mardonius behind in Greece to complete the invasion, but all he managed to accomplish was to get routed in the Battle of Plataea, bringing a disastrous ending to the invasion. So yes, Leonidas lost the battle, but sometimes inspiring a nation with a noble defeat yields better long-term results than a short-term victory. Wouldn't you agree?" The double meaning is not lost on him. It wouldn't have been lost on Winston Beaumont either.

My eyes dare him to open his mouth, but to his credit, he doesn't. He shakes his head and walks away, following the aisle up to the doors leading out of the chamber. We have come full circle. My first real conversation as a congressman during my term ended with Speaker Albright walking up that same aisle while plotting my demise. Now it ends with him walking up it trying to stop his own. Who said irony was only for writers and poets?

"Michael, you're the Roadrunner of modern politics." Members who supported us wait to offer congratulations and various accolades, but none of them surprise me as much as the man who belongs to that Barry White-esque bass voice.

"No matter how many traps we set for you, or how many anvils we try to drop on you, you're still smart enough make us be the ones who fall off the cliff," Thomas Parker muses, finishing his rather appropriate Looney Tunes reference.

Despite all the political disagreements I've had with him, I have to admit the guy is growing on me. And it's not just because he saved my ass last August. He's a staunch conservative, but that's a reflection of the voters in his very Southern district. He's a gigantic pain, literally and figuratively, but at least he's here for the right reasons.

"Beep, beep." That earns a smirk from the distinguished Republican.

"See you next year, Congressman. It ought to be a very interesting one."

"We just found something we can agree on, Reverend," I say, offering my hand. "Merry Christmas, sir." He shakes it, gives me a nod and heads off.

Once again I am nearly alone in the center of the House chamber, the heads of my staff peeking over the railing in the visitor's gallery above. Déjà vu all over again, as Yogi Berra would say.

"You're the talk of the kingdom, my liege," Cisco says, giving me a bear hug from behind. "Courtesans will fall to your feet and minstrels will sing songs about your victorious exploits."

"Cisco, have you been watching *Monty Python and the Holy Grail* again, or were you wrapped up in a game of Dungeons & Dragons during the vote?"

"Eh, leave me to my fun, man. I haven't had a reason to smile this much since my girl bought me mag wheels for my lawn mower. Come on, we have a horde of press to impress on the steps."

"Mag wheels on your lawn mower. You're turning yourself into a walking stereotype nobody will take seriously, my friend," I say, putting him in a headlock as we make our way out of the room.

"Only to you, buddy. I make everyone else call me Congressman Reyes."

SEVENTY-ONE

SENATOR VIANO

I watch as Michael and Francisco walk out of the chamber like a couple of frat brothers who just scored at a sorority house. There's professionalism at its best. Across the gallery, I see his staff pile out, presumably to go meet him outside in the hall.

Gary has also tired of the game. With his boss now unemployed and my star not shining so bright, he left to work on his résumé right after the final votes were cast. He is a loyal foot soldier, but after watching every plan we hatched go down in flames, he cut his losses. With the drama over and the House adjourned, I am alone.

"You didn't come through, Marilyn." Well, almost alone. He can't know that everything I have tried has failed.

"Nobody could have seen that turn of events."

"Yeah, right," James Reed says, taking the seat next to me. "You knew he would never go for the third-party thing. It was all bluster. If you really wanted him to take that course of action, there were dozens of ways you could make it happen. You were hedging your bets on the outcome, and now you've turned on me."

"I haven't turned on you, James, but I will. I am a mercenary in this, and the price for my loyalty just went up."

"You think you're in a position to make demands?"

"I think I am the one still in the game and you aren't."

"You think that makes a difference?"

"It does if you want results. I spoke to Bennit before the vote. I will get back in his good graces. He makes the same mistake all new politicians make—he still believes in people. He's a fool, and I'll use that to my advantage. Eventually, he'll come around, and once he does, I'll be in a position to influence his caucus. Once I do that, I'll own them."

"A caucus is not as powerful as a party."

"Who says they'll be a caucus forever?" I respond with a hint of a smile. "Some of the greatest movements the world has ever seen started with a loose-knit core of dedicated people. I can make them congeal into something more powerful and influential. Once they get a taste of that, forming a party will be a foregone conclusion. The only question to be answered is whether you will still be involved when it happens."

"What do you want in return?"

"I don't just want a seat at the table. I want to run the whole show. You want to call the shots behind the scenes, fine. I won't settle for just getting back in the game. I want to be the starting quarterback. If I make this happen for you, you're going to help me become president of the United States."

"You don't ask for much," he replies sarcastically.

"You are going to get everything you want. Why shouldn't I get the same?"

He checks the length of his fingernails, thinking over my proposition. It's a big gamble with a weak hand, but I'm all in.

"You are making some pretty big promises for someone who hasn't delivered anything."

"I delivered almost eighty independents to the House."

"Bennit delivered that. What makes you think you'll ever be able to control them?"

"I picked their names for a reason. Yes, eventually, I know I will." I only hope that's still the case. The problem with bluffing is you run the risk of another player calling it. My hand is weak, but I'm betting a seasoned player like James Reed knows his is weaker.

James lets out a hearty laugh. "You know, I thought you might pull something like this, so I already made a call to include you in some plans I'm working on."

"How forward thinking of you," I say dryly.

"Oh, I think so too. Well," he says giving me a pat on my knee, "we should talk after the new Congress forms. In the meantime, you don't want to be late for Bennit's presser and miss your photo op. I want you standing right beside him when he gloats over this victory."

SEVENTY-TWO

SPEAKER ALBRIGHT

"Mister Speaker," my secretary says as I enter the room, "the majority leader is waiting for you in your office." Oh, that's just great. He isn't wasting any time, is he?

I walk in to find the smug bastard I call a friend sitting in the chair behind my desk. The only better signal of his ambitions other than comfortably ensconcing himself in my office is catching him measuring for new drapes.

"You may covet that chair, Harvey, but I strongly suggest you remove yourself from it until it's yours," I say in as harsh a tone as I can muster.

"That day may be closer than you think," he responds, rising from it and circling back towards the front of my oversized desk. "That vote sealed your fate, Johnston. The committee wanted no part of your continued leadership next Congress before this disaster, and they certainly won't after it."

The Republican Study Committee is the most conservative and largest element of my membership. It is also very influential when we ballot for leadership positions every two years, and Harvey owns it.

"And you think you are going to curry favor with them? What will they say when they find out you were the architect of all this?"

Blame avoidance is a way of life on Capitol Hill. Nobody takes responsibility for any negative action that can ever show up in an opponent's television ad. The same axiom applies when jockeying for positions of power in Washington.

"All I did was pass on the concerns of the members."

"You're the one who put me up to all this! If you had listened to me in the first place, Bennit would be gone and there would have been no icandidates."

"Inaction was not a feasible alternative. Nobody was willing to bury their heads in the sand and hope he didn't become a problem later. I think the party thought you were capable of handling Michael Bennit. Do you think Gingrich or Boehner would have failed so miserably? Hell, even Pelosi could have navigated these waters better than you."

Comparing any political leader to predecessors in that manner is an incredible insult. Stepanik is trying to get me emotional so I say something stupid, but I'm not going to take the bait. I have played this game for far too long.

I pull the Macallan out along with the pair of tulip-shaped glass tumblers. How many drinks have I shared with Harvey Stepanik in this very office? I pour us both a couple of fingers and hand him his glass. He accepts it apprehensively, no doubt wondering why I am offering to drink with him as he plots my political downfall. Frankly, I'm wondering the same thing. Politics makes strange bedfellows, but rarely does your most trusted political ally become your most ardent political adversary.

"Do you know how South Carolina got the nickname 'The Palmetto State'?"

"What?"

"You aren't deaf, Harvey. You heard me. Do you know?"

"No."

"It refers to our state tree, the Sabal Palmetto, which has a historical significance dating back to the American Revolution. In 1776, we repulsed the British fleet's attack on Sullivan's Island. Colonel Moultrie had a palmetto-log fort built that withstood a withering barrage of British cannon fire until the fleet retreated."

"You're starting to sound like Bennit." He's right, I do. "You think you're going to survive the bombardment heading your way?"

"That's the idea."

Stepanik presses his lips together and nods before taking a long sip of his scotch. What is he up to now?

"What will happen when it's made public that you knowingly colluded with a major lobby group to frame Michael Bennit for accepting a bribe in an attempt to expel him?"

"I did no such thing."

"Yes, you did. We know James Reed sent you the pictures and you knew it was a setup. We wanted you to get rid of Bennit, not compromise the integrity of the party. Add to that this debacle we just witnessed—"

"Harvey, I swear, I had no idea those photos were—"

Harvey holds up his hand to stop me. He swirls the last of the scotch in the glass before drinking it in one swallow. He places the glass down on my desk and we just stand and stare at each other for a long moment.

"You're a liability now, Johnston. You're out as Speaker, regardless how things play out next month. That's only half your problem. The party wants someone to pin the blame on, and you're the sacrificial lamb. So you're going to resign your seat for health reasons before the next Congress starts."

"I won't."

"You will. Otherwise, you'll be in and out of hearings about your behavior more than A-Rod was. You'll face a barrage of embarrassing questions you really don't want to answer. As a friend, I don't want to see that happen to you."

"A friend? Is that what you're still calling yourself? A friend?" I ask incredulously. He has some nerve. "Get out of my office." He obliges, walking across the spacious office overlooking the National Mall that I have called mine for a long time now.

"You wouldn't dare cross Reed. Not just to get me out of this office."

"Do you really want to test us on that?" he responds, stopping at the door. He's right. The Republican Party has shot itself in the foot over far less over the years. "For perhaps the last time, have a good day, *Mister Speaker*."

-SEVENTY-THREE-
MICHAEL

There are strictly defined rules about where the media can go and what they can film on the Capitol grounds. Aside from the press briefing rooms in the Capitol and the various office buildings, there are countless areas that allow portable coverage for interviews. Since I don't like the idea of being the typical politician that slithers over to the closest camera after a vote, we decide on a semi-impromptu gathering at the base of the House steps at the southeast corner of the building.

It is cold out, but not bitterly so, yet I hold out the hope that the temperature will help keep this brief. Even with my wool overcoat and countless days freezing during Ranger School and Mountain Warfare School while I was in the Army, I prefer being warmer than I am right now.

I stop a few steps from the bottom, just beyond the roped off area of the steps where only members are allowed to proceed. A gaggle of media are gathered at the bottom, microphones and cameras at the ready. The group is nowhere near the size of the hordes of media that followed our first campaign, highlighting just how little the average American understands what just happened here.

I have no opening statement, and sensing that, the press launches into the questioning. I am flanked by Blake and Chelsea to my left, Cisco to my right, and Viano a step behind me. The rest of my staff is a few steps higher and way off to the side, content to watch from outside the limelight.

"Congressman Bennit, you ran a social media campaign to try to sway opinions on this vote. Do you think that's the future of politics?" Interesting first question, but one I'm happy to comment on.

"I hope not, because it failed miserably."

"What do you mean?" the reporter asks after looking at his colleagues with a slightly confused look on his face.

"It didn't work. Americans weren't paying attention to this vote, especially once news of the fake anthrax attack spread. Nobody got caught up in the excitement of this vote outside of the Beltway. They simply were not invested in the outcome. If this lame duck session accomplished anything, it's showcasing the limitations to the effectiveness of social media when it comes to how government legislates."

"Why do you think that is?" a young female in the middle of the scrum follows up.

"Because it's almost Christmas, and the people want to spend time with family, shop for gifts, and get on with their lives. Americans went to the polls to choose their representatives in November. They did their job, and now they want us to do ours. The public doesn't understand what we voted on today, and honestly, I don't think they really care. It is why we have a representative government: so they can remain indifferent about what happens here and focus on what matters in their lives."

"So what does this victory mean?" one of the intrepid journalists up front asks. She looks like she's been out here for a while and is in drastic need of a warm fire and a hot chocolate.

"Every piece of legislation that is passed justifies the Founding Fathers' optimism that elected representatives can govern a free and diverse nation. Sometimes the same is true for legislation that gets defeated. Today, we defeated an assault on that optimistic vision. For too long Americans have questioned whether the people they elect are truly dedicated to serving their best interests. I hope we can once again restore our citizens' trust and confidence in our system of government."

More questions get shouted from the group. I wonder the same thing every other American does. If they just spoke one at a time, these conferences would go much faster, smoother, and a lot more questions would get answered. Instead, I wait until a clear question emerges.

"What makes you think the independents who got elected will be any better?" Good question.

"I don't think that for sure. What I do know is they did not take large campaign donations. Big oil, big tobacco, big labor … none of them can lay a claim. The independents that ran along with me are beholden to nobody other than the constituents who elected them. They are not people with career political aspirations—just some of our best and brightest citizens who don't want to just be a representative in

Congress, but a distinguished one who works toward solutions to our problems. Over the past several decades, we have seen an exodus of legislative statesmen and women. I think the American people elected some new ones."

"What would you say to your critics like the Tea Party and the ACLU who think your desire to compromise may damage the country?"

"God bless America for them being able to articulate their opinions, but I would challenge any claim they make that the extremism we have seen over the past couple of decades has made this country a better place."

"And you think compromising will help achieve that goal?" a man with a tape recorder remarks sarcastically from my right.

"Except for on the rare occasion when there is enough dominant consensus on an issue where it isn't needed."

"When does that happen?" asks a pretty woman from the middle of the group, causing a few laughs amongst her peers.

"The resolution supporting Veteran's Day is all I can think of," I answer, eliciting some more laughs. "For the rest of the issues we face in this country, legislating will inevitably mean compromising. That's what making policy in a democratic system is all about. No single person, faction, or interest can get everything it wants."

"Congressman, are you categorically stating you will not be forming a third party?" a voice shouts from the back of the group.

"Yes." I want to say something more clever, but I don't want to it come across the wrong way.

"Is there any truth to the rumor this new caucus you will form with the other independents will challenge the president when it comes to setting the agenda for the country?" Not sure where he got that tidbit of information from.

"The administration is responsible for day-to-day management of a huge bureaucracy which has, by default, made it a dominant force in politics. The president has been empowered to become more involved in the activities of Congress, resulting in less laws and policies being initiated by this body."

"You didn't answer the question, sir," the reporter presses.

"I know," I say with a smile. "The founders lived in simpler times and never could have imagined the increasing complexity of American life. In some respects, it makes sense that the chief executive sets the direction in the country. But coequal branches of government no longer are. Over the past century, a succession of presidents has asserted the supremacy of executive power. I think we need to reinstate the balance the Framers envisioned."

"So you're saying that you and this new caucus are planning a more aggressive role for the House of Representatives?" I really don't want to go down this path. It isn't going to earn me any late Christmas cards from the power brokers in this town.

-SEVENTY-FOUR-
CHELSEA

"The Framers intended Congress to be the engine of American democracy," the congressman says, responding to a question from CBS that he looks like he doesn't want to answer. "This building should be a venue for working out the country's most difficult problems, not Sixteen Hundred Pennsylvania Avenue."

"Are you saying the president has no place setting the course for the country?"

"No, I'm not saying that at all. But the era of the president issuing executive orders to cover for Congress's dysfunction must come to an end. All regulations should be tied to legislation approved by the House and Senate. For that to work, partisan brinkmanship must cease and the process of lawmaking in this country must be more efficient."

"What do you think the Speaker of the House will say about that?"

"You'll have to ask him when he gets elected."

Under any other circumstances, Mister Bennit's badinage with the press on this serious of an occasion would not be received warmly. Somehow, he pulls it off. The only other politician I have seen be this direct with the media without rankling them was Chris Christie in New Jersey.

It dawns on me that this will probably be the last press conference I ever attend. Well, at least for a very long time. It's amazing how used to reporters and cameras I have gotten in the last couple of years.

I'm not sure if my decision is the right one. All the insecurity over the past year and a half has brought me to this point, and up until now it was the right thing to do. I wanted out, and now I got my wish. I can see what college is all about and why Xavier, Amanda, Emilee, and Brian enjoy it so much.

I don't want to leave Vince and Vanessa, but I know they will be just fine. Vince may speak poetically about the trappings of college life, but I know there is no place he'd rather be. As for Vanessa, I get the feeling the only place she ever wants to be is by Vince's side. Funny how I never noticed that until now. Maybe they are a couple and I don't even know it.

Listening to the congressman answer questions, I realize just how far we've come. Had we called a press conference last spring, we would have been lucky if only Kylie showed up. Now I look out at a mass of humanity armed with cameras and microphones, recording every word for both posterity and immediate communication to the American people.

We started a movement that has begun to give the power back to the Americans on whose backs this nation runs. It's a proud day, and probably my last and most substantive achievement in the time I spent here. I wonder how many more I would have had if I decided to stay.

But I need to start a new chapter in my life. For as sad as I am to leave the congressman, Vince, and Vanessa behind, I need to do this for me. Heck, maybe I will even start school with a new boyfriend if the guy standing next to me sticks around. Either way, it is going to be an exhilarating experience, and I can't wait to get started.

A lone individual makes his way through the mass of journalists, probably trying to get a close-up of Mister Bennit as he addresses the country. There is a lot of pushing going on, and it reminds me of videos I've seen of 1990s mosh pits. He manages to break out in front, only a matter of six or eight feet from us before I notice he has no camera or microphone. I freeze when I realize what he does have.

I hear the first "pop" and see the congressman fall backward before it even registers what is happening. Journalists in the crowd react immediately and push to get away while some dedicated cameramen try to keep their lenses trained on the unfolding events around them. Everyone gathered around us on the stairs looks for any kind of cover they can find. There is none. A split second later, the man targets someone to my left and I hear another "pop, pop."

Finally, I see the gun point in my direction, but am frozen in fear in disbelief. Is this really happening? This can't be real. How could …

I am abruptly grabbed and forced down strongly by someone pushing my small frame violently toward the steps. Whoever grabbed me is now blocking my view, because I can't see the gunman. I hear more "pops," but have no idea who they're aimed for. Things are happening too fast … who is grabbing me ... I'm falling ... I feel a warm ooze dripping down my face and neck.

I hit the stairs hard and feel a sharp pain register in my head, causing my vision to burst into bright stars before ... nothing.

Acknowledgements

As always, my sincerest thanks go to the readers who have become invested in the journey of Michael Bennit. *The iCandidate* was years in the making, and I am proud to continue Michael Bennit's journey in *The iCongressman*.

Now, a few personal shout outs. Michele, thank you for your considerable support and patience throughout the process of writing this novel. As with the last book, I simply could not have done it without your love and encouragement. I also would like to thank my parents, Ronald and Nancy, and my sister, Kristina, for everything they have done to help introduce Michael Bennit to the world. I appreciate all you've done!

Special thanks go to the people who have been instrumental in making this book a reality. Caroline, my editor, her husband Gary, and BubbleCow did another amazing job helping me overcome some early shortcomings. Diane for the copyediting job on this book and for the revised edition of *The iCandidate*. Through your diligence we avoided many of the errors that plagued the first edition of my first book. Last, but certainly not least, Veselin Milacic did an amazing job with the cover design, far surpassing the lofty expectations for what I wanted it to look like.

A Note from the Author

Sequels are much harder to write than the first book of a series. Capturing the same magic is rarely done, and I have agonized over some of the directions this book went. Let me start with undoubtedly one of the most controversial parts of this book.

It was very difficult making the decision to not include Kylie in a first person narrative. She is a beloved character, and I love her as well. Unfortunately, the only way she fit into this one was to add a fifth first person account, and I didn't want to do that.

Kylie was a huge part of Michael's success in *The iCandidate*, but didn't play as active a role in this part of the journey. Sometimes life just works that way. To include her would not have done the justice she deserves, so she was omitted from the first person perspective. Rest assured, Kylie will be back with a vengeance in the third book of the series.

The other controversial part will be the cliffhanger. I know many will think of it as a ploy to read the third book, but honestly, it was just the natural place to stop. The events of the last chapter were planned out even as I was writing the first book. As I told my copyeditor, to continue past that point would have prompted me to rename this *iWar & Peace*. I beg your forgiveness if you have to wait for the third book to come out to learn what happens that fateful day.

As much as I wanted to keep the entire staff together, it would have been too unbelievable if they all had skipped college. Even bringing them together for the campaign begged some indulgence from the reader. I tried to offset that by making their contributions unequal, which would be expected in real life.

Before I get angry e-mails questioning why college kids would go through this again, remember they became close through the first election, and I imply they were all best of friends after the second and up to their graduation from high school. They have a shared experience few could identify with, and that bond is a strong one.

Michael Bennit is Michael Bennit. He's a fish out of water in Washington, and he knows it. He is also driven, has a deep love for his country, and wants to make a difference. It's hard enough to do that in the capital when you are surrounded by friends and allies, so it's no surprise he struggles without any.

Chelsea is facing struggles of her own. No doubt many people with question why she was ever made chief of staff. The simple explanation is that Michael believes in her, and as a teacher, just considers this an extension of the learning experience in *The iCandidate*. The same applies to Vince and Vanessa. Chelsea made the decision to leave, but who knows what will happen after the events of the last chapter.

Francisco Reyes sprung from a combination of my sophomore year roommate at Marist and a close colleague that I worked with several years ago. Much of the self-effacing humor is derived from that former coworker. He is a great family man, loving husband, and fantastic father, and it was fun bringing some of his personality out in this character. Cisco is an interesting guy, and this book should be considered only as an introduction to him. He will play a prominent role in the next two volumes.

Likewise, Terry Nyguen is based loosely on a soldier I have the honor to serve with and have engaged in numerous debates with on a myriad of issues. Nyguen is an enigma wrapped around a mystery, and not everything is as it seems with him. We will be seeing a lot more of him to come as well.

Marilyn Viano, Johnston Albright, Jack Reed, Harvey Stepanik and Gary Condrey, like most characters, are completely made up but resemble some of the politicians I have met throughout my life.

In life, we all run into sold acquaintances. The characters that made an appearance – Chalice, Robinson Howell, Charlene and others are a link to Michael's past, but will also play a role in his future to come.

Michael's old fiancée Jessica Slater is keeping her distance, but don't be surprised if she shows up unexpectedly in the third book. Madison, Roger, and the former Congressman Winston Beaumont are currently doing hard time. However, like Jessica, there may be a point where they cross paths with Michael and Kylie again.

About the Author

Mikael Carlson is a screenwriter and acclaimed author of *The iCandidate*. This is his second novel.

A nineteen year veteran and current non-commissioned officer in the Rhode Island Army National Guard, he deployed twice in support of military operations during the Global War on Terror. Mikael has served in the field artillery, infantry, and in support of special operations units during his career on active duty at Fort Bragg and in the Army National Guard.

A proud U.S. Army Paratrooper, he conducted over 50 airborne operations following the completion of jump school at Fort Benning in 1998. Since then, he has trained with the militaries of countless foreign nations.

Academically, Mikael has earned a Master of Arts in American History, and graduated with a B.S. in International Business from Marist College in 1996.

He was raised in New Milford, Connecticut and currently lives in nearby Danbury.

Life will never be the same …

The iSpeaker

–Third Book in the Michael Bennit Series–

Coming Fall 2014

WARRINGTON
PUBLISHING

Discover other works and learn about future projects by Mikael Carlson at: www.mikaelcarlson.com

Follow Mikael on:

Facebook: authormikaelcarlson

Twitter: @mikaelcarlson

Google +: mikaelcarlson

For additional content, he also can be reached on:

Tumblr: mikaelcarlson.tumblr.com/

Pinterest: pinterest.com/carmikael

Linked In: linkedin.com/pub/mikael-carlson/75/476/97b

Instagram: authormikaelcarlson

CPSIA information can be obtained at www.ICGtesting.com
Printed in the USA
LVOW10s1712301015

460434LV00001B/144/P

9 780989 767323